KISS MY JAGGED FACE

KISS MY JAGGED FACE

Isabetta Andolini

LUMINARE PRESS
WWW.LUMINAREPRESS.COM

Luminare Press
442 Charnelton St.
Eugene, OR 97401
www.luminarepress.com

LCCN: 2022923747
ISBN: 979-8-88679-174-7

To my mamma.
In moments big and small,
You're here, there, and everywhere.

"I'm not telling you to make the world better, because I don't think that progress is necessarily part of the package. I'm just telling you to live in it. Not just to endure it, not just to suffer it, not just to pass through it, but to live in it. To look at it. To try to get the picture. To live recklessly. To take chances. To make your own work and take pride in it. To seize the moment. And if you ask me why you should bother to do that, I could tell you that the grave's a fine and private place, but none I think do there embrace. Nor do they sing there, or write, or argue, or see the tidal bore on the Amazon, or touch their children. And that's what there is to do and get it while you can and good luck at it."

—Joan Didion

LIME AVENUE

HAMPSTEAD HEATH

GAINSBOROUGH GARDENS

PRIMROSE HILL

ST. JOHN'S WOOD

PANZERS DELI

REGENTS PARK

GINGER PIG

MARYLEBONE

MAYFAIR

HYDE PARK

CHELSEA

RICHMOND PARK

London

LONDON

WHAT A STRANGE sensation to no longer know yourself.

What is happening to me? Is this it? Is this the beginning?

She tipped her head toward the knotted gold chain and electrical wire that supported a simple, rectangular glass chandelier encased in gold on the first floor landing. "Look at Where We Are" by Hot Chip filled her ears and silenced the sound of her breath. She had passed the light fixture every day for a few months, never noticing it beyond her peripheral vision. This time, she stopped on the final riser before the landing and stared at the chain.

If she were lost to the world…

Keep going.

Up to the next floor.

The next.

The next.

A hollow formed in her throat as she slowly ascended the wide, shallow, thinly carpeted treads. '*Won't you come back to my heart / There's something I'm trying to say.*' Alexis Taylor's soprano and the synth-pop pulse matched her motions, a weighted beat between each footfall, her shoulders heavy.

I wish I could ask you, Is this what it's like? Is this how it feels?

By the time she reached the top level of the Hampstead mansion, unlocking the door to the final set of steps up to the garret, she was crying forcefully.

The flat was precisely as Margherita had left it when she had dragged herself out for a walk to Primrose Hill, where she had sat on a bench in the fog and pursed her lips at passersby. Once inside again, she flipped on the overhead lights and looked around. Suitcases pushed into a corner, flimsy pillows on someone else's worn sofa, boxes she had shipped from Italy and Mustique that she hadn't ever opened. She hadn't lived anywhere that felt like "home," like *hers*, since before the pandemic, and most of her belongings were stacked in storage across the various land masses on which she had temporarily lived.

She tossed the plastic bag of rice crackers and a single banana on the kitchen counter—her dinner lately—and opened the large swing window in her makeshift bedroom. The sweater and jeans she had worn to see Nick the previous evening lay in a pile on top of the dresser, where she had removed them and immediately crawled into bed, burying her face in the pillow. She hadn't even bothered closing the thick curtains to block out the drippy morning light, the fleeting appearance of which was so ephemeral she no longer bothered to catch it.

The roof terrace wasn't much of a terrace, more like various levels of wooden planks where one could stand, crawl, or crouch. The mansion had a pathetic backyard, with old stones leading to a weather-worn bench in its corner, abutting the fence that separated it from the manicured garden of a single-family home. Beyond, North London rambled, cascading down from the height of the Heath to England's Lane, then on to Primrose Hill and Regent's Park beyond, where white and red brick buildings sat forlornly ensconced in January mist. Above her hovered the ubiquitous white winter sky, swathed in opaque clouds that swirled around nonsensically, never revealing anything.

She eyed the cement wall that served as a railing. It wasn't very high. Who would possibly find her if she tipped over its edge? Who would possibly know how to identify her?

Isabetta Andolini

The wind was so strong on the top floor that it dried her tears before they had a chance to reach her jawline. She wished it would stop. All the crying. She hated it.

As she crouched to crawl back inside, she hit her head on the windowpane and winced, holding her hand on the potential bump and catching sight of herself in the bedroom mirror. She looked a pathetic misery; her long dark hair desperately needed a fresh cut, her glasses were murky from the mist, the circles beneath her green eyes were aubergine and one revealed a violet vein running along its perimeter, an unwelcome reminder of her upcoming thirty-second birthday.

It was the expression, however, that instigated a fresh round of tears. She hated the *sad girl* staring back at her, the one who had run her wet, smudged palm over the glassy screen of Margherita's usual courage, confidence, and energy.

Was this how you felt? she asked her reflection. "Why didn't you ever explain it to me? Tell me what to look out for?" she asked out loud.

She rubbed her head where she had hit it as she limply picked up her phone from the bed and wandered to her stretch mat.

Margherita: There's a song by The Acorn, he sings 'you could spend all your days waiting for the night'
Margherita: That's how I feel
Margherita: But then night comes and I'm waiting for morning again
Margherita: And round and round and round
Margherita: until what or when or who I don't know
Margherita: 'it's up to me' blah blah blah I know
Margherita: I wish it wasn't. That's a pathetic thing to say. I know.

Noah: Uh oh
Noah: sounds like someone's depressed
Noah: don't get fat

Noah was her oldest friend. He had worked in the New York office of Merrill Bates Lee, the architecture firm where Margherita had held her first job after graduating from Yale. He was always dependably dry and stoic, even from his current address in sunny Los Angeles.

Margherita: thanks that's exactly what I needed to hear.

But what if I'm becoming her?

With her back flat on the mat, she sent her legs into the air and watched her toes take turns covering the overhead lights. Tiny extremities protecting the darkness.

There had been too much of that in London of late—darkness—and with her dreary moods, Margherita couldn't help but worry. Bipolar disorder could come on at any age. As she lay on the stretch mat, she reminded herself that she, as a human being in the world with her own set of ups and downs, was allowed to feel appropriately depressed, especially during an ongoing pandemic.

But what's appropriate?

The next afternoon in the Planet Organic in Hampstead, as something to do, Margherita ordered a power greens juice. Her fridge was barren, and though it was past three p.m. and already dark outside, she hoped it might inject the bleak Sunday with inconceivable positivity and energy.

A mother and her small child stood behind her, staring up at the drinks board.

"Do you want a hot chocolate?" the mother asked.

"I'm not vegan," the small child said. "The sign says *vegan* hot chocolate."

The mother looked at her child with impatient disbelief. "So do you want chicken in your hot chocolate?"

Isabetta Andolini

Margherita smiled to herself as she paid six pounds for the powerful frozen zucchini blended to nothingness. Outside, young families stomped up and down the hill, en route to the butcher or headed home from the Heath. Boots muddy. Smiles genuine.

Jack would be doing something of the sort. Returning from some Sunday activity with six pairs of muddy boots in tow. A dog. Laughter. Brothers ganging up on sister. Jack asking them what they wanted for dinner.

She took out her phone and scanned her WhatsApp chats. His name sat there like a blinking cursor, though he rarely texted her in the app. His existence alone, in conjunction with the knowledge of his spending weekends with his family, was enough to embolden her loneliness. She, on the outside. He, on an inside.

MUSTIQUE

December 31, 2020

THE FULL MOON starlit a singular hint of turquoise in Macaroni Bay like a soloist on the stage. It illuminated the now familiar body of water right in its center, a witchy stretch of glimmer that shortened and lengthened toward her, like a slinky. On her AirPods, "Gentle Storm" preached the words of the hour.

2020 was over. At long last.

The high sides of the beach darkened the shallow spit of sand on which she sat, and she looked from side to side and behind her, as if someone else on the island might have the same New Year's plans and suddenly appear on her turf. In a normal year, the beach would have been dotted with visitors in expensive beachwear day in and day out, into the evening and beyond, but that year—that "unprecedented" year—the island was a hideout for a select few. Those who owned one (or more) of the prestigious villas, or who were otherwise considered regulars of the tiny island and had the means to pay their way through travel restrictions and private planes made up the entirety of her human interaction.

Margherita and her father passed the first year of the pandemic in the ultimate of bubbles, and while at the beginning she had been lonesome, emotional, and highly anxious, as so many were in the great unknowns of The Beginning, she had easily fallen into the habits of that highly unique version of life on Mustique, a tiny island in the Grenadines. She relished the nearly empty island, her alone time, her hikes, bike rides, and peculiar set of "friends." Oddly, with everyone she knew from New York to Italy being sequestered away for so long, her friendships, though distant in physicality, had never been stronger. She was in touch more than ever with friends in Italy, with her oldest friend Noah, who remained in Los Angeles where he had moved nearly a decade prior, and with her brother Benjamin, who had rented a house in southern France with his wife, two-year-old, and new baby, working remotely and learning to bake fougasse in the ancient oven or uncovering the secret to the thickest rouille. Margherita had thought he was joking when he recounted his quest to find the spiciest chili peppers for the sauce and was amazed when her brother, rarely seen out of a custom button-down shirt, sent her a video from his rustic kitchen. Their mother would have been speechless—another rarity.

She stirred her toes in the sand. The sounds of Nat King Cole's "Cappuccina" tumbled down from the Octopus villa, and drunken laughter, yelps and baritone triumphs spilled into the night. She slid open her Spotify and changed the track to Franco Battiato's "Summer on a Solitary Beach." Though not summer, and though she was in no mood "annegare" (to drown), it was befitting for the occasion, and one of her favorite songs she had discovered while living in Italy.

Margherita spun her head toward the villa at a shrill scream. She remained motionless for a moment, awaiting a follow-up explanation, which came in the form of one of the island's most fabled visitors.

"Pipe down, Meredith, or I'll tie you up!" Gerald roared to the island's most notorious divorcee, laughter ensuing.

She and her father had been invited to the decadent soiree but politely declined. They were in the Grenadines as employees, nearly enough, and her father felt it wasn't right.

"Aren't you the least bit curious what a party like that looks like?" Margherita had asked Tommaso, one eyebrow mischievously raised as her father sat with his elbows on the table concentrating on a revised set of plans.

"Not a bit," he said blandly, without looking up.

"Maybe I'll go by myself," she tested.

"No." He looked up at her, his thick-rimmed glasses on the lower bridge of his nose, his once asphalt-black hair a gravelly mix of white and grey. "I don't think it's right. Some of these people are the ones who approved these plans. So, in a weird way, they have supported my income here. And thereby, yours too, in your current unemployed state. It's not appropriate. Besides, you've been to a few of these things this year, I'm sure it's no different from any other night at Gerald's."

Margherita raised her eyebrows and tipped her head in response, knowing the New Year's Eve festivities were beyond notorious on the island.

In the sand, she imagined her mother at a party like that; surely, she would have defied Tommaso and gone, even if it meant going alone. No one stood in Francine's way.

"You would have despised this year," Margherita said out loud to the navy sky before her and the lapping water. The moon hung over the sea, keeping her company. She could hear her mother's snarky words, her deep, throaty voice and crisp English accent—what she might have said at the pronouncement of the extended stay in the farthest throes of the Caribbean. "Fucking imbeciles. I can't work from Mustique for a year, Tommaso. That CDC is a lot of lazy bastards. We need to go back to work!" Margherita hugged her knees, her mother's voice in her head. That St. Andrews intonation.

Margherita wondered constantly what her mother would have done that past year; would she have spent more time at home? Wherever home might be. Would she have worked less? Would she have been interested in Margherita's hotel idea?

She pushed her toes into the sand and extended her legs straight, lying down with her head resting on her palms.

"I'm working on something, Mom. I think you'd be proud. I think it's going to be big. It *has* to be big," she said to the moon. "Fucking littles," she finished off in an English accent. "Don't be a fucking small, little human Margherita darling. Be fucking brilliant," she imitated her mom.

"I'm going to be fucking brilliant, Mommy," Margherita said, a tear escaping down her freckled cheek.

MUSTIQUE

December 31, 1975

FRANCINE TIED THE beaded string of the halter top around her neck while she eyed herself in the shell mirror. The villa was a ridiculous show of shells and rattan. She rolled her eyes every time she stepped foot inside the living room: a mishmash of Caribbean 'shabby chic' that Rodney's decorator had compiled the year before.

Farce. Total complete farce, Francine thought to herself as she spun around to look for her lipstick, her eyes grazing the elaborate rattan legs of the round dining table and the bowl of shells sitting on its surface.

"Right, darling, ready to go? The kids are probably waiting for us." Rodney appeared from the hallway leading to the bedroom wearing all white: a pair of wide leg trousers with a short-sleeve white button-down tucked in and a collar with arms so long and sharp they nearly reached down to give his nipples a flick. He jerked his head to flip his neck-length hair out of his face, revealing his long sideburns and perfectly shaven face.

"Oh gosh, just had a fleeting vision of Bea and Cole with kids," she said, eyes falsely wide.

"Heavens. I hope not. That smarmy little twerp."

"Cole or Bea?"

"Cole, of course. He's no Keith, I'll just say that. I swear I saw him with another Bea look-alike at that fussy little place on Elystan a few weeks ago."

"Oh, like Bea's so virtuous," Rodney laughed as he stood behind Francine in the mirror, pouting his lips and fussing with his hair. "Come, darling. Ready now?"

Francine inspected herself, turning left and right, provocatively. Her skirt was short, but she had the legs for it—this she knew—and she'd layered on a nice tan in the week since she had left London. An image of her father standing in the doorway of his brick Upper Cheyne Row house flashed across her mind, his forlorn expression as she climbed into Rodney's taxi en route to Heathrow. He was likely spending that evening nursing one additional Old Fashioned and a weathered book from his library, with an after-midnight phone call to Francine's mum. Though divorced for more than a decade, her father often checked in on her mother on holidays, an impulse likely brought on by guilt, loneliness, and the rush of emotions holidays tend to put forward. She thought of her mother lying in bed in the Hampstead house in one of her silk kimonos, an old Ava Gardner movie on the television, the volume all the way down, and looking toward the ringing telephone thinking: "there he is."

"I suppose. How do I look?" Francine asked Rodney, turning to face him.

He looked her up and down seriously. "Like Patty Hearst after a bank robbery."

"Rodney! You cunt," Francine exclaimed, throwing a shell at him.

"Ow! I was kidding of course. You are the farthest thing from that vagabond. You are smashing. You look positively smashing. I could fuck you right here," Rodney said, coming toward her with his hands outstretched to grab her cheeks and kiss her on the mouth, flamboyantly.

"Too bad you're fucking Horatio the tennis instructor from St. Vincent," Francine said playfully, hitting her friend on his shoulder with the back of her hand.

Rodney's eyes grew large. "How did you know!"

Francine rolled her eyes. "Oh come, love, the whole island knows."

"Oh, gosh, how scandalous. Fantastic." Rodney appeared to digest this favorably. "Right, let's go. Stop faffing about, now. Come, come. Time to celebrate 1976. And to your father not allowing you to go to New York. I hate you wanting to leave us for Gotham, Francie, it's so dirty to think of you on those streets. The grime. The noise. Horrid. Just horrid."

"Just want to do one thing first," Francine said, and she reached for the bowl of shells on the glass dining table. It was heavy, and she used her full upper body strength to carry it out to the porch, where she rested it on the railing and tipped it over onto the sandy path below. When she returned with the empty bowl, Rodney gave her a quizzical look.

"Let's go, sweets. I don't want to miss the good drugs." She held her arm out to Rodney, who looped it with his.

"You are my queen, Francie," Rodney said and kissed his friend's cheek. She rolled her eyes but smiled.

"*You're* the only queen here, darling."

MUSTIQUE

January 6, 2021

MARGHERITA ROSE FROM her four-postered bed and lay down on her stretch mat in the dark, her phone beside her. She stared at the beamed, vaulted ceiling and watched the floor length curtain beyond her feet bend to and fro in the night breeze, like a ghost. Her father constantly told her to lock her porch doors but she couldn't bring herself to close them. She loved to listen to the night sounds of the island.

The ceiling fan spun around in slow, concentric circles, and she watched its legs turn round and round its center, a slight wobble once every turn. It made a soft whishing noise, like a blanket being dragged across a wooden floor. Oftentimes she could hear the undertones of music coming from the villa next door, where her neighbor Thayer evidently wasn't much of a sleeper either. Though Margherita wasn't sure if it was due to insomnia or if he was one of those wildly productive night owls, working on his next film. Or maybe it was a bit of both.

Thayer, an Englishman who had quickly risen to Hollywood gold as one of the most prestigious and highly paid film directors, did not emerge from his cottage until mid-day. The overgrown Morrissey hair, purplish undereye rings, and growing forehead creases were evidence that the island failed to relax his mind. Margherita felt sorry for him; broken-hearted after his recent divorce from a prominent, best-selling murder mystery author and reeling from a disastrous bomb of a film—endless rewrites, two years of shooting, and a $94.6 million shortfall. When a movie budget is $105 million and only grosses $10.4, the director isn't promptly welcomed back into town.

It was doubtful Mustique gave him the breathing room he likely needed. Though filthy rich and steeped in *Town & Country*-worthy stories, the island was a concentric circle in itself.

When Margherita's father Tommaso had been invited to stay in one of the cottages in order to be close to the new hotel development, she had assumed it would be a short stay—a month or two, maybe three. The virus was only weeks-old in the headlines, and none of them had expected stagnated life to go on indefinitely. Alas, the world and its insatiable pandemic had other plans, and month after month went by in the same pair of jean shorts and knock-around beach dresses. She had found a bicycle and begun making plans for herself, for 'when she returned to the world.' The time-out had proved reinvigorating and enabled her to focus in an extraordinary way, having so few distractions and no real need to go anywhere or see anyone.

There was, however, the sporadic night in which she took the ten extra minutes to blow dry her hair and partake in the island's infamous soirées. Standing inside one of the billionaire 'cottages' made her feel simultaneously out of place and a necessary character in the ridiculous, fictional lives of the island's inhabitants.

Thayer, who had rented the island's infamous Plantation House in the wake of the burying box office reviews and legal suits from producers, wore the same faded tee-shirt and beat up flip flops to the extravagant parties. Though his conversation was five words long on average, his somewhat awkward presence was a comfort. Margherita would make eye contact with him across a massive veranda overlooking the sea and smile facetiously. He would raise the corners of his mouth, shake the long hair that humidity charged upwards into the sky—opposing gravity—raise his ridiculously thick eyebrows in a mock expression and take a sip from his Pyrat rum.

"Tell me about the best sex of your life, darling," Meredith had once asked her at a party that had run past its usual three a.m. dwindle.

Margherita had just then raised herself from the sofa, deciding she would walk back to her cottage, when tiny little Meredith approached her. Meredith, a three-time divorcee, had given her adult-brat offspring the keys to her Gloucestershire estate for the year while mummy traipsed between Mustique, Dubai, and yachts in international waters. Her skin was as taut as sailors rope and her eyes as wide open as a frog's. Despite the frontal misses, Margherita found herself jealous of Meredith's impossibly athletic figure. From behind, she was approximately eighteen. From the front, she was five or six times under the knife.

"The best sex of my life…" Margherita pondered as Meredith rested her tiny chin into her palm, losing poise after a long night of debauchery. This topic of conversation was typical on Mustique.

"Yes, darling. Well—so far!" Meredith added with a jolt of the head, grabbing Margherita's wrist with her bony, topaz clad fingers.

"It has to be a tie," Margherita decided, thinking of the two males in her life who had been the toughest to shake. Sharks in the water.

"Why? Was it a threesome?" Meredith asked quizzically.

"Ha. No. Each in their own country."

"And what languages were they whispering in your little ears?"

"Italian," Margherita said, thinking of Paolo. "And Anglo-Saxen." Nick.

"And was it love or just general superlative fucking?"

"*Il primo…*"

"The first," Meredith confirmed her amateur Italian.

"The first was… puppy love. Lust. Craze. Obsession. Secrets and sneaking and hotel rooms and motos in the night. Fabulous restaurants, raw fish, great wine, the city, the sea. An absolute hunk of a man. The sexiest man I've ever met. The sexiest man *anyone* has ever met. Deep, soothing, quiet voice. Liquid blue eyes. So much throw-down," Margherita reminisced, smiling.

"Che favoloso," Meredith swooned, her bulging eyes glued to Margherita. Her version of story hour.

"A wife and three children," Margherita tipped the scale.

"Fuck them all," Meredith waved her hand in the air. "And the second? Anglo man?"

"Anglo… boy. Gorgeous. Charming. Smart. Articulate. Selfish. Center of attention. But sweet. When it served him. Secrets and sneaking and our own beds. One broken heart—mine—and lots of miscommunicated feelings and unnecessary confessions and stubbornness—mine again," Margherita shrugged.

"I can see everything in your face, darling," Meredith said, leaning against the back of the sofa. "You are young and gorgeous—don't dwell. Get what *you* want. And get out!"

Margherita laughed and shook her head dismissively. *If only it were that easy.*

"And I know what you're thinking. It doesn't always work that way. But let me tell you. Life is short, but life is *long*. If you get stuck up in someone's ass for years and decades, you'll miss all the opportunities of someone getting stuck up in yours," Meredith said, her bulging eyes not blinking, her eyebrows closer to her hairline than her eyelashes.

Margherita grimaced. "Lovely," she said. "I think I'm going to head home now."

And that had been Margherita's most intimate girl-talk with Meredith the divorcee from Gloucestershire.

Outside, a palm leaf swayed in the distance, draping a shadow back and forth across the dark lawn beyond her porch. She looked back up at the ceiling fan. *Whish. Whish.* On her middle finger, she turned a gold serpent ring around and around. It was too quiet.

Growing up, in the townhouse in the charming nucleus of

Carnegie Hill on Manhattan's Upper East Side, there was always noise emanating from somewhere, from wherever her mom was. Wherever Francine went, there was a hum ranging from lively to inexcusably cacophonous. She slept only a few hours each night, and the rest were spent watching an old black and white movie on full volume, listening to Fleetwood Mac or Cat Stevens at ravenous decibels, or baking something superfluously floury. It could be July, and Margherita would come downstairs at three a.m., bleary-eyed, to find her mother making Scottish shortbreads, stollen cakes, or mince pies, listening to Van Morrison and singing and talking to herself.

"Oh hi doll, did I wake you? Did your dad finish the butter again?" Francine's voice cut through her ear, years later. That unmistakable boarding school accent. Cheltenham Ladies College and St. Andrews entwined. Tommaso would sometimes wander down too, if his earplugs were not strong enough, and sit at the counter watching his wife like a spectator.

In the too-quiet room on the island, Margherita reached for her phone at her side and held it in front of her face, taking a deep inhale and exhale before tapping the phone symbol on a contact named simply 'N.'

"I am in the mood for… something," she said when the phone stopped ringing and she heard the rustling of covers in the night.

"Hello." A sleepy voice.

"Hi," she said, resting the phone, on speaker, on her diaphragm. "I don't know what for though. That's the thing. I am antsy and I don't know why." She rose her right leg in the air and drew it down around and up, in the shape of a letter 'D', as if she were in a Pilates class.

"Okay." She imagined him speaking with his eyes closed.

"Were you dreaming?" she asked.

"I don't think so," Nick yawned into the phone. "I haven't heard from you in ages. How are you? Where are you?" He sounded like he was propping himself upright.

"I'm in the mood to snuggle. That's what I want."

"You? Snuggle? You can't get to the edge of the bed fast enough."

"You don't know me. I'm not made of glass."

"Your words…"

"Anyway," Margherita said, as she raised the other leg in the air, making D shapes, "I like to. Snuggle."

"If you were here, I would snuggle you."

"Where are you?" she asked.

"Dorset," he said. "Where are you?"

She ignored him and let a beat pass.

"It must be almost morning there."

"Mmm," he moaned, sleepily.

If he was at home in England, where was his girlfriend? The last time Margherita had exchanged a text or two with Nick, that previous September, he had told her he was in Cadaqués with her family. It had landed like a subsonic cruise missile after months of not being touch. Barely detectable on his side, injurious on hers—all the more so because of its nonchalant delivery.

She hesitated, then ventured forward. "Where is your girlfriend?"

"We broke up. Fairly recently."

"Oh. I'm sorry," she said, genuinely. "That's rough."

"Yeah. I'm okay."

She blocked the thoughts piling in her brain and quickly searched for a decoy flare. No good would come of wondering why they broke up or who did it, or what he had been doing since, or with whom. It was surprising, however, that they had lasted so long, considering his self-serving tendencies.

"Can you believe nearly a year has gone by since this thing started?" she asked, changing the subject as she watched the curtain dance up from the floor and billow into the room. It was windier than normal. "I haven't been on a date in ages. Or to a movie theater. A bookstore. A crowded bar."

Images of her heels dangling below her bar seat floated across her vision. A fabulous New York restaurant. Violet eye shadow, a gin cocktail, and loud, flirtatious laughter.

"I know." His voice was like balm to her, it always had been, though she never understood why. Their secret affair had persistently slinkied her from chafed and hollow to blindly hopeful, adrenaline gushing. Her own obstinacy in the face of unrequited feelings morphed into masochism—she kept going back for more, as if the outcome would magically change. Margherita had met Nick soon after she returned to New York from Italy, at a time when she was desperate for distraction, and though they had never truly gotten to know each other in any real way, and though their tryst was mostly sex and random chit chat and fire bursts of built-up emotions that had been left unvoiced, she had felt an inexplicable attachment to him from the start. She felt he understood her in a way others did not. She was both strangely comfortable and completely out of her element with him.

"How's home?" she asked.

"It's good. Lots of walks. Lots of nature."

She sat up, her feet on the ground and her legs bent, her elbows propped on her knees. She held the phone as she looked out into the night.

"Do you ever feel lonely?" she asked.

"Um, no. My best friend from school is here. And my family. Why?"

Her eyes drifted to the framed black and white photo of Francine on her desk. In the photo, Francine held a one-year-old Margherita in the driveway of their Connecticut weekend house. Her mother's elegant hand, with Francine's mom's serpent ring, sat on Margherita's bald head, her other hand wrapped around her pudgy baby body.

Margherita stood, pulled the muslin net back from her bed, and placed her head on the pillow.

"Are you still there?" Nick asked.

"Mmhmm," Margherita said in a little voice.

"Why can't you sleep? What's on your mind?"

She stared at the ceiling and her throat constricted.

"I miss my mom," she said, in a completely different voice.

"Oh, Marghe," Nick sighed.

"I'm sorry I woke you. Go back to sleep."

"Don't be sorry. We can chat."

Margherita tried to swallow the tears that were lurching up her throat. "No. I'm going to try to sleep. Goodnight Nicky."

A blue light lit the room and she heard her phone ping a sound she hadn't heard in a very long time—a low ba-boom; an ominous sound that used to catapult her stomach into somersaults.

Nick: Listen to this
Nick: "Skin" by Glimmer of Blooms
Nick: It was nice to hear your voice.

Margherita silenced her phone and slipped it underneath her pillow with one hand as she swatted a tear running down her cheek with the other. She turned onto her side and pulled her knees into her chest, burying her right eye into the linen bedding and wishing for morning.

LONDON

AT KEITH'S FLAT on Sheffield Terrace, Cole stormed through the living room energetically. "Where's Keith?" He looked from one girl to the other, but neither responded.

"In here, mate," Keith called from the kitchen. The flat spanned two floors of the brick house, which he had purchased outright the year before. Sensible, responsible Keith let the top floor to a quiet, older single woman, and he lived by himself in the rooms of the first and second floors, a regular meeting-place for the tight-knit group of friends and anyone additional they pronounced worthy. Francine, Beatrice, Rodney, and Cole would appear unannounced, Keith ever welcoming and reliably mellow.

He emerged, holding a jar of jam in one hand and a knife in the other, his face a proud display of joy and satisfaction.

"Well?" Cole asked. "Fuck off, man! How was it?"

"Wicked. Brilliant. Charlie Watts… ace."

Cole disappeared into the kitchen.

"Oh, hi to you too Cole," Bea yelled sardonically from the sofa.

Cole stuck his head around the doorframe. "Bea, did *you* go see the Stones at Zuiderpark? No." He disappeared into the kitchen again.

"I hear Richards isn't gonna stick around. Band drama," Bea shouted.

"Yeah, that's public knowledge. Where've you been?" Cole appeared again, slightly miffed, the jam jar now in his hand.

Francine listened to their conversation from the other side of the long, narrow sitting room, where she made a mess of records on the carpeted floor.

"Where is your Fleetwood Mac?" she yelled to the boys in the kitchen.

"What?" Keith peered into the room, one hand holding a piece of toast.

"Fleetwood Mac, Keithie!" She had ripped a few records from their sleeves and was about to yank open the third cabinet door when Keith came up behind her. He bit on the end of the toast, half of it hanging out of his mouth, and grabbed Francine's slim, naked arms.

"Franschine," he said through his toast.

"Stop it, Keithie!" she shouted as he attempted to drag her away from the pile of records.

"Let her be," Bea said, bored, as she flipped a page of *Woman's Own* magazine.

Francine began to hit Keith with an old Joni Mitchell record, hard enough to ruin it. He threw his toast down on the floor and grabbed her underneath her arms, pulling her to standing. Her babydoll dress rode up her body as she swam her legs up toward Keith's chest.

"Francine!" he yelled as he held her like a baby. She continued to wriggle and scream. Bea continued to read her magazine, unperturbed.

Francine's bare feet found the ground and she crouched below Keith to escape his outstretched arms. She went to the telephone and asked for the operator.

"Rough Trade Records, please. Kensington Park Road. Please hurry, it's an emergency. No—not a medical emergency. No, I'm fine. Oh for fucks sake, operator, please!" She stood with the phone to her ear and one hand held out at Keith.

"Geoff! Thank God. Do you have Fleetwood Mac's record from last year? It's an emergency." She paused, giving Keith a demonic eye. "Do *not* sell that album, Geoff. Don't you dare. You promise? We will be right there."

She hung up the phone and grabbed Keith's hand. He held his weight in place.

"Keith!" she yelled at him like a protestor in the street.

He rubbed his forehead.

"Keith. You don't understand. When daddy and I went to New York a few weeks ago, we watched this show on the telly—'The Midnight Special.' They've got two new band numbers, Fleetwood Mac I mean, and this blonde chick who sang "Rhiannon"—Keithie. You *don't understand*," she said with eyes wide, her hands running through her hair. "She was a force I've never seen before. She was rock. With this goat-like voice. But so fucking sexy. All black lace and the most feathered hair I've ever seen. And the look she gave the new lead guitarist. His hair! Their love. Keithie, you cannot live another day until you have this album. We are going to Rough Trade, we are buying the record, and we are coming straight back here to listen to it over and over and over without eating or sleeping or making love for days. We *must* drink it. You didn't see how she smashed it at the end. You didn't see her *fire*."

Francine's head nodded fanatically, and she slapped her palm with the back of her other hand. Bea hadn't looked up from her magazine, and Keith's expression had morphed from frustration to pity to acquiescence. Cole watched from the kitchen doorframe, taking regular bites from his toast as if watching an episode of 'Love Thy Neighbor.'

"Francie," he began.

She grabbed his wrist and pulled. "We can walk fast. We can walk so fast. Fast. Fast walking. Fucking fast." She pulled him toward the front hall.

"Francie, you're not wearing shoes."

"I don't care. I don't care, Keithie! It's spring! We're in Kensington! Why do I need shoes? You live on fucking Hyde Park!"

In the hallway she stopped abruptly and turned around to face him. "Have you ever heard Lindsey Buckingham play the guitar? The guitar solo, Keithie. He played it just for me. I felt it in my cranium." She looked up at the ceiling and opened her mouth in shock. "I think I orgasmed listening to his solo. You know how you can *feel* sounds? I've never heard anything like it. And the most gorgeous boy too. This big curly afro that almost swallows him," she motioned her hands around her head. "But these innocent eyes, like really innocent. All he wants to do is play and sing and love." She leaned her body into Keith's chest. "I want to play, and sing, and love," she said as she wrapped her arms around him.

"Where are your shoes?" he asked, as her arms groped his back.

"I wasn't wearing any today. I wanted to feel the Earth. Shoes have been blocking my connection to the Earth. I only wear them to sleep lately, in case I need to run."

"You came over here without shoes?" He pushed her shoulders backward in order to look at her face.

She dove in to kiss him, and he pulled away.

"Jump on my back, Ruby Tuesday."

Isabetta Andolini

MUSTIQUE

February 2, 2021

MARGHERITA TURNED OFF the golf cart's ignition and waited in the dirt driveway for Tommaso to finish for the day. She propped her feet on the dashboard and hugged her knees to her chest, wishing she had brought a sweater. She couldn't remember the last time her father was on a job site nearly everyday, but the circumstances being what they were, and them living on the island, what else did he have to do?

On Mustique, Tommaso kept an eagle eye on the GC's team and ensured all of the materials delivered from both the UK and the US were correct and in excellent condition. The hotel, overlooking Macaroni and Simplicity Bays, was jointly and privately owned by a Greek and an Englishman. The latter was the main person overseeing the project while he sat out the pandemic at his villa in the south of France, so close to her brother that the two had actually forged a pandemic-era friendship.

Margherita had seen Sloan a few times on video calls as she passed behind her father in their cottage's kitchen, where their kitchen table had become Tommaso's de facto desk, plans spread out since day one. This man, Sloan, with his crisp English accent and linen button-downs, appeared to be very handsome, and she wished he would come visit the island, spice up her pandemic life a little. Her father rolled his eyes at this and instructed his daughter not to cross romance with professional contacts.

She winced. In New York, a few months prior to the pandemic, Margherita had had to come up with a plausible story for why she had been let go from her job in boutique development at the esteemed jewelry company, Lolato. Alexandre, the CEO, who Margherita had met while living in Milan and with whom Margherita had had a brief, secret romance, had offered her the role when Francine died. It had given Margherita an opportunity to return to New York to be near her father at a time when she felt she should be, though the job itself was a horrific trifecta: a two-faced, impossible to please, and despicably behaved female boss, unsatisfying, monotonous work, and the uncomfortable position of remaining entangled in the trail of Alexandre's wounded ego. When one of her boss's evil accomplices witnessed Margherita and Alexandre saying goodnight after a work dinner in Paris, the typical two cheek kiss, the young co-worker had somehow finagled a photo that read inappropriate, and a formal accusation formed in which Margherita was sleeping with the CEO. In order to save face and appease Margherita's boss, Alexandre had asked Margherita to resign.

Embarrassed, hurt, and somewhat disgusted with the human race, Margherita enrolled in unemployment and returned to Italy to clear her mind. When the first wisps of the virus had come through the news, Tommaso had sent his daughter a one way ticket to return to New York.

Tommaso strode up the sloped driveway toward his only daughter. The weight of the pandemic had not affected him in the slightest; he was so invested in the hotel project with so much enthusiasm, that if anything, he looked better than he had in years. The island had given him a healthy tan, and his muscles had grown from so much walking and being on site every day, lifting things unnecessarily, much to Margherita's dismay. It made her happy to see him looking so fit, though every time she thought of it, her mind whiplashed with the stark contrast of the tired, too-thin, haggard version of Tommaso she had gotten used to seeing a few years prior. Her mother had led him to carry so much stress and worry for so many years, and in the aftermath of her death, his pale color had worried Margherita so much she insisted he go for monthly bloodwork.

"I'm fine, Marghe, I'm just in mourning," he would say. And she would scrunch her eyebrows together and pout, unsure how to make it all better, terrified that he would grow weaker and weaker in his loneliness.

"Did you see the roof going on over the restaurant?" Tommaso asked as he looked backwards at the property. He paused to take it in from their higher vantage point.

She felt a twinge of jealousy—was it jealousy? Or impatience perhaps? Hunger. That was it. She was hungry to get going on her own project and eager to be in that position—standing back, admiring physical progress after the long development phases. The last time she had felt that tangible satisfaction was in Milan; there had been nothing during the last few years in New York that had rewarded her with that *closeness*, that zeal.

"Very exciting!" Margherita said, nodding. "So, Basil's?" The beach bar was the fan favorite on the island.

"Yes, yes I'm ready," Tommaso said, as he turned back around and hitched himself into the golf cart. "You hungry? I've been thinking about the fish burger since lunch."

"You have the fish burger at least three times a week." She rolled her eyes as she turned on the ignition and looked behind her to reverse.

"Well I like to keep it easy. You're the most difficult customer on the island. I bet you're the only one who has dishes specially prepared. Is that Gerald?" Tommaso squinted toward the golf cart approaching from the southern side of the island.

Margherita waited for Gerald and his big hat and sunglass-covered guest to pass before pulling out of the site's dirt driveway. "We are the only ones on the island without a chef at home. And Dad, their version of 'light bites' is fried lobster and crispy jerk wings."

"Yeah but you're going to turn into a rabbit soon. Did you hear he just bought a third villa?" Tommaso kept his eye on Gerald's straw hat with a Gucci leather band around it as they followed on the winding roads that crossed the island. Clearly he too was making his way toward Basil's.

Margherita shrugged. Of the 120 villas on the island, it was not unusual for a private owner to one-up someone else for the sake of it. "Remember Bunny Shits A Lot?"

"Oh God. I haven't thought about Bunny Shits a Lot in years. You had to have that thing. I told your mother a thousand times: 'we should have got the dog.' A bunny is no companion for a young girl. And who cleaned up all that shit?"

"Betsy."

"Ah, yes. Poor Betsy. I wonder what she's doing now."

"Probably still in recovery from being locked in the bathroom and forced to cut Mom's hair off, only to be fired because of it the next day. And rehired as soon as the mania wore off."

Tommaso guffawed. Their old housekeeper put up with a lot.

"Do you think I should get the brownie tonight?" Tommaso asked, like an excited child.

"Vey," Margherita said.

"Vey!" Tommaso repeated, affectionately placing his hand on his daughter's shoulder and bringing her toward him. "Poor girl. So much time with her father."

"Yeah. Vey!"

Father and daughter decided to sit at the bar, their usual spot, and Tommaso recounted the events of the day: a long anticipated delivery of stormbreaker, sound-dampening windows and doors, and a final decision on the whimsical yet sophisticated bathrooms, in line with the aura of an oasis disconnected from the prowess of the world, with sparkling bay views, elevated rain showers, and adjustable floor-to-ceiling exterior glass walls.

"You can stand on top of this pristine beach, as if you are alone in the Grenadines, in the nude, feeling the sea breeze on your chest and literally touching the Frangipani with an outstretched arm, and no one in the suites on either side can see you, because of the way we've positioned each 'plateau,' we're calling them, all the while rinsing the sand off and washing your hair. The water is cleansed, purified, and re-used for laundry. I aim to cut that ten percent average utility bill to five." Tommaso had barely touched his fish burger, so impassioned was he to describe his current work to his daughter, whose matched enthusiasm was the best gift the man could wish for.

"What if they've had one Mustique Mule too many? Will they literally shower to their death, nude body on the giant rocks, found on the morning's bird watch walk?" Margherita asked.

"No!" Tommaso triumphed, sitting back in his bar stool. He smiled proudly. "No, because I have designed one foot of exterior balcony with treated white oak, and a retractable overhead for further protection for said oak. It will be heaven."

"How's it going over here?" the young waiter asked, leaning his hands into the edge of the bar and smiling sociably at first at Margherita and then Tommaso.

"It's good, Cal, thanks for checking. Though I've been eying Woody's rib eye tacos over there and already thinking about them for tomorrow." Tommaso tipped his head across the pentagonal bar at the infamous rib eye tacos, with spicy pico de gallo and cabbage slaw.

Woody, a gentleman about Tommaso's age, ate neatly, a glass of chilled Casamigos Anejo before him and a book unopened next to his woven placemat. Margherita couldn't make out the title on the binding, it was too much in the shadow.

Woody caught the uninvited attention from Cal, Tommaso and Margherita's eyes and nodded back at them, raising his tequila glass.

"Taco jealousy," Margherita smiled.

"Ah. Cheers," he replied curtly in his English accent.

Tommaso and Margherita returned their attention to their own plates. They were equally perplexed by Woody's quietude and introverted tendencies. After so long on the island with the same group of rather extroverted people, everyone had come to an odd sort of familiar, clubby, and companionable status, like a never-ending episode of "Love Boat." Margherita imagined flamboyant Gerald as the Captain, aka Merrill Stubing; Cal as Isaac Washington the bartender, Meredith as cruise director, and herself as a permanent passenger with an innumerable quantity of days at sea.

"Tommaso, fine Italian gentleman, how are you doing this evening? Here with your lovely offspring. Marghe, have you met Remi? She is my guest for the week at Jacaronda. I just *had* to rescue her from Bordeaux. It is so dreadfully dreary there this time of year."

Margherita tipped her head toward Gerald, who had placed one hand on the back of Tommaso's bar stool and the other on Margherita's, gliding his narrow head toward a lithe, red-headed woman one step behind him. Remi flirtatiously placed her hand on Gerald's upper arm and smiled graciously at him.

"My savior. I cannot imagine missing a season on Mustique. What an inferno France is right now," she said, in a thick French accent. "This virus! I've been vaccinated, I don't know what all the fuss is about. They even closed Le Bonne Marche in Paris! Horrible!"

Margherita smiled and allowed her father to speak for them. "Very nice to meet you Remi. Welcome to island confinement. There are just a handful of us here this year— no Mick, I'm afraid. It isn't the high season you are used to. But thanks to Gerald's connections, we're all jabbed too."

"Ah, we are the crème de la crème, aren't we? Tommaso is designing what will be the Caribbean's most modern, glamorous resort. Thirty-five suites and guesthouses. Discreet, pristine, exclusive," Gerald announced.

"Comme c'est fabuleux!" Remi said. "And you, Marghe, do you work with your father?" She pronounced Margherita's nickname with a soft French 'g', like Mar-jay, instead of the hard Italian consonant which gave the name its poetry: Mar-gay.

"Margherita is working on something of her own," Tommaso said proudly.

"Ah, you are? I did not know. Do tell!" Gerald exclaimed as his eyes grew large with false enthusiasm.

Margherita did not have as much patience as her father for quacks and phoneys; she was quite like her mother in that way. It had always been Tommaso who pacified an oncoming quick witted retort shamelessly presented with an eye roll, while Margherita could not help but silently grin at Francine's lack of restraint. Although, it was that same lack of restraint, on other occasions, that had left Margherita frustrated, abandoned, and guiltily bitter.

"Yes, I'm putting together proposals for a small beachfront hotel on the Ligurian coast, in Italy. I've designed it, and I'm speaking with a few private investors. The property is already in existence; a dilapidated house on a baia. It needs to be revived, which requires a buyer, but I aim to be very convincing."

"Margherita, how smashing! What news! I'd love to hear more. Maybe I can help. You know I have so many contacts who would be interested in something like this. Let's go to lunch tomorrow. The Cotton House? One o'clock? You're not busy, are you?"

"That sounds lovely, thank you Gerald," she said with a smile.

"Fantastic. How wonderful for you. What an enterprising daughter you have, Tommaso."

"Yes, that she is. Good to meet you, Remi," Tommaso said, as he picked up his fish burger once again.

"You think this is just an opportunity for him to brag? Boredom?" Margherita eyed Remi's eight-hundred-dollar sandals as the pair glided away.

"Hey. You just. Never. Know," her father wagged a potato wedge between his fingers.

The next morning Margherita woke early to go for a run from Pasture Bay to Britannia Bay and back. After the initial months of acute anxiety at the beginning of the pandemic, she had reached, with the aid of the island sun and dewy humidity, a version of emotional homeostasis; she felt abnormally balanced. Of course, there was still the news to deal with, horrific virus stories and heartbreaking tales of elderly couples at one another's side for seventy years only to be prematurely torn apart by death.

Life had never felt so precious.

At Basil's, Cal made her an espresso; after the first week she didn't have to ask. As soon as he saw her approaching he would grind the beans.

Woody was often at the bar early mornings for an iced coffee. Margherita would give him a pursed-lip smile and a nod, not overstepping as he clearly wasn't much for morning chit chat. She noticed, however, that he tended to regard her with a bit of side-eye, as if he were judging her in some way. Was it not chic to jog in the morning?

"Creatures of habit," she deigned to say that day.

"My preferred way to start any day on the island since 1967," he said, stoically raising his cup, condensation already encircling it in the heat of the morning. He looked at her with sad, slightly drooping eyes, which locked with hers, and for a split second it seemed he might say something else.

"1967!" Margherita repeated.

"Yup. Woody's got more stories than all three thousand (usual) residents combined," Cal nodded at the older gentleman while placing Margherita's espresso cup on the bar.

"I can imagine! If you ever feel like sharing, I'm all ears," Margherita said as she took her first sip.

Woody smiled and raised his eyebrows at his sun spotted hands on the wood bar. "Cheers, Cal. Have a good day," he said to Margherita, and started walking toward the pathway that connected Basil's with the bright pink and purple gingerbread houses-cum-shoppes, where, in a few more hours, one could buy expensive SPF and six-hundred dollar women's bathing suits. Margherita watched his slightly uneven stride.

"You know, in the six or seven months I've been here, I've never seen Woody in shorts. Or bathing trunks," Margherita said to Cal. "Not even on a boiling hot day. Actually, I've never seen him in the water. Or on the beach, come to think of it."

Cal was silent as he retrieved her empty espresso cup and rinsed it in the sink.

"Did I say something wrong?" Margherita asked, reading the awkward moment.

"No. Woody's got a bum leg," Cal said quietly, leaning his hands on the counter, his shoulders riding to his ears.

"Really? I never would have known. Since always?"

"No, not since always," Cal said.

"How do you know?"

"My dad told me the whole story. But we don't talk about it. We're not a gossipy bunch," Cal said, a fair amount of warning in his voice. Margherita felt like she had overstepped and was slightly embarrassed.

"I won't say a word," she said. "He's so quiet; it's hard to figure him out."

"He's a really great guy. Not a bad bone in him. I think he doesn't want to be figured out, if you know what I mean," Cal said, opening the dishwasher behind the bar and unloading glasses that had run the night before.

"Gotcha. Okay. I'm off. See you later," she said, as she began the second half of the run.

She returned to the path that ran along the edge of the hill. That morning, brightly colored fishing boats took up most of the narrow, crescent shaped beach, practically toe to toe with lush flora and fauna at the edge of the protected shore. They were so close to the forested hills, that it looked like a scene out of a pirate fairytale. Out in the turquoise water were a smattering of larger sail boats, not nearly as many as one might find in a non-pandemic year, and perhaps all the more picturesque for it.

Margherita spotted one of the island's white-jacketed security people on the stout dock, walking out to greet a boat that had just pulled up. From where she stood to stretch her calf beneath a palm tree, stepping on the end of the trunk with a tipped-up foot, she could tell that whoever had arrived was a friend or perhaps another staff member. Security on the island was stricter than TSA at JFK; everyone that had a heart beat was registered upon arrival, whether it be from air or sea. There was no hiding anyone, or anything, on Mustique. The false cloud of 'discretion' was one of the island's claims to fame. Margherita shook her head at the paradox of it all; celebrities and the world's elite claimed Mustique as a beacon of privacy, but really they just wanted to feel the prying eyes of their peers.

She could not help but wonder about Woody. Was he so virtuous that Gerald, Meredith, and their nefarious minions truly left him in peace? Now she really wanted to know. Maybe Thayer would fill her in.

Isabetta Andolini

LONDON

December 12, 1976

FRANCINE TURNED THE corner from Smith Street onto St. Leonard's Terrace. She preferred to do a long-about way, taking the quieter streets to Eaton Square—Turk's Row and cutting through Holbein Mews—anything to put off meeting her father's newest find. Dr. Uwe was visiting from Munich for less than a fortnight, and Francine's father had arranged a special visit.

All Francine heard in this pronouncement was: a new pill regimen. A new set of moods out of her biological control, or, the more likely scenario: a *lack* of moods. And certainly a long list of side effects.

The wet winter cut through the fur chubby she had borrowed from her mother's wardrobe that day, and she tried to cross her arms over her chest to hold in the warmth. Beneath it was the floor-length, fringed Paco Rabanne dress she had bought with Bea the previous weekend, blowing her entire month's salary.

The chubby didn't have a proper closing, but it did have a matching hat that she thought was quite fabulous. Surely Dr. Uwe would view her stylish choices as conflations of a manic personality.

Fuck them all, she thought to herself as she eyed a suited man walking with his hound in Ranelagh Gardens. Watching them through the black gate rails made her dizzy.

"You look smashing, darling," her mother had complimented Francine as they both looked into the swing mirror in the dressing room. Francine had smiled at the reflection of her mother's delicate arms wrapped around the fur, trying to close it over Francine's bosom.

When she was a little girl, Francine would sit on the floor watching her mother choose an outfit and jewelry, apply her make-up and re-adjust her set hair as she smoked half a dozen Viceroys. It might take two hours from start to finish—three if she indulged in a long bath first. She had moved the record player closer to her vanity table, and they would sing and hum along to Sam Cooke and Glenn Miller as they paused at each Jacques Fath skirted suit set and belted couture, Norman Hartnell lamé dress and coat, Thea Porter chiffon gown, and custom Belinda Belville. Francine would giggle in fits of delight when her mother danced and spun around in her corsets, slips and garters. Her father might appear in the doorway, likely just home from work and assuming Francine's mother to be ready and dressed. His face would bemoan impatience and annoyance but with one cheeky smile from his beautiful wife and a turn of her hips, he would loll his head and return with a half-grin, spinning around the room for a chorus or a bridge before he was shooed away. Francine thought her parents were the most glamorous, charming, and amorous people in the whole wide world.

That afternoon, her mother's dressing room was the same slightly dusty, amply lit ghost it had been since the divorce, but with the anxiety of meeting a new doctor looming, she felt the gravitational pull toward nostalgia.

Francine tilted her head toward the illuminated windows in the elegant, cream-colored mansions on Chester Row. Dusk rolled in like a billow of pollution off the rear of a truck as she cut through the damp early evening. She wondered who was pouring a cocktail in those upstairs rooms, who was sitting miserably in an armchair waiting for their significant other to return, who was scut-scutting a lover down the service stairway, and who was slipping on a pair of gloves on their way to Rules in Maiden Lane.

She turned left onto South Eaton Place, then right onto Eaton Square, where she felt her face scrunch into dismay. A porter took her coat at the door, and she climbed the carpeted staircase to the second floor, where the rooms were deathly quiet and, to Francine's surprise, modernly decorated, with every piece of furniture shaped in a curve of some sort, dressed in primary colors, and bold shapes as art on the walls.

"Francine, I presume," an older gentleman said, rising from his comfortable seat.

"Yes, hello." She moved toward him as if to shake his hand, but he did not extend his toward her.

"Please, sit." He motioned toward a bright red chair. Francine watched him look her up and down.

The man sat on a similarly colored sofa with a pad of paper and a pen in hand. He crossed one wool trouser leg over the other and his sweater vest bunched at the bottom. He had a greying beard and a bushy mustache, and he reminded Francine of the famous Dr. Kraepelin, also from Germany, who had declared psychiatric disorders biological and genetic.

Francine had read about it in a textbook she had found in her father's office when she was seventeen. She had gone looking for answers about her mother's recent prophesizing, to find some piece of information that might calm her down. Her mother had begun to visit Francine's bedroom in the middle of the night, to tell her daughter about the imminent ending of the world, but not to worry, because mummy would save everyone. Mummy had all the answers. And not to listen to anyone else, not even Bob Dylan. Francine's mother would go on and on about the curly-haired man listening to her phone calls, and about war and combat and how the Heath was sinking.

But instead of reading about hallucinations, the kind of text her corporate lawyer father did not have anyway, she had found the few books he had on his wife's mental illness. The same mental illness that Francine had been diagnosed with the previous year. Reading about its disabling, lifelong effects in great detail had catapulted her into weeks of despair, hardly lifting her head from her pillow; convinced she was a lost cause, and with no cure or way out of her condition, she had asked her parents why they 'made her continue to live.'

That night was the first time she had heard her father cry.

"My name is Dr. Uwe, as I am sure you are aware."

Francine pulled her ankles closer into the legs of the chair, so much that she felt her calf muscles strain.

"Your father has shared your medical history with me. I have read everything; there is quite a lot," Dr. Uwe said, lifting his pad to reveal a thick folder beneath it. He flipped it open, balanced on his thigh. "Seven hospitalizations. Four suicide attempts. Nine disappearing acts. Three arrests and other countless run-ins with the law, not only in England. Thirty-three different medications administered at various points and stages. Sixteen psychiatrists, three psychoanalysts, four clinical psychologists."

The puddle of saliva that had been sitting in Francine's throat caused her to suddenly cough.

Dr. Uwe looked up, as if he had forgotten she was sitting there. "Hmm." He looked back down at the folder, moving pages from right to left and back again for what felt like eons. Finally he closed the folder and moved it to his side, where it sat on the red sofa like a character in a horror film, about to spur legs and come alive at any moment.

"Your father tells me you have a few very good friends," Dr. Uwe said, crossing his hands over his knee.

"Yes," Francine replied.

"I find it fascinating that you have managed to grow and maintain friendships throughout your… eventful life. As a rapid cycling manic depressive."

The skin above Francine's eyebrows formed two crevices. "Right," she said crisply. She looked down at her own hands, folded in her lap, and squeezed her entrenched fingers together. Her knuckles took on the hue of the cream-colored mansions outside.

"Tell me, Francine, what is the most frustrating element of your illness?"

She sat in silence, waiting for him to elaborate on his question. He did not.

"I don't understand," she said.

"What is, the most. Frustrating. Element. Of your illness," he parsed, enunciating each piece through his thick German accent, irking her.

"I suppose. The most. Frustrating. Is. This." The menace in her eyes and the tautness in her jaw was a storm that descended on the flat like a mid-August afternoon bolt of thunder.

"And. By This. I suppose you mean having to deal with the rigmarole of incessantly treating yourself." He paused, awaiting her response, but she said nothing.

"The unremitting undertaking of applying, re-applying, and finding of a new, band-aid," he continued. She remained silent.

"The constantly growing barrier between your mind and your dreams, between you and the rest of the world," he said, absent-mindedly drawing a rectangular shape on his empty notepad.

"Sure," she said curtly.

"Add to that the need to meet doctors such as myself, from near and far, to appease your father. But also with the small—perhaps increasingly minuscule—hope that there might *be* hope, after all."

Francine bit her inner lip and stared down at her knuckles. She unclasped her fingers and purposefully laid one hand over the other more gently.

"So. That brings us to the agenda of this meeting. I have with me a new mood stabilizer, direct from Switzerland, which has been approved in Zurich but is still awaiting approval in England. I have the ability to administer this, in a low, slow dose at first, with the careful and close attention of your current doctor. It has been proven to be very effective with depression, but not mania."

"How wonderful," Francine responded dryly, looking down at her hands.

"I'd like to ask you a few questions. Is that alright?"

"I'm sure I've been through them before. Go on."

"I'm sure you have, but for my own notes, you see. Do you hear voices? In manic episodes or otherwise?"

"No." Francine knew what to say.

"Hmm. Do you find you are… promiscuous, sexually? In manic episodes or otherwise?"

"Sexually promiscuous. Never. I am quite chaste, actually."

"Right. Do you spend a great deal of money, during manic episodes or otherwise?"

"I have an allowance when I'm between jobs," she spat out stickily.

"Hmm. Have you ever had your kidneys checked?"

"What for?"

"Well you see, lithium can do a great deal of damage to the kidneys."

Francine thought of her mother.

"Yes. I am aware."

"Do you sleep normally?"

"Every night, like a lamb."

"Right. I see how this goes. Well, the most important thing is that you find your even ground in the most health-conscious way, and that you are able to feel most your self. That is what I'd like to help with."

"My self." She huffed.

"Yes. A sense of self exists, in everyone. And we have a good chance of revealing it in a way you've never felt before, with this new drug from Switzerland. And if we combine it with lithium and haldol…"

Francine watched her right hand rub her knee cap. She slid her thumb and forefinger down around the outer edge and slowly back up again. Down and up, ever so gently, the way Keith did when they were sat next to each other. She wasn't listening anymore to Dr. Uwe. If there was a mood stabilizer on planet Earth, she had taken it at some point, mixed with two or three more at the same time to 'conquer' both her depression and her mania and to keep her at a certain level of constancy throughout the day. All her life, between her mother's illness and her own, she had been listening to doctors pronounce a series of odd-sounding names: carbamazepine, divalproex, lamotrigine, loxapine, ziprasidone, olanzapine, lurasidone, fluoxetine... Whatever was put in her pill box each day was out of her control, anyway, so what did it even matter?

When Francine was reunited with her mother's fur and once again ensconced in the humid December mist, she walked back in the direction of Chelsea. She found a pay phone on Pimlico Road and dialed Bea.

"Is there somewhere we can go near you for a drink before Susan's's party? I'd love to arrive a little more loose than my current state."

"Oh, Francie, can't you just come here and I'll pour you a glass of something? You know there's no where worth going around Chelsea Common."

"I'm wearing my Paco and my mum's chubbie and I want to have a drink with my best friend, out in the world with other fucked up people. I am a person of the world. I want to mix," she said defiantly.

Bea exhaled on the other end of the line. "Fine. I'll meet you at that clubby spot on Elystan. But I'm not getting derailed here; we are going to Susan's birthday straight after."

"It's early yet. Don't worry. We will be there for cake and candles."

Francine continued on toward Elystan Street, huffing and puffing her frustration at the evening's meeting.

How do you have friendships with such an 'eventful' life? she mimicked in her head. "Fuck you," she said out loud to the sidewalk. "Fuck all of you."

"Was that meant for me?" She heard a male voice coming from Franklins Row, the street she had just passed as she continued on the Royal Hospital Road. She slowed her step and turned her head, ready to give the stranger a dirty look and keep walking. But when she saw his tall, wide shouldered frame, his jet black shaggy hair, his olive complexion, and his irises, bluer than the Aegean from where she assumed his accent to originate, she couldn't help but smile flirtatiously.

"What if it was?" she asked, letting her hands drop to her sides.

"Well, I'd have to ask you what I did to deserve it." He stepped toward her on the sidewalk. The night light from the park's tennis courts illuminated the space between them and she could see his provocative eyes light up at the prospect of a tease.

"Interrupt my inner dialogue, for one."

"I don't come across many beautiful women swearing to themselves in the street. Maybe over in Whitechapel, but not on the Royal Hospital Road," he said, tucking a piece of black hair behind his ear. Francine followed his hand as it slowly dropped down to his waist, where he held it, his suited elbow sticking out into the night.

"I swear wherever, whenever I want. In Dalston. In Kensington. At myself, at other people. Whatever I want."

"And when you're not swearing?"

"I'm fucking."

"Wow," he raised his eyebrows.

"Have I stumped you?" Francine asked, a mischievous glint in her eyes.

"Hardly. Where are you off to?"

She looked behind her, as if her destination could be seen. "A birthday party. Actually a pre-party drink. Where are you off to?"

"Just leaving actually—my drummer's mum makes a killer brisket."

"Your drummer," she repeated dryly.

"My drummer."

"And what does that make you?"

"Lead guitar."

"Of course you are," she said.

"Not easily impressed, I gather."

"Not especially."

"Well, we can give it a go. Maybe you change your mind? Do you need a date for this birthday party?"

"No, I don't."

"Do you *want* a date?"

"I wouldn't find it extremely disagreeable," she stepped toward him and touched the bell-bottomed sleeve of his jacket, then raised her eyes slowly to his cheek bone and grazed her fingers along it. He watched her as he raised his hand to cover her fingers, gently, as they traced his cheekbone to the hair above his ear.

"I think that's the best I'm going to get. And as an added bonus, you can swear at me all you want," he said quietly, a glint in his eye.

"Or fuck you," she said quietly, confidently, still focused on his hair.

She brought her eyes back to his, and they exchanged a glance of committed roguery.

"One quake at a time…?"

"Francine."

"Francine," he repeated, slowly, taking her hand in his and bringing it to his thick lips. "Christos." He kissed her fingers. "I like your dress. Let's go show it off and get to know each other."

MUSTIQUE

MARGHERITA CLOSED HER iPad in the middle of a cheesy YouTube tutorial on the most foolproof tactics for onboarding external investors in a business venture. She was tired of watching young boys in bright green polo shirts point at white boards and make declarations about successful start-up businesses only to follow each sentence with a self-promotion and suggestion to subscribe to their pathetic little YouTube channel.

She exhaled deeply. She needed to speak to someone who had been through this, first-hand, and someone who could help her figure out how to configure what her own stake might be. Margherita's goal in The Villa project was *not* to get rich; quite the contrary, she really could not care less about the money aspect of it. She wanted to be proud of something, to create something on her own, to prove to herself and to whoever else that she was capable. She wanted to begin the path to something *big*.

On the cottage porch, she leaned back in her chair and rested her hands on the edge of the stone-top table. Her hands, once fair as porcelain, were noticeably more weathered and tan.

"Don't be like Bea and bake to death," her mother used to say. Margherita had never met Bea, her mother's best friend from childhood, who had passed away from skin cancer when Margherita was a little girl. She had seen a photo of Francine and Bea, lying out in Hampstead Heath in short-shorts, silk scarves tied through belt loops, another head scarf around each of their heads, and bandeau bikini tops. Francine had her eyes closed, her forearm thrown over her face, and her other arm outstretched on the blanket in the grass, while Bea had her legs in the air, laughing. Whoever took the photo had been standing over them. Margherita couldn't help but wonder if her mother had been hungover in the photo; she looked like she was in a crabby mood.

Margherita had sent a few emails to various people in her network, kindly requesting their input and advice on a variety of topics. Man was not an island. She was pleasantly surprised by how many people had written her long emails, had carefully picked apart her presentation decks, had spoken with her for an hour, multiple times on different Zooms and calls, to teach her about hospitality business models and return on investment, taking money from private individuals versus small business loans, and more.

There was one other friend, or if 'friend' was not the right word, person, who Margherita suspected would be helpful, with whom she had yet to share the project. Nick had, after all, been a founding member of a successful co-working company with multiple locations. He had been the one to raise capital, all three rounds of it, maybe more for all she knew, and he was the one who had done the due diligence, the outreach, and presentations.

Margherita reached for her phone and opened a new chat. He was online. She hated to write to him while he was online, assuming she was interrupting him. Maybe he was talking to a girl. Her eyes closed for an extra beat and she shook her head gently.

Whatever. Who cares. I have a goal here.

Margherita: I've been working on something.
Margherita: Can I tell you about it? I'd really appreciate your advice on a few things.

It was her style with him—a new WhatsApp chat sans formal greeting. In fact, if either of them began a text conversation with any kind of formal greeting, it signified some kind of missile was en route.

He took a few minutes to open her message, and she wondered where in the world he was. Was he still in England? She had no idea. He had never been one to voluntarily share, while Margherita had, uncharacteristically, volunteered more and more. He had taken what she gave him in his palm and tossed it somewhere out of sight.

Nick: Hiya
Nick: Yes.
Nick: What are you working on?

Margherita: I've drawn plans for a small boutique hotel in Italy. I am trying to find an investor or two.

She raised her shoulders to her ears and looked up at the porch ceiling fan. Margherita still felt silly when she said these words out loud to anyone, especially to someone she knew. Writing an outreach email to a stranger was peanuts; she had all the confidence in the world, but admitting her grand plans to someone like Nick, or even talking about it to her brother, she felt belittled before they even responded. Nick had a way of making her feel small without saying very much. Her brother Benjamin was a pillar of dismissiveness: 'Oh Margherita, twiddling her thumbs in Milan,' was the general assumption, compared to his successful career in London, his wife and family, his stability.

Don't let anyone make you feel small. Her mother used to say it. Sometimes Margherita heard Francine saying it to herself, when for instance, she might have gone looking for her mom in her dressing room in the morning, needing Francine to sign something for school. There Francine would be, sliding shoes on for work and fussing with her hair, muttering with force under her breath.

Nick: wow!
Nick: impressive!
Nick: do you have a deck?

Margherita: Yes.
Margherita: I'll send it to you.

Nick: I'll look at it today. And we can talk tomorrow? What time zone are you in?

Margherita: EST ☺

Nick: Okay great. Tomorrow, 8am your time?

Margherita: Perfect. Thank you ☺

Nick: of course.

"The Mamas and the Papas," Thayer said as he wrapped his arm around the large square-shaped banister and stood with one foot on a porch step, one foot hanging off.

"Great song."

"Catchy, right?"

She put her phone down on the table. Thayer looked behind him toward the palm trees blowing in the breeze and then skimmed his eyes over the bougainvillea that wrapped the porch like a nest.

"What are you up to?" he asked.

"Work," she said. "Unpaid work, but work. I don't think I've ever worked harder on anything in my life." Margherita stretched her arms into the air and rolled her wrists.

"Ah yes, this is just the beginning."

"What are you up to?" She dropped her forearms and stretched each of her triceps, pulling at one elbow.

"I was thinking about taking the boat over to Canouan. Lunch at the Mandarin," he said, idly, as he climbed the rest of the porch steps and sat down at the stone-top table next to Margherita. He absentmindedly picked up a few of her notes and put them down before casually crossing his hands over his stomach. "What do you say? Break time? I've been craving spring rolls for days."

"You need a buddy," Margherita laughed.

"Just being neighborly."

"I have so much to do." She pushed her lips to the side of her face.

"Did you know there is a KFC on Canouan?"

"Really? That's disgusting."

"What if I treated you to a spa day?"

"Thayer! Is this how you make friends? Spa bribes? Though it is tempting."

"Fine. I'll ask Woody if he wants to go." Thayer looked up with his eyes pinched and his mouth in a pout. "Though I'd have to find a life vest. Have to get one from the club," he said to himself.

"Yeah, especially for the ride back, you lush."

"I'll have you know I am an exemplary captain, lush or no lush."

"Thayer, can I ask you, and I hope I'm not being rude, but what is the story with Woody? He's such a loner; that kind of behavior feels so out of place on Mustique."

"Ahh… poor Woody." Thayer pitched the tips of his hands together like a teepee. Margherita waited for him to continue. "Robyn Hitchcock!" he exclaimed as Spotify moved on to the next song. "Such strange lyrics."

"What happened with Woody?"

"Woody. Woody is a prime example of a good sail sent out into a bad storm one too many times." With that, Thayer stood up and stretched his own arms over his head. "Right, you little blighter. Stay here and do your work. I'm off to spring rolls and a Thai massage. Maybe a body wrap. Ohh, maybe an 'oriental scrub.' You know, I think they're the only company in the world not ostracized for using the word 'oriental.' Good thing no one who reads the *New York Times* goes to Canouan."

"Next time!" Margherita called after him as he hopped down the steps. The dark hair in the middle of his head, longer than the hair on the sides, flew backwards in the breeze.

The next morning, after an especially early run and a quick shower, she quickly blew a hair dryer over her hair, pulled a dress over her head, and patted a little undereye concealer over the dark circles. The shade was no longer consistent with her tanned, freckled skin, and she felt a little raccoon-like, but it would have to do.

Margherita set herself up on the porch, her pandemic-era office, and began the first Zoom that had ever made her nervous.

"Hi," he smiled at her. That charming grin. Those white teeth. The energetic blue eyes. He had a little scruff on his face, a few days worth, and he was just as adorable as she remembered. "Where are you?"

His voice was just as smooth. His boarding school accent. She smiled, despite herself.

"Hi. I'm in the Caribbean."

"Oh! You do look quite tan. Look at you in your dress. How did that come about?"

They chatted for a bit, about their geographic locations mostly (he still in Dorset, she in the throes of the Caribbean Sea), and about living so far from New York, from metal and fumes and the insistences of a Manhattan social life.

"So. Tell me. This project. I looked at your presentation. It's gorgeous. Why this property? Why this project?"

"Okay well, I'm not sure if I ever told you, but when I lived in Milan in my twenties, I spent a lot of time on the Ligurian coast. It's a really easy getaway from the city and it's a dreamlike orgasm for the senses."

"Wow! Orgasm for the senses."

"Yes. It's the best way to describe it. If I could transcend the scents and the aura and the tan Ligurians and their fabulous swimming costumes and the bright colors and shades of turquoise on this Zoom, you'd be moaning. I promise you. But more than that, it is incredibly chic, and back in its day, very elegant, all in this salty, sexual, swim-out-to-the-rocks, hikes-in-the-sky in a bandeau bikini and a head scarf sort of way. And there is this property that I always used to pass when I'd get off the train at Santa Margherita Ligure and walk the thirty minutes to Paraggi, this incredible baia with my favorite beach club where I used to lay out for the entire day and swim and have lemon sorbetto at four p.m. When it got really hot, I'd climb down the ladder into the water, which is a thousand different shades of gem blue, and I'd swim along the jutting coastline to the shores of this villa. It *draws* you. Like it has stories to tell but it's too discreet and classy to tell them. And it sits right at one of the sharpest curves on the coast road —you risk your life pulling out of there, I bet, I've never tried —and so it sits out on its own promontory and has water on all sides practically. It feels like it's speaking to you, whispering to you. Think 1960s Italian black and white film. Monica Vitti. Antonioni. The gorgeous Italian families in late 1950s Slim Aarons photos. Modernism. Style. Lapping water. Salt. Cocktails. Crisp, finely dressed men. Think *class. Sprezzaturra.*"

He watched her with a closed lip smile, as if he was trying not to break character.

"What's sprezzatura?" he asked.

"It doesn't translate. It's something everyone wants to emanate. It's that effortless elegance, that natural moviestar quality—untouchable, yet warm and lovely. Sophisticated. Charming. Anyway. I want to bring back a slice of this. A return to sprezzatura. And the area is really lacking for this kind of hotel. Portofino, down the road, has become so tacky. All these instagrammers passing through. Here on this tiny promontory, there is a chance to create something cinematic—a moment in time that is more present and alive than any dumb, falsified TikTok in glitzy Portofino. At this property, guests will not be taking photos—they will be *living* the property. The Villa."

She sidestepped the nerves he induced in favor of passion. Then she got to the questions that made her unsure. The investor-related questions. He answered with sincerity. He offered advice and encouragement. He gave her ideas. Made her slow down a bit.

"I want this to really *be* something, Nicky. I'm not just biding the time until the virus is over. I want this to be big. An architectural feat. I didn't work my ass off at Yale and pay my dues for ten years for nothing."

Pay her dues she had, especially at Lolato in New York.

"I know you do," he nodded, a confident grin on his face. "And it will. Just remember that you are working both sides of this—the creative and the business/strategy, and you've got to get the latter buttoned up before you can dive into the former. You can call me whenever you have any other questions. We can talk again. Call me whenever," he repeated.

"Thank you, truly."

"It's my pleasure."

When they disconnected, she stood from the table and went to wash her hands. Her palms were sweating.

It had been one year since Margherita had seen Nick face to face, and she felt afresh the desires she had always felt with him, all of which had made her so fearful of the consequences of having feelings for someone. Of feeling attached to someone who wasn't attached back.

Those desires reappeared after speaking with him, like having just one bite of dark chocolate… it was nearly impossible to walk away from the fridge door without diving back for a sneaky second piece. She felt once again the longing to tell him things. Random things. Big and small. To ask him things. Random things. Big and small.

She had felt things for Nick which she hadn't felt since Jack, at her first job at Merrill Bates Lee. Though her secret romance with Jack had never become intimate beyond a kiss, whereas she had never seen Nick without having sex.

What had she wanted? Simple things. To slide her hand into his palm. To fall asleep next to him. To curl herself into the warmth of his body. To stay there, and not feel like the wedged-in puzzle piece that would never truly fit.

In her bathroom, she patted her hands dry and unzipped the dress. She slid on a pair of jean shorts and threw a tank top over her head. Her Mustique wardrobe.

Back out on the porch, she noticed a new email. It was a response to a query email she had sent the previous week, one which she was certain would go unanswered. The prominent venture capitalist was esteemed for his activities in small retail, entertainment, and real estate companies, and for turning them from nobodies to multi-bid sales.

She excitedly shared the news with Nick.

Margherita: it's just an intro chat. But still.
Margherita: Smiling ear to ear

Nick: Me too
Nick: Proud of you

She grinned at the screen. Why did his approval mean so much to her?

A moment later, her excitement faded at the realization that he was not planning to dig any deeper, ask any questions, or talk to her about it further. She got a pat on the shoulder.

How had she not yet learned that it would never be more? And why was she allowing his reaction to dampen this positive event of the day?

Let old habits die, she thought.

There was one other person she would have loved to share

that little bit of news with. Her mother.

Her mother would have known of the highly esteemed investor. She would have been impressed. She might have given Margherita an enormous smile and luminous eyes. That Francine vibrancy that felt like winning the lottery when it shone from her face.

Looking out beyond the porch toward the grassy yard that separated the property from the sandy beach path, Margherita imagined her mother suddenly appearing between two palm trees. Her long, full, chestnut hair. Her green eyes so unnervingly emerald they sometimes took on an animalistic light, and her long, never-ending legs. Margherita pulled at her top lip with thumb and forefinger. Her mother had been magnificent. She would have been a stunner on the narrow beaches of Mustique.

Margherita looked down at her jean shorts and her legs, not nearly as long as her mothers. She wrapped her hands around the width of her thigh. What would they have done together on Mustique? What had Francine done when she was her age? When Margherita had asked Tommaso about it, he'd shrugged and smiled and said: "I'm sure your mother was either driving the men crazy with her teasing and aloofness, or teaching the island how to dive. Whatever it was, she was the life of the party. And sometimes the death of the party too!"

"Don't say that," Margherita had said, pouting slightly.

Tommaso changed his expression. "You're right. I'm sorry. That was the wrong word. She was the drama of the party. Let's say that. And thank goodness for her escapades here. I'm not sure I would've won this pitch without knowing the island so well. It's been a good twenty years since we've been back, but not much changes around here."

Margherita put both of them out of her head and carried on with the day. She spent a few hours with the financial planning, taking into consideration Nick's advice in relation to real estate appreciation, and before she knew it, her stomach was grumbling for leftover two p.m. Niçoise salad.

A low ba-boom threw a wrench in her appetite.

Nick: Hey I had a thought while you were talking
Nick: I'm sorry if my behavior toward you ever hurt you
Nick: I was being so selfish always
Nick: And not particularly kind at some points
Nick: And I felt a pant of guilt about that on the call
Nick: And I hope you knew it was never your fault or anything about you
Nick: Just me being a selfish jerk
Nick: *pang

Margherita stared at the messages. They were unexpected. It was the first time Nick had ever alluded toward their strange history, and the first time he had acknowledged that perhaps his behavior had been less than chivalrous.

Margherita: Thank you.
Margherita: Was going to say pant maybe not the right word there.

Nick: lol
Nick: I felt my pants.
Nick: You didn't deserve to ever feel insufficient

Margherita: I wasn't particularly kind either
Margherita: And I really regret the way I acted with you throughout. I was immature and irrational and I'm sorry too.

Nick: It's okay
Nick: I forgive that

Margherita: But I don't want you to help me out of guilt

Nick: I'm certainly not
Nick: It's just a separate thought I had
Nick: I enjoy this stuff

Nick: And fun talking with you
Nick: And you looked hot on the video
Nick: So…

Margherita: that gets an eye roll from me.

MUSTIQUE

January 1, 1977

FRANCINE EMERGED FROM Rodney's villa in a white one-shouldered, one-piece bathing suit, leaving the delicate, booming sounds of Ellen McIlwaine's "Can't Find My Way Home" playing on the record player. She had slept until two that afternoon, with the help of a few extra flurazepam, and her head felt foggy. Rodney was nowhere to be found, and the only clues of how the previous night had ended were her dress in a rumpled pile on the porch, her panties on the gold rod of her headboard, and an inexplicable number of the island's yellow-green bananas crowding the coffee table in the living room, though none of this led to any reasonable conclusions. The bananas were strewn amongst the usual ashtrays and bottles of Nolet's Silver Dry, which Francine was always forgetting to put back in the freezer, much to Rodney's dismay. Francine plopped one of each in her bag on the way to the beach—a banana and a bottle of gin.

The overgrown parakeet flower bushed into her arms as she passed, but she barely noticed the thin strikes on her forearm. She shielded her face from the sun as she emerged from the shaded path and refocused her eyes. Floaters darted all over her vision, dropping in like big fat raindrops and disintegrating too slowly. Walking down to the beach, she had the strange sensation that the lower half of her body was not connected to her top half, and she watched each of her legs descend the sandy, wooden steps. Her left leg bent slowly, then her right.

Strange, she thought.

"We thought you were dead!" Rodney called out. Francine looked up. Rodney lay in the sand, propped up by one elbow, his white bathing suit as tiny and tight as could be, his oversized sunglasses hiding his hangover, and his hair a disheveled beach mess. Francine squinted and rubbed her forehead.

"Was going to check on you darling. Promise. But I had great confidence you were still breathing up there," Rodney said, shading his eyes as he looked up at her once she approached. "Is that McIlwaine I hear? Can you put on something a little less sad? Look at this sun."

Francine closed her lids beneath her sunglasses. "She's not sad. She is original and alluring," she said, insipidly.

Next to him, Bea lay on her stomach, her arms straight out by her sides. Her skin was as fair as it was years earlier, when she and Francine spent summers lying out by the men's swimming pond on the Heath, smoking cigarettes and pretending to watch their friends race each other across the pond. Poor Bea, as English as could be.

"Is she sleeping?" Francine asked, motioning toward her oldest girlfriend.

Rodney made a show of putting his face near Bea's head.

"She isn't snoring, so no."

"Fuck off," Bea said, her voice muffled. She blindly reached her arm out to Cole at her left, who sat with one hand as a doorstop, the other holding a cigarette and looking out toward the water.

"Cream, Cole," Bea's muffled voice said.

Cole looked down at Bea's back with dread. He turned his face toward Rodney and then Francine, as if to pass the task onto them.

"You're fucking her. You fuck, you cream," Rodney said, shaking his head to flip a long wisp of hair away from his face. "Actually that's a very accurate statement."

Francine looked out toward the turquoise sea. Her body felt like it was floating beneath her, and she grazed her palm along the top of her left thigh, to ensure its status as a limb still protruding from her hip. She recognized Keith lurching himself out of the water, shaking his head, his long locks shirking excess like a cocker spaniel after a bath. His swim trunks stuck to his solid thighs and his chest glistened. Francine was certain she was seeing two of him.

"Can you go back and do that again, please?" Rodney said facetiously as Keith approached the group. Keith smiled and regarded Francine as he pushed his long hair back and away from his face with a large, wet hand.

"Fran, you there?" he asked, tipping his head.

Francine barely registered his presence before her, where she continued to stand, half awake. Keith placed his salty hand on her bare shoulder and brought his pointer finger gently under her chin.

"Hey, love," he said quietly, searching for her eyes behind her large sunglasses.

Francine turned her head and Keith's finger fell to the side. She put one foot in front of the other and went to sit down next to Bea, who smelled of jasmine. Bea snuggled toward Cole a smidge, vacating a piece of the towel, and Francine lay down next to her childhood friend, facing the sky. She calmly folded her hands over her abdomen and closed her eyes. Voices formed a cocktail around her, and the only thing she could hear, though not certain it was heard by anyone else, were the sounds of bananas being yanked from the trees, not quite ripe, but nearly there. She couldn't figure out where her legs were. She assumed them to be floating, the way they sometimes were—a sensation no one but Francine seemed to experience.

I must have mixed something. She thought backwards to the previous morning. Had she taken Dr. Uwe's new regimen? There was no way she could remember what she had swallowed, imbibed, and snorted at the New Year's party, and the cloudiness etched out anything that came before.

She felt a presence on her arm that was not a part of her own being. She sat up abruptly.

"Whoa, it's just me," Keith said, his hands raised in protested innocence. Francine's eyes were a mosaic of confusion beneath her sunglasses. She slowly placed her delicate hand on Keith's strong forearm and held on. Maybe he knew why her legs were floating. She looked into his eyes, two flags of concern and pity.

"Francie?"

"Keithie, there's a banana in my bag," she said motionlessly. "I feel a bit sick."

Keith reached for her bag, which she had dropped at her feet. He removed the greenish banana and began to peel it for her. She kept her grip on his forearm, sticky from the salty sea and slightly rough with hair.

"Keithie?" she said in a small voice, looking up at his face as he held the banana. Two tears slid down her face from beneath her sunglasses.

Keith quickly glanced at the others. Rodney was recounting a story of the night before to Cole, who was barely listening, and Bea was still facing the sand. Keith wiped Francine's tears with his thumb, and guided the banana toward her lips.

"Here, small bite, lovie," he said quietly. "Small bite. You'll feel better. You're just hungover, that's all. Nothing to worry about." He held the banana in one hand, the same one she grasped, and he placed his other hand on her shoulder blade. "You're okay."

"Keithie, what is happening to my legs?" she asked, her voice quivering.

He looked down at her legs. They lay stretched out before her, lithe, tan, and exactly as they had looked every other day of the ten years that he had known her, since they had met that first of September at St. Andrews.

He took his hand off her shoulder blade and placed it on her upper thigh, rubbing it up and down. "They're here, darling. They're right here. I'm touching them. I can feel them. They look gorgeous. You have the most gorgeous legs. Come, here, have a bite of this."

She took a small bite of the banana.

"Did you take something this morning?" he asked as she chewed.

"I'm not whole. I'm certain of it," she said, turning her hands over and staring blankly at her palms.

Keith was awash in concern as he guided the banana back toward her lips.

"You're looking at me that way. That way you do."

"No," Keith said.

She shook her head.

"I can do it myself. I can figure it out. I'll find my legs," she said, quietly, but defiantly.

Keith wrinkled his nose, his jaw clenched.

"Do you have your doctor's phone number here?"

Francine looked out toward St. Vincent across the turquoise water. She put her hands to her temples and lay back down on the towel, covering her face with her arm.

MUSTIQUE

March 6, 2021

MARGHERITA SAT AT the porch table, a glass of pineapple and carrot juice before her, a yellow pad at her right, and eyes in full squint mode before an Excel graph. She had at least twelve tabs open, most of them articles and YouTube videos on how to make five and ten year financial plans for new ventures. Conceptual design, architectural planning, project management, networking—these were all talents she claimed to possess with great confidence, but financials, statistics, algorithms and the like… well, these stumped her.

It had always been a sore subject with her mother—her lack of financial prowess in the face of Francine's innate and profound talents in anything to do with numbers and money. Benjamin had clearly sopped up her genetic skills, marching up the investment banking ladders of London's most prestigious financial institutions, now sitting pretty as one of the youngest partners at the U.K.'s most prominent private equity firm. Francine had treated Benjamin like an equal because of it. They would debate stock picks for hours, retelling tales of CEO's past failures or successes, trading their guesses into the future of publicly traded companies, and calling each other whenever someone of great note was interviewed on CNBC, so they could huff and puff and self-congratulate in the other's company.

Margherita, meanwhile, was viewed as the "artsy" child; i.e., the less financially stable, the less relatable, whose future was a wavering, indiscernible question mark. Only Tommaso understood his daughter's path in commercial architecture. Only her father had gently encouraged her to pursue a degree at Yale. And it was Tommaso who, with an impatient, smiling face, creased at the eyes, held his tan, weathered hand over his daughter's shoulder as she opened her acceptance letter, erupting in a "whoopee" sound so loud he left Margherita's eardrum ringing for hours.

"Yale, Francie!" he'd exclaimed, eyes alight, hitting his palm on the kitchen counter with pride.

"That's fantastic, darling. You must be so proud," Francine had said, without emotion or enthusiasm. She had been in a dry funk for a few weeks, a numb slump that was one of the many versions of her mother Margherita was accustomed to.

The only one not proud here is you, Margherita had thought, as her mother robotically walked toward the staircase and up to her bedroom, where she stayed horizontal for the entire weekend.

From the porch, Margherita could hear the sound of Thayer opening and closing his porch doors. Her eyes grazed toward him without moving her head; she refused to be distracted in the face of so many confusing numerical symbols, and she noted him at his veranda's edge with his hands on his hips. An older gentleman approached and Thayer held out his hand to pat him on the shoulder. Woody joltily ascended the few steps, and the two men sat down in a pair of deck chairs.

That makes sense. Two sad, lonely, men. It's good they have each other, Margherita thought.

She checked her calendar. She had a Zoom call with a potential investor from Vienna in a half hour's time.

After applying a few dots of under-eye concealer and a swipe of barely used lipstick, she double-checked her reflection on her laptop camera and began the Zoom call. The Austrian gentleman was in his mid-forties, with good to very good English and a pleasant demeanor. Margherita dove into her spiel about her experience, her ample familiarity with the Italian market, and the propensity for current hospitality investment within the resort stratosphere.

"So, Margherita, I looked at your presentation document briefly, and I do agree with you that there is great opportunity in this area of Liguria for this level of luxury hotel, but can you tell me more about the timeline for this property?" the Viennese man segued. This was likely a polite way of getting to the subject of money and the investment schedule.

"I aim to take advantage of this moment in the market. Public markets are volatile right now, but private equity is sitting on cash and is eager to invest. Rates are low. The luxury market has never experienced such built-up desire, and along with their desire is their growing cash pile. I want to move quickly with the development period, start immediately, and take advantage of a 'hit the ground positively flying' opening. The Villa, as I have temporarily named it, will have just twenty-four suites. I have highlighted a few choice selections for the build team, and it should take no more than fourteen months to complete the renovation. Landscaping will be young, but we can bring in older trees and bushes so that it looks historic. The biggest risks insofar as build schedule are the usuals—permits, licenses, and the newest hurdle in today's world: supply chain and material delays. My hedge there is to use all Italian materials, which why wouldn't we do anyway? They are the best of the best. I foresee an opening date of September 2023."

"That is extremely ambitious, Margherita," the Viennese gentleman said. "A new hotel of this size, on a cliff side no less, takes at least three years. Even at just twenty-four suites. Permits, supplies, infrastructure surprises…"

"I intend to keep this very streamlined. Simplicity is key, and half of the battle in building is already done. There is no need to review architect pitches; I have completed the plans. There is no need for anyone to debate, change, or approve plans; there is no board or whinging family members. I have my team ready to go, all of my materials chosen, all of my sources lined up and prepared. I just need the capital."

The gentleman's glance was one ounce too quizzical for her liking, as if he were minutely entertained by Margherita's confidence and zealous approach. She felt a rush of impatience run through her as she tapped her foot on the porch.

"Well," he said, looking down at his folded palms. "It is certainly a fantastic property and a stellar design, in one of the world's most beloved playgrounds of the rich and famous. I do not doubt that you have worked very hard at this. However, as you may know, a development process is always behind schedule, and hiccups must be accounted for. With only twenty-four rooms, it will take, I believe, far longer than you foresee to begin seeing a return on investment. Let me look at your presentation again, and make some notes, and I will get back to you," he said, a hint of condescension dripping from his Germanic accent.

"Of course," Margherita said crisply.

"I take it you have incorporated the cost of your work and your own salary throughout development, pre-opening, and post, into your ask?"

"I have incorporated the most minimal annual salary for myself," Margherita replied. "This is *my* project, and it is more important to me that it is brilliantly delivered and successful, rather than my being paid some silly figure. I do not consider myself any Deborah Berke, but I believe my talent will appreciate with time, and certainly with the completion of The Villa."

He nodded and smiled politely. "Do not undersell yourself, Margherita. That is one of the biggest mistakes in this process," he said.

"Of course. Well, I don't want to take too much of your time. Please let me know if you have any questions," she said, perfecting her posture and enunciating each word.

"Wonderful. Thank you Margherita."

She pushed back her chair and allowed herself to slouch completely, throwing her head backwards and running her hands through her hair.

"Good chat then?"

She picked her head up and looked to her right toward Thayer's porch. He stood on it's edge with his hand on the railing, while Woody remained in the chair behind him.

"Could you hear that?" she asked, still slouched in the chair, her legs outstretched.

"Some of it. Why are you talking to Germans? You want a German telling you how to live la dolce vita? Doesn't sound right," Thayer said.

"He was Austrian."

"You need a Greek. Look how much freedom and finesse your father is allowed with this project."

"I need money."

"Care for a rum something instead?"

"Maybe later," Margherita said. "I've got graphs to stare at."

Thayer nodded and turned back around toward Woody.

Fuck me, Margherita thought to herself as she opened the Excel once again, hating the sight of it. Her phone pinged.

Noah: My ass is getting flat.
Noah: old age

Margherita: you're like 35

Noah: I am 41

Margherita: What?!

Noah: Yes, you may not be aware, but each year, I turn one year older.

It was true; Margherita had a vision of Noah in his mid-thirties permanently ingrained in her mind's eye. In truth, he was younger than that when they had met eight years prior, at the architecture firm in New York where they had both worked. She was drawn to his aloofness and dry humor, his British-isms that felt so familiar to her with her very English mother, and his odd but comfortable way of befriending her whilst remaining strangely cold, detached, and tough-loving. It was one of a handful of relationship types that seemed to fit her best.

> **Margherita:** I haven't put on a full face of make-up since March 3 2020. I've no clue how to apply mascara anymore.
>
> **Noah:** You've given up.
>
> **Margherita:** basically.
>
> **Noah:** I'm trying to wear good clothes around. Someone mentioned my neighbors were the "best dressed in the neighborhood" and I was devastated I wasn't considered
>
> **Margherita:** are they though
>
> **Noah:** I think I'm better on my day
>
> **Margherita:** start a drama. Everyone needs a little drama these days.
>
> **Margherita:** look at this. Speaking of best dressed.

Margherita sent a photo she'd taken on her hike that morning of her arms covered in SPF protection sleeves, white slips from her knuckles to her elbows.

> **Noah:** did you get burned? You look like a burn victim
>
> **Margherita:** That's horrible!! I wonder if people think that.
>
> **Margherita:** I'm protecting my Vivien Leigh skin
>
> **Noah:** wasn't she cancelled?

Margherita: don't get me started. Ok I need to concentrate. I am doing cost analysis.

Noah: this doesn't sound good.

Margherita: I need to forecast five years. Do you know how impossible it is to forecast five years financials with a million moving parts, without even having the keys first and knowing actual costs in real time?

Noah: that's my cue. Buh bye.

Margherita turned her phone upside down and held her head with her fingers at her temples, staring at her spreadsheet. A ping rose from the table.

Noah: are you going to watch Meghan and Harry's Oprah interview

Margherita: was that meant for me? Have we met?

Noah: England has never experienced such a whinger in the royal family. It's a disgrace.

Margherita: I can't be bothered. The world is dying.

Noah: Are you still sad about the pandemic? I thought you were moving past that phase.

Noah: I think you need to go on a date

Margherita: who should I date. I'm on the world's richest version of Survivor.

Noah: Precisely. Isn't there some sad, aging rock star you can go be your reckless self with?

Margherita: Yes, but I do not think I'm the trophy fuck they're looking for, and I really can't be bothered. Dating is the farthest thing from my mind at the moment.

Noah: whoa who is this girl

Noah: I miss your wanton ways.

Noah: you were such good entertainment. Like reality TV but better.

Margherita: oh so this is about you being bored.
Margherita: have your own affair then

Noah: ha no. I leave all things heedless to you, dear.

Margherita: I'll send you a postcard when I'm fast and loose again.

Noah: should I have salmon for dinner or chicken

Margherita: I thought you never do the cooking

Noah: I don't but I need to submit my wishes.

Margherita: brat. Let me concentrate!

She turned her phone to silent and set it face down underneath a pile of notes. *Basta.*

On the next porch, she could hear ice cubes clinking. She eyed Thayer's tall, Morrissey hair.

Strange. I haven't even pondered the possibility.

Was it because he was a little sad, or had her over-sexed mind turned to mute without her even realizing? She decided not to dwell on it. Better not to muddy the Caribbean waters.

LONDON

June 7, 1977

"THE SET LIST is meant to be longer than my tongue; I'm not leaving yet!" Rodney yelled over "Killer Queen" just as the triangle rang through Earl's Court Arena. Francine's eyes rolled from her friend to the stage and Freddie's colorful, skin-tight costume with a chest cut-out and Roger's checker-print bodysuit.

Francine huffed to herself, still wondering why she hadn't heard from Christos. He had promised he would be at the concert, though halfway through, he was nowhere to be seen. She debated finding a pay phone but knew there was no chance in hell he would be at home.

She hadn't seen him in nearly a month, having spent the better part of May in bed, numb to the world in a too-long bout of "Francine's Lows," as her parents referred to her waves of depression.

Bea had come to visit with the new Cat Stevens album. Her friend sat on the frilly chair by the window and judged each track, ultimately declaring the album pathetically lightweight and plinky. Francine lay on her side in a fetal position and stared at Bea as if in a trance. The tiny, athletic body hung over the tufted chair, legs flapped in the air, neck scrunched and head pushed into the arm rest. Keith had knocked on the door at that moment.

"It's been a pathetic year so far for music, hasn't it Francie?" he said from the doorway.

"Rumours!" Bea shouted.

"Ha, yeah, and that's about it," he said as he approached the side of the bed nearest Francine and looked down at her expressionless face. He pushed a lock of hair behind her ear and turned to Bea, who shrugged and offered a "this is the best I've seen her," look. Keith kicked off his Samoa sneakers and climbed over Francine's lithe body curled in a ball. Then he adjusted the pillows behind him and picked up a book from the bedside table. "The Bluest Eye" by Toni Morrison. He flipped through it.

"I was just about to go downstairs to make tea. Keith, you fancy a sandwich or something?" Bea stood from the chair and changed the record to Simon & Garfunkel's 1970 "Bridge over Troubled Water."

"Oh—yes. Haven't eaten in hours."

"Was just being friendly. But at your bloody service," Bea said sarcastically as she headed downstairs.

Francine remained curled in a ball facing the window as "The Boxer" began its intro. Keith rubbed her back.

"Francie," he sang slowly. "Fra-a-a-a-ncie."

He pulled her shoulder to turn her around, and shifted her onto her back. With one hand on each of her shoulders, he turned her another ninety degrees to face him. His top hand stroked her hair.

"Fra-a-a-a-ncie," he sang quietly.

"I'm tired," she whispered.

"I know." he said as he ran his thumb around the periphery of her hairline, along the top of her forehead as she closed her eyes.

"I want to sleep."

"Okay. How about having a little tea, and then Bea and I will leave you to it for a while?" He kissed her forehead and lay with her until Bea returned with tea and cheese sandwiches.

It took her longer than usual to emerge, and it was not until Dr. Gavison made a house call with an extra dosage of lurasidone that she managed to get dressed, brush her hair, and meet Bea for lunch in South Kensington.

Too frustrated and distracted to enjoy the concert, she itched for something to set her mind afloat.

She spun on her heel toward Bea and Susan, who had crowded themselves around a makeshift ledge on a sidewall. She snuck up behind her friends and put a hand on each of their shoulders.

"Girls! Can we go now? Ohh, what's this?" Francine eyed the pills that both of their petite backs hid from the rest of the arena.

Bea flashed obvious big eyes at Susan, who matched the 'oh shit' expression.

"Oh, fuck off, the two of you," Francine shouted as she dived her hand into the fishbowl.

"Ay!" Bea slapped her friend's hand away.

Francine gave her best friend a deathly glare. "Those are fucking disco biscuits Bea, you're going to have *one* each. Don't be a fucking hog."

"Fran, no. I'm sorry. But no! You can't!" Bea shouted, blocking the pill assortment with her body.

Francine felt her blood curl, but she knew Bea would not go down without a fight. She came as close as possible to her face, with a glare so horrid Bea actually took a step backward toward the wall. Then, with sudden force, Francine grabbed her by the arms and kissed her on the mouth before spinning on her heels and leaving the arena.

Outside, the June air was warm and dewy, and crowds of people were strewn all along the street, some sat on the sidewalk smoking, trading PCPs, or maybe even mescaline for all they knew, and speaking to each other with eyes half open. Two lovers, probably strangers, lay on the pavement kissing.

She fell in step behind three guys who appeared to be about her age, maybe a few years younger, and at what felt like the right moment, she skipped in front of them. They stopped short.

"Where you off to?" she asked, taking in each one, one at a time. They eyed one another, entertained by the surprise encounter.

"Madame Jojo's. Want to join?" the one in the middle asked, placing his right foot closer to Francine's booted toe. He looked her up and down carefully, from her wide legged, high waisted trousers, to her short sleeve, skin-tight, ribbed cardigan with its plunging v-neck. Francine watched his gaze until his eyes met hers. She raised her eyebrows.

"Depends," she said.

"On?" the one on the left challenged her.

"What are you bringing?" Francine nodded toward their pockets.

The boys eyed each other again until the one in the middle nodded.

"Rainbows," the one on the left said, tapping his front pocket.

"Black beauties," the one on the right said, flexing his arm muscles as he dug his hands into his pockets.

"One of each?" she asked, flirtatiously.

The boys looked at each other and laughed.

"Fine, love. But you're coming to Jojo's."

Five days later, Francine landed at London's Luton airport feeling hollowed and dirty. She didn't have any belongings with her, and she wasn't wearing any underwear beneath an oversized sweatshirt that covered the tops of her thighs. She smoothed out the sides of her hair as she slowly waded through the terminal, passersby eying her warily.

Near the restrooms was a pay phone. She quickly looked around and stopped a businessman in a hat striding toward his gate.

"Excuse me, sir, so sorry to bother you. I know I must look a right mess, and very curious, but, you see I lost my wallet, and I need to make a call…" She gestured toward the pay phone.

The man's worn face regarded her with a mixture of pity and judgment. He placed his small suitcase on the grimy floor and dug in his pocket to retrieve a few pence, which he dropped into her palm without a word.

"Thank you. Thank you so very much. That's very kind," she said to his back as he strode away.

She carefully slid the coins into the slot and pushed the numbers round the dial, holding the phone cord and watching people walk to their gate, all of them dressed and fully aware of their place in the world at that moment.

"Keithie," she gasped. "Thank God."

"Francine where the fuck are you? We've been looking for you for five days. Fuck! Francine?"

Francine closed her eyes and inhaled deeply through her nose, nodding in silence. "I'm sorry. I'm sorry."

"Where are you?"

"At the airport."

"What airport? Why?"

"Luton."

"Where are you going?"

"No where. I've just come back."

"From where?"

"Amsterdam?"

"With who? Why? Since when?"

"Um, Keithie, listen it's a long story. Don't worry. It was fantastic. Wild. Loved every minute. But I'm not wearing any panties, and I have no money on me. Can you get me, do you mind?"

She could hear him exhale frustration across the line.

"Come, darling, your Ruby Tuesday needs you," she pleaded, innocently.

"Stay where you are. Don't fucking leave the airport, Francine, I mean it. Meet me at baggage claim. Don't. Leave."

The phone clicked and she hung the piece on the receiver. She stared at it for a moment before she erupted in laughter in the booth.

As she made her way toward baggage claim, following the signs, she felt warm tears on her cheeks.

She sat down on the edge of an unengaged baggage belt and leaned her head into her hands, gripping her dirty hair hard between her fingers.

"I fucking hate myself. I fucking hate myself," she cried into the pit in her stomach. "I fucking hate myself. I fucking hate myself."

MILAN

April 26, 2021

IT WAS AFTER two in the morning, but Margherita couldn't sleep. The jet-lag was worse than normal, which she attributed to "getting older," though Noah rolled his eyes at this. She had been in Milan only a week, but something felt off—different, than when she had last been there pre-pandemic.

Of course, she had to allow it that. The Italians had experienced one of the worst lockdowns in Europe, and as they were amongst the first to be ravaged by the virus, with a disproportionate amount of deaths and army vans circling ancient villages, constant sirens twenty-four hours a day for months, and the strictest of rules, it was bound to feel like a war-torn, depressed battlefield. This was not helped by the complete lack of tourists, in a country so buoyed by tourism. The people were emotionally scarred, the mood heavy, the negativity and despondency substantial.

The landing was, luckily for Margherita, extremely comfortable. Thayer had made an introduction on her behalf; an Italian friend of his ex-wife's who kept a flat in Milan kindly allowed a random friend of Thayer's to rent it at a fair price in an open-ended agreement.

"He intends to flog it, says he hasn't used it in years, but the market in Italy is bleak. Positively funereal, if you will. He might as well just let it sit and have the odd gypsy girl check in on his Taikan nihonga." Thayer had been absentmindedly watching Margherita pack up her bedroom on Mustique. He sat on the floor with his back against the bed while Margherita rolled bathing suits into tootsie rolls and stuffed them into the perimeters of her suitcase.

"Wouldn't he be more concerned that this odd gypsy girl would steal his Taikan nihonga?"

"The average odd gypsy girl has never heard of a Taikan nihonga and has no idea its value."

"Right."

"Example. Do *you*, Odd Gypsy Girl, know what I am referring to when I say Taikan nihonga?"

"Haven't a clue."

The modern flat was Japanese-inspired, with high ceilings, a narrow corridor lined with structural frames that let in slats of light from the living room beyond, and a shoji screened bathroom. There was also the extremely large painting by an artist named Taikon, in what was, Margherita finally learned after googling, a traditional matte style called nihonga. It should have inspired tranquility, but it clearly wasn't working on Margherita.

She stood at the bedroom window, looking up and down a quiet Via Manzoni. Occasionally, a moto zoomed by, driven by a man in a suit jacket or leather bomber, on his way home from somewhere in the middle of the night. She reflected on the many times she had rushed down the busy street's sidewalk in the thick of the day, with traffic honking at the intersections and motos weaving between cars, women hurrying over the tram tracks in high heels while men turned their heads to get a second look. Her old apartment was a few blocks away, and she had traversed those crosswalks hundreds of times. A lifetime ago, it felt like.

She shifted the blinds closed again, climbed back into the low to the ground king-sized bed, and tapped her phone screen. Thayer had messaged an hour previously.

Thayer: how's that wabi-sabi spirit

Margherita: fittingly imperfect, impermanent, and incomplete

Thayer: ah. As defined, then.

Margherita pressed the play button on her iPad (the apartment's television was so high-tech, she still, after one week, hadn't figured out Netflix), but she couldn't concentrate. She looked up at the coffered ceilings and began to count the squares from one side of the room to the other.

She paused the show again and turned her Spotify to shuffle in an attempt to mellow her mind with music, then picked up her phone and searched for someone with whom she could chat absent-mindedly.

Every chat with 'N' was a new chat, according to WhatsApp. Every chat that she had ever had with him in the past three years was deleted, sometimes a few days afterwards, sometimes immediately. When it came to Nick, she was either indulging a feeling or suppressing it, and there wasn't a whole lot in-between. Besides which, she didn't want to be reminded of the things she had once said to him—the feelings she shared in moments of weakness, the anger she unleashed in frustration, the countless ignored messages she had sent in search of a friend.

And she definitely did not want to be reminded of the few times he had been even minutely thoughtful, and she had taken it for more than it was worth.

He was likely confounded as to why she wrote to him, as to why he was the recipient of her random thoughts, her music or book or movie suggestions, her stirring questions.

"Courage" by the Villagers began to play and she rolled her eyes at her phone. *Pure coincidence.*

She could picture herself on the Canal Street subway platform that winter night, on her way home from a date. After a long bout of silence, she had sent him a song, and he in turn sent her "Courage." She remembered listening to it as the trains rumbled past. The E that was practically six per minute. The A that rarely came at all.

She pressed the call button.

"Hello," Nick said sleepily. Margherita could hear blankets shifting.

"I'm watching the most ridiculous show. Her husband dies in a car crash. Then she falls in love. Then her new boyfriend gets shot. Then his house burns down. Then she saves the local drug lord's life. It's so dumb and yet."

"And yet. You're still watching it."

"And yet, here I am. Episode after episode," she sighed. "Were you sleeping?"

"Yes, yes I was," Nick said. Margherita could hear sounds of sitting up.

"Do you want to go back to sleep?" she asked.

"No, no."

"Okay."

"Where are you?"

"Milan," Margherita said. "Since last week. Took me a month to get documents."

"Ah. Well done you. Must feel good to be back. Ready to run the town? Enchant all those suited Italian investors? Build the dream?"

Her stomach flipped. The anxiety had been worse than ever; the instantaneous rupture of tears came on unexpectedly, nausea and self-doubt hung at disturbing levels. What she found so alarming was not the anxiety itself, which had always arrived in bursts and waves, but the fact that it flowed through her blood in relation to her move to Italy.

Years earlier, when she had picked up and moved to Milan at the impressionable age of twenty-five, she had experienced nothing but an exhilarating and prolonged honeymoon-like high. She thrived on the open-endedness of it, and the beauty, charm, and potential of what her life could become. Now, at thirty-one, she felt she was free-falling in an unfamiliar cloud of doubt and regret.

"Do you think I'm an idiot?"

"No. Why would I think you're an idiot?"

"For leaving my dad. For moving to a country that doesn't function very well. For devoting so much time to a preposterous idea that probably will flop. For spending so much on moving—again—" she rattled on.

"Margherita, darling, you are living. You are daring to live. You are making your life interesting. You are adding to your future obituary."

"Morbid," she said, dryly.

"Yes, but… it's true."

She squeezed her big toe between her thumb and pointer finger, nodding to herself. "Do you want to watch this show with me? It's so ridiculous."

"Sounds like a bunch of poppycock. What is it? And what episode are we on? Catch me up."

After they finished an episode, Margherita stifled a yawn.

"Tired?" he asked.

"A bit," she said, though she didn't want to hang up. She rolled onto her side, her right hand facing the ceiling in the shape of an upside down crab. How sweet it would be if there was someone next to her to slide a warm palm into it.

"Time for sleep. That's a ridiculous show. I'll probably have dreams of drug lords and gun shot wound surgery on trail hikes. Never knew the Pacific Northwest was so wild."

"Sorry. You know I love a little drama."

"Yes. I do. Goodnight darling."

"Goodnight, *dahling*," she said, and ended the call.

Margherita recalled one evening in New York, one of the instances in which she had tried to tell Nick off and end their affair. "I think you enjoy the drama," she had said. He had flung it right back at her.

The truth was, they both enjoyed the drama.

The next day she woke early for a breakfast meeting with a senior partner at Matteo Cassino, one of the most highly regarded architecture firms in Italy, with projects ranging from modern flagship boutiques to the most highly anticipated luxury hotels, community complexes, leisure centers, and university libraries. Emiliano, a friend who her former Milanese lover Paolo had once introduced her to, had kindly agreed to meet with Margherita to offer an opinion on the plans for The Villa. Every relationship in Italy was based on introductions; one didn't accomplish anything without a network.

They were set to meet in CityLife, the modern mixed-use district north of Parco Sempione where new construction had been prolific for a decade, with a great deal more to come in its transformation from barren industrial wasteland to premier work/life destination. The road to arrive in the zone was wide and spatial, far from the colorful, elegant, old palazzi of central Milan that Margherita loved. Planned green spaces, modern high-rises and residential developments, all vying to be most avant-garde, became more and more frequent as her Uber approached the café. So many of the big names in architecture had a foothold there: Daniel Libeskind's PwC tower with its 40 meter-tall crown comprised of 600 tons of steel and glass (containing, among other integral components, a rainwater recycling system), Bjarke Ingels's incredible 'portico'—a hanging roof structure connecting two buildings complete with a rooftop bar overlooking the Alps, Zaha Hadid's twisting Generali tower and shopping complex where each floor's rhomboid shape was fractionally reduced from the floor below, as well as her distinctive, serpentine condo building. Margherita recognized the works of Carlo Ratti, Arata Isozaki, and of course, Andrea Maffei's Allianz Tower.

Two empty espresso cups sat before them as Emiliano spoke freely about the current environment in Milan, his legs casually crossed and his left shoulder into the back of the chair. He raised one or both of his hands every few seconds, every concept and statement supported by gesticulation.

"So you think I'd have better luck elsewhere, is what you are telling me. Not very uplifting, Emiliano!"

He shrugged, his furry eyebrows raised toward his curly hair. "Margherita, I want to be honest with you. What you need is not here. You want to build out a team. You have no firm. Nothing to stand on. No one will take your project seriously until you have that. Everything is hierarchal in Italy. Everything is on a smaller scale. People are spread thin. We can barely finish what we've started amongst ourselves, let alone be the cheerleader for an uncommissioned job."

"I don't need a large team. I don't need anthropologists or environmental psychologists. No specialties. Understanding the DNA of the project is all I require. How will guests live in the space. How will locals use it, pass through it, engage with it. It's simple. I doubt it will be a high-paying project to work on, but it will be highly visible, for a firm who wants to champion it. With me." She followed his gaze to her vibrating foot, which she had not noticed was shaking.

Emiliano nodded slowly. She could tell he was ready to move on from this coffee.

"Tell me about your materials."

"Limestone. Glass. Stone. It's all about sensibility, thoughtfulness, and style of course. It's about the connection of Paraggi's fabulous history with a sustainable, forward-thinking concept. Less closed doors, more spatiality, more luminosity. Room to breathe without forgetting style and fantasy. Less power requirements, more oculus for daylighting."

Emiliano checked his watch.

"Do you have to run?"

"Yes, actually, I have a meeting with a client in an hour and want to review a few things. But listen, Margherita, I think what you've done here is great. It's a great start. Just don't... get your hopes up, right? So many of these kinds of projects, even the most promising ones, die in the water. Even the ones coming out of the most famous firms in the world."

She pursed her lips and nodded.

"Right. I know."

"Have you seen Paolo?" he asked as they both stood.

"No, not yet."

Margherita had not yet told Paolo that she was in Milan. She was determined not to fall into old habits, to be a wiser, more mature version of herself than the twenty-something girl who traded dinner for cocktails with men twice her age and slept in half a dozen hotel rooms with someone else's husband.

Though, she missed that girl. And that time period.

A lot.

Later that evening, after three more espresso meetings with former contacts, all of whom suggested she get a job, keep working on her contacts and continue to build her resume, she wandered around dusty Parco Venezia. She landed on a green bench, where she watched dogs jump into the fountain for a lick of water, shaking themselves off wildly before joining the others for a gallop in the field.

Her phone vibrated in her jacket pocket.

Noah: Alive today?

She smiled down at the screen. Noah's satire was always warmly welcomed. They basked in the joyousness of cynicism, usually Noah more-so than Margherita, but she could be easily swayed to the dark side.

Margherita: Lingering headache and lots of anxiety and stress
Margherita: but yes I remain physically alive
Margherita: And you?

Noah: I'm alive too
Noah: lingering anxiety and dread. Generally thirsty
Noah: but physically alive, yes

Margherita: we are two real positive humans

Noah: lol really into these Monday morning blues vibes. Just life dread. I have life-envy
Noah: And I have to do my team call where I go full blown American positivity

Margherita: Ugh the horror
Margherita: can't you go British on them and just be miserable

Noah: Jeesh I wish.
Noah: Thank god you're fifty percent English misery. We'd have no common language otherwise.

LONDON

IT HAD BEEN a few months since Francine had last visited her mother in Hampstead. Since secondary school, when her mother's emotional and mental state had begun to deteriorate, Francine had developed a push/pull with the house in Gainsborough Gardens. Inside was a melange of idyllic and upsetting memories; moments of childhood that came to mind so vividly she could practically smell the lilies in the garden, could practically hear the crisp pages of her father's newspaper, her mother's voice calling them into the den after tea for an old black and white movie. She could recall on which step she sat as they put on evening coats, furs and hats, long gloves and elegant umbrellas, on their way out for the evening. She could hear her mother giggling from their bedroom Saturday morning. And she could see her father's hand on her mother's chestnut hair at the kitchen table, stroking it, twisting it, and kissing her neck.

Upsetting memories began when her mother's psychologist had changed her medication, and unmanageable side effects having to do with a distressed kidney sent her into hospital at least once a week. For as long as Francine could remember, her mother had taken a cocktail of multi-colored pills from a bathroom cabinet, never once explained to Francine. There had been instances in which her mother would pass a few days in bed, or do something extraordinarily spontaneous, like the time she had taken a five-year-old Francine to Land's End one autumn day, the two of them nearly blowing right off the cliff's edge. When they returned to London, her father was frantic, having no idea where they had vanished to. But for the most part, Francine's mother had been just like all the other mothers in Hampstead, only perhaps more beautiful, more vibrant, and more colorful.

Something in her mother's chemistry had shifted, and her doctor wasn't able to land on a combination that worked without further damaging her internal organs. The impeccably-dressed, perfectly-manicured, highly-socialized, ultra feminine woman who had raised her had morphed into another being entirely; an unpredictable, untamed, embarrassing version Francine had never known. For two years, her mother went on and off her meds, see-sawing between chronic kidney disease and extreme bouts of mania and depression.

All the while, Francine's own mental illness, diagnosed at sixteen and clearly inherited from her mother, was changing form every day.

Francine's father, with two manic-depressive women at home, grew weaker and wearier. As he watched the love of his life slip away, he became more dogged about Francine's treatment. He was determined to keep his daughter out of the same treacherous, thorny path, and he was fearful of how the stressful environment could be triggering for Francine.

The divorce was like separating oil from water; neither person truly wanted it to happen, and there were many reasons out of their control for its enactment, but her mother had become so alien to both of them, and so disruptive, that a re-allotment of the family members seemed the most sensible answer. Francine's father decided, though it broke his heart, that he had a duty to his daughter. He did not want Francine to witness her mother's extreme bouts so often; it only made Francine sink farther into a hole populated by one; depressed, convinced she was looking into a crystal ball of her future. Her mother was left to test the boundaries of her moods on her own, assisted by a hired nurse.

Out moved one broken-hearted man, torn between love and responsibility, and one teenage girl, more aware than most of life's modulating icebergs.

Francine loved her mother, and she understood her illness better than her father. But that did not mean it was not depressing to see her in bed for a month at a time. One morning, Francine had gone over with still-warm crumpets, thinking she and her mum would have breakfast in the garden, next to the daffodils which surely would have bloomed in the warm April sun. When she arrived, she found her mother curled up in the dewy grass, sticks in her hair, carpenter ants from the nearby wood bench crawling on her ankles. There was, according to her mother, a stranger in her bedroom who would not leave nor stop talking to her through the night.

Francine's visits became less and less frequent; she could not bear to see her beautiful mother deteriorate, and it was too awful a reminder of what she herself must look like sometimes, in her swing states.

Though her father would not let her live on her own, she managed to evade his house on Upper Cheyne Row a few nights a week by sleeping at Christos' flat on Circus Road, much to her father's concern. He had never met Christos, and though she assured him that he was a charming Greek gentleman (once in a while this was even true), her father was wary of any detail of Francine's life he could not himself control. He fretted over her movements as if she were a child, not a woman in her late twenties.

Francine was on a mostly solid streak during the week. In the mornings, they would pop into Panzers Grocer for coffee, smoked salmon and bagels, then make their way toward Regents. She insisted on taking in the morning light in the park, soaking up the spirited dogs off-lead before she got on the tube at Marylebone. It had been a few months since starting as a receptionist at an American investment bank, and so far so good; she hadn't mucked it up. While her father and Dr. Gavison were wary of her committing to full-time, worried she would make a mockery of herself at some point, she was determined to set her own record straight.

She was deteremined to move on beyond London, beyond the vigilant limitations.

At her mother's house in Gainsborough Gardens, just across the road from the Heath, she quietly shut the front door behind her and bent down to collect a handful of old newspapers and unopened mail haphazardly tossed next to the ribbed, brass brolly holder. When Francine had been a little girl, she had never seen a thing on the floor unless she herself had mindlessly left it there. Her mother's pristineness had diminished acutely, and though Francine was just as scattered, she grated her teeth at the disarray in her beautiful childhood home.

As she walked down the main hall toward the kitchen at the back of the house, placing the newspapers and mail on the round table with its dried and deadened flowers, she could not help but notice the stagnant, closed scent. It reminded her of the patients' rooms at the Landor Road Day Hospital in South London, where she had often spent the night after a too-difficult-to-handle manic episode. Her father would bring her in with horror and exhaustion and heartbreak in his eyes, unable to do anything to calm his teenage daughter from the treacherous lurches of her own mind. The rooms smelled like damp closets, starchy bedding, and the nurse's hairspray. Francine would smell it oozing from her follicles for days after she was freed to go home, even after dozens of baths or lake swims. It seeped into her skin in the same way her pores reeked of alcohol after a bender.

"Mum?" Francine stuck her head into the kitchen, which appeared abandoned save for a half drunk cup of tea on the counter, an open packet of crisps, and three soft and bruised pears begging to be tossed. She took them by their weak stems and launched them into the bin. The black and white checkered floor was in dire need of a mop and broom, and the light green cabinetry that had always felt so cheerful in her childhood, sunblotched and matched with fresh flowers from the garden, had never appeared more sad, cast in the shadow of the sun-less afternoon.

"Mum?" Back in the hallway, at the foot of the stairs, Francine craned her neck upwards. She climbed the steps, one hand on the large banister, exhaling, preparing for gloom.

Her mother had grown more and more depressed, less erratic than she had been in recent years, and a great deal slower and quieter. In the last twelve months alone, she had seen her mother dressed in presentable clothing only a handful of times, and any food she brought her was left to rot in the fridge.

"Mummy?" Francine called out again as she slowly ascended the stairs.

She peered into her old bedroom as she walked down the upper hall, where her old maths books sat in a pile on her desk, and an array of concert ticket stubs remained stuck to the wall, faded and softened.

At the end of the corridor, the door to what was formerly her parents bedroom was ajar, and Francine pushed it gently and stuck her head into the chilly room. All three windows were pushed up and the cool September air streamed in. Francine breathed in the outside, the dampness coming off the Heath.

Her mother lay in bed in a fetal position, facing the window that overlooked the center garden. She wore a silk robe and her hair looked like it had been recently brushed. Perhaps the nurse had just left—though if she had been there, why hadn't she cleaned up a bit?

Francine lay down on the side where her father used to sleep and scooted closer to her mother, wrapping her slender arm around her. Her mother's bony hand grappled for Francine's, and she wrapped her chilled fingers around it, feeling the diamond-studded serpent ring that never came off.

"Mummy, how long have you been in bed?" Francine spoke quietly into her mother's hair.

Her mother turned around to face her daughter. Her face was dry and colorless. Only her eyes, green as emeralds, showed any vitality. She said nothing.

"Mummy?" Francine squeezed her mother's bony hand.

Her mother pushed a wisp of hair out of her daughter's face. "You're so beautiful, Francie," she said, smiling wistfully.

Francine rested her cheek on her forearm.

"Don't waste away here. I kept telling your father. Let her go. He's so damn protective. I said, let our girl be a woman. You can't squash her with doctor whatsit and doctor whossit all the time. Just don't let them make you feel small. Don't let those fuckers win," she said, squeezing her daughters hand.

"Who?" Francine asked.

"All of them. Be big. Be bigger than them." Her mother's green eyes widened and bore into her.

"Okay."

Her mother wrapped her thin arms around her daughter and squeezed her tightly.

"You are not alone, my darling," her mother said into her hair. "You are never alone, never alone," she repeated.

"Okay," Francine whispered, more nervous for her mother's sanity than her own, and more alone than ever.

MILAN

May 12, 2021

JUST AFTER NINE, Margherita exited the zen apartment, crossed Via Manzoni, and turned onto the uneven stones of Via della Spiga. The shops were still closed, and she noticed one of the cafés that used to be open reliably early had gone out of business.

Via Montenapoleone was so quiet, Margherita could hear a window slide open above her head and a cigarette sizzle on the sidewalk as she entered her favorite café, the same café she had frequented nearly every day when she last lived in Milan. She quickly found, however, Marchesi wasn't the same when everyone entered in a mask, and all of the familiar faces behind the counter, in their tuxedo or vintage smock dress uniforms were covered in Pandemic-Wear. The café had once been a key fixture in the routine of so many chic Milanese; those who lived or worked in the infamously stylish Quadrilatero D'Oro. So many of those people now spent the majority of their time at their second home, outside of the city, or had not returned to the office, leaving the café to wither and wilt.

The neighborhood was known as one of the best dressed and most desirable shopping addresses in the world, and in the Prada-designed café, lined with glass display cases artfully filled with *marmellata*, collectible tins of pralines, pastel-colored candies and jellies, exquisite cakes and pastries, panettone and Gianduiotti, the people watching at the counter was— pre-pandemic—nothing short of cinematic. Sophia Loren lookalikes—women with their hair just blown out, exquisite cat-eyes, outfits from the future pages of Vogue, and their shoes or six-hundred-euro sneakers in constant competition with the pair next to them—stood shoulder to shoulder with bespoke suits. Men wore fine leather shoes, their skin glistened from the sun, their hair was neatly combed. Everyone exchanged pleasantries and affectionate jokes with the long-time staff behind the counter as they sipped macchiatos, espresso, cappuccino, and took effortless bites from sugar-dusted, buttery brioche, filled with honey or jam or pistachio cream.

When Margherita entered, however, the café was quiet, and the two patrons at the counter were expressionless, having their breakfast in an otherwise banal setting, the colorful displays a sad leftover reminder of the spirited Milano that had not quite found itself after the pandemic's somber winter. There were even a few new faces behind the counter, and Margherita felt at once the dissociation with a place that had long been a link to a sense of community and belonging. She had her espresso quietly and stepped back out onto Via Montenapoleone, a ghost of its former self. On the corner of Via Verri, she slid into a taxi and tried to refocus her mind on the meeting ahead.

In a modern glass building in Via Tortona, Margherita stood over the paper plans and looked around the table at the three middle-aged men whose private equity firm focused on real estate development. She was taking every meeting. Every potential contact was worth her time.

They were cold and dry as a three-day-old porchetta sandwich. She had thrown "female founder" around, she had tooted diversification of assets, she had name-dropped every impressive architect for whom she had worked. They had very few questions, very few comments, and were mostly interested in why she had left America, in a pandemic above all, to try her hand once again in Italy.

Which she had ignored.

She tried to find the balance between pushy, direct American and polite, refined, submissive Italian, the latter being more culturally acceptable to three middle-aged Italian men. She tried to channel Francine. She pretended she had her own architecture firm, assumed a confidence she didn't have the right to.

But at the conclusion of the one hour block, they thanked her, declined a hand shake (COVID), and wished her the best of luck. Hotels were not a business in which they were interested at the moment. Perhaps check back in a year or two.

After the meeting, Margherita returned to the center to meet Camilla for lunch. They had been as close as sisters when Margherita had last lived in Italy, and though there were days during the pandemic when they exchanged messages from morning til night, the truth of the matter was their friendship hadn't entirely withstood distance and time zones.

The hardest test of their sister-like friendship was the rushing river into motherhood. Margherita had made her best effort to stay in touch with Camilla throughout her friend's pregnancy, but as soon as baby Dalia had been born, Camilla's priorities and attentions had been directed elsewhere.

"So, tell me about this 'project.' I don't understand what you're trying to do," Camilla squinched her eyes condescendingly at Margherita once they'd placed their order at Giacomo Bistrot. The café did not yet allow indoor seating, and the two sat outside in Via Sottocorno, across from the petite pasticceria where Margherita used to buy wedges of panettone at Christmastime, having eaten the entire thing by the time she reached the Parco Venezia.

"Well, it's a boutique hotel. On the way to Portofino. In an old villa jutting out over the sea."

"I don't understand. You're going to build a villa?"

"No. It's already there, but it's derelict and basically abandoned. It's sitting in a trust with the bank, and we are going to buy it, skivvy it down to its bones, and bring it back to its glory."

"Oh so you're not doing this by yourself!" Camilla smiled and laughed. "I thought you were doing this all alone. I was like, is she crazy?"

"No—I *am* doing it alone, but with investors, and then with a team of course. Eventually."

Camilla's face was confused again. "So you have an investor? Wow!"

"Well, not yet. But that's what I'm working on now."

"So, you're all alone so far?"

"Yes. I've done my homework, trust me, I've been working on this for a year. I have interested parties. I have the plans ready to go. I just paid for building and demolition permits—they could take ages, so I needed to get that under way. And I'm working with lawyers to free the property from the bank."

"You bought the property? Yourself!?" Camilla's contorted face of disbelief and confusion was one step too far, and Margherita felt the beginnings of steam in her ears, the indignation growing red hot at her fingertips.

Margherita took a sip of water and shot a dirty look at the smoking man next to them who heedlessly blew into their faces. "No. I hired the lawyers to work on unraveling the red tape, so that when I have an investor, the purchase is swift, and we'll have our permits, and everything will be ready to go."

"So you invested all of your own money into these things before you even have an investor?"

"I have to have skin in the game, Camilla, or they'll think I'm a flighty rich girl looking to make a TikTok reel."

Camilla laughed. "It's so interesting to me how you take these risks. You move here, you move back, you change jobs, you move again, you 'invest' in things with no idea what will happen. Good thing you don't have kids or a family or anything!" Her false smile and disingenuous cackle pierced the dull sidewalk as the sullen waiter brought them a basket of gluten-free bread and asked if they were ready to order. Service had soured since the pandemic, and all around her Margherita felt as if the city she had once called home was wearing a different mask other than an N95. It was a mask of surly antagonism, an inhospitable and embittered facade that Margherita did not recognize.

After they had each ordered a plate of spinach cooked in the pan with extra garlic and chili flakes and a chilled seafood salad, Margherita attempted to change the subject.

"So, how is Dalia? How is being back at work? I can't believe you're a mamma!" Margherita slapped a smile on her face, knowing this was a safer subject.

"Oh. Fabulous. Everything is fabulous. I told you about my promotion, right? And I got a raise. I was like, no way in hell you're giving me more work without more money. I already practically run the place," Camilla rattled as she flipped her long hair with her manicured fingers. "The nanny is fantastic. I mean, it took me a few. The first three or four were horrific. Horrific! But we've got it down now. We're working remotely from Noli for all of July. August on Elba. We rented a villa with a few friends and their babies. It will be adorable. I can't believe everyone has kids now. It's like, how did that happen!"

Margherita concentrated on her octopus and spinach as she smiled along. Camilla always had loved to brag, but on the back-end of the morning's unsuccessful meetings and then coupled with her friend's condescension, Margherita wanted nothing more than to get up from the table, buy herself an enormous panettone across the street, and eat the entire thing in her wabi-sabi apartment. Fuck traditions—Christmas or not—she yearned for nothing else but that spongey cake and a tall glass of silence.

MUSTIQUE

January 2, 1978

FRANCINE TIPPED HER head back to let the cold water splash her clavicle and run down her chest. A ribbon of hibiscus lined the tip of the wooden slats that blocked the outdoor shower from the pathway, and she eyed each one, bright in color. There was something so pure about bathing in the open air, surrounded by the tropical flowers and the sticky sweet smell of rum rinsing from her pores. Bea shamed her for showering outdoors, where one could supposedly see her in the nude, but she didn't care. She felt free.

She wrapped a linen towel around her body and combed her wet hair. The record player skipped on 'Sound and Vision' and she went to rebalance the arm, lighting a cigarette from the sideboard table and blowing out coolly and slowly as she stood in her towel, glancing at herself in the round mirror on the wall above the record player.

Keith sang as he approached from the porch. Francine could see him in the reflection of the mirror where he stood in the open doorway, the floor-length curtain swaying at his side. He leaned into the doorframe with his forearm and placed his weight on one side, accentuating the shape of his chest.

Francine smiled with her eyes.

Keith carried on as he slowly stepped toward her.

"Blue, blue," she said into his shoulder as he wrapped her moist body in a hug. She carefully held the cigarette a few inches from his shoulder blade.

He sang as he rubbed the towel into her back. They turned in place.

She looked up at him.

"How was your shower?"

"Gorgeous," she said, taking a drag with closed eyes and her head tipped backward.

"You're late. We're waiting for you at Basil's."

"Am I?" she said flippantly. She disengaged from his tan arms, put out the cigarette in the ash tray on the sideboard, and padded with wet feet down the hall toward the bedroom. He followed, still humming along to Bowie.

Francine dropped the towel on her bed, aware of Keith's eyes behind her. She reached for a crochet baby doll dress with a fringed bottom and deep v-cut that revealed her stomach all the way down to below her belly button. She turned to him as she pulled it on. He watched with a closed lip smile.

"What do you think?" she asked, as she bent to slide on her shoes.

"You're beautiful, Francie," He leaned his head into the doorframe.

She stood on her tippy toes and kissed him on the lips.

There were no other lips that felt more comfortable, more like home, than Keith's. She had gotten to know them well over the years, starting with a close friendship that had morphed into a grey area of romance at university, and a grey area of romance that turned to a pasticcio of love and attachment in the years afterwards, constantly thrown into disarray by Francine's intermittent turbulence and unhealthy relationships with other men. Keith, in Francine's eyes, was best kept as her friend and confidante; she would never want to completely subject him to the unpredictability of her mind. She would never want him to be in her father's position: blocked in, broken-hearted, and helpless.

Well into their twenties, their bond had felt unbreakable,

and while Francine never addressed any lingering feelings her friend might harbor, she was confident that Keith would always be there, a uniquely forever presence. Christos was fire; Keith was earth and water. There was no one else she preferred to climb into bed with in the middle of the night and talk about both the mundanely quotidian things and the big dreams, the boring and the brilliant, the truths and the lies.

"We're both beautiful. Let's go, darling," she said, and led the way down the hall.

At the party at the Plantation House, Francine's long fingers were wrapped around one Caribbean Sour after another while a cigarette sat perpetually between her fingers and her eyes sat on Cole's brother. The night was a debauched olio of music that could not be loud enough and hands that could not be felt enough, and she maintained a firm, inexplicable grip on Bea's wrist. She held it even as she guided Cole's brother's fingers beneath her dress. She held it even while she slid her tongue around his mouth.

Bea laughed and tried to pry herself away from the uninhibited Francine, but Francine would not let her.

"Looks like it will be three of us?" Cole's brother raised his eyebrows.

"No, Francie, not this again." Bea shook her head.

"She won't sleep with me." Francine turned toward Bea. "Why won't you sleep with me Beatrice?"

"I don't want to, love. I'm sorry." Bea giggled. She yanked her arm but Francine dug her nails into her.

"Francie, let go."

Triggered by Bea's hard refusal, Francine broke into an incoherent whirl about manifesting one's sexual destiny and the tremendous thrills of re-purposing one's body for science, and how at night, a woman named Vasha came to her bedroom and spoke to her about the connection between consciousness and desire.

Keith approached at some point and pried Francine's fingers from Bea's forearm, which had grown red and irritated. Francine shrieked and kicked and broke a bottle of Flor de Cana. Everyone looked on for a moment, laughed uncomfortably, and partied on. It was, to most everyone, a girl who had drunk too much, or swallowed too many, or mixed in a dramatic way. Nothing special or extraordinary.

———————

Francine remained in bed the next morning with a wicked headache, too drained and limp to face the day on the island.

When Keith walked into the bedroom and raised the blinds around high noon, the sun cast a glaring shadow above her headboard. She closed her eyes and rolled over onto her stomach, her face into the pillow.

He lay down next to her in his swimming trunks and stroked her hair.

"Francie, whatever you're taking isn't meant to be mixed. Maybe you need to take it easy for a bit, give the partying a pause. See how you do."

"I am nothing but a Petri dish." She turned her face toward him, her left cheek plunged into the linen pillow cover. Her mascara smudged. "That is the culmination of my life."

"Only if you let it."

"Oh. Easy for you to say." Her mouth twisted and her nostrils flared as a salty, jagged diamond skidded down her cheek into the pillow. "Would like to see how *you* handle being a manic depressive. Though you're a *man*, so it's already easier."

"What about Virginia Woolf?"

"Suicide."

"Hemingway," he suggested.

"Shot himself in the head. You knew that." She rolled her eyes.

"Hmm. Well, man or woman. You have so much life to live. Think of all those geniuses who accomplished so much.

Churchill. Roosevelt. Picasso. Beethoven. Vivien Leigh."

"So much tragedy in there. So many sharp moods. So much antagonism." She swiped at her face. "Scarlett O'Hara was manic depressive?"

"Yes. So much zest and brilliance and fortitude."

He pulled her body toward him and kissed the top of her head. "Let's think. Who will you be one day, Ruby Tuesday, besides my gorgeous best friend? What will you accomplish with all that genius?"

The next day, at the small airfield, Francine stood motionless as Keith tightened the silk head scarf around her hair. He gently guided her toward the prop plane, the wind from the propellers cutting against her bronze skin. She dreaded each inch that brought her closer to London, to the cloud of her disheveled, erratic mother, to her father's watchful eye, to the omnipresence of Dr. Gavison and his suffocating, unannounced check-ins. Francine felt she had become his guinea pig, the vehicle to enhance his ego and stature in London's greater psychiatric community.

"We'll be at the forefront of this new pill, Francine, and they will name you in university textbooks and publications. We will show everyone how well you do on this, just trust. Just trust," he'd say.

"I do not care to be named in university textbooks, Dr. Gavison. I only care to be me, whoever that is. I only care to be happy," she had finally said, after so many afternoons sitting in sullen silence in his stuffy corner office at Claybury Hospital near Woodford, where her father would drive her once a week and wait in his car smoking a cigar and reading *The Times*. The trip from Upper Cheyne Row was more than an hour each way, and not once had her father asked her what had been discussed with Dr. Gavison. He would recount to his daughter what he had read in *The Times*, followed by mutual silence in favor of old hits by Crosby, Stills, and Nash. From the privacy of his home office, he would call Dr. Gavison to discuss his daughter, giving her no doorway to participation in her own treatment.

"Happiness is a delicacy in life, saved for a select few," Dr. Gavison had responded dismissively and with great indifference, making notes on his pad with his glasses halfway down his nose. "Now, Francine, no recreational drugs this time. No alcohol. It will only play against this regimen. We must ensure the success of your treatment; do you not agree?"

"Right. Dr. Gavison," Francine said quietly, knowing the only course to take was the helpless, spineless, submissive one.

Imperious asshole, Francine thought to herself as she sunk into the narrow window seat on the small plane.

Next to her, Keith absentmindedly stroked his thumb and forefinger around her knee, sliding them up and down like forceps, as he peered out the tiny window beyond her head. Francine took in his face, his kind, handsome face, with eyes that sung of patience and understanding, and wide, symmetrical, full lips whose pillow-like touch she could feel in her mind. How many times had she imagined gentle Keith when she felt blue or anxious or aggravated? On how many occasions had he cleaned up her mess and put her back together again since spotting him in the back of her orientation group—that tall, athletic, Robert Redford-lookalike at university all those years ago? How many times had she looked up in a crowded room to find those kind, personable eyes making someone feel at home, making someone feel seen?

Why couldn't she be with Keith?

Because I'll ruin him, she answered herself.

He turned his face to hers at that moment, tipping his head downward and raising his eyebrows at her.

"Smile, darling," he said, squeezing her knee.

She smiled for him. It was the least she could do. She rested her head on his shoulder and stared at the felt barrier before her.

"I can't go back there," she said.

"I know," he said, and turned to kiss the top of her head. "We'll get you out. Promise."

MILAN

June 2, 2021

JUNE, MAY, APRIL, March, February, January, December, November, October, September… "Wait a minute. Can it be more than 10 months?" Margherita counted backwards out loud and exclaimed to herself as she froze with her outstretched fingers hanging in the air. "I haven't had sex in more than ten months?!"

A woman in head to toe Loewe gave her an odd look and a wide berth as she passed Margherita with a quickened step. Margherita pursed her lips.

Walking along Via Passione, she tipped her nose toward the afternoon sun. There was a bag of just squishy enough apricots in her tote, and her gem drop earrings clinked against her AirPods.

A ping interrupted Cass Elliot's "Make Your Own Kind of Music."

> **Paolo:** Ma sei tornata? Ho visto il tuo instagram. Per quanto sei a Milano? *You're back? How long are you in Milan?*

Margherita stared at her screen. It was like he was watching her count the months. She looked up at the palazzi around her.

> **Margherita:** Si… sono arrivata due mese fa… non so per quanto. *Yes, I arrived two months ago. I don't know for how long.*

Isabetta Andolini

Paolo: Com'è andata l'anno a Mustique? Che vita che hai. *How was your year in Mustique? What a life you lead.*

Margherita: Bella ma arriva un punto in cui devi rientrare nel mondo in generale. *Beautiful, but there comes a point when you have to re-enter the world at large.*

Paolo: Facciamo una cena questa settimana? Cosa dici *Let's have dinner this week? What do you say*

She continued to stare at the screen. The irony.

Was this really her present tense, a scene that looked so much like something she had experienced five years prior? Was he expecting once again the uninhibited actions of a twenty-something Margherita? Would he even still be attracted to her? God forbid he sleep with a thirty-one-year-old woman.

Margherita: Chi viene a cena? *Who is coming to dinner?*

Paolo: Just us two. I can enlarge the table if you want.

"Okay. June, May, April, March, February, January, December, November, October, September, August—fuck this is nuts. July, June. Was there really no one?! May, April, March. March. March 2020. Jesus Christ," Margherita had run out of fingers as she continued to talk out loud to herself. "A year and a half!"

Margherita: No no no. Solo noi due va benissimo. *No, no, no. Just us two is perfect.*

The next morning she woke early to catch a local train to Varenna on Lake Como, from where she would hop on the ferry to Laglio to meet with a potential contact for The Villa project. She received a 7:30 a.m. text from Paolo as she rushed out the door. She imagined him just waking up, a somehow safe time to make plans with women who were not his wife.

> **Paolo:** Margherita, domani va bene per cena? Dove vuoi andare? *Does tomorrow work for you for dinner? Where would you like to go?*
>
> **Margherita:** Boh non conosco nessun posto che sarebbe nuovo a Milano. Conosco sempre i stessi posti. *Hmm I wouldn't know anywhere new. Just my same places*
>
> **Paolo:** Per me va bene qualsiasi cosa piaccia a te *Whatever you want is fine with me*

"I don't even want to sleep with him," she said to Camilla the next day. Camilla was working an event at a hotel where Margherita had finished a coffee meeting. They had happenstance crossed paths and decided to sit down for a quick lunch.

"And I don't want him spending the night. It's not exciting like it once was. I'm not twenty-six anymore." She took a bite of her raw tuna. "But…" she weighed her hands in the air. "I haven't had sex in a year and a half!" she whispered.

"What!" Camilla screeched before letting out a cackle. "Are you a virgin again?"

Margherita rolled her eyes. "Wouldn't that be nice." She sat back in her bar stool with the stem of her wine glass between her fingers, studying the enormous bouquets dancing on the black marble center bar. "Is that possible?"

When she arrived at Langosteria, nearly twenty minutes late, she walked around the chef's bar to find him on the far side, talking to the restaurant group's head chef. Paolo looked just as gorgeous as he had that balmy night five summers before. Those azure eyes and their jolting effects.

Margherita took in his tan. His tall shape. His wide shoulders and suede loafers. His wavy hair that had turned salt and pepper. When had those blonde locks lost their pigment? She looked down at her left hand. She could practically see the soft blonde hair that she had gripped between the crevices of her fingers.

"Eccomi," she said with a smile as he stood to give her a hug and two kisses.

"Eccola!" His eyes glimmered, his face beamed. How vital and alluring he was; how powerless her inner battle was in the face of that expression.

Fuck me, she thought, ironically. *Still so gorgeous. Just why.*

"Margherita, meet the chef, Luca."

"The legend! What an honor." Margherita shook stout Luca's hand.

"Here," Paolo pulled out the counter stool for Margherita as she tried as gracefully as possible to sweep herself and her long silk dress onto it. Paolo sat back down on the stool next to hers, his strong, long legs facing her. She looked down at them and already wanted to put her delicate hands on his sturdy thighs, dig her nails into them.

He glanced at her again, that mischievous smile on his face as he continued to chat with the chef. He reached one large hand out to the side of her face, grinning as he did so, with his fingers extending around the back of her head in a sweet embrace. He brought her close for another kiss on the cheek. Incredulous perhaps, that there they sat after five years.

"Isn't Margherita the most gorgeous girl in the room?" Paolo asked the chef, still looking at Margherita with a glint in his eyes.

She shook her head and smiled. "We have the biggest charmer in Milano here."

After the chef went back to his post, Margherita and Paolo exchanged yet another excitable embrace. A reunion of two testosterone and estrogen overloaded humans. Dopamine and norepinephrine ran in perpetual circles.

"What are you drinking?" She eyed his Negroni-looking cocktail.

"Americano."

"That's my drink!"

"That's *my* drink," he said flirtatiously as he asked the white shirted waiter for one more for the lady.

The wine list arrived, as did the menu. Nothing was off the table with Paolo, in all categories.

There would be linguine with Breton blue lobster, amberjack and red prawns tartare, Fines de Claire oysters, seabream tagliata with crunchy capers and Amalfi lemon, langoustines and foie gras tartare. There would be grilled octopus with paprika, Catalan-style red prawns with tomato, celery and Tropea onion, and Royal snapper carpaccio with citronette. Two different bottles of white wine—a Ligurian Vermentino and a Gris from Friuli Venezia Giulia—to start them off. All presented with the utmost style, sophistication, and flair.

"How is Taddeo? I haven't seen him yet," she asked about their mutual friend.

"He's good. Honestly, I have not seen much of him this past year. He has a girlfriend now!"

"Really? That's great! Good for him. How old is she?"

"Twenty-seven."

Margherita laughed. "He gets older every year and their age always stays the same."

"I know. I try to encourage him to find someone a few years older, but he's always been that way. And if you have the choice to date a twenty-six-year-old or a fifty-year-old…"

She rolled her eyes. "You men."

He asked her to elaborate on her project, which she did, though he could not quite grasp her enormous actionables; her determination to create something so large with little to nothing behind her. They exchanged vulnerable lockdown stories and spoke of his children. The topic of aging floated, surrounded by truths, jokes and advice from one to the other. Margherita felt more confident with Paolo this time around; she was no longer a young, impressionable thing. She felt for the first time that he spoke to her, and she to him, as two adults, rather than adult and plaything.

"Do you have any idea how much anxiety I had that first night?"

The first night she met Paolo would be ingrained in her memory forever. She thought about the stormy July evening. The black marble bathroom in which she got ready. The stubborn thunderstorms. The rain that trickled down her back as she skipped from the taxi to the front door. Paolo's face when she entered the dimly lit restaurant. His tan. His strong arm draped around the back of her chair. His azure eyes that trailed her as she stood to go to the ladies room.

The text message she received the next day. The satisfaction, adrenaline, and bucket of nerves she had felt when she read it.

The beginning of so much.

"We came here. Do you remember? We sat over there." He pointed towards the velvet booth.

"And I slept at which hotel that night… I can't remember."

"Well, you were supposed to…"

"That's right. I never did in the end."

"We sat outside. And you said you wanted to watch a film." He exaggerated the word film.

Margherita's eyes enlarged. "How do you remember this?!"

"Of course I remember."

Margherita was shocked. "And you fell asleep two minutes into it."

"Which film was it?" he asked, genuinely curious.

"I have no idea."

And the next week you slept at the hotel near the Stazione, and we went to sushi."

"I can't believe you remember all of this. It was five years ago!"

"And you are just as bellissima. And still divertente." *Beautiful/fun*

"Meno male!" she laughed. *Thank goodness!*

The divine seafood kept on coming, as well as the Gris, and the after dinner drinks. It was the most fun she had had on a date in years. By dessert, the same they had always ordered in each other's company—exotic and seasonal fruit with a special request of very dark chocolate—hands wandered in places they perhaps should not, when in a restaurant or in any public place with a married man, and as the last sip of Moscato d'Asti went down, with the restaurant quiet, ardent kisses—wet and heated—contrasted the room's energy.

Damn him. He still had it.

"When you used to write to me to come to New York to make your legs shake... oh," he sighed in ecstasy.

She grinned with her lips closed.

"You used to send tremors down my insides, you know."

He affectionately pushed a mass of hair behind her shoulder and eyed her. Such was the trickery of Paolo: fond and tender mixed with carnal lust.

When a gentleman approached to say hello, giving Paolo kudos simply for being Paolo, as so many men curiously felt compelled to do, as if he were some sort of five-star general responsible for bringing a people to the highest world status, Margherita felt like she was with the king of cool. He was a high, Paolo, and she didn't know how he managed to keep the embers stoked.

"Don't tell anyone you saw me here," Paolo said to the gentleman friend, who shook his head conspiratorially. Margherita rolled her eyes at him. As if anyone cared in Milan, as if anyone thought Paolo was actually faithful.

They walked outside into the galleria and he took her hand, guiding her toward his moto.

"I'll take you back," he said.

"It's a ten minute walk to my apartment."

He took out a second helmet and placed it gently on her head, holding the sides of it and bringing her in for a kiss. On the moto, she held her hands gently around his ribs, and he picked one palm up and placed it purposefully on his chest.

Damn his big hands. Damn that breeze. How she had missed them both.

Afterwards, he dressed, a satisfied grin on his face, and he teased her about how she sat in the low bed. She smiled and rolled her eyes at him as she watched his extraordinary chest disappear underneath his tee.

"Ti vengo a cercare," he said as he kissed her passionately. *I'll come find you.*

After he'd left, she looked at her naked body in the mirror. 'Sensual,' he had called her. It was true, her petite frame had taken on a curve or two in the five years since she had first met Paolo. She had been so thin then, and now, using fertility as a baseline, she was officially on the decline.

Not so twenty-something anymore, she thought, as she pulled the skin at the height of her cheek bones in an upward diagonal, falsely tightening it. She sighed, feeling far more sober than she had been when Paolo was ripping her floor-length dress. Or was it she who had undone the silk belt and the buttons?

How ridiculous it was, she thought, that she was yet again having sex with Paolo. In how many hotel rooms had they ravaged each other? How many times had she heard his low, sexy voice moan "si" while holding one of her legs in his giant hand? How could it possibly be her reality that the first person she slept with after the pandemic was the man for whom she had fallen so insolvably hard when she first moved to Italy? He epitomized her idea of Milan, of Liguria, of Herculean sex, seduction, and charm. Adultery, mischief, and indefatigable temptation.

But something was off.

This doesn't feel as sexy as it once did, she thought as she curled up in the low, Japanese-style bed.

She thought about her twenty-something self in her old apartment with its four sets of French doors overlooking the church piazza, just a few blocks from where she currently lay. What a different girl that Margherita was. Glowingly confident and enticing with an indomitable spirit and endless energy. That girl felt like a stranger, so completely out of her grasp. What a different future that past version had had before her, what a different world she had lived in, so easy and carefree.

Who ever thought how much five years, the death of a parent, a global pandemic, and a broken heart could change everything?

The next morning, as Margherita twisted her long hair to ring out the water, singing along to 'Candy' by Paolo Nutini on her Spotify, she heard a series of low ba-booms emanate from her phone. She combed her wet hair, sprayed it with something that probably did nothing but was part of her repertoire anyway, and patted at her chest and inner thighs with her towel before tiptoeing into the bedroom, feet still damp.

Nick: (photo)
Nick: I understand now, your love for Milan.
Nick: It's gorgeous
Nick: (photo)

She inhaled sharply. The photos were in Corso Magenta, she could tell without clicking on the conversation. What was he doing there?

Nick: I'm here for a wedding on Lake Como this weekend.
Nick: Thought I'd take a few extra days
Nick: If you're in town, and if you want to, I would love to take you for a tea.
Nick: I am prepared for you to say no
Nick: But I am asking anyway
Nick: In the hope
Nick: That you will say yes

She looked closer. The photos were of a few colorful palazzi in one of the city's most beautiful zones. One had a young woman gliding by on a bicycle, her blouse fluttering behind her, her ponytail perfectly fixed. She dropped the phone onto the bed.

Why hadn't he told her he would be in Italy, so nearby?

She continued to regard her phone as if it held the winning number to a lottery and she was too superstitious to touch it, so simultaneously innocent and dangerous as it lay on the white comforter. She huffed and turned toward her wardrobe. There was no time to search his messages for double meaning, no time to stare at a screen with her thumb nail between her top and bottom teeth, contemplating a blasé response.

"Take me at face value," he had once said to her, at the very beginning of their 'situationship' as she affectionately named it. She recalled her response to that text so vividly. It went something like: "What the *fuck* does that mean?"

He wanted to have his cake and eat it too. He wanted to hear from her occasionally, to know that she still thought of him, but he never, with the exception of that day, wrote to her first. He never said: 'I'd like to see you,' nor sought her out to ask: 'How are you?' He never picked up the phone to call her. Every exchange was of her own doing, was Margherita's initiation.

In her mind she saw him sitting on the floor of her New York apartment the last time he had come over, days after she returned from Italy, where the first bits of news about a strange virus had started to trickle in. Margherita had assumed she'd be in town for a few weeks at the most, after which she'd return to Milan and get back to job searching.

She had been on a date that evening with a guy a year younger than her, an age group she was trying to force herself into the habit of, as opposed to spending time with men who had twenty years on her. Margherita was determined to develop a crush on someone new, even if only to pass the time for a few weeks.

He had made a great steak and afterwards they kissed and fooled around on his sofa. Margherita was in 'put it on' mode, forcing herself to view it as fun, but as soon as she sensed that the only reason he had bothered with the T-bone was to take out his own T-bone, she felt the mood around her deflate. True, she was promiscuous by nature, but sex with someone for whom she had no strong feelings was momentously lonely and depressing. If he did not make her heart flutter, there was nothing appealing about the act.

She had picked herself up, called an Uber, and texted Nick. "Do you want to see me?"

"Yes," he had immediately replied.

She had just enough time to get home, change her clothes and brush her teeth before he arrived. They hadn't seen each other for a long stretch, not since before she had impulsively flown to Italy after she had been forced to resign from her job, and something about him was different. She didn't ask him about his girlfriend; she assumed they were still together, though she had no way of knowing. They had sex, listened to some music, made a joke about the 'virus' in China. "Do you have it?" he had asked her playfully. "No, do you?" Both of them completely unaware of what lay ahead.

As usual, when he stood to get dressed, he lingered. He sat on her floor, pulling the leather of his sneakers outward as if about to put them over his feet, which he did, very slowly. Margherita had sat down on the floor before him, and he had patted her legs. She remembered that, somehow. He rubbed her thighs up and down, as if warming her after a cold run. He seemed melancholy. He had said something to that effect, but she couldn't recall what it was, specifically. She remembered thinking how little she knew of his life, of his day to day.

He said something like, "do you wish we had never met?" And she had said some variation of: "Yes, I do. I do wish we never met." And then the memory became fuzzy, but there was a static moment of discomfort between them as he tied the laces of his low top sneakers, or maybe he hadn't put them on yet.

She had put something to him then, something that annoyed him, about how poorly he had treated her, or how he had never really apologized. For his selfishness. For his dismissiveness of her feelings. For carrying on with her for a year, all the while knowing how she felt, knowing how much she wanted to end it but how she couldn't find the discipline to do so. He allowed it to continue on his schedule. Replied to her messages intermittently. Was sweet when it suited him.

At some point, Margherita had stood up and gone to the kitchen. She opened the fridge for something, she couldn't recall what, and when she closed it and turned back around, she saw his shoulder disappear down the hallway. He had barely said goodbye before he let himself out.

She had said to herself at that moment that she did not care. She had asked him over for sex; she was perfectly entitled to the same cake which he had always enjoyed.

But that was never really the case. Of course she cared.

The next week was the beginning of lockdown fever across the world. Italy was hemorrhaging, and Margherita felt a magnified loneliness without Francine to call or text. A few months in her apartment by herself was making her crazy, and watching the death count rise each day in the country where she felt so at home caused her great pain.

Then Tommaso received the invitation for an extended stay on Mustique, in order to work on the new property uninterrupted by the world's ailments and delays, and he had insisted his daughter come along, refusing to leave her in New York alone. Something within her clicked back on as soon as the boat brought them to the dock; a strange sense of community, of forced conviviality and the absence of FOMO enabled her to smile freely once again. Maybe Thayer's fellow loner tendencies and omnipresent clinking ice cubes had something to do with it.

At that moment, in the wabi-sabi apartment on Via Manzoni, she didn't have the luxury to indulge Nick. She didn't have time to be sidetracked or emotionally distracted. One evening with Nick would reverberate for months, while to him it was lost in stacks of evenings with a series of various girls; none of whom weighed too much in his mind, none of whom outlasted their initial shine.

She had a job to do. She had investors to find, a hotel to build. And in that moment, she needed to get dressed to meet Thayer for a quick coffee before her train to the coast. He was in town to scout possible film locations in the Dolomites for an upcoming project.

Outside, at the corner of Via Manzoni and Via Senato, she looked down at the weight in her hand, the appendage she sometimes wished she could toss into the night sea. She would not click open Nick's messages. She stared at them in her list of WhatsApp chats, his name on top of Paolo's. A tram screeched by, a foot away from her face. She shook herself back into reality and crossed the uneven stones toward Via della Spiga.

When would there be someone new, someone with whom she could create a life? Maybe someone with whom she could buy a little beach house in a pastel colored beach town. Have a few kids to chase in the sand. Where was that guy? That was what she wanted, lately. Or at least she thought that was what she wanted. A big love all her own.

As she walked along Via della Spiga, with its magnificent boutiques and window displays, sporadic women in heels traversing the uneven stones and a few beautiful bicycles carefully cycling along, Margherita was tempted to turn down Via Santo Spirito where the hotel she had spent a few years assisting to develop was still an enclosed, private worksite. All construction had come to a halt at the beginning of COVID, and the team had not yet begun again. She had of course been in touch with Elisio, her former boss. Elisio had, after all, given Margherita a running start in Milan; he had seen in her an energy, enthusiasm, and—ironically—commitment, which had enabled her to be so involved in the development from such a young age. He had also been the link to Paolo; it was Elisio who had invited Margherita to the portentous work dinner on that stormy July evening five years prior.

Margherita momentarily forgot which photogenic street the Four Seasons was on as she lost herself in the steamy memory of that night and the many nights that followed, from elegant Milan to the bougainvillea-draped beach town on the Ligurian coast.

Magic July. It was the first time she had heard that Italian expression. Magic July; freedom. Children and mothers at the sea or in the mountains. Men in the city.

Ample rope. Prerogative plentiful.

What I wouldn't do to experience it all over again, she thought, as she walked past the sophisticated, elegant menswear shops, each more quiescent than the last.

The Four Seasons in Via Gesù was also quiet that June morning, the travel restrictions still weighing heavily on Italy's hospitality industry. There was a smattering of locals chatting over coffee in Italian-made porcelain cups, and Margherita heard a few guests speaking German, others with crisp English accents.

She walked through the lobby, smiling politely at the bellmen, through the main restaurant to the outdoor tables in the elegant courtyard. It was a beautiful morning; perfect blue sky and the scent of jasmine everywhere, even in the center of the city. Thayer was seated at a table half in the sun and half in the shade, clad in sunglasses and a casual-chic look of light-colored trousers, a crisp button down, and expensive sneakers. It was a step up from his Mustique wardrobe, but he hadn't cut his Morrissey hair.

Margherita felt a feeling of familiarity wash over her, though Mustique already felt so far away. A memory of a distant anchor which she had abandoned in order to once again feel afloat, and now, looking at Thayer grazing over a fancy breakfast menu, she yearned for that anchor once again.

A salty sea breeze whipped Margherita's long hair around her face as she stood on the curved road in Paraggi, the turquoise baia where she had often spent summer weekends in her previous Milan life. Below her, bikini-clad, leather-skinned bodies sat on enormous rocks, in search of a somewhat secluded spot to layer their tan and submerge freely into the chilled water. Margherita envied them.

Vittorio, her main contact from the bank overseeing the property, stood in a crisp button-down and long pants, his silk tie whipping around each time a strong current passed over the cliff. He was accompanied by Ferdinando, one of the lawyers from the Milanese firm handling the building permits.

"See this?" Ferdinando gestured toward the neighbor's driveway, which visually seemed to belong to The Villa but took a sharp right parallel to the curved road. "This is our biggest problem right now. According to the *commune*, there was never a clear division between these two properties. We need to work with these owners to request new site division lines, or we cannot get the permits."

Margherita could feel the grievance lines on her forehead growing deeper by the second.

"So, who does that? Do you do that?" she asked Ferdinando, her eyes on her precious Villa, sitting decrepit beneath years of overgrown ivy and lined with broken terracotta potters, knocked around by the winter wind and never removed.

Ferdinando sighed and shook his head heavily, his hands on his hips. Margherita knew what was coming: a complaint lathered in laziness.

"Boh. We are busy, Margherita. That is not really our job."

Margherita eyed him wordlessly.

"I can try…" His head moseyed from side to side, begrudgingly.

"I can't just knock on their door. There's got to be a process here. You have access to this information. You know how this works. I certainly don't."

Ferdinando nodded languidly and pulled up his belted trousers while Vittorio stood with his arms crossed, staring out to sea or watching the errant car whip around the hairpin turn.

"You know, if they find out about your plans, they could contest it. If they do not want it next to them," Vittorio interjected.

"And what then?"

"Well, everyone's got a lawyer, or a price." Vittorio said and rubbed his fingers together, as if to signify a potential pay-off.

"I don't have money to bribe someone," Margherita said flatly.

Both men cocked their heads to the side and turned in a slow circle. In other words: "Well… that's your problem."

———————

Later, in a basic hotel room a few streets back from the harbor in nearby Santa Margherita Ligure, Margherita studied her bank account in a split screen with her project budget. Nausea was her new best friend; there every step of the way.

Margherita: Do you know any property lawyers? Who I might be able to ask a few questions?

Benjamin: No. What's going on

Margherita: Nothing, I just want to educate myself

Benjamin: What difference does it make anyway? Nothing is by the book in Italy.

"True," she said to herself.

She peered out the window as a young boy's voice pierced through the alleyway. The evening had turned to cotton candy and the light was awash in pastel reflections, the setting sun bouncing off the daisy and baby blue buildings.

Eyes back on her screen, she swallowed at the figure that signified what was left of her savings.

What have I done?

Later, with the glass door ajar and a crescent moon waning to near nothingness in the night sky, she finally clicked on Nick's chat.

She started to type. And stopped. And typed. And deleted. And typed. And stopped. And deleted again. What would she say to him, if she were to see him? He might ask about the project, although, maybe not even, and she would have to say: no progress yet. No news. No anything. And his gallivanting around with friends and pretty girls and going to weddings—the whole *belonging* thing—would be salt in the wound at a time when she did not want to be reminded of how alone in her lane she felt.

He came online.

She clicked out of the app.

Her phone lit up her dark room.

Paolo: Non ho pensato che siamo rivisti *I didn't think we'd ever see each other again*

Margherita: Ah, no?

Paolo: Super surprise. Che bello rivederti Margherita. *Super surprise. So great to see you.*

Margherita: E mi fai tremano le gambe come sempre ☺ ;) *And you make my legs tremble, same as always*

Paolo: Dovrei fartele tremare un po' spesso… ;) *I should make them tremble more often*

At least Paolo was a turf on which she still felt a semblance of her old self.

LONDON

March 12, 1979

WALKING ALONG FLOOD Street, Francine eyed two little girls in school uniforms just home from prep, their mother trailing them with perfect hair and a tight face. They skipped ahead and entered a beautiful brick home with hawthorn hedges out front. As Francine passed, the mother looked back from her pedestal on the top step. She pursed her lips, entered the well-lit hallway and shut the door.

Perfect lives. Perfect lives.

She looked up at the next house, and the next one, and the next one, all beautiful, expensive homes with a sprinkling of flowers in the front, planters on the steps, a stately knocker on the door. She felt like an outsider in the neighborhood; it wasn't hers, really, it wasn't the Hampstead she knew from childhood, where each day ended with a romp into the Heath. And it wasn't hers as an adult either—she wasn't married with two little girls in school uniforms. She wasn't even treated like an adult in her father's house. She was an outpatient, a child, a prisoner.

Francine took in a deep, aggravated breath and clenched her jaw as she approached her father's house, her gym bag hugged tightly between her arm and her rib cage and her wet hair dampening her sweatshirt. She prayed her father wasn't home.

When she entered the front door, however, she could hear him speaking to Greta, the housekeeper.

Isabetta Andolini

"That's fine. I'll pick them up myself tomorrow. Not to worry, Greta," her father said as Francine quietly approached the staircase. Her father passed the main hall from the kitchen, heading toward his study.

"Francine, how was your swim?" He stopped to greet her, legal pad in hand.

"Fine," she said, apathetically.

"Your hair is damp." He walked toward her. "It's been one of the coldest winters in the last century. I hope you didn't walk from Great Smith Street Baths all the way here with a damp head."

"I did. It's a lovely walk from Westminster."

"With all that rubbish in the street? I'm surprised there was ample room on the sidewalk," he huffed. "I can't believe this ordeal hasn't yet been properly addressed." He turned around, aggrieved, back down the hall. "Damn unions."

"At least they have jobs," Francine mumbled.

Her father turned and regarded her with frustration.

"You'd like to pick up refuse, now, is that it?"

"I'd like to choose my livelihood, at least."

"No one is setting rules around your employment, Francine," he said crisply.

"Just irrefutable limitations on female mobility. And a ludicrous forbidding on my obtaining a job anywhere but London."

"Did this country not pass the Employment Protection Act a few years ago? Wasn't that in favor of women in the workplace?"

"To not discriminate them for having babies, which is absurd. The bastards do it anyway, and there's no way to actually *prove* their ubiquitous discrimination. But it has nothing to do with the types of roles actually given to women. Just a false sense of protection if a receptionist wants to fulfill her duty to procreate."

Her father rolled his eyes and turned once again toward his office.

"Right. Walk away. That's how you discuss things."

He stopped.

"Francine, I have a great deal to do before tea. Greta is leaving early to catch a train to Manchester to see her family for the weekend, so it's you and I in the kitchen tonight. We can discuss this another time."

She watched her father disappear down the hall, her frustration bubbling as she gripped the banister with all her might.

She tossed her gym bag on the floor in the parlor hall and stomped past the kitchen, through the sitting room, into her father's study.

He looked up from a file in which he was already immersed, a legal pad next to it and a pen hovering in the air.

Francine plopped herself onto one of the leather chairs before his classical pedestal desk, a beautiful piece with dentils carved beneath the desktop and square handles on the drawers. He had brought it with him from the Hampstead house; it was one of those scenes ingrained in her childhood memories: her father sitting at the pedestal desk, a thick file and a legal pad before him, once in a while her mother standing at his side to deliver tea, his arm wrapped around her waist, a stolen kiss.

There was hardly ever anything more on the desktop than the specific case he was working on; he was as neat as a pin, while her room was affectionately nicknamed 'Francine's Shanty.' Clothing, records, and paraphernalia for each of her short-lived hobbies draped chairs, closets, bathroom sinks, window sills, and the floor, much to Greta's dismay.

Her father exasperatedly placed his pen down on the pad and bent his head forward. He rubbed his temples with his thumbs.

"Yes, yes it's me again," Francine said in response to his body language.

He looked up and held his palms together, fingertips to the coffered ceiling. "Francine, I am unsure what you expect of me in this moment. I am sorry you are bored, and it would be wonderful if you could find a new job, but need I remind you, you had a perfectly good one, and it is no one's fault but your own that you no longer have it, and that you are here in this house every day."

"It was a crap placement, anyway. You think I should be satisfied with making tea and answering the phone. 'Better than being a teacher! At least you're in the thick of it!' In the thick of it my arse. On the side, more like, in a glass enclosure. I see these rats day in and day out, incapable and ridiculous and embarrassing. Taking a piss *at me!* 'Francine, you're not gonna throw a wobbly are you?' 'Have you lost the plot, Francie?'" She imitated in an obnoxious male voice. "Tossers. I can do their job. I can do *all* their jobs. Better than most of them! And they know it!" she bellowed into her father's study, not even at him in particular, but into the hollowness of her external world, which seemed to swallow all of her efforts and desires without ever considering them.

"That's enough, Francine," her father said sternly, raising his voice ever so slightly.

She jolted up from the tufted leather chair and went to stand at one of the three, eighteen-paned windows overlooking the double-width garden that abutted the church. She had learned from one of her father's neighbors that the crypt had been an air raid shelter in World War II, and on one September evening in 1940, an explosive had hit it and exploded in the crypt. It was one more symbol of confinement and doom in and around her life at her father's house on Upper Cheyne Row.

To which, her heart responded with guilt, for though it was her father who confined her, she knew he did it out of love and responsibility, and not out of menace.

On the edge of the garden, lilacs drooped in the rain, battered by the wind, which always felt stronger this close to the embankment. The grass was so green it was practically yodeling, a vociferous reminder of the beginning of spring in London. The city needed it; it had been a bleak, depressing, and *angry* winter all around, for everyone.

She pushed her hands into the sill as if she could turn the wood to smithereens, as if she could push herself out of her anger.

"I want to go to New York," she said sternly, but calmly. "London is ramshackle, and you know it. It is going straight into the toilet. I want to go where there is hope. Excitement. Opportunity."

Her father sighed—frustrated, or tired. She remained facing the garden, her jaw clenched, her eyes shrewdly focused on a daffodil bloom whiplashed in the wind.

She waited for her father's response but there was none. She spun around to face him.

"I want to go to New York," she repeated. He opened a drawer and pulled out a file, ignoring her. "Daddy. Can you please talk to me?"

He looked up at his daughter. His upper eye lids drooped heavily, and his ears seemed to have grown half an inch overnight. He was not a middle-aged divorcee anymore; somewhere in the years since Francine had left for university, he had aged. His stomach, once flat, protruded over his wool tartan trousers, and his legs, once strong, thick, and vigorous, had thinned. Francine suddenly felt a pang of melancholy for the father who, she was sure, had done the best he could, in the face of a never ceding challenge; an unknowable, unpredictable, constant situation.

"I know you do," he said then, breathing out, placing the file flatly on his desk. "I know you do," he repeated.

"Daddy, can't you see that I am suffocating here? Can't you see that I can do more? In New York, the firms are so much bigger, there are so many more of them, and there are *women* doing the jobs only men are doing here! I read about it. There are female analysts and account managers and salespeople… they are paid so much more and they are treated equally."

"Francine. I find it hard to believe that there are no women doing these same jobs here in London."

"I need space. I know you don't want to hear it. But I need space. Desperately." She picked up a pen from his desk and distractedly tapped it on her wrist. Her father watched it fly up and down in a one-inch whirl.

"How do you even imagine going about getting one of these jobs in New York?" he asked, languidly. "Please stop that."

"I write letters all the time. To make connections. Contacts. So they'll think of me if something opens up." She stopped playing with the pen and placed it purposefully on top of the file before him.

"You do?"

"Yes."

Her father rubbed his forehead with the thumb and forefinger of his left hand. "Francine. You've been fired from a highly reputable family office. You disappeared for ten days, have you forgotten? You—capable, intelligent, mature you that you claim to be—arrived high off God knows what, picked up and left an hour later, and were next seen on the news protesting the Iranian revolution in Tehran. Have you forgotten this chain of events? Who knows what escapes your memory—who knows who took advantage of you there, or what might have happened if you were one of the sorry youth whose life was cut short at that scene. Who knows what might have happened if that manic period went on longer than it did? Do you know how much money I paid to hire someone to find you? Do you know how many phone calls I made to the embassy? Do you think I ever imagined, in my whole goddamn life I would be searching frantically for my little girl in a tumultuous revolution in the Middle goddamn East?"

Francine clenched her jaw and stood in silence.

"It was an extremely important—"

"Don't." He held up a hand in protest, his elbow on the desk.

Tears welled in her eyes despite her determination to appear as controlled as possible. Her frustration was so venomous inside of her, so overpowering, she could not control its outward face.

With her fists clenched, and her throat thick, she wordlessly started toward the door.

"Francie…" Her father's voice was mild and softhearted, and it only made her feel weaker. She turned and leaned against the doorway.

"Daddy, I may have 'Francine's Low's' and the odd manic episode. And I may have an inclination to try a substance or two, but that doesn't make my views, or beliefs, or knowledge any less potent or meaningful or worthy than the next person. Can you try to believe, for a moment, that it is possible that I have more courage than others? That, manic episodes aside, I am capable of *more* than other girls—schoolteachers and receptionists and babymakers? That my dreams are of a slightly larger scale? And that, incurable diagnosis or not, I am entitled to a life of my own making? Can you allow me that?"

He regarded her with an unreadable expression, and she left him to his endless files and fancy pens, and views of battered daffodils.

ALASSIO

June 28, 2021

AT A FOCACCERIA a dozen or so towns west of The Villa property, a petite curly haired girl with sharp arm muscles gave Margherita evil, distrustful eyes and pushed her espresso across the counter with distaste. It wasn't just a Ligurian culture thing. This little fire pocket knew about Paolo. Other patrons received their morning cappuccino and plain, oily focaccia with affable recognition. Margherita would have to walk to the other part of the village for her espresso.

The trip to Alassio on the Ligurian coast was the first she had made in years; she had hoped it would offer a sense of connection to a place that held so many sticky sweet summer memories. In her mind, however, every step she took in the cotton-candy-colored beach town was spat back out, every apricot she chose at the fruttivendolo was met with a grimace, every beach club was full and unaccommodating. It remained in every way the quintessential scene of Italian summer: the promenade still overlooked the glistening Ligurian sea with rows and rows of colorful beach umbrellas, the children still shrieked with delight as they ran in and out of the water, and the evening passeggiata was still filled with pastel cotton dresses and multi-hued gelato. But the little village where Margherita had passed numerous sun-filled days and summer storms with Paolo's best friend Taddeo didn't give her the same bounce it once had.

Around dinner time, with more restlessness in her belly than hunger pangs, she went for a run along the coast road. Cars whizzed around the ebbs and flows while she maintained a steady pace on the single-person-width sidewalk. She ran all the way to the next port town, where dozens of boats of all sizes sat in the harbor and the restaurants were in full aperitivo swing. On the way back, in Alassio, she looked out over the banister at the beach clubs below the promenade. At the beach club she knew to be Paolo's, there were still plenty of bathing suit clad sun worshippers soaking up the last bits of daylight. It was nearly eight p.m. and kids were still playing in the water, while a family or two packed up toys every few minutes.

And there, outstretched on a lounge chair turned ninety degrees clockwise to face the evening sun, was the unmistakably athletic, long formation of a tan Paolo. One arm casually bent behind his head. One leg bent on the chaise. And there, at the foot of it, her body leant toward her husband, was his wife.

Margherita had never before seen her in the flesh, let alone had she ever seen them together. Their kids were likely somewhere in the water, and what were they discussing—their parents? Their children's swim lessons? A friend's imminent divorce? Margherita watched them from the promenade, her heartbeat fast from her run.

Who am I, she thought. *The other woman. One of many, surely.*

She fell asleep early, only to be awoken near midnight by the sound of cheers and horns and fireworks. Italy had beat Belgium. The national soccer team was in the international semi finals and that night, up and down the country, everyone was celebrating. She lay her head on the too soft pillow, not so much bothered by the celebratory ruckus as finding it endearing. Such a proud nation. Such a united group. She had so badly wanted to feel a part of it for so long. To be included.

It was becoming clear; she would always be an outsider.

She couldn't fall back asleep. She pictured her mother in the glow of her laptop, those times that Margherita would find Francine sitting in her home office in a silk robe, a bar of very dark chocolate next to her and the monitor constantly changing figures as she kept an eye on the global markets.

"Mom, it's 3 a.m.," Margherita would say.

"Yes, doll, go to sleep. I'll let you know if anyone tries to rob the joint."

Sunday afternoon, on her way back to Milan, Margherita stopped in Paraggi to stand on the periphery of the Villa property.

"You've had a dull few decades, but don't worry. I'm going to bring you back to life," she said out loud to the faded sherbet-colored façade, with its yellow shutters and stone base that touched the chilly sea water. She imagined the Riva boats that might pull up to a new built-in portico, a guest stepping out onto the veranda with a glass of chilled Vermentino in hand, a handsome, tanned bellhop in a crisp white shirt greeting a new arrival with a warm smile. "I'm going to save you and make you fabulous again. We're gonna show 'em," she said to the villa before she walked the thirty minutes or so to the train in Santa Margherita Ligure.

On the regional line back to Milan, Ferdinando called.

"Margherita. Bad news and good news."

Margherita stiffened.

"The bad news is we have to re-draw the property lines according to new town rules. The existing ones are dated, and we can't move forward with the demolition permit without these. So we need to pay for this. And it will take time because they are behind in their work because of COVID, et cetera. The good news is that I was able to find the lawyer of the neighbor. He is a friend of my cousin. My cousin put in a good word. So at least we know who their lawyer is if we need to involve them."

"How much?"

"Scusa?"

"How much to get new drawings from the town?"

"Ah. I don't know. It changes every day…"

"So… how do we find out?"

"Ah. Well. I have to ask."

"…Can we do that, then?"

"Yes. Yes I will. I will ask."

"Wonderful," she clipped. "Let me know."

Margherita prayed it would not blow her out of the water. She increasingly felt like she was trying to catch goldfish between her fingers.

"I don't understand why I can't have even a piece of it," Margherita had asked her father on a recent phone call.

"Never question your mother's financial planning. She was the most brilliant money person I knew. She had her reasons."

"Right. Like not trusting me."

"Your thirties are for working hard, Margherita. She wanted you to learn to be independent. To go get it. To figure it out. And your fortieth birthday is a long way away, so you better get hustling."

"Who's talking? Mom? Or you?"

"I have to talk for her sometimes. She very generously left this trust for you for after you learn the lessons of working. She didn't exactly leave you in the cold, Marghe. If you want to do this project with the Villa, you're going to have to budget out your savings. Or find a job while you do it. Some people don't quit their day job."

I didn't quit my day job, I got ousted, Margherita thought.

She sat up straighter on the regional train and put her feet on the cheap seat fabric, trying another position to get comfortable on the long ride with its incessant stops. The stations of tiny Ligurian towns passed one by one. Bogliasco. Sori. Recco.

She thought of Paolo, still there in the tiny town with his wife. They would leave the beach soon. They would make their kids dinner at home before meeting friends. She thought about the life he had created. That image of him on the lounge chair with his wife sitting at the end of the chaise, him with one eye on the ocean, her leaning over his long legs. A stolen moment from his real life. A moment he was not sexy, free, Mr. Cool. She couldn't get it out of her mind. His life, how she watched it from the promenade, how sordid she had felt in that moment.

There she was on the mostly empty train, returning to an empty apartment with none of her own things. Just a few framed photos and a closet of clothes. Jewelry her mother had left her, most of which she was too scared or emotional to wear. Ceramic mugs she had bought with Francine in Big Sur, years earlier, which she carted around everywhere, one breaking with every move. Notepads filled with plans and sketches for a project that was becoming more and more daunting. And a woman who she recognized less and less staring back at her in the bathroom mirror.

LONDON

May 2, 1980

FRANCINE INHALED DEEPLY on her cigarette as she watched a mother chase a toddler around the model boating pond. The Heath was in its full spring splendor, entering its most colonized season with everyone eager to soak up the first scents of glowing pear and cherry blossoms. The wisteria was once again bountiful on the beloved pergola, and the colorful azaleas around Kenwood House breathed pure felicity into even the most perpetually sour North Londoner.

The toddler's little arms flapped wildly as he took little steps that must have felt like lightening speed for his miniature body. His stomach bulged beneath his pocket-sized sweater, and when his mother finally caught up to him, he was alight in beams and giggles. Francine smiled to herself behind her cigarette.

Will I ever be that woman? she wondered.

"Ey!" she heard her friend's voice shout from the direction of Highgate. Francine turned her head to see Bea coming toward her with her gym bag in hand, her hair a messy, feathered affair. Francine took a long inhale from her cigarette as Bea spun circles on the grass, laughing.

"Beatrice, what the fuck are you wearing?" Francine asked, flatly. Bea was a vision in yellow spandex, yellow tights, yellow legwarmers, and a wristband.

"What? I just came from aerobics. It's fab, Francie, such a good sweat. I signed up for jazzercise tomorrow if you want to join?"

"I'm sorry, I didn't realize I was having tea with Debbie fucking Harry," Francine laughed.

"Oh fuck off. Have you seen my tush? It's never looked better," Bea said, turning around and glancing over her left shoulder, then her right.

Francine nodded with wide, sarcastic eyes. She hummed 'Turned The Beat Around' as she stubbed out her cigarette.

Bea swung her gym bag at her friend.

"Ouch! What do you have in there!?" Francine yelled, grasping her forearm.

"Maybe we should get you a hamburger. You wouldn't be so delicate if you weighed more than six stone."

Francine rolled her eyes as they started toward the tennis court café.

"They're skinny in New York, you know. Have you seen Jerry Hall's collarbone lately?" Francine asked, eying a passing mother with a little girl on her shoulders.

"So?"

Francine twisted her lips to the side, nervously.

"Stop right there. Francine!" Bea halted and clenched her friend's arm. Finally, Francine locked eyes with Bea. "Are you— did you get a job in New York? Are you actually doing this?"

Francine bit the inside of her lip and a smile slowly spread across her face like a blooming tulip.

"I did. I am. I did, and I am!" She bit her lower lip. "Fuck, I'm scared, Bea."

Bea threw her yellow arms around her friend and held her tightly. "I cannot believe it! Francie!" she said in an excited whisper. When she pulled away she proceeded to jump up and down.

"Stop it, Bea, people are going to think you're really out of your fucking mind if you start jazzercising all over the Heath in that outfit."

"How did you convince your father?"

"Long story," Francine said, taking her childhood friend's hand in hers and guiding her toward the café.

The previous evening, in the chaos of her messy bedroom, with Springsteen's "Born to Run" on the record player, Francine slammed the phone on the receiver. She had been trying to reach Christos for days, had even taken the bus to St. John's Wood to bang on his door, but he was nowhere to be found. His disappearing acts were not uncommon, but their quantity did not desensitize her furor. Each time was a mountain of bruised wrath and days of foaming, apoplectic rage that usually ended in something smashing—his living room window, the windshield of his car when she found it in Westbourne Grove, one of his prized guitars when she finally caught him at home.

She stood one meter from her desk and stared at the phone. She lunged for it and swiped it from the surface, sending it to the floor with an unsatisfactory rumble and a ping from the line. The ping continued, irritating her further, so she kicked it hard, causing the cable wire to dislodge. All was quiet, save for the sound of her breath heaving up from her chest.

"Miss Francine?" Greta's voice sounded from downstairs.

Francine clenched her jaw. She grabbed an errant sweater from the mishmash of apparel piled on her chair and stomped out of her bedroom like a cloudburst.

Square-shaped Greta, unvarying, modest Greta, stood with her hand on the banister, looking up at the dust storm heading down the staircase.

"Is everything alright?" she asked. Francine was used to her meaningless inquiries into her moods; Greta knew how far Francine could go but feigned a decent amount of composure in the face of it, remaining in her place, a glass box of Service.

"What's all the ballyhoo Francie?" Her father, concerned but slightly irritated at the commotion, came toward her from the hall, a legal pad in one hand and his glasses in the other.

"I'm going out," she erupted as she charged out the door and slammed it behind her.

On the sidewalk, with a cold blast of English evening air on her burning skin, she felt a small spring loosen. Her shoulders dropped a few inches.

It wasn't enough. She needed something. Ecstasy maybe. GHB maybe. *Liquid ecstasy*, she thought, turning the words over in her mind. *Yes.*

But when she turned the corner onto Oakley Street, the sweetness of an outstretched rose bush causing her to wince, she walked right into a familiar body.

"Whoa! Sorry! Oh, Francine! Where are you going? Whoa, why so angry?" Keith held her upper arms and took stock of her facial expression. In a pair of blue jeans, a denim button-down, a camel colored leather jacket, and his layered blond locks as soft and tantalizing as ever, he was the last person in Chelsea a young woman would try to dodge on the sidewalk.

But Francine's mind was one-track.

Release. Desensitization.

She shook her head dismissively. "I'm on my way to Rodney's. What are you doing here?"

He held up a white envelope as a grin expanded across his face.

Annoyed, she held out her hands. "What?" she snapped. "What is it?"

"It's from Lazard, Francie."

"It's probably another 'thanks but no thanks, little London receptionist.'" She started past him on the sidewalk, heading north, but he grabbed her arm and spun her around. "Don't worry, I'll stop giving them your address. Might as well let my dad find the rejections."

"Or… just maybe… it's a: 'We'd be chuffed to put your big obnoxious brain to good use at Rockefeller Plaza.'"

"How do you know where their office is?"

He looked down at the envelope. "Return address."

Francine glowered. "I'm going to Rodney's." She spun around northward.

"Fine. I'll open it," he called after her. She picked up speed, the words 'liquid ecstasy' ringing just behind her eyes, pulsating at her temples.

"Dear Miss Decclestone, In reference to your numerous unsolicited letters of application and works of macro economical theory, investment strategy, and industry research, I decided to write you personally. As you know, we are a firm with a one-hundred-thirty-two year history and if I do say so myself, the most seasoned team of analysts, traders, bankers, statisticians and salespeople in all of New York."

Francine slowed her pace but didn't turn around.

"Members of our team have experience managing upwards of $1 billion endowment and have lived and traded in Asia, Europe, and North America, speaking Mandarin, French, Arabic, and German," Keith shouted down the sidewalk as he read the letter, a few feet behind her. "My team are expert quants, balanced with forward-thinking mavens on the cutting edge of innovation; they sit on industry panels and count the world's most discerning tycoons as clients and friends. While I appreciate your ample time working on a trading floor as a receptionist, I am afraid your experience for the role for which you are essentially requesting, or proposing yourself, is inadequate."

Francine huffed, shook her head, and clenched her jaw. She felt the rage run fresh through the tiny muscles in her forearms.

"Wait Francine," Keith strode quickly toward her as he continued to read, his breathing heavy. "That being said, I didn't have any of the above experience when I started, arriving on the floor with nothing but a soggy ham sandwich in my pocket and a fierce desire to learn and excel. For that reason, I would like to invite you to New York for a trial period. Show me your ferociousness, and I'll teach you what I know. It is a risk, but I am an excellent risk-taker.

You're a bet I'm willing to play. I expect you at 8:00 a.m. Monday morning, second of June. If you do not appear on time, I'll assume you found a better offer. Regards, Jed Samuels, Head of Trading."

She spun around and stared fiercely into Keith's ecstatic eyes. "You just made that up."

"Francine!" he exclaimed, holding out the letter, folded three times, its creases fresh.

"Did you make that up, Keith, tell me right now!" she shouted.

He held the letter out, extending it toward her. She grabbed it and scanned her eyes over it, reaching the end.

You're a bet I'm willing to play.

Her heart raced.

"Francine!" Keith said again, slowly, an enormous smile on his face. She looked up at him with eyes wide, disbelief striking outwards from her barely opened mouth.

Keith enclosed her in a tight hug, lifting her from the sidewalk of Oakley Street and shaking her like a Pez container.

When he put her down, her face was still awash in shock.

"My father."

Keith looked behind him, as if he was standing there.

"He'll never let me go."

"Francie, you can't let him say no. You just can't," he said flatly. "Rodney can wait. Tonight, you've got a battle to win." He grabbed her cheeks and kissed her on the lips. "Off you go. Be ferocious. Not *too* ferocious." He tapped her bum and pushed her in the direction from which she had come.

———————

Back at the house on Upper Cheyne Row, Francine knocked on her father's office door, the letter, folded into three, hidden in her hand behind her back.

"What is it, Francine?" He didn't look up from his notepad as he scribbled away, holding open an enormous law text with his left hand.

Francine slipped the letter beneath her bum as she sat down on a leather chair before him.

"I would like to discuss a plane ticket to New York," she said, hesitantly, suddenly less sure of herself in the face of answered prayers. Unprepared for hopes to become reality.

"What for?" His voice remained half-interested as he scribbled away a note from the law book.

She didn't know what to say for a moment.

For a new life. For my freedom.

He glanced at her, his eyes above his glasses, which sat low on his nose.

"We spoke about this. And now it's real."

"It's not real, it's your fantasy. And I am sorry, Francine, I must finish this article of incorporation."

The flippant dismissal was all she needed to stir her skittishness into indignant resent. She felt the letter crease beneath her bottom as she pushed her weight forward.

"Daddy, you can't lock me up forever. I am a human being. I have dreams. I have value. I want desperately to be proud of myself for something. I was smarter than all the girls in my class—you know that. You sent me to St. Andrews. For what? To teach kindergarten? Let me do something with that. Let me *be* someone."

She thought of her mother's words. *Be big.*

"You keep me in this nebulous, prohibitive world where implosion feels more and more likely each day. You and Dr. Gavison on your high fucking worthless horses…"

He pushed his head backward as if shot with a rubber band and looked up to meet the intense rancor in her eyes.

"Francine, you are my child—"

"I'm NOT—"

He held his hand up. "Let me finish. You *are* my child. *My* child. My love. My life. You and your mother…" He drifted off. "I have been unlucky with my love. Your mother, she was resplendent in her day. She was vigorous and lively and sweet. And we had a beautiful love that sadly could not stand above the water line of her illness, as much as I dearly wanted it to, and though you may not believe me now, perhaps you will understand later, that we agreed, in a moment of lucidity, that I would do anything and everything to protect you from a similar trajectory. I never imagined our conclusion looking quite the way it did. However, I wouldn't give it back for the world, because it brought me you. And you, my Francine, are just as resplendent, vigorous, lively, and sweet. But you *must* understand, there is a piece of your insides that takes this away sometimes, and through no fault of your own, we must all face the realities of this 'other' living thing inside of you. We mustn't ignore it."

He handled a pen between his hands as he spoke, something to focus on rather than his daughter's intransigent expression.

"When you are not in control, you cannot protect yourself. You cannot make smart decisions. You cannot be safe. You cannot hold a job. You cannot raise a child. You cannot be in a healthy marriage. You cannot keep friendships. You cannot hold up your reputation. And I am responsible for this. For all of it. For you, your life, your job, your marriage, your friendships, your reputation. As your father, I am responsible. And I will not risk any of it obligingly."

She bolted up from her chair. "This is bollocks," she raged.

"Sit, Francine," he said. "I am not finished."

She stood with her arms folded.

"Sit, Francine."

She sat down again, shaking her head in vexation, staring out of the window with her jaw clenched.

"I understand your desire to escape these conditions. You think that I do not empathize, this is not true. I know that before me stands an intelligent, capable, sociable, charming, and sensitive person. I know that you have immense potential in this changing world, Francine. I know that if there exists anyone to walk onto that trading floor in New York with hundreds of blood-thirsty, impolite young men yelling and drooling—"

Francine softened and rolled her eyes.

"Well, they will be—drooling. When they see how beautiful my daughter is. Well, I know that if there is to be any female taking on their challenges and their stares, it is you. So, I have done my research. I have spoken at length with the Director at Bellevue. He has agreed to take you on—personally—as a patient of his. You will see him twice a week—"

"Twice!" Francine shouted.

"You will see him twice a week for six months. As a test period. He will be in charge of your pharmacological treatment and will ensure that you remain as steady as possible during that time. If after six months, everything is going smoothly, you may see him once a week. If you slip, Francine, if you decide to take your regimen into your own hands, or mix it with too much cocaine or ecstasy or whatever you are favoring these days, you will return to London. No second chances."

She sat before him, her arms still crossed, slightly embarrassed at his bringing up her party drugs directly to her face, but also slightly dumbfounded at his capitulation in her decade-long battle to leave London.

"You knew about this offer, didn't you?"

He looked at her innocently. "No. I didn't. But I knew you'd get one sooner or later. That I knew."

LIGURIA

July 17, 2021

MARGHERITA HAD NOT risen in hours. It hadn't been easy to reserve a last minute chair on a summer weekend—she'd had to catch a local train to a village a few stops farther toward France in order to find availability. It had been so long since she had taken a day off from the project that she found herself in a stupor of laziness. Not even octopus on the beach club's menu enticed her, and she once again wondered where her spirit had disappeared to, her vigor for all things Italian summer. *Middlemarch* sat dejectedly toward the end of the chair, stained and tattered tales of frustrated love and disillusion no different than those of the present day. She felt among kindred spirits as the characters second-guessed classic definitions of morality with misinterpreted egotism and naivety.

From underneath her sun hat, she watched a woman, fortyish, approach the aging lifeguard. The woman, in a frumpy cover-up, tilted her head toward his high perch and chatted familiarly. Margherita imagined he had been the lifeguard since his teenage years. Now he sat beneath a head of white hair, his skin as brown and leathered as every tourist-shop handbag in Florence, and his relaxed disposition attributable to a long, simple, if not monotonous life in a small Italian seaside village. All around them, babies, toddlers, and young kids spurted to and fro with blow-up toys and floating devices of varying shapes. Parents and friends, who had frequented the same beach clubs since they were their children's age, congregated in small groups, constantly talking, constantly socializing. Such was the culture in Italy. She pursed her lips in a smile at a mother who trudged by, dripping salty sea water, a toddler affixed to her hips.

Margherita was the elephant in the room, alone at the beach club—an alien concept, to be alone—and sat still for hours on end, rising only for a fresh from the oven slice of super thin *farinata*. She was mystified by the Italians' never-ending energy and gregariousness. Didn't they ever want to sit still, be quiet, and not talk to anyone?

Surrounded by families, she could not help but wonder if she would one day be one of these people. Would she hold a baby under an umbrella and watch as other beach club goers gravitated toward her like mummies, all wanting to see the baby, touch the baby, play with its little hand and take turns holding the baby? Would she stand at the water's edge with her hands on her hips, watching her child kick his or her (or their!) legs up over the gentle waves, running into the water with mouth agape, over and over? Would her beach bag ever be filled with toys and children's SPF, instead of George Eliot and a bag of potentially life-threatening, choke-hazard grapes? She lowered the back of the chair and turned over onto her stomach, resting her cheek in her hands.

Margherita remembered going out to the beach as a little girl, the turkey sandwiches Tommaso used to make for lunch under the umbrella. She could picture him sitting in an upright chair in his swim trunks, a yellow pad on his lap, sketching something. There Francine would be, on the phone with her office, complaining about service and going back to the rented beach house for a better connection.

She probably never packed a bag of beach toys in her life, Margherita thought. *I guess that's one thing we have in common.*

Margherita remembered one summer trip to Patmos, where her parents had rented a beach house and Benjamin, by then attending boarding school in England, had joined them for the summer. Only Francine had ended up commuting from London, working from her firm's London Bridge office and taking a plane back in time for very late Friday night dinners. Benjamin, a teenager, convinced a distracted Francine to allow his high school girlfriend to join, leaving Margherita to play on the shallow beach by herself. Tommaso would pass her a yellow pad, and she would sketch a ridiculously out of scale house, with the powder room as big as the living room, and Tommaso would laugh affectionately.

Margherita: do you ever think about what kind of dad you're going to be?

Nick: Yes
Nick: Rich
Nick: And distracted

Margherita: oh. winning.

Nick: lol

LONDON

November 7, 1980

FRANCINE AND KEITH sang along loudly to REO Speedwagon's "Keep on Loving You," Francine kicking her legs into the air, the two of them flat on Keith's bed.

He rubbed her arm as she headed into the chorus, but she wouldn't stop singing.

"Francie!" he yelled. "Ey, New Yoykah!"

She giggled and stopped.

"New Yoykah," she imitated. "New Yoykah," she said to the ceiling.

"That's you, now, Ruby Tuesday."

"That's me now. Isn't it? Isn't it wild? I never thought I'd get out of here."

Keith propped himself up on one elbow and turned to face her, focused on her long neck.

"Hey." She energetically shifted onto her side to face him and gripped his hand.

He tipped his head but didn't look up.

"Ey! Keith. Look at me."

He looked up. His eyes were sad.

Hers were electric.

"Francie. My Francie. I really miss you." He rubbed the top of her hand. "It's nuts. It's only been six months since you left London, and every day is longer than the last."

She brought her wide silly smile down to the serious moment

and bit her lower lip.

"Keithie—"

"What?"

"Nothing. It's silly." She rolled over onto her back and waved her hand in the air.

"Tell me."

Taking a deep breath, she turned her face on the pillow. "I was just, thinking. Well. Come back with me. To New York."

"What? Are you crazy?"

She stared at him blankly. "Well, as a matter of fact…"

"I meant. Come on. I'm not going to follow you to New York. New York is all yours. For your fresh start. To do as you please. On your meds. But as you please."

"No one said you'd be following me. I just…" She swished her eyes around his face. "I just thought… Well, you and I—"

"No. No," he said dismissively as he rose to change the record. "You made it through your trial period. Smashed it. Impressed the hell out of everyone. I'm not going to mess with that. Or slow you down. This is your time."

She sat up with her hands as doorstops behind her, watching him. He hadn't let her finish.

"You wouldn't be—"

He put on a new record. She recognized the first sounds of "Sara" by Stevie Nicks.

"I thought you didn't like Stevie?" she asked.

"*You* like Stevie."

She smiled, but suddenly felt a weight on the day. Keith remained standing before his bedroom's bay window, overlooking an enormous, golden-hued chestnut tree, its autumn leaves grazing the pane, as if eager to be let inside.

She leaned forward and crossed her legs on the bed. "I miss you more, Keithie."

IN THE SKY

Margherita: I'm on a plane
Margherita: And I am veryyy very antsy
Margherita: And I really really wish someone were here to be antsy with me

The plane jerked and she grabbed the siding, as if one could possibly hold onto a flat surface. She darted her eyes around, in search of affirmation of her fears.

Please stop, please stop, please stop, she pleaded with the turbulence.

Nick: Hi
Nick: What kind of antsy

She inhaled and bit the insides of her cheeks. Distraction was necessary.

Margherita: The kind where I can feel a heartbeat in unusual places

Nick: What are you imagining

Margherita: Are you alone?

Nick: Yes

Nick: Tell me

As Margherita typed out a few explicit daydreams, she leaned into the siding and hoped the person behind her couldn't read her screen. Planes had a strange affect on her; she was either sexually excitable or anxious. A triple jolt of turbulence rumbled through and her eyes went wide as she rammed her head into the back of her seat.

Nick: If we were in the same city I would gladly bring all of these fantasies to life with you

Margherita: That would be nice.
Margherita: Where are you now?

Nick: About to board a plane myself. Had a wedding in Singapore.
Nick: Phenomenal week. One of my best friends married our other best friend's sister.

He sent her a photo of himself in a tight white tee-shirt, cuffed linen trousers, and very blonde hair. Two guy friends sat to his right on a balcony beneath a night sky. He looked gorgeous. Sexy as hell. And happy.

He didn't ask her where *her* plane was headed, she noted. Typical.

Margherita: There is a crazy amount of turbulence on this flight.
Margherita: I am the looney girl gripping the arm rest and looking at a flight attendant's face every time it feels like we are riding through Dorothy's tornado.
Margherita: What kind of flier are you

Nick: Very calm.

At the next enormous bump in the sky, she squeezed her eyes shut and clasped her hands around the arm rests.

Imagine sitting next to a calm Nicky. Imagine sitting next to a calm Nicky.

Margherita: I'll be in the city this weekend
Margherita: just for the weekend
Nick: oh?

Margherita sat with her thumb nail between her upper and lower front teeth.

Margherita: Maybe we can have a drink. Catch up in person.
Nick: I would like that.

The next night, at Margherita's favorite restaurant on East Houston, with the windows open onto the main thoroughfare and the city making every effort to normalize after its COVID winter, she sat at a bar seat next to Noah, their first post-pandemic reunion, and it was as if no time at all had passed. Margherita was every bit Noah's "little one," the same vivacious, outspoken twenty-three old girl who had started her architecture career on the fourth floor of Merrill Bates Lee, where he'd worked for years before moving to Los Angeles, and Noah was every bit the dry-humored, tough-loving, pretending-to-be-miserable Brit, though he was decidedly more LaLaLand after nearly a decade in the leafy Los Angeles neighborhood of Los Feliz.

A tray of oysters with a yuzu koshu mignonette sat on the marble bar before them, a plate of raw fluke and uni at its side. A bottle of Vermentino. GENTS, Big Black Delta, and Violent Femmes on the playlist. A full restaurant. Manhattan at its best.

"I can't believe you haven't been dating. Weren't you desperate to get back in the pool after the pandemic? What's happened to you?" Noah plodded, politely swinging back an oyster.

"I am celibate," Margherita said, poised and deliberate. "No penises in my pool. I swim alone. It is delightful."

Noah rolled his eyes. "Bugger off. You're like our modern day Jane Fonda. She didn't officially close up shop until her eighties."

"Well, abbreviated version: masturbation is actually more satisfying ninety to one hundred percent of the time, and I don't have to put make-up on or drink alcohol to do it, the end."

Noah turned an empty shell over on its stomach. "Unnecessary."

"Who am I supposed to date? I don't meet any eligible guys. Any thirty-something guy in Italy is married already."

"Heading towards a mistress."

"Exactly."

"What happened to the sexy guy you used to have a fling with?"

Margherita sighed and rested her fingers around the base of her wine glass. "Is it really pathetic that I slept with him again this summer?"

"No. I mean, isn't that the whole point of him?"

"It doesn't feel as exciting. The first night—fabulous. So liberating. So fun. So sexy. Best date I'd been on in years. He is, and you know I hate this idiotic word with a fiery passion, 'literally' the most charming, most sexy, most hypnotic man I've ever met. But then the second time it was déjà vu… pushed me to the end of the night. Straight to the crux of the deal. And I saw him once at the beach with his wife. And I felt… ick. I felt ick all over. Not toward him. Toward myself. Like who is this pathetic thirty-one year-old on the promenade looking down at someone's family? What the *hell* am I doing? It wasn't cute. I'm not cute anymore. Look at this wrinkle." Margherita pointed at the crease in her forehead.

"Stop squinting. Get your eyes checked. Go for botox."

"Yeah. You know when we went out the first night, hours and hours at that restaurant, talking so fluidly, so easily, laughing so much, just getting along so, so well, I thought: why can't I find this guy? *This* guy? Why is this evening so perfect, with a guy that already has a family? I don't get it. I never have evenings like that with anyone available, in my age group."

"So now you *want* a guy? Like, your own guy? This is new."

"Well, the pandemic was long and kind of lonely sometimes."

"Weren't you with your dad every day?"

"I can't grow old with my dad, Noah. This isn't some weird version of *Grey Gardens*. I need to find a relationship."

"A relationship! Whoa! Learning new words!" Noah smiled with eyes exaggeratedly enlarged.

"Yeah! I said it!"

"But you're celibate."

"I'm waiting for the one who makes me lose my appetite. That 'can't sleep, can't eat, jump in the air when he texts me' sort of thing."

"That sounds like all of your previous disasters. Flames to ashes in no time."

"Well, if I don't feel that, I can't get on board. I just can't. Blame my genetic make-up. I do descend from a psychotic mother, and grandmother, after all. I will wait for flames if it takes me until menopause and I have to induce them with hormone replacements."

"That's what cowardly people say. That they're waiting for the 'right one.' Waiting and waiting all their little lives. They say they won't 'settle' like everyone else does, like they're above everyone. Are you above chances? What did Auntie Mame say? The world is a banquet and most people are starving." Noah scooted his stool one inch closer to her when someone to his left coughed.

"I just took a chance on that oyster. And I'm sitting *inside* a restaurant during a pandemic with a waning vaccine that barely passed the CDC."

Noah took an impatient sip from his wine glass.

"So it's better to be with the potentially wrong person than to be alone, hopeful for Big Big Love," she declared, leaning into the brick wall behind her.

Noah turned his back toward the bar seat on his left, as if he was about to tell Margherita a secret. "Marghe, jokes aside, don't you want companionship? Not just sitting next to someone for a few hours with a bottle of Vermentino and a round of oysters in front of you?"

"Companionship."

"Yes. In its most mundane and beautiful forms. Not always exciting. Not always dramatic. Stories not always worth re-telling."

"I..." she started, and looked around the room with her mouth ajar.

"You what?"

Margherita touched her back molars with her tongue. She thought of her parents, and their unique version of companionship, of the last years of Francine's life, after her doctor at Bellevue died and she began to take dips off her meds. So many of Margherita's memories of her parents were of Tommaso acting as caretaker. So thrown had she been by her doctor's sudden departure from her life, Francine had allowed herself to rollercoaster through swing states, causing many sleepless nights for Tommaso, all too frequent trips to the hospital, and an undeniably one-sided relationship. Tommaso as water. Francine as sponge. Not exactly ideal companionship.

"You're scared," Noah said matter of factly. He picked up his glass of wine and looked dead ahead into the cavity of the restaurant.

She glanced at Noah, who raised his eyebrows at her, his face bored.

"Whatever. So when are you going back to LA?" she changed the subject.

"Tuesday. When are you going back to Milan?"

"I'm not. I need to give my bank account a little breathing room, and that apartment was just slightly more than I should be spending. Besides, Milan feels so different. It's kind of sad still. It doesn't feel like my Milan. Did you ever meet my friend Chiara? A friend of hers has this adorable top floor apartment in the hills above Santa Margherita Ligure she's going to rent to me month to month. Twenty minute walk to the villa property. One thousand euros. Can't beat it."

"Where is that Chiara girl? You used to talk about her."

"She's teaching back to back courses on renaissance art in Toronto. I've rarely spoken to her this year, actually. But she seems happy. Busy. Met a guy." Margherita shrugged.

"So what will you do in this little beach town?" Noah asked. "No one's invested in the project yet, so this villa isn't yours to touch."

"I'm going to keep trying to get this project off the ground. Focus."

"Wouldn't you have better luck in New York or Miami or somewhere with big, fast-moving, crypto-money? Why don't you get into crypto in Miami?"

"Right. Great advice, Noah. Let me drop everything and 'get into crypto in Miami.'"

"Well, honestly, have you had any actual leads Zooming random investors in Zurich or Vienna or anywhere else in Europe?" He used a hunk of bread to swish beef tartare with elderberries and sunchoke onto his fork.

"Who knows? These things take time. And if it weren't for this stupid pandemic I'd fly around a little more, meet people in person. Or if I had the funds. Italy has been less than fruitful for potential investors. I will admit it. I thought some of these people would be eager to put money into their country. My numbers are promising. The potential is enormous. But every man I've met in Milan has looked at me like a piece of meat with my head in the sky."

"Tartare or lamb chop?" he asked ironically as he took another forkful.

"I don't think cut or farm animal was of particular importance. I wish I were a guy sometimes."

"Yeah, being a white guy is a breeze. Are you going to eat any of this or is this all for me?" He pointed toward the tartare.

She grazed her fork through a top layer on her side of the bowl. "It is! All you have to do is apologize for everything!"

"So why bother going back to Italy at all?"

"Because that's where the property is. And if I leave, it's like I'm giving up. And everyone will think I gave up. But I'm actually spending August in Carmel." She took a bite of the tartare. "Gosh, I love how they do it with the sunchoke. That crunch. You know Italian cities are ghost towns in August."

"You're going to Carmel? To do what? Swim with the seals and play golf at Pebble?" he asked, somewhat condescendingly.

Margherita thought of her mom and the yearly trips they used to make to the central coast. It was just after their last trip together, when Margherita was twenty-five, that Francine had tried, once again, to overdose. She had been, once again, unsuccessful.

The next and final attempt was her most, and only, successful attempt. If one tries hard enough, they're bound to bang the door open.

Margherita imagined her mom on the little streets of Carmel-by-the-Sea, her hands shoved into the pockets of a fleecy zip-up, a relaxed smile on her face. There had been so many lovely mornings when they would walk together along Casanova Street, Camino Real, and Scenic Road after coffee in the village, admiring the dollhouses and making their way down toward the white sand of the wide beach, where the dogs ran free.

"I love to see the dogs off-lead, don't you? It reminds me of London," Francine always said. Some version of that. And Margherita would wonder what memories of her mother's London life she was stirring at that moment. What had been so wonderful and joyous in her previous life that brought that gentle smile to her face, just thinking about it?

In the restaurant, sitting next to Noah, perhaps her oldest friend, she resented feeling as if she needed to defend herself, her trip to Carmel or the fact that she was not returning immediately to Italy, to the scene of the challenge she had created for herself.

"My aunt's house is rent-free. August is a dead month in Europe—everything on pause. So I'm going to regroup. Get my head on straight again. I haven't been back in a few years." She finished vaguely, and she sensed that Noah knew to drop it.

He looked at her blankly as the bartender cleared the empty tartare bowl and replaced it with Margherita's favorite plate at the restaurant: endive with crunchy walnuts, anchovy, and ubriaco rosso.

"You need a job," he said flatly.

"Ugh!" Margherita threw her head back. "Thanks, *Dad!*"

"Or start having babies. How old are you now?"

Margherita scrunched her face.

Noah pointed at a line between her eyes. "Botox. Just a little."

"Next you'll be telling me to freeze my eggs."

"Why not? A friend of mine just had a baby at forty-seven."

"Do you know how expensive it is to freeze your eggs? Twenty grand. At least. I can barely afford a New York espresso right now."

"Well how many kids do you need?" he asked exasperatedly. "Don't we have enough little WASPs running around?"

The next day, after running through her 'don't forget' list typed out on her phone (prescription sunglasses, sketchpad, retainers, passport, ear plugs for the plane), Margherita sat in the back of an Uber on the way to JFK and watched Queens roll by outside the window. She wondered how many times Francine had watched the same scenes on her way to the same airport, on trips to London or Frankfurt or Tokyo or Cairo—wherever she had been going. It was something Margherita found herself thinking about a lot; did Francine look at this too, in the same way perhaps? And what would she have been thinking about? It was pointless really, because of course Francine saw much of the same view en route to the airport, and what difference did it make? But it was something that made Margherita feel an atom more connected to her mother; or an atom more guilty, for being there, above ground, covering the same surfaces, not accomplishing nearly as much.

In the security line at JFK, notoriously the world's worst, Margherita stood with her weight on her right leg, her hands on her luggage handle, and her eyes hidden behind her sunglasses. The mask was one more tool with which to cover her forlorn mood. New York didn't feel like home at that moment, and every night spent in her father's townhouse, *not* hearing the sounds of her mother—her midnight jaunts to her downstairs office, her bathtub running in the evening, every television screen in the house tuned to CNBC—stained her with a melancholy that seeped deep into her pores for weeks and weeks.

And even more pathetic was that she let herself be disappointed by Nick. She had hoped, though she assumed it would be unlikely, that she would see him. It had been so long since they had stood face to face, and in the absence of in-the-flesh interaction, she had romanticized the idea of him all over again. Their intermittent communications had left a door open in her mind, and though she knew she needed him as a friend more than anything else, she wanted his attention. She wanted him to *want* to give her attention, as she always had.

She pried a plastic bin off the stack using a sani-wipe and swiftly laid her carry-on suitcase on the conveyer belt. Into the bin went her sweatshirt, her sneakers, and her purse, though it always terrified her to send her purse on its way through the security belt, its exit on the other side lightyears ahead of her own person.

She tip-toed across the floor, held her arms above her head and her legs wide, and stepped through, numb to the commotion around her.

Why am I going to Carmel? she thought as she made her way towards her gate. *What the eff was I thinking?*

She inhaled and exhaled. She would spend August alone. That wouldn't help, would it? Knowing most people in her age group were gallivanting around Europe with big groups of friends? And here she was, going in the opposite direction, to take hikes by herself and be constantly reminded of her dead mother. How did she think this would be mentally or emotionally therapeutic?

In her hand, as she made her way through the terminal, her phone sounded a low ba-boom.

Nick: Are you still in the city?
Nick: I'd like to see you before you leave
Nick: I'm sorry I didn't write yesterday
Nick: I was running around looking for a new apartment
Nick: And had a party last night for one of my friends
Nick: And the weekend got away from me

"Ha," she said aloud to the screen in her palm. *Fuck you,* she thought as she read off the gate numbers.

Margherita: My flight is at 7
Nick: Quick drink
Nick: One hour
Nick: We can speed talk
Nick: Come on
Margherita: You do realize that's in two hours.
Nick: I'm sorry.

Margherita: Don't be.

Nick: This is you being terse and passive aggressive when I know you're mad.

Margherita: I assure you I'm not. Better this way, anyway.

Nick: Why

Because you are a black, black hole, she thought.

She put her phone on airplane mode as she waited to board to dissuade any additional exchange. On the tarmac, she turned the network back on and typed out a somewhat daring response.

Margherita: Because I feel not-in-control enough as it is

Nick: What does that mean
Nick: I thought you liked that feeling

She flipped her phone over in her lap and stared out the window as last minute luggage was shoveled into the belly of the plane. A tear fringed her right eye.

What is wrong with me? she thought as she pushed it into the heel of her hand.

Nick: Do you regret every minute you've spent with me

Margherita: Maybe I just want more than a rapid heartbeat for once.

She waited the thirty minutes before the plane took off for him to respond, but he never did.

LONDON

September 2, 1981

FRANCINE SWALLOWED ONE lithium and one carbamazepine. As a rapid cycler, she needed as many anti-mania pills as anti-depressants, and as a result, often found her regimen overlapped in seemingly superfluous ways. But her flight was the next day, and she needed to ensure she was on top of her game by the time she returned to the office, and to Dr. Bronsson's check-ins at Bellevue. Her doctor, though fastidious and strict, had won her over with his New York directness, honesty, and sense of humor. He sometimes felt more like a friend than a man administering her moods, and though her appointments at Bellevue were not the most convenient, she did not mind seeing Dr. Bronsson. With her father and Keith and her friends so far, he was a warm, familiar face, and she knew he genuinely wanted her to succeed in New York—with her work, with her life, with her future.

There was also Tommaso, the dark haired, fair skinned, subdued young architect she had begun dating. He was the opposite of Christos: humble, focused, and selfless, and for some reason, he adored her. Or more specifically, he adored the version of herself she had so far shown him. Surely he wouldn't be so enamored if he knew she had been having oodles of unprotected sex on the slippery rocks of a Greek island for the past two weeks. But it was early yet—no one was married.

Her vacation on Patmos, where she passed the days sleeping on the boat or the rocky beach, saving the nights for cocaine-fueled parties, ecstasy, and dancing with Christos, had been blissfully unregimented. Days blended together, sustenance came directly from the sea or arid land in the form of sun-dried octopus, bulgar salads, tahini soup, and other flavors of the Dodecanese, and her pill box was nowhere to be seen.

When she and Christos had returned to London a few days prior to her flight, she had picked up the plastic box once again and begun swallowing her rainbow friends out of his sight.

Back to Dr. Bronsson's version of Francine. Lazard's version. Tommaso's version.

CARMEL

August 3, 2021

'THANK YOU! MASKS required! Be kind! ☺'

Margherita ha-ed out loud at the chalkboard sidewalk sign.

Oh, California, you passive aggressive, overly apologetic, absurdly expensive, beaute of a place, you. She sighed and smiled as she entered the café for a much-needed espresso.

She had landed the previous evening at Monterey Airport after a short layover in Phoenix, managed to find a rental car, and made it back to her aunt's empty, peach-colored house in the Highlands just in time to watch a magnificent sunset. It was one of those Fog vs. Pink Starburst skies, where a thick layer of Karl the Fog rolled over the deep hues like a slow snail, inching farther and farther along the horizon, fluorescent candy oozing from its uneven edges. Sitting on the wooden deck with nothing but the sounds of the chimes and a possible bobcat lurking in the tall morning glory shrubbery, it was the precise moment of tranquility that Margherita needed.

Tommaso's sister Vera, who lived in Palo Alto with her husband, used the dated 1970s house perched in the Highlands on most weekends and holidays, but August tended to be a foggy month in Carmel, and she preferred to go north over the Golden Gate Bridge to reliably hot and sunny wine country rather than weather the odd emotional effects of the central coast's microclimates. Not particularly close to her Aunt Vera, who had grown apart from Tommaso with the appearance of Francine on the scene (the two women could not possibly have been more different, sparring partners at every opportunity), Margherita had suspected that her request to use the house for the month of August would be politely dismissed. She was surprised when her aunt quickly obliged and immediately assumed it to be some form of pity: *the poor, motherless girl.* That summer, finally able to travel internationally again, Vera and her husband had rented a house in southern Portugal, and Margherita couldn't decide if she was disappointed or relieved to not have to spend time with the only extended family she had.

Mornings began chilly and refreshing, sometimes misty depending on the fog, and Margherita zipped her Patagonia high up her neck as she made her way toward the farmers' market. The central coast's August breeze was deliciously welcome after the hot and humid days in Milan, the non-air-conditioned trains and the hard plastic seats that stuck to the backs of her bare legs.

From Mission to 6th Ave and all the way up to Junipero, vendors showed off their gorgeous bounties, and Margherita's eyes glowed at the sight of crisp, freshly baked seeded breads, flaky, caramel-colored pain au chocolat, mango cream puffs, and pecan scones from Bee's Knees Bakery. There was just-squeezed strawberry guava lemonade, green paper cartons of plump local raspberries and blueberries, and tables filled with colorful heirloom and multi-hued cherry tomatoes. There were wonky cucumbers that wrapped around like snakes, sweet peas and swallowtails, and always stalks and stalks of freshly cut flowers. Locals stood in lines with woven wicker baskets, their heads craning left and right and upward like rubbernecking swans, eager to have their pick of the plump strawberries. Golden retrievers and standard poodles sat with smiles slapped on their faces, a friendly water bowl always a few feet away, and a still-warm baguette within jaw's reach.

Sigh, how I love it here, Margherita thought, as she breezed through the center aisle of pedestrians, criss crossing from the north to south sides, from Nitro coffee to peaches, from California avocados to farm fresh eggs. How different life was in that idyllic, craggy stretch of coast from life in New York or Milan. How very California it was, in all the best ways.

It was not Vera who had made Margherita fall in love with Carmel; it was her mom. It was the one place in the world where Margherita had seen Francine unequivocally calm; so blissfully peaceful and content for a whole week at a time. Tommaso appreciated its beauty just the same, but as his moods were more consistent, it didn't have the same contrasting effect on him as it seemed to have on Francine, who relished the wildness of the nature, the whiplash transition between humidity and fog along the coast, and the intrinsically lyrical qualities.

"It speaks to me," Francine had once said, sitting on a fallen tree trunk in Point Lobos, seals making a ruckus beneath her. "Something about it reminds me of Hampstead. Hampstead with a craggy coast."

"How do you see Hampstead here?" Tommaso had asked, tying the shoelace on his hiking boot.

"I don't *see* it. I *feel it*," Francine had said.

Margherita breathed in deeply, recalling the memory. She could picture the creases at her mother's eyes when she smiled. She shook her head gently to jerk herself out of the visualization, and with too much fresh produce and an armful of fresh flowers, made her way back to the car and hurried home to have breakfast on the deck.

Tommaso: did you settle in okay?

Margherita: oui. I'm in heaven. the air feels therapeutic, the breezes are medicinal, the chimes fit right in, and by day two I'm nodding along to people who use words like Gratitude in every sentence

Tommaso: good. I'm happy for you. Did you write to Vera?

Margherita: yes. But Dad when was the last time they did anything to this house

Tommaso: 1972

Margherita: That's when they built it

Tommaso: exactly.

After a smoothie with fresh produce from the market, she drove down to Francine's beloved Point Lobos for a walk through coastal scrub, high above the crashing waves and groups of seals. The sky shifted from clear and blue to low hanging clouds as she weaved in and out of the pathways, veering toward the Pacific and back again toward the mountains. There were monarch butterflies, Monterey cypress, pelicans, cacti, and trees so big they could host tea time.

In the afternoon she did a self-guided yoga session on the deck, sweating in the dry heat beneath the beating sun. Toward evening, she read a book on her yoga mat, her head resting on a deck chair pillow, the horizon vast before her, and the sound of Francine singing along to 'Sara' by Stevie Nicks in her head. It was one of her mom's favorite songs and was at one time on constant rotation on their vintage record player. Later, as she made a small dinner—homemade soup from the market and California strawberries for dessert—she felt her mother so thickly in the air she suddenly had trouble breathing.

"I'm really sorry I kept leaving," Margherita said out loud to the evening breeze. "I'm really sorry I kept moving away."

A tear cascaded down her cheek and she smeared it away with the sleeve of her sweatshirt. She let the moment pass, sitting still for a long while. The evening grew chilly, but she remained cross-legged, watching the sunset and listening to her own breath.

Here I am, she thought.

As she brushed her teeth and washed her face before bed, everything silent save for the chimes and the rustling lavender, her phone pinged.

Tommaso: did you lock the doors?

Margherita: dad, I am thirty one. I know how to live by myself.

Tommaso: just checking. There could be murderers in the hills looking specifically for a thirty-one year old.

Margherita: thanks for that bedtime story.
Margherita: in the police blotter this morning, the most alarming event was this: 'Homeowner on San Juan Road reported a suspicious incident.'
Margherita: It's carmel not East Harlem

Tommaso: your mother used to leave all those doors open. Remember when the baby fox showed up to breakfast?

Margherita huffed out loud. It was true; her mother had insisted on sleeping with a door or two open so she could hear the oceanic sounds and the rustling leaves. And sure enough, a fox once strode in, looking for bagels.

Margherita: she was so different out here. So peaceful and content.

Her father typed and stopped a few times.

Tommaso: your mother loved it out there.
Tommaso: you know she grew up on the Heath
Tommaso: in tall grass and mud and ancient trees and all the drama of those foggy mornings. She always said that was what it was, some aura of the Heath.

Margherita: didn't you ever talk about moving back to London?
Margherita: I sometimes wonder if that would have been better for her

Tommaso: there's no easy solution to life's complications
Tommaso: your mother needed distance from London, and she was thriving in NY
Tommaso: that is the double edged sword of being adventurous and gutsy... picking up and starting anew.... You are always chasing a feeling of 'home.'
Tommaso: don't spend all your time out there thinking of mom
Tommaso: she'd be livid

Margherita: I know

Tommaso: make some calls to some NY firms this week.
Tommaso: it might be August in Europe but NY is still at work, and I imagine your savings is running dry
Tommaso: gas aint cheap in California

Margherita: k goodnight

Tommaso: lock the doors

The next morning, back on the front porch, she basked in the company of bright blue birds with red faces and insistent woodpeckers.

Companionship, she thought with a smile.

She breathed in the scent of lavender and sat patiently watching the fog that burned off and rolled in, only to burn off and roll in once more. The rhythm of the morning was set by the sounds of the crashing waves below, and Margherita fluctuated between drinking tea and stretching her limbs.

After a shower, the sun shone so brazenly it dried her wet hair in less than twenty minutes. She debated a drive along the jiggedy jiggedy coastline, where each day she tried to glimpse Kim Novak's old house jutting out below, but she felt glued to the porch. Her butt on the wooden slats. She didn't want to stop looking up and around from that vantage point even if it meant going blind staring into the sun. The sky was always changing and she didn't want to miss a minute.

A whole day went by on the porch, and after dinner, she felt the urge to chat about nothing with someone whose company she often craved in moments of quietude.

Margherita: are you awake?

But she went to sleep without a response.

The next morning, after parking her car on Highway 1 and descending the steps onto the white sands of Garrapata, she received a response.

Nick: Sorry I crashed out
Nick: Where are you?
Nick: Are you awake?

Margherita sent him a photo of the short, four mile beach, surrounded by layered green mountains and bluffs.

Nick: Gorgeous

Nick sent his live location in South London.

Margherita proceeded to do three timed sprints before she responded.

Margherita: are you a Peckham boy now?
Nick: Ha no.
Nick: I'm at my sister's

Margherita: which sister

Nick: oldest

Margherita: Aw sweet. Uncle making his rounds

Nick: Actually no one is here
Nick: so I'm homo alono

Margherita: ohh homo alono that's a good situation to be in

Nick: such a good situation
Nick: I have been living a quite proactively, aggressively single life the last few months

She looked down at her phone and scoffed. *Why must I know this?*

Margherita: Oh yeah? How's that going?

Nick: well
Nick: I am tanned and in excellent physical shape

Before her, half on the beach and half in the water, two young whales were entwined, their silky wet bodies flapping over one another. They appeared to be mating, and Margherita looked on in wonder. She sent Nick a short video.

Nick: and have been in some glam places
Nick: and have been trying to sex my way through my relationship processing
Nick: and it's going well

Margherita: you sound very pleased with yourself

Nick: ha no
Nick: just reflecting

Margherita: what does that mean, you're sexing your way through your relationship processing
Margherita: You think you're going to tire yourself out and not want it anymore?

Nick: ha no
Nick: more like rid myself of any lingering validating needs I have
Nick: I think my relationship chipped away at my confidence
Nick: and sense of sufficiency
Nick: so the aggressively single part is in some way to say
Nick: Look I am attractive and wanted

Margherita stared at her phone. Of all of the things he could share with her, why this? And all things considered, how the hell was she meant to respond?

Margherita: Well I'm happy for you that you feel so positive

Nick: how are you doing
Nick: I hope you don't mind my sharing

Margherita: surely self validation doesn't all boil down to sex? You never had any reason to doubt yourself there
Margherita: and definitely not a person you want to spend time with… anyone who breaks down and takes away your confidence
Margherita: anddd you don't need a reminder you're gorgeous you nimwit

Nick: I'm being reductive
Nick: how are you
Nick: what's in your heart these days

Uff, Margherita thought to herself. *What's in my heart. What's in my heart.*

You, still, she thought as she caught her ankle in her hand and stretched her quad staring out beyond the foaming sea. She ran a mile before answering.

Margherita: I'm good :)

Nick: ……..

Margherita: ha what

Nick: I'd love to know more

Would you really? she wondered. *Since when?*

Nick: I suppose I want an insight into how you're doing

Nick: what you're grappling with

Nick: enjoying

Nick: worried about

Nick: enticed by

Margherita stared at her phone and laughed out loud.

Margherita: What's gotten into you?

Anytime she had shared in the past, he had shimmied away, ignored her.

Margherita: Did you watch the mating??

Margherita: Isn't that amazing?

Nick: I did!

Nick: and you don't have to answer me if you don't want to.

Nick: I felt compelled to be outrageously honest

Nick: but I know that's just where I'm at this minute so, no biggie

Margherita: they're making babies. So sweet

Margherita: Are you outrageously honest with everyone

Nick: No not really

Margherita: Then why me

Nick: Cause you're in my life
Nick: but not in my day to day
Nick: and you're thoughtful
Nick: and insightful
Nick: and I know you'd get it
Nick: that's all

Not in your day to day, isn't that right, she thought.

Margherita: Okay :)

Nick: right I'm going for a jog

Margherita: you know I'm always happy to lend an ear, I only ask because you are not usually so forthcoming with me. But I'm really glad you are feeling so solid—in so many ways ☺

Nick: I think it's because
Nick: I don't always "feel" like being honest and open
Nick: and inspected
Nick: but today I do
Nick: so I did
Nick: xxx

Strange, she thought.

Later that afternoon, eager to return to all of her favorite places, Margherita drove out to Big Sur Bakery on Highway 1. She took the curving, cliffside road slowly, not the most seasoned driver, and she pulled over a few times to revel in the glory of the most dramatic road in her universe. The waves splat against the cliffs and everything smelled like air, the way air should smell, and salty sea.

At the now-famous bakery, an unassuming wooden hut next to a gas station on the side of the highway (or, as it was often romanticized, a 1930s ranch house), with a colorful, wonky sign—letters of all shapes and sizes—suggestive of its singularity,

Isabetta Andolini

surrounded by cacti and a picket fence, she greeted the crunchy, flannel-wearing crew. It was the sort of place where one would hear a young girl wax on about dating an earth sign, something or other about a Taurus lingering in Capricorn.

"Lunch is not served until lunchtime!" one of the flannel, bearded guys announced before she had even asked, and she followed the point of his finger to the black chalkboard menu. Margherita's mouth watered at the menu, let alone the scent of wood-fired sourdough levain, rich almond croissants, puff-pastry turnovers, and their seasonal breakfast pizzas and vegetable strudels. She had been dreaming of the August heirloom tomato salad with purslane and salmon roe all morning, and the simple but heavenly avocado toast—Francine's favorite.

Everything about Big Sur Bakery was representative of her romanticized version of that piece of the central coast—it was simple, elegant, heartfelt, honest, and steeped in community. It stripped away the slivers of presumption from urban living, and any half-baked slice of attitude was dusted away like flour on the roll-out table. Margherita had seen its magical powers on Francine. She knew they were real.

She meandered patiently to the side patio. The picnic tables were exactly as she remembered them, beneath a wooden awning. She could picture Francine there, in a red fleece, looking around at the desert fauna and the redwoods overhead, completely at ease, waiting for Margherita to return with their order number placard. Francine was so vivid at that second picnic table, Margherita was certain she could go over and swing her legs around and touch her mother's hand.

Funny how quickly tears well.

"Okay! Lunch!" she heard from inside.

Margherita inhaled and blinked forcibly.

"Okay. Lunch," she whispered to herself, turning away from the picnic tables.

Later, back at her Aunt Vera's house, more flour.

The scent of toasted dough blanketed Margherita as she walked into the peach home perched on the side of the mountain. As she approached the kitchen, she noticed a mise-en-place for bagels and lox: a cutting board with crumbs, a handful of dill in the colander, a jar of good capers opened and at the ready.

"Hello?" she called out.

Certainly murderers didn't appear for two p.m. gourmet bagels. Though she wouldn't put it past a fox.

Tommaso's wavy, salt and pepper hair appeared above the counter. Margherita walked around the island to find her father crouched down with a sponge, wiping the floor.

"I got poppy seed. Next time, sesame only!" He stood up, exasperated, and rinsed the sponge in the sink. "Never mind, about your poppy seed!" He shook his head as he dried his hands and turned around to unfold the cellophane around the lox.

Poppy seed had been Francine's favorite.

"What are you doing here?"

Tommaso busied himself with the lox. He picked up one thin slice with the prong of a knife and layered it over a bagel.

"Oh. I just thought." He shrugged.

"You thought…"

"Well, I didn't want you to be alone the whole time. August is a long month, you know. There are thirty-one days…" He looked at his daughter with a half smile, his shoulders shrugged.

Margherita chuckled. "Right. That extra day. You *really* feel it. What'd you do, get on a plane at my first mention of Mom?"

Tommaso shrugged again. "Hungry? I'm starved. Picked these up in Monterey from that bakery you love with all the hipsters lined down the block. I could have been everyone's grandpa."

"I just ate. You enjoy."

He sprinkled a few capers on with great concentration.

"Et voila. No offense to New York, but these bagels are pretty dang good. Where did you eat?"

"Big Sur Bakery."

Tommaso glanced up at her. "I hope you were being careful on that road," he said sternly.

"Vey." She turned toward the front door. "I'll be on the deck. It's my living room, bedroom, dining room, yoga studio."

"As long as it's not your bathroom."

Margherita sat cross-legged on the yoga mat and admired a monarch butterfly dancing around long stems of lavender. She looked down at her phone before her toes.

There sat her odd chat with Nick. It bothered her that he had been so nonchalant about his sex life. She didn't want it to, and there was no sensible reason that it should, but it did. What did that make her, one of the many girls he used as jenga blocks in the precarious building of his self esteem?

She typed out a message.

> **Margherita:** Not that it matters anymore, but is that why you slept with me… for some sort of validation or confidence booster

He answered immediately.

> **Nick:** No
> **Nick:** I was attracted to you
> **Nick:** and wanted the feeling of exploring you
> **Nick:** and maybe I was missing that in my relationship
>
> **Margherita:** I would hope you're attracted to everyone you sleep with… at the very least
>
> **Nick:** I meant
> **Nick:** that I wasn't blindly seeking it from any where and you would do
> **Nick:** You were glittery and beautiful

KISS MY JAGGED FACE   173

Nick: and I wanted you

Margherita: glittery!

She looked up. At that time of the afternoon, the sun was high and strong and the sky was solid blue. The fog would roll in later, but for now, the highlands were in the clear.

His answers were always annoyingly vague. Unsatisfactory. Couldn't he say something more… meaningful? Something that might make her feel like she was something *more* to someone. Not just sex and lust and glitter.

Margherita: we never really explored anything, you know

Nick: I know

You still don't know me, she thought, gripping her knees in her hands, leaning into her butt bone. He had cornered her into one definition, one version of herself, and she still hadn't found her way out of it.

She stood and poked her head into the house.

"Do you want to go to La Bicyclette for dinner tonight?" she asked her father, who was chewing on his bagel at the table, making crumbs on a set of plans.

He swallowed and looked out the window before him, over the driveway, above the treetops, toward the Pacific Ocean beyond.

"Mommy's favorite," he said, in that sad voice Margherita hadn't heard since before they had left for Mustique.

"Yeah," Margherita said quietly, biting the inside of her cheek. "We don't have to. We can make a big salad. I have lots of things from the market."

"Whatever you want to do, amore." He said, rubbing his eyes with the fingers of his left hand, the half-eaten bagel in his right hand before his face.

"No, let's stay here. You're probably tired."

"Okay. Yeah. Salad sounds great." Her father smiled with his lips closed.

Margherita went back to her spot on her yoga mat and talked a tear out of falling.

Fuck, she thought. *When does this stop hurting.*

LONDON

September 6, 1982

"FRANCIE, DARLING, COME meet Noel," Christos yelled over the crowd. Francine took in Christos' tan, which looked black as night in the shadow of the DJ's table. He had stayed in Greece for an extra few nights, and she had spent the entire plane ride roiling in thoughts of him inviting random girls he met on the beach to parties in the village or raves in Athens.

"Gorgeous." He placed his large hand on the small of her back and leaned in to kiss her on the cheek. He was sweaty. "Noel, this is my gorgeous friend Francine."

She chafed at the word "friend." She knew she shouldn't. She had been dating Tommaso in New York, who was lovely and Keith-like and had no idea how she had passed her summer vacation with her not-so-former, wild, Greek lover.

Francine exchanged a familiar eye-lock with Noel. "We've met," Francine yelled over the music. Noel didn't say anything.

"When?" Christos yelled.

"Last year. Dirtbox," Noel said, nodding as he eyed Francine's skin-tight, asymmetric leather dress. "Bloody primitive."

"Missing Belfast?" Francine yelled, looking around Substation's current venue in Roseberry Avenue. The decadent club night had moved from Camden to Clerkenwell, and Noel and his tailor-by-day brother had quickly become the hottest DJ's in London. "This is mental, Noel. Fucking mental." She could barely turn a circle on the spot, the club was so crammed. She recognized models, musicians, fashion designers—everyone on some sort of upper, downer, or looking like they had just shot up.

He huffed. "You two set? Bag of something, spliff, in my back pocket. Everyone's off their fucking nuts tonight. Special K. Fucking mental."

"Just a little blow for me. I popped a Molly on the way in." Christos held his hands up.

Noel gave him a look of disbelief. "Mate, your mum would be proud. You're a fair amount out of place in the West London set, but, fuck—your call. Anyway, we run til 8, usually. Good to see you Francie. Don't die tonight. No more heroin in the girls' toilets. Just getting started here. Knees up!" Noel backed away into the crowd toward the DJ booth in the derelict clothing factory basement. Run D.M.C.'s "Sucker MC's" boomed so loud the room was practically shaking. Covering it was a series of a cappellas. Next there were the synthesizers cut and mixed with beats on DMX drum machines. Francine breathed in the sweaty, torrid stench of the room, condensation dripping from the ceiling.

"Baby, have you been doing heroin?" Christos yelled into her ear.

"No, never, *friend*," Francine shouted back, giving him a vicious eye and turning her back to him.

As she watched a young woman rub the palms of her hands up her bare chest, unaware of the universe around her, Francine inhaled with pleasure. She missed the savageness that her London life could be, the spontaneity and vitality. She hadn't let herself admit that, but like an addict, she had moments of craving for ferality so deep she felt she would implode from order. A little wildness was all she had known before leaving London, and she found it immensely challenging to remove herself entirely from its seductions. It wasn't that New York lacked the scene; in some respects, it had begun there, but she hadn't allowed herself to participate in it. She never wanted to be accused of 'being off her trolley' again, and she had convinced herself she could break her mind's habits with sheer will and determination. She was the one making decisions, she was the one getting stronger, she was the one feeling respected for once, and it couldn't possibly *all* be attributed to Dr. Bronsson's pills.

Christos grabbed Francine's face and kissed her hard. "Don't be dramatic. Let's dance, baby," he yelled, as he pulled her hand into the masses. She let him lead her, feeling the beginnings of the line she had just done off Rodney's forearm in the saw dust-covered hallway leading to the exit.

The next day, in Keith's car on the way to Heathrow, with Nina Simone on the cassette player, Francine rubbed her right temple with her pointer finger and stared out the window at the signs on the M4.

Gunnersbury, Brentford, Ealing.

Keith was oppressively quiet.

"Straight to work tomorrow?" he asked, changing lanes.

"Hmm-mm," she said.

"How's the new guy? What was his name? Thomas?"

"Tommaso," Francine pronounced purposefully.

"Tommaso," Keith said slowly, in a near whisper.

Neither said anything.

"So? Are you still dating him?"

Francine cleared her throat quietly.

"I'm zonked, Keith, can we talk about it another time?"

Keith huffed.

"What is your problem?" she asked harshly.

"Nothing. You took a summer vacation and spent the majority of it with your asshole ex-boyfriend, and I get to drive you and your salty mood to the airport. That's fine."

"Oh please! Were you not in Spain with Louise for a week?" she threw back at him.

"A week. Whatever. Do you even know what you took last night?" he asked, more aggressively. "How many more suicide Tuesday's can you withstand? Fuck, Francie, we're not twenty-five anymore."

"Yes, I am aware," she said with a biting edge.

"Does Tommaso do this shit? In New York?"

"No." She turned up the volume on Nina and continued to stare out the window.

Keith turned the volume down.

"So why not give him a chance? What's your excuse?"

She didn't say anything.

"I'm sure he's head over heels for you and can't figure you out," he said, with continued edge.

"Yeah."

"Does he know you fuck Christos when you're in town? *If* he can even fuck after all that E," he added under his breath.

"Of course not," she snapped, annoyed. "And of course he can," she said under her breath, facing the window.

"Well, what do you reckon he'd say? Tommaso?"

"Alright Keith. Can you stop being such a blighter? I get it. I'm a shit person. I get it."

"Don't get so cheesed off; I just want to know if you've considered him. I mean, for fuck's sake Francie, your actions aren't in a vacuum. You *do* have the capability of affecting others, not always positively, either."

"Give me a break, alright?" she whined, rubbing her temple.

"What happened to the straight and narrow you've been on? The promotion? The twelve hour work days? Giving up on that already? Too hard?"

"No," she said under her breath.

"What was that?" he asked, diving his head down as if he could not hear her.

"No, I'm not! I'm not giving that up, okay? It was a break. I had a wee break. Forgive me!" she yelled, in mock martyrdom.

"Ha. Yeah. A break. We all need a few nights high off our asses, unable to take a piss, blood laced with everything in the bowl, to cheat on each other and spend half the day sleeping—instead of visiting your ill mum by the way—in order to get from one day to the next. Yeah, Francine, fuck. The *utter* depravement. I hear ya. A break."

"Fuck you, Keith. Not all of us have every detail of our lives organized to a fucking T, with a law degree and natural, easygoing charm and graciousness that makes everyone think you're God's greatest gift, and a perfectly clear head on our shoulders, exemplary and noble, and a perfectly fucking perfect moral compass. Lily-white you are!"

"Right." He clipped. "You know the risks you take with these breaks, right? If this shit is still in your blood by your check-in Tuesday you're fucked."

She didn't respond.

"Unless that's your goal. Self-sabotage."

"Fuck off, Keith. I didn't know my *father* was driving me to the airport."

They sat in silence from Slough until the first turn-off for the airport.

At the terminal drop-off, Francine silently got out of the car and came around to the boot, where Keith slowly removed her bag.

"You have more control than you think, Francie," he said, more evenly, as he offered her the bag strap.

She readjusted it on her shoulder and looked around her before facing him head-on.

"I have control of my pills. You're right, Keith."

"You have control of so much more than that. Don't play the pity card. Your heart is your own. Those pills don't tell you who to hurt or treat poorly," he countered.

"Not even you have control of your heart. Or do you? Are you *that* repressive?"

Keith looked to the left of her at an older Korean woman saying goodbye to her son, perhaps sending him off to college. She was crying openly, uninhibitedly. Francine followed his gaze.

He sighed and rubbed his forehead with the heels of his hands. "He doesn't love you Francine. He loves himself."

"You don't know him." She shook her head dismissively.

"Neither do you. You know his charm. And, to state the obvious, he doesn't know you. Not in the way someone who *loves* someone knows that person."

"You don't have to know every detail of someone to love them. Sometimes less is more."

"Maybe. But if he doesn't know the details, what's so special about you? You're replaceable."

She huffed and nodded her head, insulted, as she turned toward the automatic doors.

"Francine," he called out from behind her.

Fuck this, she said to herself as she carried on toward the door.

"Don't stomp off, Francine," he yelled, inviting the attention of travelers around them.

She kept walking.

"Francine, don't you dare." His voice was determined. Strong. Heartfelt.

She stopped. *Fucking fuck*, she thought.

She turned and he approached her, wrapping his arms around her.

"Let this guy be good to you. This Tommaso guy. Let someone treat you wonderfully. Even you deserve that. Daisies are truer than passion flowers," he said, holding her by the arms.

She looked him in the eye. Those eyes she knew so well. Those kind eyes that had put up with so much of her shit. Those eyes she missed so much she could barely bring herself to look at them anymore, for fear she'd never be able to get them out of her mind every time she woke up, every time she left her apartment on seventy-first street—knowing she wouldn't see him that day—and every time she had dinner with Tommaso.

"You do. You deserve wonderful. You do," he repeated. He kissed her on the forehead and playfully pushed her toward the door. "Off you go. My New Yorker. Goodbye, Ruby Tuesday."

CARMEL

August 7, 2021

THE SOUND OF sizzling steaks blended with single chirps from nearby sparrows as Margherita lay on her back on her yoga mat, reading from a book she had bought from the shop on the Valley side of Highway 1. At the grill on the side terrace, beneath the drooping wisteria hanging off the side of the house, her father was talking to himself.

"The steak-ah!" he declared as he flipped them, and a new rush of sizzle sang out.

Margherita laid the book down next to her and sat up.

"How's the steak-ah?" she called down to her salty-haired father.

"Almost ready. You like your steak cooked or raw?"

The next morning, after a run in Yankee Point, admiring the homes sitting directly on the water between Big Sur and Carmel-by-the-Sea, Margherita walked up the steep hill toward San Remo Road. She held her hands on her hips and put her knees into it, feeling the incline at the backs of her legs. As she looked upward at a pyramidal Deodar Cedar tree, she spied a perched owl glaring across the road at a stunning euphonia—a dual-hued bird dressed like an LSU mascot: swathes of purple and yellow.

She smiled to herself, her skin moist from the run and the fog layer. Maybe this was it. Maybe this was her place. She could stay. Maybe meet a man. Have a few kids. Get a dog. Life wouldn't be too bad. Maybe Francine would have liked that idea. Maybe, if she were still alive, she'd have been thrilled. She'd visit. She'd be more attentive. Maybe she'd eventually retire in Carmel and be close to Margherita.

Mom is dead, Margherita reminded herself.

She turned around on the steep road to check on the fog's progress over the horizon.

Thirty-one. What should she be doing at thirty-one?

What had she accomplished? Not enough. No, she wasn't ready to give up the pursuit of big and brilliant. Though she felt for the first time, especially in the tranquility of the central coast, less eager than ever to dive into everything so alone.

She slid her phone out of her zip-up pocket.

Margherita: do you know what's scary
Margherita: homo alono was released almost 32 years ago
Margherita: there's something I'm grappling with lately. Time. It's flying

Back up at the peach-colored house, she found her father sitting over an enormous set of plans. Margherita went to press the button on the electric kettle and leaned against the counter as it boiled.

"Is that for Mustique?"

"No," her father said, his hand outstretched across the table, leaning on the paper and tracing something with his other hand. "New project. Private home." He turned around and slid his glasses up his nose. "Montauk." He raised his eyebrows.

Margherita raised hers in response. "Ah."

She poured hot water into a mug and squeezed half a lemon into it.

"Am I ever going to afford a house in Montauk?" She went

to stand over her father at his chair.

"Not if you stay out here staring at birds all day." He turned the plan around semi clockwise.

"Humph. You can make money out here. There's tons of money here."

"Yes. Tons of money. Made elsewhere, though. Here they come to play golf and admire their twenty million dollar view. What are you doing today?" he asked without looking up.

"Humph times two. Don't rain on my Carmel parade or I'll send you back where you came from."

"I was thinking of driving out to the valley for lunch? Earthbound? And the butcher. We need a few things. You only shop for rabbit food."

"Yeah that sounds good. I'll be on the porch if you need me."

She returned to her yoga mat with her steaming lemon water as her phone pinged.

Nick: why do you feel so short on time

Margherita: hi

Nick: hiya

Margherita: I don't know. I miss my twenties. They didn't seem to go by so quickly.
Margherita: they were fun. Easy and flighty and free. Less pressure. All the time in the world at your fingertips.

Margherita thought of getting dressed in her apartment in Milan, applying lipstick before an evening out. How excited she was each night, at the potential and the possibility. The 'anything can happen' adrenaline she hadn't felt in so long.

"Get dolled up and take yourself for a glass of something. You never know who you will meet," Francine used to say.

Margherita: And. Also.

Margherita: This is going to sound silly and maybe I'll feel differently in the future… but I want to meet someone sooner rather than later. I want to grow with someone… instead of meeting when we've both got 40 years behind us and it's like you'll never know such a massive chunk of that person's life

Nick: yeah I get that

Nick: Mike Nichols, three times divorced, married Diane Sawyer when he was 55 and she was 42. And they were madly deeply in love in ways they never had been before. Together until his death.

Nick: how old are you poppet

Margherita: 31!

Margherita: and that's sweet and lovely but also not what I want to hear. Imagine not being in big love until you're halfway done. That makes me sad.

Nick: 31. shove it

Nick: you're a sprout

Nick: the only thing I'd say is

Nick: it won't feel like that, like there's so much of someone you'll never know.

Nick: it will feel like it only could have happened then and there

Blah, Margherita thought.

Margherita: yeah

Nick: And it will feel perfect

Nick: Because it happened at that point and couldn't have happened at any other time or place

Margherita: how do you know

Nick: because that's how life always ends up feeling

Margherita winced. She thought of that day, three years prior, in the café in Soho. She could see her Missoni hat. She could see his face when she sat down. She could feel his eyes. That moment. That moment that could have only happened then, and there, not at any other time or place.

CARMEL

August 29, 2021

THAT EVENING, AFTER lunch in the sunny, blistering hot valley and a few hours sat outside at the Carmel Valley Ranch, Margherita dropped Tommaso off at the airport and returned to the village for a solo walk.

She descended the wooden staircase at the end of Santa Lucia Ave and pulled her sneakers off, holding them by their insides with one hand as she padded closer to the water's edge. The sand was plush and she wanted to feel her feet sink with each step. She stopped at a safe distance from the crashing waves and sat down in the sand, her sneakers next to her.

The sky was softening, its blues slowly cascading into a yellowish hue as the sun began its descent. That end of trip melancholy was grabbing hold hard and fast, and she acknowledged that for the first time in her life, she was very much *not* looking forward to returning to Italy. *Returning to what?* had crossed her mind many times in the last few weeks. She knew what her mother would say: "Your Italy fixation has been fulfilled. It's time to move on."

"Gypsy" by Fleetwood Mac came on her shuffle. She picked up her phone and huffed at her Spotify.

Fucking internet mind-readers, she thought. She absent-mindedly opened and closed a few apps before landing on WhatsApp.

Isabetta Andolini

Margherita: Where do you feel most at home? Like if someone asked you and you had to answer in three seconds, do you know what you'd say?

Nick: My parents house.

Margherita: And what about, do you know where you want to make a life for yourself?

Nick: Less sure about that one.

Margherita: I feel like everyone I know is so settled. They live in NYC and they always have and they have no plans to leave, or London, or Paris or wherever—they're just content. I wish I knew their secret.

Nick: They're not as curious
Nick: Or courageous
Nick: Or bold
Nick: As you.

She smiled at her phone.

I miss you, she typed, and then deleted it.

Margherita: Everyone thinks I'm nuts.

Nick: No. They're just jealous. And in five years they'll be divorced and you'll be madly in love with someone you met when you knew who you were.

She dropped her phone in her lap and hugged her knees, looking up at the ocean and a teenage boy catching the evening's last waves. A few yards from where she sat, the boy's mother watched him, her hands on her hips, a smile on her face. Her son.

Am I ever going to have that? she wondered. She leaned her chin on her crossed arms, hugging herself even tighter, the evening temp dipping already.

"I miss you," she said quietly. To the ocean. To nobody. To

the air. "I miss you," she said again, her throat thick and her eyes suddenly full.

She imagined her mother on the narrow path between houses leading up to San Antonio Avenue, while behind her the sky was a salvo of plum and apricot streaks, stripped down fruit, deeper at its core. Francine constantly spinning around to watch it grow more vivid.

"Come on, Mom," Margherita had said, ahead of her on the path.

"Come *where*? This is *it*, Marghe!" Francine had pleaded, turning around to stand triumphant, hands on hips, reflections of juicy, perfectly ripe stone fruits in her eyes.

LONDON

November 14, 1983

FRANCINE CROSSED THE footbridge connecting Regent's Park to Prince Albert Road and took the scenic route, past St. Mark's Church and the pastel-colored homes on Regent's Park Road. At Primrose Hill, she meandered slowly toward the ascent, beneath whitebeams and hawthorn trees, as she watched dogs run off-lead in the vibrant morning sun. Rays bounced between the ancient trunks, and she was momentarily blinded when she stopped to watch a husky sprint from one side of the meadow to the other and back again. They had such freedom, such vitality, such happiness. She sometimes felt that if she watched the dogs in London parks long enough, she too might feel more free, more spirited—happier—simply by osmosis. That was one thing New York lacked—her hometown's glorious parks.

At the top of the steep hill she turned around to take in the panorama. London's skyline shone yellow beneath a beautiful November morning, and around her, a few joggers stopped to stretch a quad while taking in the view.

"Fran!" She turned around, still squinting.

Keith approached from the Ellsworthy Road entrance, holding a paper bag and wearing his Ryan O'Neal suede coat. Francine had found it for him in a vintage shop in Glasgow after they had gone to the cinema to see 'Love Story.' Keith reminded her so much of preppy Ryan O'Neal's character, from his longish blonde hair and thick lips to his gentility and generosity. Keith wore the coat everywhere, and Francine adored him in it.

"Blueberry," he said, holding up the paper bag as he trudged up the hill toward the plateau. She delicately opened its top and dipped her nose in to smell the fresh, warm muffin.

"Gorgeous day, isn't it?" He looked out toward the City. "And I found parking. All around brilliant morning so far."

"Mmm. I do miss this," she admitted.

He nudged her playfully. "Fuck off. You're smashing it in New York. One day of sun and you're missing London again?"

"Come, come Keithie. There's room in my heart for all of you."

They sat down on one of the benches and Keith broke the muffin in half. Francine crossed her legs and held her half in her palm, breaking off bits of it with the other hand. Keith sat slouched into the bench, his long legs outstretched before him.

"Where's Louise?" she asked him, mid-chew. "I assumed she'd come along, attached to your hip."

He shrugged.

"Keith…" She pushed a finger into his upper arm. "Spill."

"Louise is… gone." He stared straight ahead, watching a dog dart down the hill.

"What happened?" Francine asked, turning her body toward him.

"Nothing. She's just. She's just not for me."

"But she was so wonderful. And you seemed so happy with her. Maybe a few sandwiches short of a picnic… but sweet."

He finished his half of the muffin and rubbed his hands together to wipe off any errant crumbs.

"Francie, do you ever wonder if love is a real thing?" he asked, without changing his demeanor, or tone, or facial expression.

"Um." She blinked a few times in confusion. "Gosh which pub is first to open around here?"

"I'm serious," he said, leaning forward, bringing his legs up beneath him and resting his elbows on his knees. "The kind of love that two people feel for each other *at the same time*. That kind. That 'fuck me' I think I'm going to be sick, kind of love."

"Keithie, I didn't know you were such a cynic."

"Yeah. Well. Maybe I am. Maybe I'm not. But I think it's a total wad of codswallop. I think, and just consider it, I think we're all mental for trying to find it. Or chase it. Or whatever licentious, self-indulgence we participate in, in vain efforts to capture it. All this searching for something that's not real."

"Oh, Keith. Jesus. The sun is out!" She tried to lighten the mood, but his face remained soulful and stoic.

Francine put her hand on Keith's leg affectionately. "Okay. Well. No, it's not solid or in the flesh, but… Okay, but then what has everyone been whinging about for centuries if it isn't quote on quote 'real?' If it isn't worth it? If all it is is grandiose licentiousness? You've been in love. You know it exists."

"The last time I was in love, she didn't love me back. If you recall. And so, what good is that?" he asked with a smile on his face, but marred emotion in his voice.

Francine's eyes softened and she rustled his dirty blonde hair, tucking a strand back away from his face and watching his eyes stare out across the meadows before them. He smelled of blueberry and fir body wash. "Keithie, I wasn't good enough for you. Never was. Never will be." She leaned her elbow on her knee and sat her chin into her palm, inches from his face.

He turned his head to face her, eye to eye.

"Francine you're better than all of them combined. You just don't see it."

She watched his eyes continue to graze her face until he gave up and glanced back out toward the dogs running across the hill, their owners meandering down the various paths. Francine wished so hard in that moment that she was someone else, someone who *knew*, with confidence, that she would be able to be the same person one minute that she was the next. The same person one week, with the same capabilities, the same moods, the same dependencies, strengths and personality traits, that she possessed the next. Without the assistance of a melange of psychiatric drugs.

She would never be someone like that. And so, in her mind, she wasn't worthy of someone like Keith. She wasn't worthy of Tommaso either. But Tommaso didn't know her history like Keith did. Tommaso knew the current-regimen, the current pill set. He knew *that* version of her. And so far, that version had been consistent, at least in his presence. So far, that version of Francine had not disappointed anyone, and that version of Francine had not shown the weakness and disorder and helplessness that Keith had witnessed more times than she could count. The heedlessness or the listlessness, the manic desires or the indifference to the world—the this or that life which had been such a burden to everyone to whom she was close.

Keith squeezed her knee with his thumb and index finger, hitting a spot that he knew sent shivers down her leg.

"Right. Better get going if you want to walk. Do you think your mum will feel up to a wander on the Heath? Too gorgeous not to. Parliament Hill must be a wonder right now."

Francine sighed and stood, shaking crumbs off her legs. "I hope so," she said, knowing full well her mother would not leave her bed, not even to spend time with the daughter she hadn't seen in over a year.

He held out his hand. "Come, Ruby Tuesday. To the village that raised you."

IN THE SKY

September 5, 2021

MARGHERITA WATCHED THE tiny plane on the screen before her make imperceptible progress across the expanse of the country of her birth. She cracked her knuckles and wiggled her foot, raised above her body. Four hours to go. Four hours to landing, packing her bags again, and getting on another plane.

Her Carmel time-out had been blissfully restful, a feeling of contentment shrouding most of her days, and though introspective and slightly too emotionally molten at times, the latter was to be expected in the land of peppermint gums and sycamores. And visions of Francine. Then had come the departure, and all was swallowed by nerves and whiplash anxiety all over again.

> **Margherita:** I'm on a plane
> **Margherita:** On a lay-flat to be specific
> **Margherita:** With my legs in the air
> **Margherita:** I actually googled this because I was really starting to wonder why this happens to me so often, and it is a scientifically proven thing that people are horny on planes.
>
> **Nick:** Is it
> **Nick:** What are you thinking
>
> **Margherita:** well, do you have a moment to participate in this?
> **Nick:** Yes.

Margherita: I have been going through scenes in my head for about two hours now. May I share them

Nick: Yes.

Margherita: Okay. The very first thing that I absolutely must have, is your hand, very slowly…

LONDON

FRANCINE OPENED HER eyes at the first jolt in her stomach. She reflexively put her hand over her skin, as if her own touch could calm her innards and sat upright when she felt a wave ride up her tummy. Her hand went to her mouth.

In the bathroom, she rushed to the toilet bowl and pushed the door closed with an outstretched leg. What had she drunk last night? Maybe she hadn't eaten enough. She felt positively rotten and remained on the cold floor a while longer, leaning against the bathtub, in case she needed to be sick again.

The flat was still dark, and with the wet, rainy day, she had no idea what time it was. A light from a passing car illuminated the floor en route to the kitchen, where she ran the faucet while she searched for a clean glass. Christos' apartment was typically barren of domestic essentials. Where there should have been a dining table, there were oversized pillows on the floor, and where there should have been plates, there was an overflow of his record collection. Guitars stood leaning against one wall, and the only thing one might find in the fridge was feta, which Christos' brought back from his frequent trips to Greece, along with his family's olive oil. Francine had been enamored of the flat in the early years of dating, feeling in it a sense of freedom and dissolution from the confinements and predictabilities of her father's house on Upper Cheyne Row or her mother's house in Hampstead. She loved to lie on the oversized pillows watching him write music with his guitar on his lap and a pencil behind his ear, before his musician friends arrived, each toting a different drug, and they would sit around listening to music, indulging, and deciding what to do that night.

Skip forward a few years, and Francine still found his flat an escape from her parents, though the charms of their youth dissipated with each visit. After four years in New York, she felt less zealous for Christos' lifestyle, and more frustrated with herself that she hadn't been able to shake him free. She seemed incapable of letting go of that chapter in her life, for what reason, she could not say, and more simplistically, she could not refuse his charms or physical allure.

She returned to the bedroom and reached for a tee-shirt sticking out of a dresser drawer. As she pulled it over her head, she glanced at Christos' sleeping body. He lay face down, his head turned to the side, his legs splayed out as if frozen, mid-air, doing a belly flop. She took in his form for a moment, his shapely calves and the hollow running down the center of his back. His muscular, brown upper arms. His large hand, motionless and empty in the spot where she had extricated herself. He was just as sexy as he was years earlier when they had met on Royal Hospital Road and he had accompanied her to Susan's birthday party on Ranelagh Grove. That night, with the help of one peach colored tablet each, unaware of the world around them, she had been swept away by his thick accent, addictive glance, and seductive hips as they danced to the Steve Miller Band, Supertramp, and Donna Summer, sweating profusely from the closeness of their bodies and from the ecstasy. Their relationship had been hypnotic and intense from the start, all sex and desire and immediacy. All drugs, alcohol, and blurred-out nights. Music, self-rule, and mischief.

He never tried to tame her. She never felt like he was baby-sitting her. He was diverting. And diversion—from her parents, from her doctors, from her own mind and the frustrations of her own life—was among the most desirous of states.

Tommaso knew nothing of her ex-boyfriend, who wasn't officially her ex yet, considering the errant visits. She'd stop her medication a few days before taking off for London, knowing that Christos would not be entertained by a muted version of herself—which wasn't even a version of *her*, it was the pills taking chemical control.

An hour later, after laying in bed with one hand on her tummy and one rubbing her temples, in the vain attempt to ease an oncoming headache, Francine decided to throw on a sweatshirt and head to Panzers herself. She could not stop thinking about pickles and chocolate, an interesting hangover craving, but a manageable one at Panzers, just a few minutes walk away. She turned her head toward Christos' splayed body; his breathing was even and deep—he wouldn't be awake for a while yet.

Later that evening, when Francine returned from the shops, Christos' apartment was empty. There was a note on the kitchen counter next to an empty bottle of Glenlivet. 'Gone to a show. Back tomorrow,' he had scribbled.

"Well thanks a fucking lot," she said out loud. She tossed the empty bottle in the bin and reached for the biscuit tin. Francine had taken a week off work—a ten day trip if she included the weekends—and it was frustrating as all hell that Christos treated her visit so nonchalantly.

Tommaso appeared in her mind's eye and she suddenly felt guilty. She grimaced as she opened the fridge, reached for a bag of carrots, and returned to Christos' unmade bed. Carrots and biscuits was as good a dinner as any for a duplicitous manic depressive.

The next day, at Bea's local café on Chelsea Common, Francine felt her stomach rumble again. They had just ordered two cups of tea and egg sandwiches, and the thought of moist egg sent her throat into convulsions.

"What is going on? You've just turned white as a night-out," Bea said, concern draped across her face.

Francine bolted from her chair and ran toward the loo in the back of the café. Sickness was not uncommon in her life; between the party drugs, the periods of withdrawal, the lithium and the valproic acid, vomiting, changes in appetite, and headaches were customary. But she hadn't done any hard drugs in a while, and even if she had, her body had become so numb to so much of it, she could weather quite a bit.

When she returned, her hands on her tummy and her face looking drab, Bea regarded Francine with a grimace.

"Yuck, Francie," Bea said, as she picked up her egg sandwich.

"Sorry. I don't know what's up lately. I feel quite tired this week. Which I can understand. Work's been busy. But I've also been vomiting. Random times of day. And the only thing I've changed lately was *not* taking my meds." She shrugged.

"You haven't changed your medication at all?" Bea asked.

"No," Francine shrugged.

"When's the last time you had your period?"

"Well, my period has never been regular."

"Maybe you should take a pregnancy test?" Bea suggested.

"No…" She shook her head dismissively and made a face at her egg sandwich.

"When you were here in July for my birthday, did you see Christos? Tell me the truth," Bea looked into her friend's eyes.

Francine avoided Bea's glance and clenched her jaw, twisting her mouth to the side.

"Francie!"

Francine exhaled and rolled her head backwards. "For fuck's sake, yes. Okay? Happy? Yes. I'm a shit person. I know."

"I'm not saying that. I'm just wondering… if you're pregnant… you don't *really* know whose it is?"

Francine bit the inside of her cheek again before claiming: "I can't be pregnant. There is no way. I cannot imagine my body is capable of cultivating anything with the amount of drugs I've taken." She looked askance and drew her attention toward her hollow stomach. "Not possible."

Though, really, she had no idea what her body was capable of.

Bea bit the inside of her bottom lip and stared at her friend. "I think you're pregnant," she decided. She picked up her sandwich again and nodded to herself.

"You're such a drama queen, Bea."

In her mind, the number ten sent waves of worry through her veins. *Ten percent.*

Ten percent. That was the probability of passing her disorder onto a child. It sounded low, but the fact that it had happened with her mother made it somehow feel more inflated than it actually was.

Three days later, by late evening, Christos had not returned to his flat, and Francine's return flight to New York was the next morning. It had been nearly two weeks since she had taken her meds, and she could feel the energy congealing at her fingertips.

In the kitchen, she twisted off the cap to the pickles and threw the glass jar at the tile wall. She snapped off the end of a pickle with her molars and launched the rest of the slimy rod at the same wall.

At the telephone, she dialed Christos' drummer, but he didn't answer. Neither did the lead vocalist in their band.

Fuck this.

In the bedroom, Francine opened and closed dresser drawers, unsure what she was looking for. On the bathroom vanity, she threw his things into the rubbish bin one by one. Deodorant, shaving cream, face wash, toothbrush.

"Guess you don't need these things!" she yelled at the mirror.

In the living room, she picked up one of his guitars and smashed it against the wall. Anything that could be raised in her hands, Francine picked up and threw it.

Another sound trumpeted through the flat and she looked up with curiosity. It came from the front door. A banging.

"Lost your key?!" she yelled as she approached the door and swung it open.

But it wasn't Christos on the other side. It was his downstairs neighbor. In her robe. Not looking very pleased.

"*What* is the ruckus, dear? What in the world is going on?" the elderly Polish woman asked, suddenly fearful at the sight of Francine's disheveled hair and livid expression.

"Do you know where Christos is?"

"Well of course. He went to Athens with his girlfriend. He mentioned he might have a cousin coming to stay. You Greeks with your enormous families. Can you keep it down? It's late, dear!" The woman turned back around and shuffled toward the narrow stairway.

"Cousins! Ha! Yes, we cousins! There are so fucking many of us!" Francine screamed after her and slammed the door.

Cousins. Her brain raged. There was no mercy for a single item in the apartment.

After she had ripped cabinets from their metal hinges and written the word 'cunt' in large letters on his living room wall, she decided she couldn't bear the sight of the flat for one more minute, and she called Keith.

"Hello?" he answered groggily.

"This fucking bastard goes around calling me his cousin. His cousin! His cousin who he fucks! He probably *does* fuck his actual cousins," she rattled on. "Where do you even think this concert was? If there was one. It was a lie. I'm sure of it. Well nothing here has been saved. All of it ruined. I ruined everything. I ruin everything. I am the ruiner of things. Families. People. Pickle jars."

"Whoa. Whoa. Francie. Slow down." Keith's voice was quiet.

"I can't stay here any longer. Can I sleep with you tonight? Can you come get me?"

"Ugh," he groaned.

"Please Keith. *Please.* Please. Please. Please. *Please.*"

"Alright. Alright! I'm coming. What time is it?"

"I don't know. I don't know. I can't sleep here. I can't. He left me here! And Bea thinks I'm pregnant! And I ca—"

"What? You're pregnant?"

"No! No, Keith! I don't know! I hope not. But I don't know. So can you please come get me *please* right away?"

"I'm coming. I'm coming. Don't move."

Exhausted by her own outburst, she sank down on a pile of pillows and curled into a ball. Tears flooded sideways toward the old carpet, and she held her knees for dear life, as if she were being rocketed into the air without a seatbelt.

A half hour later, still no Keith. She paced the flat and called him again, but he didn't pick up. She kicked the door and started bawling, wave after wave.

Finally Francine was so fed up with waiting she decided to call a taxi. She checked her purse for a fiver and presumed that if she were short, Keith would make up the difference once she got to his house.

"Yes, I need a taxi please. 45 Circus Road, please." She pulled at the cord. "That long?! Please!" she cried.

"Yes, madame. It's the time of night, you see, and there's been an accident, you see, on Park Road, just south of you actually. So there's a bit of a wait, I'm afraid," the taxi operator said.

"Oh for crying out loud!" she exclaimed and hung up. She eyed the phone as if it would suddenly ring and then abruptly yanked the cord from the wall.

She waited on the front stoop for the taxi to arrive. Her tears were dry but her eyes were engorged and she was irate at Keith for abandoning her.

"Sorry miss," the taxi driver said as he turned to watch her climb into the black cab. "Bad accident on the Park Road."

"Yes, yes I heard," she mumbled. "I'm going to Kensington. Holland Street, please," she said, moodily.

"Right-oh," the driver said in a thick northern accent.

They came to a halt on the Park Road as they waited for traffic controllers to wave them through. Siren lights silently blared through the dark, misty night, so bright she could hear them in her ears.

"Suppose the road was slick, and fella must have been in a hurry. Maybe he had a bit of the slosh," the driver said, as they slowly inched through the scene.

Francine watched police officers and clean-up crew take away a front bumper and two tires that had come away from a car that she could barely make out, flipped over on the grassy side of the road.

How horrible, she thought, as she pulled at her lip, unable to take her eyes off the scene.

"Do you think the driver was okay?" she asked.

"Got me. From the looks of it, was pretty bad. Can't imagine comin' outta that in one piece."

She looked behind her at the overturned car as the cab began to move again, squinting to read the plate, but she couldn't see clearly. It was too dark, and between the mist and the fog, the air was too thick for decent vision. Something in her stomach flopped.

In Kensington, Keith's driveway was empty.

She asked the driver to wait on the road. She rang the doorbell a dozen times, shouted at his window on the second floor, and ran around the back to see if any lights were on. Her heart thumped so hard she held out her hand in case it leapt out of her skeleton.

She ran back to the cab. "St. John Hospital," she yelled breathlessly.

"What? Madame, are you alright? I mean, we just came from there—"

"St. John Hospital!" she yelled at the driver, eyes fierce and wide. "Fast as you fucking can!"

She tapped her foot on the floor of the cab, scratching at her leg with her hand, saying Keith's name under her breath a thousand times a minute until they reached the hospital just next to Circus Road.

When they arrived, she bolted from the cab toward the ER.

"Ey! You didn't pay!" she heard the driver yell, but she was already mid-sprint.

"I'm looking for my friend!" she yelled at the nurse behind the desk.

The nurse regarded her dully and gave her an expression as though she was considering the likelihood of Francine's sanity. She must have looked a right mess, after all, she had been crying and screaming for hours, ripping Christos' apartment to shreds. Her long hair was a tangle and the black tights beneath her black denim shorts were ripped, a long run from hem to ankle.

"I said I'm looking for my friend!" she yelled again, slamming her palm into the counter.

"Please lower your voice," the nurse said, her eye a warning.

"His name is Keith Maddox-Stone, and I need to know if he's here."

"I cannot share that information."

"Please," Francine began to cry. "Please. It's my fault," she cried. "It's my fault," she tried to control herself, to sound as strong as possible. "Please. Keith. Keith Maddox-Stone. I need to see him. I need to know that he's okay. Please. Please. Please."

The nurse stood from her chair and came around the front of the counter, leading Francine to a seat up against the wall.

"I'll bring you a glass of water, how's that?" the nurse said, calmly, but with trepidation.

"I don't want water!" Francine shrieked. The nurse jumped back and other hospital staff in the corridor stopped what they were doing to look on. A few began to approach as back-up, weary but stern.

"I'm sorry. I'm sorry," she whimpered. "I don't need water, I just need to know if my friend is okay. Please tell me, please can you tell me?" She looked up at the nurse with eyes that begged.

An older, white coated doctor who had emerged from a patient's room stood in the middle of the corridor watching the scene. He pushed his glasses up his nose and slid the clipboard in his hand underneath his arm. He went to Francine.

"What is your name?" he asked.

"Francine," she sniffled. "I'm his best friend. Is he okay? Do you have Keith? He has dirty blonde hair, to here," she motioned halfway down her neck, "and he has blue eyes. Beautiful blue eyes. And the warmest smile. And strong, soft hands." She held up her raw, shaking hands and turned them front to back, her eyes wide as a water bug's.

The doctor sat down next to her and held her hands together. She looked down at his large, crepey skin covering her white fists. Her head slowly rose to look him in the eyes, her face frozen.

"What?" She searched for answers. "Oh God. Oh God. Oh God."

The doctor squeezed her fists. "I'm Dr. Haddlestone. Your friend Keith was in a terrible accident tonight. He's in surgery. He has many broken bones and a head injury. He will be fine, Francine."

She inhaled loudly, tears cascading down her face and her throat thick from crying. "Oh thank God. Oh thank God." She rocked into her lap with the doctor's hand trapped between her legs and her head.

"Francine. He's going to need you to be strong for him. He's going to need you, and his family, and his friends. This is going to be a difficult time for him. A long road ahead," Dr. Haddlestone said peaceably.

"But, but why? You said he's fine," Francine looked up, confused, eyes blotchy as an ancient patina.

The doctor licked his lips. "Francine, his body was very badly constricted in the car. He was smashed under the weight of it, when it flipped, and spun in ways no body should ever be spun. You see, we have to remove his leg. That is the surgery he is in now. He will be fine, in the grand scheme of things, but this will be a very challenging adjustment for him. Especially for such a young, fit, strong man as your friend Keith."

Francine's eyes narrowed as she dug a hole into the doctors face with her stare. Her expression moved through phases of utter confusion, denial, and horror. She felt herself on the verge of gagging.

The nurse, who stood a few feet away, quickly grabbed the waste bin from the nurse's station and put it before Francine's feet.

Francine vomited. Twice. The doctor patted her back and rose to his feet.

"Francine, promise me you will be there for Keith," he said, standing over her as she spit into the waste bin and wiped her mouth with her forearm.

She leaned her head into her palm, her heart racing, her brain blaring an incoherent, blurry buzz.

It's all my fault, she thought. *It's all my fault.*

The last thing she could remember from that horrific day was watching the kind doctor stand to attend to his clipboard at the counter, and how he glanced back to look Francine in the eyes, his glasses halfway down his nose. The piteous expression on his face as she vomited once more into the bin.

NEW YORK

September 6, 2021

MARGHERITA DECIDED TO stop at the Barnes & Noble in Union Square on her way downtown. A coffee table book or a biography was always an acceptable gift, though she felt silly buying *anything* for Gregorios, a man who could purchase all of Mustique during a breakfast meeting if he so desired. Her stomach grumbled as she made her way down the aisle of historical biographies, and she remembered she had a peanut butter protein bar in her bag. Dinner probably wouldn't be served for another two hours, at least, with the long and drawn out cocktail hour first and foremost, and she hadn't eaten lunch.

As she stood before the music and film industry biographies, imagining Gregorios reading gossipy tales of Jagger in the 1970s and re-framing them as his own at his next dinner party, she took small bites of the bar and leaned toward something predictably enjoyable like Jimmy Page. A young girl, possibly in her twenties, gave Margherita a dirty look from a few sections down.

"Can you please not eat here?" she said, annoyed.

Margherita looked down at the three inches of protein bar in her hand.

"It's a power bar. Not a fish fillet."

"Still."

Margherita looked around. "We're at Barnes & Nobles in Union Square. It's essentially a homeless shelter."

The young girl gave her another dirty look and exited the aisle. Margherita shook her head and finished her protein bar in peace.

At Gregorios' Beach Street triplex in Tribeca, Margherita was relieved to find Thayer nursing a whiskey smash. The evening was meant to be a celebration of the one year marker since ground had been broken on the Mustique hotel, bringing together a few familiar faces. It had been a remarkably productive year; the hotel was on track for a spring 2022 completion, and her father was in high spirits. He was in the city for a month, to catch up with his team and give the crew a few weeks rest during the island's hurricane season.

Gregorios, tall, tan, and very Greek looking, with dark hair, a pronounced jaw line, and falsely white teeth, placed his giant hand on Tommaso's shoulder blade as a hired cater waiter appeared with a tray of mojitos. Gregorios raised a toast to the group.

"To the boss—who has championed each day of this past year with grace, innovation, and rigor. I couldn't be more proud of this project. Yasou!"

"Cin! Sante! Bravo Tommaso!" The various styles rippled through the group. Margherita smiled and clinked her glass with her father's. His humility wasn't made for moments like these, and Margherita bumped his shoulder with pride.

"Now, let me give you all a tour. I've just finished this little pied-à-terre, bought at the perfect moment at the bottom rung of the pandemic, and I want opinions. I'll probably sell it in a few months and make a hideously ridiculous profit. Fuck I love this city." Gregorios put down his glass and clapped his hands together. His triplex was easily five-thousand square feet in one of the most prestigious addresses in Tribeca. Not really the one bedroom pied-à-terre the term was made for.

After the tour, including the wrap-around terrace, the group made their way to the solid zinc and petrified wooden dining table, with a sculptural aspect; forty-eight legs cascaded down to the floor like a waterfall. Margherita glanced under the table to better understand how the work of art was constructed.

Thayer: $1.1 mil

Margherita read the text in her lap and her eyes expanded like a cartoon character. If only she could pass her Italian legal bills along to Gregorios. He'd think they were from the dry cleaner.

The extraordinary table was littered with colorful glitter (the designer of the one-of-a-kind piece would have a conniption fit if he knew), and multiple small vases of anthuriums and exotic Cattleya orchids created a vibrant, tropical aesthetic. Margherita was sitting next to Sloan, visiting from London—or his house in the south of France, where he had passed the summer—and one of Gregorios' latest fifty-something hangers-on; a woman from Dallas named Claire, whose Harry Winston Colombian and Emerald ring gave Margherita double vision every time she looked toward that side of the table. The emerald weighed ten carats, and Claire had purchased the Art Deco, late twentieth century piece on her 1stDibs app while she had her nails done the week before.

"Only $575,000 more than the manicure! But isn't it sweet?" she asked Margherita.

Margherita's face belied a fraction of a sneer but Claire was already snapping gently at a cater waiter for another cocktail. Across from her, Thayer twisted his lips to camouflage his smile. Margherita purposefully brushed back the hair at her temples, her hands creating a teepee around her face so only Thayer could see her eyes roll to the grass cloth walls behind her.

"So, Mathilda, what do *you* do? How do you fit in here?" Claire asked, a fresh mojito looking all the more green behind the tint of the emerald.

"Margherita. I am also an architect, like my father." She exaggeratedly made eye contact with Tommaso. "I lived on Mustique with him most of last year."

"Oh, bless! I didn't realize the man of the hour is your father! How fantastic. How utterly fantastic! And what kind of architecture do you practice?" she went on with her pretentious drawl.

"Commercial. And what do *you* do, Claire?" Margherita said with a smile smacked on her face. Tommaso adjusted himself in his seat and imperceptibly cleared his throat.

"Well, I'm glad you asked Mar-gher-ita. Because I've just begun a new, *fantastic* project with Gregorios here. We are starting a digital newsletter, along with some of my friends from *Vanity Fair*. For worldly cosmopolitans and the finest journalists. It will be a *smash*. Like the way *Vanity Fair* used to be."

"Fascinating. Is there an editorial focus?"

"Sex, drugs, Ponzi schemes, the dirty dirty royal family, the nasty business of the art world, scandals in Burgundy…"

"So unconventional. Sounds like a modern edition of *The Official Sloan Ranger Handbook*. I love it," Margherita said, her sarcasm cleverly masked.

Claire looked up at Gregorios with a hint of confusion in her eye. Tommaso shook his head and looked down toward the floor at Sloan's dog.

"Is that a book by you, Sloan?" Claire asked, a half smile on her face, trying to regain her step.

Sloan coughed mid-sip of his mojito and fought back a laugh.

Margherita locked eyes with Thayer who licked his lips and let a small huff slip through.

"No, no. I didn't write that bible." Sloan cleared his throat again.

"What was the byline?" Margherita looked around the table, entertaining herself. "'The First Guide to What *Really* Matters In Life.' Oh, you'd love it Claire. Order a copy. It will be so inspiring."

"So, Margherita, what is the latest on your hotel?" Gregorios changed the subject, obviously having caught Claire's deflated expression.

"I'm looking for the right investment partner. And I've got a few lawyers working on releasing it from the ancient jaws at the bank. It's been sitting abandoned for decades, so if we have the right buyer, they should let it go pretty swiftly. Though, 'swift' is not in any Italian dictionary."

"I'm trying to convince Margherita to spend some time in London, actually," Tommaso said as the waiters served plates of green jerk shrimp with pineapple and apple. "With her big brother."

"Oh? Do you have a project there?" Sloan asked, reaching his hand down to pet his dog.

"No. It's just an idea. There is admittedly a more promising pool of potential partners there. But I'm not giving up just yet on Italy." *Though I need a job*, she thought.

"Doing a bit of a float, are you Margherita?" Gregorios posed.

"Well, no. I've been quite purposeful this year, actually."

"Sounds like the run of the mill thirty-something, single, lost, Pandemic Float. Sort of not really working, traveling, indulging, sleeping around, et cetera," Claire said, speaking to the table, rolling her head from left to right to emphasize the 'lost float.'

Margherita glanced at Tommaso, embarrassed by the utterance. *Fuck off*, she thought.

"Fuck off, Margherita's been hustling more than all of the thirty-something, single, Pandemic-era floaters combined," Thayer said.

Gregorios smiled confidently. "Well! Thayer, man, maybe you can take a lesson from her. When's your next film, man? You've got to prove yourself again!"

Margherita noticed the immense difference in the two gentleman's demeanors; they couldn't have carried themselves more differently if they were two actors on a stage.

"I'm always working, man," Thayer said dully, gyrating the cubed ice in his glass.

Margherita sliced through a shrimp and exchanged an unreadable glance with her father, who she imagined was feeling rather uncomfortable.

"Margherita has been very busy this year. She has a lot to be proud of right now," Tommaso said kindly, his eyes on his daughter.

She appreciated the lift but was nevertheless embarrassed by the piteous condescension. She didn't want anyone to feel she needed pathetic words of encouragement, which only belied the undeniable fact of her failure. She had always imagined words of congratulations.

Why was I so damn sure of myself? she thought as she pushed half of a shrimp toward a piece of pineapple. *Who did I think I was?*

Margherita made her way through a slew of heavy Caribbean dishes: slowly cooked pressed ham, BBQ salmon, and a pumpkin, cranberry, and red onion tagine, remaining above line sociable with each person at the table, avoiding the temptations of simpering rebuffs and quick retorts. Francine would have been proud, or more likely, disappointed.

As dessert was served, Margherita eyed the other guests. Her father laughed politely at one of Gerald's snobbish jokes, Sloan picked up his Schnauzer and fed him pieces of leftover bread, Gregorios' booming voice—enhanced by a disproportionately imbibed amount of alcohol and possibly other drugs—recounted his most raucous evening of the summer aboard his Russian friend's yacht, complete with a police chase across the Bosphorous, and the rest of the table was wildly, falsely or genuinely engaged.

Margherita smiled at the server who set a bowl of pistachio parfait with amaretto, pink grapefruit, and biscotti before her, and she quietly got up from her chair as if she were going to the bathroom. Instead, down the hall, she unlocked the enormous, eleven-foot steel doors leading to sweet escape and stepped outside.

Beyond the terrace's edge, her former neighborhood glittered like a faraway memory. She imagined stretching before a run while saying good morning to lower Manhattan's stunning skyline—how many times she had done that in the years before the pandemic.

"You've got a talent for a table," said a male voice behind her.

She turned around to see Thayer walking toward her, a half empty glass in his hand. He gestured behind him toward the dining room.

"Ah," Margherita said, turning back toward the illuminated city.

Thayer stood beside her, his back against the railing.

"Taking a minute," she said as she casually intercepted his glass.

"Yeah. Yeah. I get it."

She took a large sip and eyed him sideways.

"How's life, Thayer?"

"Can't complain."

"Are you officially a divorced man?"

"That I am." He leaned back farther into the railing.

"How does it feel?"

"It feels... How does it feel?" He focused his eyes on something in the sky. "I am a rock."

"Did you know Paul has said he is no longer proud of that song? That he wouldn't write those lyrics again?"

"Is that so?" He glanced at her.

"Maybe you won't be such a rock in a little while."

"Time heals all." He raised his eyebrows and nodded slowly.

"Give time time."

"And you? Something tells me you're not as brilliantly happy as you put on in there," he said, gesturing toward the large doors which reflected their forms beneath the night sky.

She regarded him blankly.

"You've got a talent, like I said." Thayer turned to face the city.

"How do you know?" she asked, her face toward him.

"That you're not brilliantly happy?"

"Right."

"It's *my* talent."

"What's that?"

"Stating the obvious."

"Ah. And what do you *do* with this talent, dear Thayer?" she asked, still expression-less, as she looked down at her bare shoulder and brushed away an errant piece of glitter.

"Put the obvious on the big screen. Make people feel less alone, I guess," he said humbly, as he took the empty glass from her and flipped the long hair on the top of his head out of the evening breeze.

"You think it works?" she asked, as she gripped the railing with both hands and leaned over it, looking down at Beach Street below.

"I don't believe in pretending. You can count on that." He hooked a finger around the back of her dress, where the shoulder straps made a cross in the middle of her spine, as if holding on to a leash.

"And I didn't need your godlike presence on Mustique? I don't remember you reading into my moods porch to porch." She stood upright again, leaning backwards into his pull.

"Ha. No, actually. You were palpably fulfilled. Productive. Enterprising. You had a fire under your rear."

She nodded slowly. "And now?"

He eyed the bottom of the empty glass. "Your fire is out."

Margherita continued to look toward the hollow Tribeca street ten floors below her. She nodded her head again.

Yup, she thought.

There was a building on Beach she had always loved, imagining it to be the perfect architectural studio for her father, with its big rounded windows. She thought about Tommaso sitting in his apartment uptown too many consecutive nights a week. She wished he would sell it, to move on from the decades of memories, but on the other hand, she didn't want to be torn from those memories any more than he did. How does one grieve and move on simultaneously, without offending the deceased?

"Anyway," Thayer said, turning around again to face the dinner party inside.

Margherita turned around as well.

"Anyway," she said, staring at her reflection on the dark glass door. "I think I need more than a movie." Margherita smiled with her lips closed and her outer eyes creased.

He smiled back and nodded. "Yeah. Me too, kid."

As the evening crept to an end, Margherita said her thank you's to Gregorios and called an Uber for herself and Tommaso.

"Tommaso, congratulations again. You will be the most in-demand hospitality architect after the opening. I guarantee it," Gregorios said cockily, one hand on her father's shoulder. Tommaso looked worn next to Gregorios' robust form and head of dark hair. Her father smiled humbly and tipped his head to the side, uncomfortable with direct praise.

"That would be fantastic." He shook Gregorios' free hand and bent down to pet Sloan's dog. "Sloan, see you next week." He shook Sloan's hand.

"Can't wait, boss," Sloan said, tapping Tommaso's upper arm.

"And you, young thing. Don't turn stumbling blocks into a 'Road Closed.' Power through," Gregorios advised Margherita, looking her sternly in the eyes as if he were her guru. "When I was building my business, I had countless assholes say 'no' to me. And look. Look at me now." He gestured to the expansive Tribeca duplex in which they stood.

Thayer appeared behind Gregorios' massive frame and rolled his eyes. Margherita hid a smile as Thayer slapped him on the back. "Cheers, G. See you in London," he said, leading the escape route toward the front door.

In the Uber, Margherita let out the exasperated air she had kept wound up throughout the evening. "That's such bullshit. People said no to him. Who the fuck cares who says no to you when your father is a Greek shipping magnate? What a load—"

"Don't swear, Marghe. It's so unfeminine. Your mother swore like a dockworker. It sounds terrible."

"I think it suited her," Margherita said, looking out the window toward New Jersey as the car made its way up the West Side Highway.

Back at the townhouse, Tommaso took a glass of port into his office and Margherita wandered upstairs. She absentmindedly found herself in her mother's dressing room, where she often gravitated when she felt blue. Not a thing had been touched in the few years since Francine had died, and Margherita grazed her eyes over shelves of framed family photos as if she had never seen them before. One of her favorites was an ancient, fuzzy photo of Francine laying on a carpeted floor with a fabric headband around her head, and her short, sleeveless dress with buttons down the center barely covering her long legs. She was having some sort of giggle fit, twisted up with a guy who looked like a cross between Ryan O'Neal and Robert Redford, his longish hair cut by a stylist who clearly loved to layer. Francine had her hand over his chest, laughing, while he held his hand over her hand and looked toward her youthful face.

"Who is this?" Margherita had once asked her mom.

"An old friend," Francine said, looking at the photo wistfully.

"Who?"

Francine had taken the framed photo into her hand and admired that long-ago version of her self. "Someone who used to be wonderful and treat everyone with love and patience. Life isn't always everything it's cracked up to be," she had said, as if speaking to herself and not her daughter. "Happiness is a delicacy. Savor it."

Margherita put the frame down then, hearing her father ascend the stairs. She tip-toed back to her own bedroom and pulled her dress over her head, draping it on the window seat. Naked, she picked up her phone, swiped it unlocked and twisted her mouth side to side, biting the inside of her cheek, before decisively typing out a text.

Margherita: Are you awake

Nick: Yes

Margherita: Are you alone

Nick: Yes

Margherita: Would you like not to be

Her phone began to vibrate.

"Hello?"

"I didn't know you were in the city."

"Yes, a layover of sorts."

"Would you like to come over?"

"Yes, please."

"Come. I'm just finishing some work. We can watch a movie and cuddle. Would you like that?"

"Yes."

"I'll send you the address. Text when you're in an Uber."

———

She buzzed and walked up two narrow, carpeted flights in the old Charles Street townhouse. He had left the door ajar and when she stepped inside, he shut his laptop and put an empty glass on the kitchen counter.

"Hi," he said, with that glint in his eyes, that non-existent smirk she swore existed beneath his lips. That 'I won' look. That 'told you so' look.

"Hi," she said, slipping her sandals off, as if she visited his apartment all the time. As if it had not been a year and a half since they had last seen each other.

He looked the same. His summer tan was strong, his hair blonde, his stubble dark, and his eyes just as cobalt. Electric. But soft at the same time.

He approached her and slid his hand into hers, kissed her lips. "What do you think?" He spun his head around at his new apartment.

Margherita took in the oversized windows with their beautiful panes, original to the townhouse, and the working fireplace, the crown moldings, and the little kitchen, newly updated. "It's very charming!"

"Yeah. I love it. Took forever to find. Come," he said, guiding her toward his bedroom.

"Whoa, what's that?" Margherita asked, stopping to admire the enormous birthday cake on a glass stand atop the table. 'Happy 35th Birthday Nicholas' was written in frosting.

"Ah." Nick glanced at the cake, cocked his head and winced. "I had a birthday. Two days ago."

"I see. But how come no one's eaten the cake?"

"My best friend Greg just dropped it off. His girlfriend made it, but then she went into labor. And I felt weird eating it by myself."

Margherita walked over to the little kitchen and opened a drawer or two.

"What are you looking for?" he asked.

"A fork and knife. You can't let a beautiful birthday cake just sit there. How sad!"

She found his silverware and brought over a small plate from a cabinet above the stove. Margherita sat down at the table and he sat down next to her, bashfully.

"It may not be a celebration with best friends but a celebration with a sort-of stranger will just have to do," she said sweetly and kissed him on the cheek. "Happy birthday, Nicholas."

"You're not a proper stranger anymore, you know that right?" He watched her carefully slice through the marigold buttercream.

"Ohhhhh!" she exclaimed. "I love that movie. Natalie Wood." She set the triangular slice on the small plate. "'Love With a Proper Stranger?'"

"I haven't seen it," he said, as he took the fork in his hand.

"Oh no! She plays an innocent young woman living in the city and she has an affair with the uber hot, couldn't-be-sexier Rocky, played by the king of cool."

"Steve McQueen," Nick said before swallowing.

"Yes. And I won't ruin it for you. But something happens. This, that, and the other, sex…" Margherita twaddled her fingers in the air. "And he tries to do the right thing. Messy situation, two gorgeous people. Mistakes and strong points of view, et cetera et cetera."

"Et cetera et cetera," he repeated, regarding her with a pursed-lip smile. "Love," he said, as he cut the fork through the cake's layers.

"With a proper stranger."

He was silent for a moment. His finger roamed across the numbers 35. He licked it off his finger.

"How is it?" she asked.

He winced. "Sweet."

"Ah. Yes. I dislike frosting."

He looked at her with a sour, punctured expression. "Yeah, me neither. Awful shit. Who eats this?"

"But the cake part looks good." She took the knife and skimmed off the frosting. He turned the plate for her while she performed the medical procedure.

"There," Margherita said, satisfied, admiring the naked cake.

"You fixed it. God you're handy."

She smiled and bumped his shoulder with her shoulder. He put his arm around her while he took another bite from the naked cake.

"My proper stranger. You look like her a little."

"Natalie Wood?"

"Yeah."

"You look like Steve McQueen a little."

"Really?"

"No, not really. More young George Peppard. Who, by the way, I read was a horrible, misogynistic, controlling, a-hole."

"Oh! I accept, based on looks and charm, not misogyny of course. But I'm not young anymore. Thirty fucking five."

"I'm thirty fucking one."

He looked at her with simulated disbelief. "You need to stop with that."

"I have white hairs."

He peered at her scalp. "You're ridiculous."

She knitted her brows and stroked her scalp vulnerably.

"Here. Eat this." He lifted the fork to her mouth and she took a bite.

"Good cake. I just ate gluten for the first time in years."

He kissed her on the lips as she chewed.

"I'm really glad you're here," he said.

Nick stood to get a glass of water and took her hand, leading her into his bedroom.

"So, are you happy? To be back in the city?" Margherita stood at the end of his bed and watched him open a dresser drawer, from which he retrieved a tee shirt.

"Here," he said, handing it to her. "Yeah. I really am."

"It really is such a sweet place. You were tres lucky to find this," she said, peering out the oversized window into village gardens as she unbuttoned her jean shorts and slid them off. He watched her as she removed her lightweight sweater and bra and as she slid his tee shirt over her head. She looked down at her chest. A university tee.

He climbed into the bed and flipped the comforter back, inviting her. She climbed in next to him and sat upright, the comforter pulled over her crossed legs.

"What did you think you'd be doing at thirty-five? Ten years ago, when you thought about thirty-five."

He watched her adjust the pillow behind her back and gently leaned her forward so he could puff it and fix it for her.

"I probably thought I'd be riding a lot higher than I am now. But I have to get things in order. I don't think you can find your life partner until you've got yourself straightened out."

"I suppose. And maybe you never find a 'life partner.'"

"Maybe not."

"Maybe you endlessly date girls who say things like 'bless' and pronounce initialisms out loud instead of saying the whole words."

He huffed. "Initialism."

"That gen-z stuff. 'IMO' 'AMA.'"

"Oh. Ask me anything."

"Yeah."

"When's the last time you had sex?"

"No, I wasn't being literal you knob." She rolled her eyes. "What are we watching?"

"I looked at our choices. Are we feeling funny, dumb, funny/dumb, sad, depressing, romantic, romantic/sad..."

Nick pulled her body toward him as he rattled off the choices and she snuggled her head into the nook below his arm, her cheek on his chest.

"Sweet, smart romantic. Easy. Respectable," she decided.

"Sounds ideal." He peeled himself back just enough to be able to look at her face. "It's really nice to see you. Really." He kissed the top of her head. "And you smell good."

"I spent the evening next to a dozen anthuriums."

"What's an anthurium?" he asked as he weeded through the movie options.

"A tropical flower. It can either smell like marzipan and blueberry or dog poo and vomit."

"Lovely!"

"I assume I smell like the former."

"You assume correctly."

As Nick flipped through the choices, he pulled her hand onto his chest and covered it with his palm. She relished the closeness. His touch. The ease and comfort and tenderness.

Though at the same time, she was aware of every pore of flesh that touched his; how many girls had he done this with? It came so easily to him.

It felt so alien to her.

"Don't let me fall asleep," she said.

"Why not?"

"Because I'm not sleeping here."

"I don't understand this refusal to sleep in my bed. Why is it bad? Why *must* you leg it every time?"

"Every time? I haven't seen you in ages," she said with a smile.

"Yeah, and you were always legging it."

She shrugged into his chest and said nothing.

Hours later, she woke to the sound of silence and a dark room. A shadow of a light danced in from behind the thin floor-length curtain, and she felt Nick's hand resting on the mattress in front of her chest. His body was wrapped around hers, both of them facing the wall. She gently moved her hand on top of his and rubbed her thumb into his skin.

Margherita turned slowly around. His face was motionless, and she could feel his breath on her nose. She stroked her thumb from his forehead to behind his ear, over the round of his shoulder, slipping down to his hip bone.

"Nicky," she whispered.

She gently squeezed his upper arm.

"Mmm," he stirred, his eyes still closed.

She quietly kissed him on the lips. He didn't move.

She kissed him again, with slightly more pressure. His eyes fluttered open.

She stared straight into them. Those ocean blue magnets.

The lantern light from beneath the curtain made them brilliant in the dark room. He put his hand on the back of her head and leaned in to kiss her, quietly, gently. Always more tranquil than her, more calm. Smooth and steady to her nervous energy.

She rolled over on top of him, and he flattened out on the bed. Straddling him, she ran her fingers up his tan, rippled chest. It was soft and warm, and as she grazed her fingers back down again, his fingers seemed to suddenly wake up and he gripped her hips.

They had sex and fell back asleep.

———————————

When she next woke the room was bright, the sun strong beyond the diaphanous curtain and the walls an art installation of morning shadows.

She turned her neck to make sure he was still asleep, and as quietly as she could, she slid off the bed.

He grabbed her hand.

"Don't you dare. Don't even think about it."

She stopped and stood facing him, his warm fingers wrapped around hers.

"I'm going to the bathroom."

"If I hear that front door close, I will come sprinting after you," he said, opening his eyes and looking at her.

"Just the bathroom."

"Give me your handbag."

She stood at the end of the bed. Her handbag sat on the chair at her side, next to the window.

"Give it," he repeated, closing his eyes again and holding his arm outstretched.

"But I want to brush my teeth. And there are a few things in there I'd like to use on this highly anticipated trip to the bathroom."

"Okay. Give me your house keys."

She rolled her eyes and dug her keys out of her bag.

"See? Drama queen," she said as she took her bag to the bathroom.

He huffed and dug his face back into the pillow.

She peed and flushed, washed her hands and her teeth. As imperceptibly as she could, she opened the front door and skipped down the two flights of stairs.

Her dad would be at home to let her in.

"Late night?" Tommaso raised his eyebrows at his daughter as she entered the foyer. She clucked her tongue and walked past him as he slapped her on the back playfully.

"Thirty-one, dad," she reminded him as he followed her downstairs to the kitchen. She picked up the electric kettle and went to fill it with water. Tommaso stood at the counter and ruffled distractedly through a pile of mail.

Her phone pinged a low ba-boom and she jumped.

"What?" Tommaso's eyes enlarged.

She shook her head of the sound and swished her phone screen open.

Nick: Can't believe you did that
Nick: But also can

She ignored it for a moment while she poured herself a cup of tea.

"So, you all packed? You arranged the car to the airport?"

"I'll just take an Uber."

"No, get the car service. I don't trust these Uber drivers. Could be anyone. Could be Bernie Sanders."

"He's dead."

"How do we *really* know, though?" Tommaso asked facetiously as he ripped open an invitation from one of the city's most prominent architecture firms.

"What is it?" Margherita asked, taking a sip from her tea and nodding toward the invite.

"Oh, just another dinner. Celebrating another project. Another dinner. Another celebration," he said, bored, and placed the invite on top of the pile.

"Margherita, I know you don't want to be told what to do—you're 31–I get it. And I know your mom was better at this than I am. The whole career guidance thing. But I think it might be time you leave Italy. What is there for you now? You tried your hat at this thing. You put your all in. It doesn't mean it's dead. But you need an income."

"I know," she said, sheepishly.

"Maybe think about coming back to New York."

"No." She put her mug down on the counter. "No, I don't want to do that. I don't want to be here," she said adamantly. Her father sighed and stared down at the invitation.

"Maybe you should go to that. It's good to be out and about," she said, encouragingly.

He continued to stare at the invite.

"I will go. If you think about getting a job."

"Ha. Dad. That's not exactly the same thing. But I know I need a job. I know. You don't need to tell me. I am aware. Please let me figure it out myself."

"Okay. Okay," he said, his hands up in mock defense. "No advice. You're on your own. How's that?"

"More my speed. Thanks."

Tommaso regarded his only daughter with concern. He tapped the edge of the invite on the counter.

"Margherita, amore. I worry you are living in your own world."

"I'm going to get a job, dad. But not in New York," she said. "I'm sorry. I just can't."

Tommaso's chest filled. "Okay. Listen, Marghe, I'm not going to tell you where to live. I suggested London. I think it might work for you. You wouldn't be alone, with Benjamin there. But go where makes you happy. You can't be a gypsy anymore. That's all! That's all I'm going to say. You happy?" He looked up at the ceiling, as if he were talking to the sky.

Margherita's heart hiccupped. She had seen him do it a few times—talk to the ceiling, or the sky, or the roof of the car—and she couldn't bring herself to wonder how often he did it when he was alone.

He walked around the island and brought her in for a hug. "I know you're going to figure it out. Feet on the ground, head in the sky. That's my girl. Just make sure you've got feet on the ground once in a while."

He walked away and dragged the invite with him toward his office.

She looked outside toward the back garden. It had an L-shaped sofa where Francine used to lie with one leg crossed over the other, a cigarette in one hand and a glass of gin in the other. Her father would spot her from the kitchen, and Margherita would play a game with herself of how many seconds it would take for him to storm outside and demand she put out the cigarette.

"Francie, why? Why?" He would shake his head as he'd rush into the kitchen to put it out under the faucet. Francine would roll her eyes and laugh at him.

"Let me have a Moment, Tommaso," she'd say. That's when she'd pitch up on her elbows and turn her body enough to lock eyes with Margherita in the kitchen. She'd toss her eyes to the sky as if to say, "Your silly father."

Margherita looked down at her phone on the counter where Nick's message sat.

Margherita: thank you for the cuddle

Nick: you are the strangest girl

She didn't reply.

Nick: when are you back

Margherita: who knows

He hadn't ever asked her where she was going.

———————————

Later, she sat on the plane thinking about her father. How guilty she felt for not staying in New York with him. But she just couldn't. She needed to make her own roads. Her own space in the stratosphere. New York was pain and grief.

Her phone vibrated.

Nick: I showed my best friend the virtual plans for The Villa
Nick: he was blown away

Margherita: that's nice to hear

Nick: He's so impressed
Nick: As am I

Margherita: thank you ☺

Nick: He said where is this girl I'd like to meet her

Margherita: And what did you say

Nick: I said she is adventuring. She's finding herself

Margherita stared at the screen and nodded slowly. She scratched the side of her nose and lost herself in the cloud formations.

Is that what I'm doing? she thought.

Nick: Marghe even if you don't come back with any answers, it doesn't make the adventure any less worthwhile

Come back where? she thought. She flipped the phone over on her stomach as she turned onto her side, trying to maneuver into a fetal position on the lie-flat. It pinged again. That low ba-boom.

Nick: No risk, no story.

"Ha," she said out loud.

Margherita: dance hall days
Nick: precisely.

LONDON

December 31, 1985

"HE'S FINALLY GONE to sleep," Francine sighed, exhausted, as she collapsed into the sofa. She put her feet up on the fringed ottoman and turned her head toward her father, who did the same. Two sets of feet in thick winter socks. One Christmas tree, bejeweled and bedazzled, with Bea and Rodney's help, a plate of leftover, sugar-dusted mince pies, and *Auntie Mame* on the telly.

"Here comes your mum's favorite line," her father said, a slight smile on his face, his eyes tired and heavy.

"'She's not English, darling, she's from Pittsburgh.' 'She sounded English.' 'Well when you're from Pittsburgh, you have to do something!'" he mimicked.

Francine looked at her father. His crepey skin, the bags under his kind eyes, his thinning hair, and his big, fatherly hands that used to wrap around her own. She could still feel his hand grasping hers crossing the high street. She could see him look out into the traffic, his hand stretched behind him, fingers splayed, as if to say: "Not yet." And then he would quickly glance behind him and wave his wrist around, as if to say "Okay, now!" And he'd hold her little meat pattie in his grasp, and he wouldn't want to let go even once they were safely on the other side. "But I thought you *loved* to hold my hand!" he used to tease her as she grew older.

At that moment, sitting on the sofa in the den, he looked so sad to her, so lonely and sad and old and she would have done anything to reverse the years for him, the stress, the heartache.

She felt a knob in her throat rise and spread, like a sink drain closing, water pooling on all sides.

She reached for his hand.

"Mummy had the best taste in movies, didn't she?"

He looked down at Francine's milky white hand in his, and he squeezed it. "Yes. Yes she did."

Francine bent forward to reach for a mince pie from the plate on the oversized ottoman and sat back again, sugar falling onto her sweatshirt.

"Not such a bad New Year's Eve ritual, daddy," she said, taking a bite.

"It's not, is it? Better than Mustique, I imagine." He reached for a mince pie.

"Ha. Well, I'm not sure a nine-month-old would be allowed at that party."

Her father tapped her knee affectionately. "Proud of you, Francie."

"For not bringing my baby to a rager in the Caribbean?"

He regarded the star-shaped mince pie in his hand as if it was about to tell him what to say. "No. For managing everything. The job. Benjamin. Making it work with Tommaso. Everything with poor Keith. Losing mummy. You are the most resilient person I know."

Francine was momentarily embarrassed. It wasn't the sort of thing she was accustomed to hearing.

"Surely it's the meds," she retorted, turning her attention back to Rosalind Russell.

"No, it's Francine. You shine through; don't ever think the rest of us can't see it."

The phone blistered through the room, and her father's face went ashen as he watched it jump from its cradle with every ring.

"What?" Francine asked, getting up to answer it. "Hello? Who?" she said into the phone. "No, you have the wrong number I'm afraid."

She hung up and sat back down next to her father, who rolled his face through his hands and massaged his forehead with the the heel of his palm.

"What?" She looked at him confused.

He shook his head and re-focused on the film. "No one ever calls on New Year's Eve. It's always *me* calling mummy."

SANTA MARGHERITA LIGURE

September 10 2021

THE APARTMENT WAS large; it extended from front to back in an off-white tenement townhouse a few blocks back from the port, where small boats bobbed and fishermen stood on the docks with a ubiquitous slice of focaccia in hand. Beyond the apartment were the narrow roads that led steeply up the mountain, where larger villas surrounded by acres and acres of olive trees had private pools and sweeping views of the Ligurian sea.

The sides of the railroad-style apartment were dark, but the kitchen had one perfectly square window overlooking her elderly neighbor's arcadian gardens—roses and sunflowers and even flowering raspberries beamed in the late summer sun. Each morning, afternoon, and evening, the old lady, in an elegant skirt and sweater set, would wade through it, shoulders hunched, checking and scrutinizing. She never seemed to smile; her blooms were like one hundred orphans in need of monitoring without any grand affection. Margherita could not help but wonder what this woman was thinking as she surveyed her garden—was she talking to the blooms in her head? Was she pondering her lunch choices? Debating whether or not to wash her sheets that day? And did she live alone, or had she planted the garden with a lost husband or love?

The front room, where Margherita had set up a little office, faced the village and overlooked the rooftops of the shops and cafés. If she peered out, she could see the seventeenth-century Villa Durazzo presiding over the gulf, with its orange, lemon, and grapefruit trees and Italianate garden enriched with roses, fountains, statues, and rare camellias. It was where Camilla had gotten married years earlier, before she and Margherita met, and every time Margherita saw it in the distance, she thought of her friend's wedding photos. She wondered if she'd ever have some of her own.

Evenings were still long, and Margherita made a quick habit of walking up the mountain, her fingers grazing the hanging honeysuckle along the enormous stone wall that lined the sharply curving road. Every so often there was a break in the vista, and she could look out over the verdant hills that cascaded into the sea, imagining how profoundly peaceful were the lives of the neighborhood inhabitants. They with their birdsong, scattered lemon trees, and enormous wrought iron gates. She would walk the narrow road all the way to the top, stopping to sit on a stone wall, risking mosquito bites in favor of a meditative view, the Villa—with its high hopes—in the distance.

The sun set in the west, as it did all over the world, but there on top of that seaside village, with its magnificent slopes and shapes and shadows, and the glittering, glimmering water that danced in the last light, the sunset had never felt so intrinsic, so ruminative. Every moment of those walks was a contemplation for Margherita. Every step felt more and more inward.

In the morning she did the same walk, louder on the way up with the return of school traffic, but still dotted with summer's vibrant flora. Margherita placed her outstretched hand next to a giant magenta hibiscus in full bloom; wider and larger than the girth of her extremity. How flamboyant and determined it was.

She tried to time her morning hike so that by the time she reached the back streets of the village again, the sliver of an organic shop on the hill above her apartment was open. It was, however, never open on schedule, and often Margherita stood outside from nine until nine-thirty, when the sing-songy manager finally arrived, clueless as ever about opening hours.

More and more, Margherita missed the conveniences of her own culture. Cafés that were open before eight a.m. Shops that were ready to roar by seven. Not to mention, establishments that *did not* close for four hours in the middle of the day. City councils that answered the phone and responded to email. Life in Italy was just too slow for her, it was frustratingly unrealistic and behind, and she already felt the irk growing in her bloodstream.

However, when she finally entered the shop, the wooden crates filled with the first of the season's dark purple grapes, the last of the season's soft green figs—sitting fat and proud beneath an errant leaf direct from the tree—and premature sightings of squash and awkward gourds, made her enamored of Italy's charms all over again.

Upstairs, on the fifth floor, sitting in her make-shift office and staring at her laptop screen, she breathed out forcefully and inhaled deeply.

Her mother used to do that. Take in too much air. "S & A," she would say, when Tommaso commented on it. Stress and Anxiety. Margherita used to wonder when Francine's 'S & A' might ever subside. Her mother seemed to swim in it, perpetually submerged, forever weighed down by thoughts or feelings or memories she never shared.

Margherita shook her head. *Stop it,* she thought to herself.

When she had left Italy to return to New York after Francine's death, Margherita had tried to distract herself with shallow things like dating, or her devil boss, or Nick. She had been momentarily caught up in a brief relationship—Derek—that had caused her own anxiety to ripple forcefully, due to the simple fact of being in a 'relationship.' For a year at least, she had— perhaps selfishly— managed to superficially focus on the trials and tribulations of being twenty-something. Benjamin had been far away, her father uptown—distant but not guiltily far—and Margherita had safely skimmed along without her mother too much in her thoughts.

Then had come the pandemic, and the worldwide time-out had given her so much space, so much quiet, and what practically felt like an invitation to be contemplative. She found herself thinking of her mother all of the time; she was guilty for not thinking about her enough in the year immediately following her death, and then she was bitter towards her for making her feel guilty. After all, it had been Francine's choice to take her own life.

But then Margherita felt guilty all over again, for placing 'blame' or 'faulting' Francine for anything at all. Mental illness is no one's fault.

The Villa project had been the perfect antidote. She had directed all of her energy into it, enthusiastically and willingly, and poised it as a way to connect with Francine in a positive light. It was a project that would raise Margherita in her dead mother's eyes.

But it wasn't turning out the way she had envisaged. Margherita, so eager to move it along, had perhaps jumped the gun by hiring the lawyers in Milan to work with the bank to release the property. She had perhaps written the script ahead of schedule by paying for certain permits and licenses. Margherita knew that Francine would tisk-tisk her for spending her savings on these things. Her mother would have told her she was doing things out of order. But Margherita had been determined. Stubborn maybe. But wasn't that what Francine had taught her? Be big. Be Brilliant. How could she be big or brilliant without taking risks? Weren't leaps more courageous than baby steps? Or had she been naïve? Irresponsible? Idiotic?

Night after night that week, Margherita stayed up until the wee hours. She lay lethargically on the sofa, admiring the giant luminous moon that didn't seem to get any smaller. It bounced off the mirror opposite the window and streaked across the blanket on the back of the sofa.

"I think I dug myself a hole, Mom. What now?"

The next week was a blur of hours at the desk and walks in the hills. Of lemon trees and teal shutters and high villa windows facing west. Peachy orangey patinas, villas sitting right on the stone road, villas sitting far back behind steel gates. Shadows of olive trees in dipping fields. Stray dogs. And more visits to the shop on the hill. Two apples, one carrot, one skinny zucchini with the flower flopping on the end, a handful of cherry tomatoes. Evening sun. Cerebral sunsets and reflection.

That weekend after such a dry stretch, it poured and poured and then stopped and then poured some more, like someone who needed to have a good cry. It brought with it the perfect five p.m. breeze to walk up the hill with a little Edwin Starr. To top it off there were still soft green figs at the little shop on the hill, so—for the moment—everything on the surface felt peaceful. Below the surface was a different story.

Sitting at her desk one late afternoon, mid-email to a hotelier based in Miami, a notification flashed across her screen.

Benjamin: what's the latest

"Ha," Margherita said to the screen. "Thanks for checking in."
She opened the message and wrote back with jaw clenched.

Margherita: all good.

Passive aggression was her only mode of confronting her brother's disinterest in her whereabouts, mental and emotional state, and general life goings-on. She could count on her hands the number of times he reached out to her first. After Francine had died, he had made a small, barely perceptible effort, but since his wife had given birth to two little ones, Margherita had dropped to a far lower rung on Benjamin's totem pole.

When she next looked up from her screen, a cat was staring at her from the other side of the window. Margherita jumped. And then laughed.

"What?" she asked the cat. The blonde creature scratched at the window and continued to stare.

"I'm not letting you in!" Margherita stood, looking around beyond the lonesome creature, but there were no other cat friends on the rooftops. It sat there for hours.

Benjamin: project? Updates?

Margherita: working on it.

Benjamin: are you still in Milan?

Margherita: … no. I'm in Liguria.

Benjamin: why?

Margherita: why not?

Benjamin: are you teaching sailing lessons and shucking mussels?

She huffed angrily and shook her head at the cat.

Benjamin: how can you accomplish anything there? What's the point?

Margherita: I can figure it out thanks Ben.

Benjamin: I don't think you can.

Benjamin: I think you need a little guidance Marghe.

Margherita: I am not a child.

Benjamin: I didn't say you were
Benjamin: but you are looking to raise capital and you won't get very far in Italy. Esp the fanciful shores of Santa and Portofino
Benjamin: And you need a job. fyi.

Margherita: I have a father thank you.

Benjamin: cut that shit out Margherita I'm not trying to father you
Benjamin: I'm your big brother, I have an opinion
Benjamin: and I know a thing or two about raising capital
Benjamin: you don't do it in a third-world economy. life isn't 'Waterloo Sunset' .. as long as you gaze up isn't the solution to everything.

Margherita: k.

Benjamin: you're not helping yourself with that attitude. You should go back to NYC. Boots on the ground.

Margherita: I am not going back to ny

Benjamin: then you should try London at least. You'd still be on this side of the pond. But it's time to get real. Re-enter the world.

"Is this what it's come to?" she asked the cat. She stood and went to the kitchen, unwrapped the jagged wedge of Parmigiano, cut off a few shards, and returned to the office window with a snack for the cat.

"Calcium is good for your bones," she said as she held each shard between her thumb and forefinger, one at a time, watching the little mouth nibble away.

Later, she stood at the kitchen window and watched the old lady a few houses down survey her robust garden. She held delicate rose stems in her swollen hand and stared into blooms as if they were old lovers reminding her of stories she tried to forget. Her hunched and rounded shoulders looked to Margherita like a giant wave suspended in mid-air. One day, it would crash down. Who would take care of the lovely garden then?

Is this a square-shaped, literal window into my future? she wondered.

What a gloomy person I am. She shook herself physically and washed a few bright red, juicy tomatoes under the faucet.

"I'm so bored," she said out loud.

Margherita: Like hi are we still friends

Noah: I've been meaning to text you for a month. Miss you. How are you?

Margherita: "I've been meaning to write you for a year darling just keep forgetting!"

Margherita: Gosh feeling special
Margherita: Blah
Margherita: Everything is blah Noah
Margherita: How's unemployed life
Margherita: I can't believe you quit. You're not a quitter.

Noah: I'm shit at texting. But think about you and sending you good vibes always!

Margherita: Oh good. Good vibes. That's the stuff friendships are made of.
Margherita: Transcontinental good vibes

Noah: Why blah? Where have you been?
Noah: Thinking of you is like 85% of friendship when covid and international time lines are a factor
Noah: I presumed you were shacked up with some older Italian man…

Margherita: Shacked up with my growing ass and a homeless roof cat that stares at me through the window all day

Margherita: What's new with you

Noah: Are you a crazy cat woman now?

Noah: Are you doing ok?

Margherita: No it lives outside. We eat parmigiano together.

Noah: Nothing new here. Need to find a new job. Unemployment is making me slovenly.

Margherita: no I am the ultimate sloven.

Margherita: The world is exhausting.

Margherita: All the politics and the apologies and the masks and the virus

Margherita: Do you know how many questions I have to answer now on job applications about my gender and sexual status and gene mutations

Margherita: Who is ever going to hire me, I'm just a white girl

Margherita: I don't fill any of the quotas. Oh. I'm job searching. Not admitting that to anyone but you.

Noah: I'm a white guy. In his forties. I'm screwed.

Margherita: You're British and Scottish in America. That's something at least.

Margherita: Yesterday I had a phone screening with a twenty-three-old for a design job for Dadados'. Everyone on this team is at least six years younger than me. I said what is the trajectory of this role and she didn't know what trajectory meant

Noah: Aren't they based in Portland?

Noah: now you're moving to Portland?

Margherita: god no, I don't smoke pot

Margherita: but I AM homeless so at least I'd be with my people

Noah: Maybe you should just go back to NY
Noah: Stop wasting your energy

Margherita: I feel like such a failure I don't want to go back
Margherita: And I'm tired
Margherita: I set myself up for all these changes and challenges and it doesn't work out and now for the first time I am starting to feel tired
Margherita: sometimes I really hate adult-ing

Noah: It's tough. Meeting and exceeding life expectations is a journey. You'll get there, it's just going to take different and multiple paths. There's no failure, just life experience. And hard decisions and choices. You got this.

Margherita: fist pump! blah thank you.
Margherita: I am thinking about going to London. But the thought of packing up everything I unnecessarily brought to Italy, sending it all back to… where? To sit in storage. Do you know how expensive storage is?
Margherita: I feel like all I do lately is send boxes around, shred my overdue credit card notices, and get on a plane again

Noah: London. Cool. For what?

Margherita: To try to find a job
Margherita: Or a man
Margherita: whichever comes first
Margherita: I am homeless
Margherita: And broke. And going grey.
Margherita: My brother thinks I need 'guidance'
Margherita: Not a particularly desirable job candidate as I haven't stayed in the same place for very long, ever
Margherita: Did you know Emily Blunt was 22 in devil wears Prada??!

———————

One afternoon, after eight hours straight at her laptop, the room turned an odd shade of golden. She watched the September rain outside her window as it fell in torrents on the decrepit roof tiles. Lightning on lightning on lightning blazed the sky, enough to make her starry eyed, and then everything was a cloud puff, like bubble wrap. The sky was yellow. Everything yellow. A yellow so bright, the weather could be described by its hue. Margherita could say "It's yellow out" if someone were to ask.

When the rain stopped, it was light again, tinged with yellow, and she decided to get out of the apartment. It was starting to feel like a cell in the sky. All day long she would sit at the desk. She never saw anyone, except for the woman at the corner shop on the hill, and occasionally she crossed paths with Chiara's friend who had rented her the apartment, in the little street downstairs. But the biggest chunk of the day was spent writing emails to potential buyers for the Villa, to family investment offices who might be interested in the project, and once in a while, job searching. Something in her felt like a ticking grandfather clock. The same noise. Round and round. All day. Part of her wished it would decombust. Send pieces everywhere. Just let it smash or explode.

Outside, she languidly walked up the hill. Her steps had become heavy since returning to Italy, and she envied the few people she saw jogging or riding bicycles; so swift their movements, with such ease. She had once felt that energy. Where had that gone?

Sitting on a bench in Villa Durazzo's park, with a bee buzzing dangerously near, she felt like she was going to burst in a morass of built-up emotion. She needed to tell someone about it, to unfurl it all to someone who would make her feel less crazy. She didn't want pity or lip service. And she didn't want someone who would just listen and tell her she would be fine. She wasn't fine. Telling someone who wasn't fine that they would be fine was in no way helpful.

She needed someone to make her feel less alone. Someone who would give her the space to be or feel whatever it was she was being or feeling.

Margherita: Can I have a moment to vent. Response not necessary, I just need to talk

Margherita: You know that feeling when your heart starts palpitating vigorously and you can hear the echo of your own voice and everything in the room feels brighter and bigger and louder like it's coming at you, or you're sleeping and wake up suddenly feeling nauseous and you shoot up and all your limbs go bizerk and you lay back down but worry you might vomit horizontally? The moments before a panic attack basically. Well I am having them like three, four, five times a day. I take deep breaths like that is the normal way of breathing, and I can't concentrate on anything because every moment feels like I just walked into a radio station recording studio and all of the lights and beeping noises are going off at once. I feel like I am actually going crazy and I don't know how to stop it.

Margherita: I thought going out to Carmel for a month would solve all of this. Would idk wash it away. Make me feel connected again. 'Sooth me.' How ridiculous right. My mom would be seething right now. Embarrassed and seething. Her daughter, failing and flailing….. and whining about it. my oh my how that would really irritate her. I don't know why in my head I think, it all seemed to come so easy to her. Success and a grown-up life. But that's really ironic, all things considered. And really unfair of me to say, because surely it's not the case. But she never shared any of her own process with me, of how she did it or got there, and so how do I know if she struggled? Or what the struggle was? Is that how parenting is done…. Make success look attainable or admit to your children that it's hard.

Margherita: I've made such a mess for myself this year. I had so much damn confidence and was so positive with my idiotic rose-colored glasses, so sure that this would all magically work out within six months and they'd write about me in the WSJ weekend magazine. And I'd be proud of myself for something 'big' and my dead mom would be proud of me and life would magically start. But it hasn't been like that at all and the only thing I feel is this total Ungluing. Everything is in flux. Everything is a question mark. The world is a question mark. And I'm just sitting here every day, not accomplishing anything, watching time go by.

Margherita: And I haven't stopped moving around. Packing boxes. Trying again. and I feel all the time like I work twelve hour days, none of it fruitful, like I don't know where any of it is leading, and doing it all by myself is starting to feel highly impossible. And I don't have any sense of home whilst everyone else seems so connected to wherever they are or whoever they're with, their husbands or their children or their enormous groups of friends, and I don't feel connected to much of anything. I used to love to move around and constantly be on a train or go somewhere new or meet someone new or do something new and now it doesn't feel good, for the first time, to be so untethered. I want to go Home. But nowhere feels like home anymore. And then I feel like a wuss for saying that because it makes me sound like I'm giving up. Like I can't handle being an adult.

Margherita: That was a lot. Feel free to ignore. I think I just needed to have someone hear that.

She exhaled and wiped the tears running down her cheeks as the bee latched to a yellow rose and sucked its nectar.

Hours later, on her way back from her walk, her phone vibrated consecutive baritone ba-booms.

Nick: owh Marghe

Nick: I completely understand everything you said.

Nick: I can relate. I was going through similar feelings until I found this new apartment. In fact, that is the word I used just yesterday: untethered.

Nick: I think as humans, we cannot be unglued in so many facets of our life at once. Job, home, relationships… we need something, one thing at least, to be stable.

Nick: it's natural to feel what you are feeling; you unglued everything at once in pursuit of something big.

Nick: So I think you should see your feelings as very reasonable and human.

Nick: And embrace them.

Nick: You're only experiencing them because you've had the guts to pursue a life that's different and interesting.

Nick: It's a privelege

Nick: Truly I mean that

Nick: You only know how it feels to lose a world cup final if you're one of the best athletes in the world.

Nick: It's a rarified misery.

She looked down at her phone and smiled as another errant tear dribbled down her face.

Margherita: I like that perspective.

Nick: Most people stay in their lanes and home towns and marry their fat college boyfriends.

Margherita: but maybe they're happy!

Nick: They're probably not.

Nick: go have a coffee with a friend tomorrow

Nick: talk to a stranger

Nick: what would Van say

Nick: it's present everywhere

Margherita: that warm love

Nick: Exactly.

Nick: And

Nick: I didn't know your mum

Nick: But I have a feeling she would be immensely proud of how brave and determined you are, and she would probably tell you that everyone has their own process

Nick: The bigger your dreams, the more complex and daunting and lengthy that process is.

Nick: Not everything comes together on the same schedule. Making your own sense of home in the world is a process too.

Nick: Don't be too hard on yourself for what you're feeling.

She hugged her phone to her chest and breathed in the beautiful evening.

You are bold. You are courageous.

The next morning, as she stepped into the corner shop on the hill, she surveyed the latest additions. Enormous cabbages as big as her head were next up on September's bounty. She bought a few bright red tomatoes, squishy green figs, a faded yellow pear, and a head of lettuce as crisp as a cucumber. Lunch would be a salad of everything, with tiny flecks of chopped ginger and shavings of Parmigiano.

As she left the shop with her paper bag, her elderly neighbor entered, hunched over, her thin white hair neatly combed.

"Permesso," Margherita said with a kind smile. The woman's enormous, glassy eyes peered at Margherita curiously, that somewhat shocked look of an older human, as she shuffled onto the linoleum floor and greeted the shopkeeper. Margherita wondered what the woman was buying. Maybe she would carry home one of the enormous cabbages. Maybe she was a brilliant cook.

Sitting at her desk, the rusting rooftop tiles before her, Margherita decided to write a few personalized emails to senior partners at prestigious architecture firms in London. She had submitted applications to a handful of random job postings in the states, even though she had no desire to return, but she had not begun to look in London. Land of Benjamin.

Maybe it was time. Maybe she needed a little tethering.

Margherita: do you think it would be considered giving up
Margherita: if I left italy to spend some time in London, where I can try to network and push this project along

She sat with her thumb and forefinger pulling at her top lip.

Nick: not at all.
Nick: it's your project.
Nick: your life.
Nick: take control.
Nick: if you need to go to london to steer it
Nick: then go.
Nick: shake it up.

She nodded at the screen.
Yeah. Shake it up.

Ten days later, after a sprint of packing, a last minute one-way ticket courtesy of Benjamin, and a mad dash exit from Italy not too dissimilar from that of a fugitive on the run, Margherita felt a surprising sense of relief. It was true, Italy had not been coming together for her this time around, and though she had been stubborn to admit it, and to 'abandon' it in some way, there was a certain amount of closure when that last box went on its merry international way. Like when a jar of a favorite face cream reaches its final swipe and is thrown in the bin; an odd thing to be satisfied about, but closure all the same.

She reminded herself that she was not giving up on The Villa project; she was repurposing her efforts. She did not need to live next to it in order to make progress. She needed contacts and a network more than she needed to physically see it, or touch it—at least at that moment in time.

The anxiety of what was to come kicked up on the day of her flight. In the car on the way to Genoa's airport, the mountains of southern Piemonte ahead and the grittiness of the port city to her right, she felt the familiar, profound desire to talk to Nick. To calm her nerves, distract or soothe her.

Margherita: Song for you
Margherita: "Make Your Own Kind of Music" by Cass Elliot

Nick: oh lovely
Nick: here's one for you
Nick: "Being Special" by Sophia Kennedy

Margherita: on theme. I like it.

He didn't say anything else. She imagined him being busy, with friends, or girls, or work, or one of the far flung trips he posted snippets of on his Instagram. His life in New York. Which she always assumed to be so full, so enormously social and fun. And as with each of those split-second exchanges that ended as full tilt as they began, she felt that frustration in the actuality of their situation, that she still wanted him to fill a hole that he had no interest in filling, and that she was, more than likely, a very insignificant person in his long list of contacts.

As she presented her passport to the young, gruff Italian at passport control, she could not help but feel as though she was doing something wrong. She folded her lips over one another and pursed them together as she watched the bald man flip through her passport with a cynical expression, as if dubious of her intentions. Margherita quickly contemplated what she might respond if he asked one of those strange questions, like why was she leaving, or why was she going to London?

"What were you doing in Italy?" he asked instead.

She was momentarily taken aback.

"Studying," she said.

"Studying what?" He eyed her as he held her passport hostage between his fat thumbs and forefingers.

"Self-worth," she said stoically.

His expression barely changed as he unhurriedly returned her passport to her hand.

On the small plane, she shoved her overflowing canvas bag underneath the seat in front of her and sat a delicate hat in her lap. The gentleman next to her was well into his sixties and had not a single belonging with him. He was well-dressed, bored, and not chatty, though he eyed the bulging bag at her feet with what felt to Margherita like judgment and dismay.

"I'm moving," she said by way of explanation. "Hence the inability to pack neatly." He checked the time on his Patek Philippe before he closed his eyes with his arms folded over his chest.

She looked out the window. *Okay*, she thought to herself. *British people aren't as friendly as Italians. Mustn't forget.* She had spoken to so few other human beings in the previous few weeks, she felt she might have become a little strange in her idle loneliness.

Margherita inhaled and exhaled forcibly as she looked out of the tiny oval window onto the tarmac, awaiting the plane's departure to yet another destination where she would live in yet another temporary flat and start again with new faces. Maybe she would make a friend or two. Maybe she would find an investor for The Villa. Maybe she would find a fantastic job at a firm like Norman Foster, meet a man, fall in love, and—

Her phone vibrated in her lap.

> **Nick:** I spent this summer having all this random sex
> **Nick:** Thinking it was how I'd get over my relationship.
> **Nick:** But it's not my relationship I've been trying to get over. It's you.
> **Nick:** And it's nuts because before a few weeks ago, we hadn't seen each other in a year and a half
> **Nick:** We've always had the strangest timing
> **Nick:** I know you are in the midst of a lot of growth and trying to figure things out
> **Nick:** And I've been doing the same
> **Nick:** And I know that these messages aren't relevant at all to what is going on in your life right now.
> **Nick:** But I needed to say that.
> **Nick:** For myself.

Margherita stared down at Nick's missives.

She quickly typed out a response without thinking.

Don't think, she had once said to him. *Don't think too much, or you'll ruin it.*

> **Margherita:** What would Paul say
> **Margherita:** *The butter wouldn't melt so I put it in the pie.*

LONDON

January 1, 1986

THE FIRST DAY of the new year was warm and humid, and
Francine decided to take the long way through Hyde Park to
Keith's house. Before nine, there were just a handful of people
in the park, everyone starting slowly and with great patience,
united in their civility and quietude. The mood veered inch by
inch away from silence, the dogs just starting to break into runs,
the light growing strong.

Francine craned her neck upwards to breathe in the moist air,
the vast sky above the park, and the absence of grime and high-
rises. She loved New York, but she would be lying if she said she
didn't miss London in some way—big or small—every day. She
missed the parks and how wrapped up and safe they made her feel,
surrounded by trees and open meadows and perpetual dew. She
missed the days of Bourne & Hollingsworth—idling an afternoon
away with Bea at the make-up counter. She missed cozy early
winter evenings huddled in the pub on days it was dark by three.

She missed the comfort of her friends, for whom she didn't
have to pretend.

She missed Keith—Keith before the accident.

"Hello-o-oo?" Francine called as she walked into the house,
the door unlocked.

"In here." His voice came from the sitting room, which currently doubled as his bedroom. Not yet able to climb stairs, the
second floor was no longer usable. At least for the time being.

"There he is. My Keith." Francine plastered a smile on her face and threw her arms around Keith's slender shoulders.

He sat at his desk and craned his head back as Francine awkwardly hugged him in his chair.

She stood up straight and fluffed his hair, leaning into the desk, where enormous tomes on trusts and corporate law sat flipped open, one on top of another. "Hell of a way to start the year, huh?"

She distractedly flipped the book to read its cover. "Woof. She's a doozy."

He regarded her with reserve, and she smiled confidently.

"You look gorgeous, by the way."

Keith shook his head, a dry expression toward the books. Everything about him was less—his weight, the color in his face, the life in his eyes, the energy at the tips of his fingers.

"Thanks, but no lies from you please."

"Not lying! Keithie, you've always been, and always will be, the most gorgeous man in my life."

"What about Tommaso?" He fingered her mother's serpent ring on her finger. She had begun to wear it after the funeral. "I thought you said he was a real head turner."

"Tommaso is very Italian looking. You are my English prince."

He rolled his eyes again and reached for his crutches against the wall. Francine moved out of the way so he could prop himself up.

"Do you need help?" she asked, holding out her arm for support.

"I can do it," he said, exasperatedly.

"Look at you go." She watched him move toward the sofa.

"Yeah. Back in Courchevel by February." He plopped down and rested the crutches against the neighboring chair, throwing his head back into the pillow and pushing his fingers gently through his hair.

Francine slipped off her boots and went to sit next to him. She curled her feet under herself and nestled into his warmth, taking his limp arm and pulling it around her shoulder.

"I missed you," she said into the room.

"Yeah."

She looked up at his face. "Keith?"

"Hmm." He glanced into her eyes and then looked straight ahead, his gloom a solid entity in a space that had once been the anchor point of so much vivacity, warmth, and intimacy amongst friends.

"Bea said you've gone back to work?"

"Hmm."

"That must be a relief."

"Hmm."

"Are we to converse in 'hmm's' for the day?" She pulled at his arm affectionately.

"Potentially."

"What do they say at rehab? How's it going?"

"It's… going."

"Well? What do they say?" She pushed away from his body to look him in the eye. His mouth appeared to be permanently drooped downward.

"They say… what do they say? They say to be patient. Takes time."

"Right. Of course. You're smashing it with the crutches."

"Yeah."

"How much longer do you think you'll be on them?"

"I don't know, Francine. Can we talk about something else besides my damn bionic leg?" he snapped, quietly, as he leant once again into the pillow and tipped his face toward the ceiling.

Francine took a lightening speed inhale and her eyes teared up. Keith took one look at them and moaned, his face went to his palms and by the time he glanced at her again, Francine had two tears running down her cheeks.

"Keithie, I…"

"Don't, Francie. Please don't." His voice was strong and deep, the same voice her father used to take with her when she had tantrums. Keith placed his hand on her wrist and squeezed it before wiping her tears, one at a time, with his thumb.

"Stop it," he said, more softly, more delicately. "Don't fucking cry in here. Go put a record on. You choose."

She sniffled and nodded her head vigorously as she raised herself to walk toward his enormous collection. He waited in ringing silence as she busied herself with the decision-making. "Cat?"

"Which?"

"Teaser and the Firecat."

"Fine. Though I don't desire to hear 'Moonshadow' ever again in my life."

"Why not?" she asked, as she slid the record out of its sleeve and opened the player's dustcover.

"Oh." Francine grimaced painfully, holding the RCA's arm suspended in the air. "Maybe a little Echo then? *Ocean Rain*? 'The Killing Moon?'"

"Oh yeah. Knife in the wound."

"You're moodier than I am. Cat it is." She returned to her spot, snuggled into his chest, feet beneath her, and purposefully wrapped Keith's limp arm around her shoulders once again.

"Where's Benjamin?" He took her hand with his other arm, his big palm over her little paw, layers of skin that had grown thinner over hundreds of blue moons.

"At home with daddy."

He stroked the back of her hand with his thumb. "How's he doing? Benjamin I mean."

"Oh. I don't know. How am I to know? Fine, I assume?"

"Well, he's still alive. So that's a fine start."

"Yeah. I guess that's all we can hope for."

"Jokes, Francie. He's just a babe. Not a lot to judge from yet."

"There is, actually. I can tell in his face. He doesn't like me."

"That's ridiculous," Keith said quietly, shifting his real leg and shaking it out.

"Cramp?" She looked down at it. A fraction of the size it used to be, all of his muscle mass gone.

"Babies only have two expressions. Hunger and constipation."

"Not true. When I come home from work, he looks at me like 'Oh crap, *her* again.' I'm a terrible mother, Keithie. I go to work. That in itself is treason. I have a full time nanny *and* a night-time nanny. Even Tommaso thinks I should spend more time with him. I know it. He says things sometimes… I just know he's judging me. I swear, sometimes I think Tommaso continues to date me because of Benjamin. He has Dad genes *and* Mum genes. It's not fair. Thirty bloody eight. I should be in full-on mummy cog."

"Ha. Well, I'm quite certain no man dates a woman purely to spend time with a newborn who is not his, born out of wedlock to a wanker. A wanker who engaged this woman in lies and duplicity. Tommaso must be made of saintly blood. That or he really *is* crazy in love with you. And I mean crazy. And I'm thirty bloody eight too. You don't see any little league paraphernalia around here do you?"

Francine scrunched up her face while leaning into Keith's chest,and spun around to look him in the eyes. "You think I'm a horrible person, don't you? You think I'm taking advantage of him don't you?" She didn't wait for his response as she nestled her head into his chest again. He stroked the top of her hand. "I do love him. I asked him a zillion times if he was sure. I gave him a zillion chances to leave, to walk away."

"I know, Francie."

"I think I owe him a lot. For staying with me. I know I do," she said, more to herself than to Keith.

"I think he's an adult. He can take care of himself. You owe him honesty and decency, just like every other honest, decent person. Anyway. I can't believe they let you fly with a nine-month-old."

"I can't believe I *have* a nine-month-old. Keithie I'm not meant to be a mother. I put on a smock to say goodbye to him when I leave for work, so that I don't have to change my blouse again. And then when I step outside, I exhale this big obnoxious breath. I hate myself for it. I couldn't *wait* to get out of the house this morning without him. What kind of mother thinks that way? I'm horrid. Steely, self-absorbed monster is I."

"Every mother thinks that way at some point."

"But it wasn't supposed to happen for me. A life-long out-patient with a high-stress job. I wasn't meant to raise a boy, no less without his father."

"Stop it with that. None of us are *meant* to be or do anything. I'm not *meant* to be handicapped. But here we are."

Her face sunk into itself, and she inhaled deeply, her eyes a torturous display of guilt. Keith keeled forward to witness her gloom.

"Oh, come now, don't sulk. Wipe that off. It was a joke. We've got to joke."

"Keith—"

"How many Cat concerts would you say we've been to together?"

Francine spun around, disengaging from his flimsy embrace, and draped her legs over his lap, her back pressed against the sofa's armrest. She could see him properly from there. The ribbed neck of his wool sweater was roomy and loose, and she could see the protrusion of his collarbone, the deep purple rings beneath his eyes, and his dry lips. "Oh. Almost a dozen."

"Those were great years, weren't they?" He closed his eyes as 'Peace Train' began to play.

She felt the tears prickle her eyes again, that sink drain swelling in her throat. How much it hurt to look at him now.

Keith opened his eyes and rubbed her ankle up and down, regarding it as if it were a perfectly fluted shell found on the shores of Britannia Bay. "Hey—Happy New Year, love," he said. He lifted her foot in its thick sock and kissed her bare ankle.

LONDON

September 30, 2021

IN THE TAXI from Heathrow, with an exceptionally kind and helpful driver and 'Back on the Chain Gang' commemorating the arrival, she sat with eyes peeled as the cab drove past Norman Fosters' City Hall, through Canary Wharf with its enormous sky-scrapers—One Canada Square, Herzog & de Meuron's cylindrical One Park Drive, the 'Walkie-Talkie' at 20 Fenchurch Street—one on top of another, through St. Katherine's, and on to the City. She watched suited men and women walk briskly (The World Again! Insert: Elation) around the Gherkin at 30 St Mary Axe, through Blackfriars, Whitehall, and St. James. Along the edge of Green Park, the environment changed immensely, from glass to brick and limestone. Then they were in and out of Knightsbridge, with its tall gingerbread houses, right through Chelsea at dusk, where young women dashed into bakeries and yoga studios and finally onto the quiet, residential Brompton streets of SW10, lined with beautiful white homes. The area was just south of the almond-shaped Boltons, known for ornate Italian and Victorian-style villas and one-time addresses of Douglas Fairbanks Junior, Madonna, and Dame Paddy Ridsdale—rumored to be Ian Flem-ing's inspiration for Miss Moneypenny.

Margherita had lined up a series of short lets for the first few months of her open-ended sojourn, not knowing how long she would stay and unable to sign her own apartment lease without a job. The first, for just a few days, was on Cathcart Road, just south of some of the most guarded and expensive homes in West London, the sizes of which she found fantastically ridiculous and impressive after her top-floor apartment in the dusty 1950s apartment block in Santa Margherita.

The first night, she set out toward Fulham Road to feel the bliss of a bustling metropolis, one in which she didn't have to pay her electric bill at the post office. One in which there were cute guys to gawk at, and ethnic food.

> **Margherita:** soooo much stufff everywhere!!!
> **Margherita:** It's like the world again! Options! Nothing is closed!
> **Margherita:** Cute men!
> **Margherita:** An abundance of gourmet stores with really good dark chocolate and exotic fruit!
>
> **Benjamin:** You are back in the land of plenty now.
>
> **Margherita:** Places accept credit cards!!!
>
> **Benjamin:** ha. Yes. A return to present day was in order.
>
> **Margherita:** What are you doing? Do you want to meet me for late dinner?
>
> **Benjamin:** Can't. I'm still in the office. Enjoy yourself. Call you tmr. Xx

Typical Benjamin. She knew he wouldn't call the next day, but she was suddenly so elated and energized, it didn't bother her.

The next few days were marathons of exploring by foot. She bought every type of nut butter she could find in every speciality stop (Italians did not stock this sort of thing), reunited with Whole Foods in Kensington, and walked around Highgate to see where her brother's wife had grown up. She ventured to Notting Hill where she stepped over Instagrammers with too much lip filler, and she walked by Benjamin's childhood home, where his father still lived, a man Margherita had never known.

By day four, she managed to figure out the bus. She sent a photo to her brother.

Margherita: I'm on a bus!

Benjamin: well done.

Margherita: It's so easy. Just tap my contactless card. In Italy you need to go to a tobacchi and buy an actual ticket.

Benjamin: I've never taken the bus. Italy is a time warp. Stop comparing the two. Running to meeting. Xx

The second week was in a sizable, stylish flat on Beaufort Street in Chelsea. She was amazed by how much the atmosphere changed after just a few blocks, and she adored the stately architecture and charm on Chelsea's old streets: the freehold terrace houses and the Chelsea dacha on The Vale, Petyt Place with its arched brick doorways, and Elm Park Gardens with double chimney stacked mansions sitting cozily behind wrought iron pedestrian gates. Then there were the ivy covered homes on Glebe Place, the classic light brick townhomes on Cheyne Row, and of course, Cheyne Walk. She visited the one-time addresses of John Barrymore, Mick Jagger and Marianne Faithfull, Ronnie Wood, T.S. Eliot, Henry James, Ian Fleming, Somerset Maugham, Laurence Olivier, Mick Fleetwood, and of course, the fictional characters invented by Virginia Woolf, John Fowler, and Roald Dahl. She tried to blur out the fact that Michael Bloomberg had acquired 4 Cheyne Walk, the Queen Anne-style home that held the blue plaque noting George Eliot's residence; this was an affront to the literary world which made up Margherita's romantic idea of Chelsea.

Toward the end of her second full week in London, she was finally getting the hang of the streets that were shaped like the letter L, the dead-end mews versus the pass-through mews, and the Park versus Lane versus Street versus Garden which all used the same first name. Though she didn't mind getting lost, constantly in awe of the architecture and elegance of her mother's birth city, on that particular Thursday she was rushing more than usual in order to meet her brother.

Margherita had seen Benjamin the weekend before, when she had visited his Richmond home to spend time with her baby niece and nephew. Benjamin himself made a brief appearance, long enough to make them each an espresso and fill his water jug before he raced off to a tennis match with his mates—his bi-weekly male bonding time which he wouldn't sacrifice for anyone, not even his half-sister.

He asked her to meet him in Farringdon, at the same place where he had just had a coffee meeting.

"How sweet, how convenient, dear brother," Margherita said flippantly.

"I am very busy, Margherita. This month has been hell on ice. I've not a second to spare, really."

"Yes, yes, yes I know. I'll see you there at 12:30 sharp."

Margherita tried not to be too distracted by the smart red doors and architecture on Clerkenwell Green. She felt so deliriously positive after such a slump, photographing everything and tipping her head upward to take in every detail of every building, that she had absentmindedly opened her chat with Nick to write him an enthusiastic message about how much she loved his city. His most recent message stared back at her, and she was reminded of the confusion which he had dropped in her lap in the middle of her transition from one culture to another.

Why hasn't he said anything? she wondered, exasperatedly, as she stared down at the screen. He came online, and she darted out of the app and entered the Palladian-style former courthouse, with its Ionic columns and coffered dome.

She dropped her phone into her tote and raised her head toward the bar as she reached the restaurant floor, where Benjamin sat at the edge of a seat, one leg fully outstretched before him, his eyebrows furrowed at an email on his phone. She watched him bring one hand up to the back of his head and run his palm over his dark hair. The two looked shockingly alike considering they had different fathers; Francine's honey-emerald eyes were clearly dominant, and both Tommaso and Christos possessed that dark, Mediterranean hair, though Margherita had a Northern Italian's fair skin while Benjamin leaned olive.

"Happenings?"

He turned abruptly toward her. "Ah. Hi." His eyes flickered between his phone and her coat. "Yes. Here," he helped her take her coat off and stopped a passing waiter. "Can you check this please?" He pulled her bar seat out for her and she pitched herself onto it, as gracefully as she could.

"Just… one… second…" He returned his attention to his screen.

Margherita's mind see-sawed toward Nick's words. She would *not* check her phone again.

"Here." Ben slid a menu toward her as the bartender filled her water glass.

She took a sweep of the room. The Sessions Arts Club on the third floor was back in full swing post-pandemic. The magnificent Victorian room, in the former Judges Dining Room, was a feast for Margherita's eyes, with its patinaed arches and walls, incredible high ceilings, and original log fireplaces.

"Right. So how was your Big Sur mental escape? Dad's good? I didn't properly inquire last weekend."

"He's thriving. And it was blissful, capital B. I miss it already. Sometimes I think I should just live there full time."

"And do what?"

She shrugged, a smile on her face. "Make a life."

"Doing what?"

"Ugh." She waved her hand in the air between them. "Maybe a simple life is okay. You're just like Mom."

He gave her a look with raised eyebrows as if to say, "Yes, and we are the successful ones."

"I don't know. Have a family. It's perfect for families."

Benjamin raised his eyebrows at his sister.

"Build a cozy house in the highlands. Be a part of the community. Volunteer at the library. Grow strawberries. Start my own little local architecture firm." She shrugged again. "Why not?"

"Margherita, being a mum isn't about 'a vibe.' It's a little more commitment-heavy than a sublet and a one-way ticket."

"Hmm. My aunt loves it. Did you see the photos I sent of that kiln? Amazing."

"She does ceramics in her garage while her husband works like a dog in Palo Alto. Carmel is for the second homes of Dallas or Bay Area millionaires. Lush, but get real."

"Hmm…" Margherita contemplated. "Her pottery is really impressive, though."

"So what are your plans for the rest of the day?"

"Ah the plans of the unemployed. Stacked high, they are."

"Enjoy it while it lasts."

"I think unemployment suits me, actually."

Benjamin looked at his sister with a dubious expression. "Here is fifty pounds."

"Benji, I don't need your money."

"My assistant is going on maternity and I need to get her a gift."

"Ah. I am not a task rabbit, FYI."

"Please…" Benjamin rolled his eyes.

Margherita sighed and folded the note into her wallet. "Fine. But fifty pounds doesn't buy you much these days. That's not even breakfast groceries at Panzers."

"Stop shopping there. You don't even live in St. John's Wood. Why are you shopping there?"

"But I love it," she said, innocently. "They play New Order and The English Beat and have the best smoked salmon. And Mom used to shop there. When she dated that musician on Circus Road. That wild, sexy, Greek, musician. What was his name again?" She tipped her head playfully, feigning forgetfulness.

"Please don't. Please don't call my father 'sexy.' Horrid thoughts. Horrid thoughts."

"He really was though. I found some old photos of the two of them together. Relics. Surrounded by guitars and cigarettes and cocaine. I'm actually really shocked you turned out so civil and… undeviating. Undeviating?"

"I've deviated."

"Have you? Deviated?"

"More deviation than you will ever know," he said sternly, his palms on the bar.

"Deviator? Were you a Deviator? Deviatrician! Deviat—"

"Oh shut up."

"Anyway, my next little rental is there, so technically it's not strange."

Benjamin inhaled and nodded his head. He pulled out another fifty pound note. "Don't blow it on matzo ball soup."

"Where in Chelsea did Grandpa live? I asked Dad but he shrugged it off."

"He doesn't want you snooping."

"I don't snoop."

Benjamin cocked his head and raised his eyebrows at his sister. "You are the worst."

"It's called curiosity."

"Anyway, it's not important. Just like it's not important where Alice grew up."

"Jeez. Was only curious."

"I hope you didn't come to London to obsess about Mum."

"No. I don't *have* to know where she lived. Just want to. But can you explain something to me? Gate, terrace, gardens, square…. Why can't they just come up with different street names."

He looked down toward her chest and scrunched his eyebrows. "Can you *do* something about that?" He nodded curtly toward her buttons. "Why must everyone at this snotty club see your cleavage? Button that." He sighed, bored. "And it's because the prestige is in the first word and real estate is worth more when you have Eaton in front of it. Even though we all know Eaton Gate is not Eaton Square. It makes people feel more superior than New Money Road."

"What about Eaton *Close*?" She raised her eyebrows as she blindly pushed one of the top buttons through a loop on her blouse.

Benjamin made a pained face.

"Happy?" She held her hands out, perfectly buttoned up.

"*Do not* traipse around here like it's Italy," he said under his breath.

"What does that mean?"

Benjamin glowered at her, and she eyed him scornfully as she slid the bills into her wallet.

"Fine. But I'm putting my name down on this gift. Love from Ben, Alice, and Ben's estranged sister."

"Not funny, but fine," he said as he hurriedly kissed her cheeks and briskly walked toward the staircase.

"I just got here!" she yelled with her arms outstretched.

"It will take me at least twenty minutes to get back to St. George Street."

She sighed and turned back to the bar where she took a sip of water and admired the great room around her.

"Will you be joining us for lunch?" the bartender asked her.

"Ah. I suppose not. Another time, with a more sociable companion. May I have my coat please?"

"To the museum bookshop we go," Margherita said to herself, as she exited the Old Sessions House and walked in the direction of Bloomsbury.

At the British Museum, her go-to, Margherita stepped

toward the bag-check desk. She layed her oversized tote on the table for the man in uniform to rummage through with his stick.

"Any knives or weapons?"

She took her AirPods out of her ears in which Depeche Mode had been turned up too high for eardrum safety. "Excuse me?"

"Any knives or weapons?" the man repeated.

"Oh, no, not today," she said cheerfully sardonic. She picked up her bag and carried on toward the museum entrance.

After a meander through Bloomsbury, a beautiful book for Benjamin's assistant under her arm, Margherita took the N38 bus to Green Park and connected to Chelsea from there. She felt, for the first time in a long time, the sweet zest and pure pleasure that she had missed so much in herself while in Italy. Apparently London, at that time, at that period, at that juncture, was just what she needed, and she rejoiced in the realization that perhaps she wasn't broken, after all. Perhaps she wasn't heading toward a mental state similar to Francine's. And this realization made her, with the aid of the city's elegance, energy, and eccentric civility, deliriously herself and at ease once again.

On the bus, as she watched the beautiful buildings of Mayfair, Belgravia, and South Kensington roll by, her phone pinged.

Thayer: Is she alive

Margherita: Tis

Thayer: Is she kicking ass

Margherita: Tisn't

Thayer: I'll be back in London soon for a stretch
Thayer: Don't disappear

Margherita: Twon't

NEW YORK

March 7, 1986

"CAN I PLEASE make a phone call?" Francine asked timorously from the doorway of her stark room. She weakly held up an empty Dixie cup and tilted it left to right like a bell, announcing her compliance.

The nurse glanced up from her clipboard and took the empty cup. She stood before Francine and seemed to take in her gaunt frame, her pale face and tiny wrists, below which two delicate hands floated, as if suspended in the air, unclenched and weightless.

She sighed out throatily. "Fine, honey. But out here." The nurse nodded toward the phone on the counter.

Francine approached it shyly and picked up the entire instrument. She carried it, dragging the cord, to a chair by the window overlooking the East River, where she curled her legs beneath her and swathed her dry, swollen tongue around her mouth. As she picked up the receiver, she turned to see if the nurse was standing close, listening.

"Were you sleeping?" Francine said into the phone, and adjusted her shoulders for privacy.

"Yes," a muffled voice filled her right ear, and Francine gripped the phone harder in her hand, as if she could be closer to him if she held on as tightly as her little hand would allow.

"Do you remember at university, when we skipped the Contemporary Lit exam to go see The Who in Liverpool? And when we got back to school, everyone was talking about Professor Parson's resignation?"

"Yes, he was in hospital for something. Wasn't he ill?"

"He came to my room once, when I was having a low. He said he was worried about me and wanted to check on me. Skeeveball. I was lying in bed, listless as usual, and he climbed in next to me. I didn't have the energy to push him away."

"What? Are you serious?"

"When I felt better, I went to his office and locked the door behind me. I think he thought I had changed my mind, like *oh la la* she's into it now. I asked him to take his pants down. Which he did, because he is disgusting. I lit a cigarette and put it out on the tip of his penis. Oh, Keithie, he howled so loud I think my ear is still ringing. He tried to hit me, and I kicked him hard. Then I took his picture, lit another cigarette, put it out on his ass while he was crouched over on the floor, and legged it."

"Are you fucking with me right now?" Keith asked.

"Course not."

"You're outrageous. That is outrageous. Well done, Francie." He quietly laughed into the phone. "Why didn't you ever tell me?"

"I was embarrassed."

"Why? He was the scumbag."

"I hate feeling like people take advantage of me when I'm like this. When I can't control it. Though all my doctors will tell me: but you *can* control it, Francine. Bollocks."

"I know."

She inhaled and spun her head around to check if the nurse was still at the counter. She wasn't.

"I've been put on one night watch. I went a little berserk, when Christos came to see Benjamin."

"What happened?"

"I told him. Finally. Everything." She absentmindedly wrapped the squiggly cord around her leg, bent into her chest. "He went ballistic. Demanded to see my doctor. Suddenly worried about 'his' child."

"Fucking arsehole. What happened with the doctor?"

"He assured Christos that I am a fit parent, as long as I take my medications, of course. Christos accused me of trickery, betraying him and Benjamin, that I should never have been allowed full custody, that Benjamin should live with him in London. And then he had the balls to *tell* me that I would have to pay him child support. Brazen, selfish, exploitative bastard."

"Oh because his lifestyle is so damn virtuous? And what would Benjamin do all day—sit in the recording studio in a rocking chair?"

"He's got a new job. Managing a Greek record label."

"Ha. Let's see how long that lasts."

"He's taking me to court, Keithie. He will denigrate me before the judge. I don't stand a chance. You know my history. They'll open everything. Look where I'm calling you from right now. 'Oh Francine's a fine parent, alright, just last week we sedated her after she threw a doctor's chair at her child's father and punched him incessantly in the face, kneed him in the testicles and poked his eyes with her fingers. But not to worry, she spent the night at Bellevue and now she's good as gold."

"Are you serious? Francine... " Keith sighed heavily.

Francine stared hard across the East River, starry vehemence streaked across her washed out face. "Tommaso said he would testify. I can't be accused of being a single parent if Tommaso and I get married, but Christos suddenly doesn't want a 'strange man' raising his boy." Energetic gulps of emotion pushed up her esophagus and came out in the form of tears. "He's my son, Keith. *My* son. I never thought I'd be a mum, and here sits Francine, in the loony bin again, because of how heart broken she is over the prospect of losing her baby. Did you ever think you'd see the day?" She tried to find the humor through her tears.

"Francie, do you want me to come? Say the word, and I'll get on the next flight."

"No, no of course not. I just need to get out of here. My doctor, who I thought was on *my* side, changed my prescription. Apparently I have been 'too emotional' on the previous pill, as evidenced by my 'psychotic attack.' *Evidently* being emotional over your idiot ex-boyfriend trying to rip your son from your arms and move him to another continent is not plausible. So now they will take away my child and numb me to the world, which I suppose is as good an antidote as any. If it messes with me at work—*that* will be the cream on the pie. And if I can't perform at work, I could lose my job. Then I'd be a 'psychotic' unemployed weight on this country, just another crazy without a green card. And *for sure* I'd lose all access to Benji."

"How numb is numb?" Keith asked.

"Who knows? I've only just started them yesterday, so we'll find out. If I don't take them, I will most certainly lose custody. The judge will see that I am 'refusing treatment' and then what?"

"Francie. Darling. I am so sorry."

"Me too." She looked down at the broken skin on her knuckles. "It's not all it's cracked up to be, is it?"

"What?"

She tightened the cord around her bent leg. "Life."

"Francie… come now. It's not said and done yet. Benjamin's still on your side of the pond. And if you have to split custody, it won't be the first time that two separated parents have had to figure out a horribly complicated puzzle, but it can be done. You'll always be his mum. He knows that."

"He's only one," she said through thick saliva. The tears returned with might. "He'll never remember being with me."

"Yes, he will. He will. You will make loads of memories together," Keith soothed. "And he will see you as this unique marvel of a mum, who is more beautiful, more intelligent, more witty, and more genuine than anyone in the world."

"Maybe," she sniffled, pushing the heel of her hand upwards on her nose, the back of her hand beneath her eyes. "Maybe I just can't do it. Maybe they're right. I'm not equipped. I'm not in control."

"Francine. Listen to me. Are you listening?" Keith was suddenly stern. Awake.

"Yes," she said through quickly flowing tears.

"This isn't the Francine I know. When did you start letting other people tell you how to feel? Don't throw down the gauntlet yet. This is *your* life. The rest of us lame kids are just living in it."

"Mm," she muffled.

"Say that back to me. 'This is *my* life.' Say it."

"Keith—"

"Say it, damnit. You woke me up, now say it."

She smiled and tasted the salt of her tears. "This is *my* life."

"Fuck yes it is."

Voluminous tears caught in her throat as she inhaled. "Thank you, love." She whispered into the phone, trying to force herself to stop crying before a nurse witnessed it and accused her of additional psychotic behavior.

"Never change," he said.

She smiled as salty droplets dripped into her mouth. "I miss you," she said. "I miss you so much. Sometimes I think… sometimes I think I shouldn't have left."

He didn't say anything.

"Keith?"

"Yeah. Listen, Francie, it's late. For both of us. Go to sleep. Be on your best tomorrow, so they'll send you home. Lots of love, okay?"

She nodded silently as more tears fell from her eyes.

"Yeah. Right. Goodnight."

LONDON

October 4, 2021

On Margherita's last evening at the Chelsea flat, she put on her favorite dress with butterflied sleeves and a short swinging hem, velvet heeled boots and a layered eye of plums and forest greens. She smiled at herself in the mirror.

So I'm not depressive, after all, she thought.

The five o'clock meeting was with the principal of London's most up and coming architectural firm at their vanguard Fitzrovia studio, which piqued her interest almost as much as Wesley himself. Margherita had been attempting to creatively contact his partner Robert, who somehow appeared the more senior of the two, but with the pandemic and so few people frequenting the office, and his emails being swished off into a black hole by his gatekeeper assistant, she had not been able to pierce the surface. She had even snail-mailed a copy of her presentation to his summer home, with a polite, hand-written note to induce a reassurance of sanity.

Finally she cracked the code on their strategically odd email handles and sent Wesley, the quirkily handsome, half smiling partner, a flagrantly uninhibited note. Her email had been confident, slightly cheeky, and sprinkled with praise—a balance of butter and succinct recognition. As she wrote, she glanced repeatedly at the article recounting Garrett Howard's project which had won them a highly prestigious award. A black and white portrait of Wesley and Robert intrigued her. There was something about Wesley's face that felt so familiar. He was cool-looking—someone who might have been elusive, flippant, and wildly talented in high school and, she must admit, more than a little bit sexy. The article had alluded to a potentially dry sense of humor, and so she took a liberty or two in her introductory letter, in which she respectfully, but directly, asked to meet.

Ciao Wesley,

I hope you are having a great week so far, and congratulations on the LEAF award. It seems every publication is featuring the university hospital in Berlin—one of the most innovative examples of technology and clean energy in a hospital the world has seen to date. Certainly this is the consensus or I would not hear your firm's name at the tip of every architect's tongue from here to Aswan. (I can only assume they are talking about you in Aswan; I've actually not been to Egypt). I yelled-in-text last night at a friend who has yet to watch the documentary about the project (gasp).

I have newly moved my base to London, and I am shrewdly looking for an opportunity in the sort of lion-hearted, progressive, and exotic world that you and Robert have created. Currently, I am putting the final notes to paper plans (I am old-school, like you) on a twenty-four room luxury boutique hotel on the cliff's edge between Santa Margherita Ligure and Portofino. A number of both private and family office investors have shown great interest, and I am hopeful to find the right partner in the not so distant future. I conceptualized and designed the entire project and have lined up my sources and build team. The process has been daunting and exciting and made all the more rewarding by the enthusiasm from everyone who has demonstrated interest in being involved.

This endeavor has made me realize two things: I have always been, and remain, and forever will be, massively passionate about statement-making projects that cross cultural visions and engage a community, and I have talent in this industry to put to good use. Ten years ago when I graduated Yale with the Drawing Prize award, I made a short list of every firm which gave the most flexibility and latitude to their team, with the most variance in disciplines and the least amount of hierarchy; we are, many of us, artists at our core, and artists must have a certain amount of agency. Your firm in particular, with your upcoming projects—from London to Uruguay, and Jordan to Osaka, has an invigorating range of style and vision, with great diversity of input and talent from one project to the next. Suffice to say, I want to be a part of these leaps into the future, both in terms of design output and team culture. As Zaha said, "There are 360 degrees. So why stick to one?" After a decade of work at prestigious firms and private companies, working on every type of project from universities to hospitals to city planning, premium fashion and jewelry flagships and luxury hotels, I know there is just nothing else for me but this world here, and when I see the projects that Garrett Howard produces, well this sounds cheesy, but it lights a fire under my bum.

All of this is to say, it would be such a pleasure to introduce myself in person if your schedule allows. Perhaps your team is looking for someone with my skill set.

Here is the link to my portfolio, and The Villa presentations with digital plans (yikes, no choice here, unless you'd like to meet), in case you are interested in seeing what I've been up to.

My best,
Margherita

Garrett Howard's enormous studio was housed in an industrial building in an alley behind Charlotte Street, a former film factory (as in, the kind that used to be developed). It was the only tenant in the building, a remarkable feat for real estate smack dab in the middle of the metropolis. Within the ancient brick and glass building with its original metal paned windows, a fusion of peace and commotion fizzed.

From the quadruple height atrium, Margherita could hear Talking Heads descending from a group of desks on the second floor, while the third floor, at which she had to crane her neck, was a series of silent heads, and above them, a riot had just erupted on the fourth floor, sending denim-clad, navy-head-to-toe, wide white jeans, and the occasional short skirt making excitable strides toward one side of the floor. They disappeared beyond her viewpoint, and in a few seconds a loud shriek of laughter erupted, followed by more laughter, and Margherita assumed a joke had been played on someone, or a cheeky birthday gift had been delivered with great success.

"Hi, I'm here to meet Wesley," Margherita said to the young man behind the reception desk.

"Of course. What's your name?" He stood from his seat and smiled at her. How very un-New York of him.

"Margherita Ricatti."

As he sat back down to type something on his computer, Margherita watched the four enormous screens on the back of the atrium wall display an inter-connected montage of the now top-ten most watched documentary. There was Wesley, scattered across four screens.

Fuck, he's cute.

"If you'd like to go up to the fourth floor, his assistant will meet you at the top of the stairs," young friendly man said. "Our elevator is out of commission."

Margherita smiled and thanked him as she began her ascent. Good thing for block heels.

"Hi, Margherita?" Wesley's twenty-something assistant held out her long fingers.

"Hi," Margherita huffed, reaching the landing. "Woof. That's a good work-out."

"Ha, yes. We all try to take the stairs every day. It keeps us in shape!"

"Good for the tush," Margherita smiled, as she followed the young lady toward a sitting room lined with architecture monographs and what looked like an extraordinary excerpt from her alma mater's library. She sat down on a cream Mario Bellini sofa with her legs crossed royal-family style and looked around the room. It certainly was a gorgeous office. She could get used to this.

A few minutes passed as Margherita sipped the water she had been offered, and just as she pulled down an enormous book on Gio Ponti, she heard a soft, smooth voice emanate from the doorway.

"I was just bidding on a walnut double dresser. Ponti. That's wild."

Margherita looked up and smiled convivially. She knew some women would approach the networking meeting with a straight face—less smiles, less personality—in order to put their skills and aspirations first and foremost and leave no room for expression. She had graduated from her architecture program with many of these kinds of people, but she felt there was room for both her talent and her personality in her workplace. She knew what she was there for: a job, and/or a meaningful contact, and she would go about it the way she felt most herself.

"Did you win it?" she asked.

He was exactly as she had imagined he would be—only sexier, more charming, more handsome. In his charcoal jeans, white tee, and light pink v-neck sweater loosely pulled over, he appeared cozy and comfortable in his skin. He stood with one hand on a small book, one hand at his side. His arms were long, his hands large, his hair just long enough to seem effortlessly hanging just-so, not styled at all, like he couldn't be bothered. On his feet he wore a pair of Fitzrovia-cool sneakers, and as he raised his hand to motion toward her, the tiny muscles in his wrist visible, she spotted a sliver of a thin tattoo.

"I don't know! I didn't want to keep you waiting." He smiled mysteriously. An energy zipped around the room, and there was that unmistakable excitability of a first meeting with someone bound to be memorable in the 'can't eat, can't sleep' category.

Margherita stood and gracefully bent toward the low sofa to retrieve her purse and her portfolio. She felt his eyes on her as she turned back around.

"Nice to meet you, by the way," he said casually. "My office is right down here. I have a sofa too." His voice was quiet, his demeanor dry but friendly. Something inscrutable. Like he was slightly entertained but holding back.

In his office, a narrow room at the back of the floor with windows onto the alleyway and an enormous table for paper plans and space for one sole 3-D rendering, Wesley sat down on one end of the sofa and Margherita sat at least two rear-end widths away from him. "A Wonderful Life" by Black played in the background on his computer.

"Love this song," she said.

"Ah, yes. 1986. Colin Vearncombe's claim to fame. Written while he was completely broke, you know."

"Dark with a twist. Done so well. Wait, Black's name is Colin Vearncombe?" Margherita scrunched her eyebrows together.

"Ha. Yes. Dreary isn't it?" he said, his eyes traveling from her collarbone to her portfolio held against her chest.

She felt like he was taking in every detail of her.

So many of her meetings in Italy had been so devoid of relatability, of rhythm and chemistry. The men, and once in a while women, with whom she met had the typical Italian attitude of false productivity. They wore the best tailored suits, they frequented the right ski slopes and Sicilian islands, but when it came time to doing deals and signing deeds, they were bunny rabbits in an open field—scurrying toward the edges or scruff brush, looking for cover. They were impressed, they were patient in reviewing the plans, but they weren't movers and shakers. They were entertained by Margherita's acute drive, her fertile passion, her ability to line ducks in rows. Then it was time for an espresso. And nothing would ever feel accomplished. They just didn't get it.

I've got nothing to lose, she thought as she placed her purse on the floor next to her feet.

"So, you're new to London."

"Yes. And no," Margherita said, her legs crossed, her hands folded over her top knee. She tipped her head to one side. "I'm actually half English."

"Ah. Fascinating. Your mum or your dad?"

"My mother. A Londoner through and through, until she became a New Yorker."

"Alas."

"But love it. I absolutely *love* London. So much inspiration, so many leafy neighborhoods. Did you know there are over 900,000 trees on London streets?! I can be walking through mud in the morning and in heels in Mayfair for lunch."

"Yes. Would be very unkempt if you wore your mud to Mayfair. And did you find a place?"

"I'm trying a few neighborhoods on for size. I started near the Boltons. Not intentionally, mind you. Had no idea what 'The Boltons' were until I arrived."

"Oh, wow. Do you live with a Sheik?"

"Ha, no. I don't think I'd be here without a chaperone if I did. Now I'm in Chelsea. Tomorrow I go to St. John's Wood. Then Hampstead."

"All very fine choices. Have you heard of East London by any chance?" He half smiled and regarded her calmly. One long leg crossed perpendicularly over his knee. One arm rested on the arm rest, the other gently bent in the space between them, his hand palm down on the cushion.

"Ah yes but I don't know it very well. My brother lives in Richmond. My mother grew up in Hampstead and Chelsea. What can I say? My blood runneth west. Though, to be honest, Shoreditch doesn't get more pretentious these days. It's just Williamsburg but with different cigarette brands. I'll get there though."

"Your brother lives in Richmond!" His tone slightly elevated, his eyes slightly enlarged.

"Yes, he works in Mayfair. He never goes in the mud in the morning."

"No, wouldn't be right."

"Anyway when it comes time to find my own place I'll probably end up in Tooting so I'm enjoying myself for now."

"Ha." He laughed. "Somehow I don't see you in Tooting."

"No, right? Me neither." She grimaced playfully.

"So, I am immensely impressed by you. You can imagine we get quite a few emails and inquiries and letters…" He gazed up toward his computer. "But yours was compelling. Fiercely. It really stood out."

"Did it?"

"Yes. You have ingenuity. And you personalized it. It made me think of myself when I was starting out. It was the kind of email I would have written."

"I'm glad."

"So, tell me about you. Tell me your story."

"Oh gosh, can we specify? Where shall I start?"

"At the beginning."

"We might be here a while," she warned, her eyebrow raised.

"That's fine. I'm done for the day. Sorry Robert's not here, by the way. I wanted him to meet you but he had to run out to a cocktail thing." Wesley motioned his hand in the air dismissively.

"Okay, well. My father is an architect, so I suppose that's where the interest came from. I went to Yale… undergraduate architecture and expedited masters program… I finished everything in five years. Never took a summer off. Was quite determined to be an adult. Which I regret hugely but that's another story."

He 'ha-ed' genuinely, his eyes not lifting from her face.

"I only wanted to go to Yale. I loved how integrated with design they were. And are. Their programs and disciplines really truly blend together, and there is so much crossover between areas that are fundamental to understanding real life practice—forestry, graphic design, sculpture, fine art, furniture, even philosophy and management. It's like Hemingway's 1920's Paris in New Haven; a true amalgamation of opinions and input and concentrations. Intellectual diversity and the invitation to disagree and be different. There is something intrinsically European about it. And Robert Stern, Norman Foster, David Childs, Maya Lin… I could name the entire alumni but I won't."

"Another time."

"Anyway, so I finished Yale and I went to work for Merrill Bates Lee."

"In New York."

"Yes."

"Very impressive firm. Their urban work ranks high."

"Yes."

"Quite a few Londoners there."

Margherita immediately thought of Jack. "Yes."

"But then you did something completely different."

"Yes."

"Why?"

"A few reasons. Specifically to the firm, it was very hierarchal. Not a lot of exchange. Not a lot of conversation. It wasn't the environment or teaching culture I thought it would be. And then, I was itching for a change. I've always had a strong attachment to Europe, and I wanted to live abroad. There is so much history to breathe in, so many cultures to understand, so many styles to appreciate… Europe has an elegance, a smooth effervescence that U.S. cities do not have."

"Understandable. So you went to Milan. Worked on the hotel project with the Leonetti family."

"Wow, you read my resume! Did I even send it to you?"

"I found it," Wesley let a shy smile escape with a flick of his hand. "Continue."

"So I went to Milan. My father is Italian, born on the Ligurian coast, though he doesn't quite relate to it in the same insatiable way I always did. For some reason, I always felt more at home there. There is a thoughtfulness to it that I don't find as much of in the states. A profound appreciation for its essence. An elegance. I had heard about this ancient seminary right smack dab in the middle of the most glamorous fashion district being bought by the Leonetti family to open a hotel. It's an enormous property; they wanted to make it a meeting place for locals, a community feeling—but chic. A discourse in the middle of the neighborhood, in this untouched perfectly symmetrical structure. You should have seen it. When we pried open the giant doors, dust up to your ankles. Webs from limestone floor to eighteen-foot carved ceiling. Better than a movie."

"This one starring…"

"Oh…" Margherita made an 'oh' with her lips and clasped her hands together. "Judi Dench! No. Helen Mirren. Amy Adams as her eager, high-voice side-irritant egging her along."

"Nothing less."

"So we sent out a brief. The family wanted an Italian architect. I went scouring the earth for the right restaurateur for three F&B outlets, spa partner, fitness center partner, retail partners… the works. It is essentially a 'plaza' with a hotel. They'll have fashion week there, and musical performances, design week exhibitions… it's very ambitious."

"Sounds like you loved it. Tons to sink your teeth into."

"I did. And yes." Margherita said wistfully, smiling with her lips closed. *Until…*

"So what happened?"

She had gotten good at this one.

"I had another offer. In New York." It was the truth, not the whole truth, but he certainly didn't need to know her life's *entire* sob story.

"Ah."

"When the world's most prominent fine jewelry brand asks you to assist with half a dozen new flagships from New York to Tokyo…"

"Sure," he said with a shrug.

"It was a great experience. But very limiting, in the end. I really missed working on different kinds of briefs. Not just boutiques and shopping experiences; I missed the variety." Another truth, but not the entire truth. She was not going to admit that she had been blackmailed into resigning, that her wretched boss had accused her of having an affair with the CEO. Her short-lived romance with Alexandre had been *before* she worked for his company, not during or any time thereafter.

"Completely understandable."

"And then… COVID. My father won the brief for a luxury hotel on Mustique right before everything went to pot, and the two private owners, an Englishman and a Greek, asked him to basically live on the island for as long as necessary, to keep the project moving along. He has a small firm and can easily be there as the only hands-on person. I went with him. I put the plans together for The Villa. Created an investor deck, started researching potentials, lined up my top-line people and resources, a really untraditional freelance team sort of thing, a consortium of diverse talents that becomes a firm once the project is greenlit, and I went to Italy. I presented to potential investor partners, I paid for a handful of necessary permits and licenses… put a little skin in the game. It's a long process, and I haven't given up yet, but I am ready to rejoin a team. I am fully capable of creating this project and breaking ground without a senior partner three steps in front of me, but at the same time, I'm not done learning, and I want to be in the center of the architectural universe."

"You are really something else."

"Is that a good something else?"

"Yes. Favorite modern buildings in London? What stands out to you, in the urban fabric?

She inhaled, licked her lips, and gave it half a moments thought before the passion started flowing. "The London Aquatics Center. The Great Court at the British Museum. That glazed canopy is such a wonder. Can always count on a hit of luminosity there, even on the greyest London day. Crossrail Palace Roof Garden. So lush. To me, London is Norman Foster, what can I say. The Bloomberg building—the ramp and the bronze fins. The metallic petal ceiling that acts as a natural coolant with the lighting coming through the metal pressings like starbursts. Have you ever walked by it at night? The gentle glow. Cinematic. Like a really gripping political mystery starring… Jessica Chastain. Using materials from the UK, supporting local industry. The juxtaposition of it against the Mansion House and St. Stephen Walbrook and the cupola of St. Paul's. How much the space energizes and feeds creativity to those lucky Bloomberg employees. I firmly believe architecture can transcribe feeling; it can *create* feelings, it can harbor them, release them, feed them, cause them to spread… it is a living organism in that way. And the design of that building is just so well-matched for what is going on inside."

"Yes, fine example. And what is your process? Where did you begin, for example, with The Villa?"

"One more," she exclaimed with eyes alight. "I was very excited for the canceled London Centre for Music."

"Driller Scofidio + Renfro?"

"Yes, but also, I really loved Amanda Levete's proposal. That would have been an incredibly moving concert hall. Imagine the goosebumps listening to performances in *either* of those proposed designs."

"A political mess, that was."

"Yes. Anyway. My process. With The Villa, I began with a series of drawings in my sketch pad… scenes and vignettes in and around the property, and as my mind stepped inside that universe, my ideas began to grow and morph slowly but surely into The Villa itself. I draw the flowers outside, I draw a snippet of what a guest might see looking west from a bathroom window, I draw the doorway in the breakfast room leading to the kitchen, I draw a fabulous banquette in the restaurant, or the center atrium with a tree encapsulated in it. The shape of the pool, a golf cart arriving in the driveway after dropping a guest in the port, a terrace with a wet bathing suit drying on the railing… I try to imagine every last detail. Including the music played, in the various areas, at the various times of day."

"So you start with details. With feelings. With the people. And the potential stories."

"Yes. And then that moves into materials, shapes, palette, and then I strategize engineering in, between, and around that, sustainability, energy, lighting… et cetera. All worked in to support the feeling, the people, and the potential stories."

"What is your favorite pen to work with?"

"It depends what I'm drawing!" She smiled widely. "A fast flowing ink nib lets me be vigorous. A point one fiber tip slows me down, which is necessary sometimes."

"And you're here to stay. Going on many meetings I suspect."

"I hope to stay, yes! And many meetings, yes. Though, selective Many Meetings. I have been around the block enough to really know the kind of firm I want to be a part of."

Wesley regarded her with his lips gently parted, his right hand still on the sofa cushion between their two bodies.

"I just think it's incredible, all that you've accomplished. You have a yearning, you go for it. You have an idea, you build on it. You have a talent, you put it to paper. You're not afraid to try things, to take chances. To put yourself out there. To feel the various corners of the room. It's really impressive."

Margherita couldn't fully tell if he was being serious or condescending. She gave a small shrug.

"It's a double-edged sword." She felt she could be candid with him.

"How so?"

"Well. Sometimes I think it would be a lot easier if I didn't have such a fire under my bum. If I was content in one place, doing one thing."

"But that's not you," he said, simply and matter of factly.

"No. It's not." She shook her head with a knowing smile.

"I think you are unique. You should hold onto that. Don't let it jar you."

"No, of course not. I'm rarely jarred," she added.

"So, I really wanted to meet you. I was incredibly intrigued by your note. And I'm really glad you're here. However, I don't have any available position at the moment that would be the right fit for you. We have a pretty tight team, and I'd basically have to add a position, which I don't have the liberty to do at the moment, unfortunately. What I'd like to do is stay in touch. And if something comes up, I'll know how to find you."

She sighed inwardly. With all of his enthusiasm and interest, she was hopeful that he wanted to continue the conversation.

"That sounds great. I couldn't ask for more."

"Wonderful. And again, I'm sorry Robert wasn't here to meet you."

"Next time!"

"Yes. Definitely." He remained seated, and Margherita wasn't sure if she should rise first. It seemed like the end of the meeting. She looked down at her purse, and with one last glance at her lips, he stood.

She exited his office before him, he followed, and she noticed the rest of the floor had gone completely dim.

"Wow! You guys clear out early! What time is it?"

"Yes. Six is pretty average for us."

"In New York we'd be here until eight at least."

"Such is a perk of this side of the pond. Any fun plans tonight?"

"Yes, I'm meeting a friend for drinks. At one of your snobby little members-only supper clubs." Her 'friend' was a first date. He had sent her the address for a club in Mayfair. "Another far cry from New York."

"Yes; they still smoke in those clubs. It's an experience everyone should have."

He walked her to the top of the stairs and took her hand in both of his large palms. "Margherita, it was a pleasure. Stay in touch. Don't go anywhere."

"I'll be here," she said. "Have a great evening."

The sound of her boot heels all the way down the four staircases, besides the quick beat in her chest, was the only reverberation in the old factory.

Outside, she called an Uber to take her to Mark's Club on Charles Street. She needed to transition into date mode, but her mind raced with two thoughts: how much she'd love to work at Wesley's firm and how extremely unavoidably attracted she was to him.

Isabetta Andolini

NEW YORK

May 7, 1986

FRANCINE'S BUTT BONES ached from the hard seat of the court room bench. She looked down at her stockings, which were still damp and catching a draft in the poorly insulated room at Manhattan Family Court on Lafayette Street, a horrible-looking building below Canal. The neighborhood was filthy—dangerous, seedy, and littered with used needles. Homeless people rested against buildings with their legs splayed out before them, or curled up and crying. Heroin and methadone addicts.

It made Francine's stomach flip, and all she could think of was her father. His anxious eyes in the hallway every time she left the house.

What if she had not been so relentless? What would her world be like, if she had allowed her father to continue to navigate her waters on her behalf? Would she have Benjamin? She wouldn't be looking into the hollow eyes and long, emaciated faces of the poor, strung-out souls on the streets of the non-named neighborhood between Chinatown and Tribeca. Their lives over.

Used up.

Her heart pinged with guilt as she stepped over wet legs, hurrying down Lafayette Street. There had been so much traffic, with the weather, and she had exited the taxi on Canal Street and run the rest of the way.

How smeared and bespattered she felt entering the front doors. How already depleted. Sucked dry by the hurdles she had created for herself.

Sucked dry by the rain.

Sucked dry by the meds.

The grey water continued to come down in sheets, she knew it, even if there were no windows in the room. She could feel it in her skin.

She looked toward her lawyer and wrapped her arms around herself, a chill running down her spine. London didn't have so many downpours; it drizzled and it misted and sometimes it came down a decent amount for twenty minutes or so, but then it stopped. New York skies could be so unforgiving—angry, bitter, hell-bent. Unreasonable.

The newspaper that morning featured a front page article covering that weekend's bombing in a West Berlin nightclub, and Francine couldn't get it out of her head. She vividly remembered nights leading up to concerts with Rodney, Bea, Keith, Christos, or whoever she was with; she remembered outfits she wore to clubs and raves from London to Amsterdam, but she couldn't recall anything that happened after the first pill. Those people in that club. That could have been them.

Her life had changed so drastically since moving to New York, since her start at Lazard, and especially since having Benjamin.

Her apartment on East 71st Street had become a life-size crib. Her dresser was a melange of expensive perfumes, baby monitors and old bottles of milk, and for every Bendels shopping bag shoved in the corner of her closet was one from Bonpoint. Onesies with velcro were affixed to Calvin Klein and Ralph Lauren suits, and baby food could often be found on the bottoms of her Manolo Blahniks. Wine glasses, sippy cups, expensive lingerie, Spring Freshscented diapers, dates with personal trainers, dates with nannies... her world as a working mother was a head-on collision. But no matter how inconvenient, mind-numbing, frustrating, tiring, and thankless life with a baby was, she was not about to let her rotter ex-boyfriend take it all away.

My life. *My* baby. *My* choices.

"Have an abortion," Christos had said after the paternity test.

My life. *My* baby. *My* choices.

But once again, her life was out of her hands. Her body, her blood, the choices she had made… lost change in a pay phone. In it went—a little bit of value, a path to purpose—down the swoop, clink, clink, and into a hole of no ultimate significance.

Her lawyer turned his head toward her and pursed his lips. He was a middle-aged, mustached Tom Selleck lookalike, with one fraction of the charm and ten times the hourly fee, but he had a good track record, and according to Francine's careful research, he had never crossed paths with anyone in her world at Lazard.

Finally the judge entered, and everyone stood. She pinched each of her left hand nails between her right thumb and pointer finger, one at a time, like a metronome. Her lawyer looked down at her fidgeting as if to say 'cut it out.' She clenched her right fist around her left thumb, as Benjamin was in the habit of doing, and lifted her eyes to where the front wall met the ceiling.

That morning, she had taken her medication, as she had every morning since the most recent overnight at Bellevue, knowing she was subject to random urine tests, but in that moment, she wished beyond anything that she had skipped it. That she'd be able to use her own might to fight for what was rightly hers.

Motherhood.

LONDON

October 5, 2021

THE DAY AFTER meeting Wesley, Margherita managed to heave her suitcases and a handful of boxes down the narrow staircase of the Chelsea flat into a black cab. As they rounded Grosvenor Place toward Piccadilly and onto Park Lane, Margherita watched the traffic and inhaled satisfactorily, a slight smile on her face. Even with all the boxes and the moving, she felt more energy than she had felt in a long time. London agreed with her.

Her phone pinged in her lap.

Noah: How's St. John's Wood

Margherita: On my way!
Margherita: Must confess something. I met a man I want to see naked and have drinks with and flirt and then see naked
Margherita: And I don't know how to go about it
Margherita: I went out last night on a perfectly nice date, after meeting aforementioned man, and this date guy is wonderful and there's nothing wrong with him, besides the fact that he knows nothing about music, which I suppose is enough right there to nix him entirely. But I have lost interest in the wake of Sexy Man.

Noah: how did you ever go on a date with someone who knows nothing about music

Noah: who is sexy man

Margherita: He is this man, who I had a meeting with yesterday evening, who owns a fantastic firm that works mostly with commercial clients and currently has this fabulous project with a university in Spain, and I knew he'd be handsome but he was much better looking in person and we talked for an hour and God help me I want to jump on him

Margherita: I want to work for him though so there is conflict of interest and also the internet said he married someone in 2015. He wasn't wearing a ring, not that that means anything, but he didn't casually mention her at all which is strange

Margherita: Usually men are a screaming cacophony of 'MY WIFE' when they want to make that clear

Margherita: And I wrote him a thank you and he said "really enjoyed our meeting. Let's stay in touch if something comes up. My number is below."

Margherita: And I want to know, why do I need your mobile number? why did he say that

Margherita: Am I reading into it

Margherita: As I look behind me at my historical comp set, I must say: wow this is all feeling very very very familiar and what the eff is wrong with me

Margherita: but we don't *really* know if he's married, do we

Noah: You're insane.

Margherita: Help

Margherita: What do you think

Margherita: I haven't had a crush in so long, I'm excited

Margherita: I am REALLY excited Noah.

Margherita: do you know what it is like to be numb to the world, without a crush for so long and then boom

Margherita: it's like a man discovering he isn't impotent after years of … impotence

Margherita: I need you to analyze it with me

Noah: Don't fuck up job contacts.
Noah: You don't want people who want you. You only want what you can't have. You are trained to try to change someone, to obtain the impossible. This is nothing new.

Margherita: Yeah yeah but do you think he is interested
Margherita: Why would he not mention his wife

Noah: Because he wasn't hitting on you and respected you as a person rather than seeing you as a vessel to hump...

Margherita: a vessel to hump! Is that a line from Jane Eyre?

Obtain the impossible. She wondered what Noah meant by that.

It was not a horribly long drive from Chelsea to St. John's Wood, but at the same time, it was a very long distance. The two neighborhoods were vastly different, from the style and architecture of the homes to their residents. Margherita's short-let was on the rear side of Alma Square, an adorable horseshoe on the other side of Abbey Road, with lovely homes that felt more humble compared to Chelsea's elegant, stately mansions. Paper hearts were taped in windows and haphazard front gardens with wild and free plantings were the favored style. There was something sweet about it.

The taxi driver, obscenely kind and generous, helped Margherita carry her three suitcases, four random boxes, and five overflowing canvas bags up the stairs into the light and airy flat. Margherita was pleasantly surprised; it looked recently renovated, with a beautiful kitchen and a dreamy bathroom with excellent lighting. The ceilings were high, the trim was tasteful, and the living room's three large windows overlooking treetops on Alma Square were gorgeous and original. She reminded herself not to become accustomed to the luxury of the short lets. Soon she would have to find her own apartment and it would not be nearly as nice.

She decided to change out of her yoga pants, put a little make-up on, and spend the rest of the day sending emails and applying to jobs from one of her favorite hotels in Mayfair, where she had been setting herself up for hours with a cup of tea. The people watching was superb and the Art Deco interiors were on point—not an easy feat. One never knew who one was going to meet.

As she skipped down the steps onto the square, intending to walk through Regents Park and hop on the tube in Marylebone, her phone rang.

"Checking in on you." Her brother sounded breathless, and Margherita could hear sounds of gate announcements in the background.

"Just absolutely loving your city. Why didn't you have me move here years ago? There's a big mess of overgrown bushel in my new neighborhood, growing on top of a white brick wall like a hat the Queen might wear, and the green door says 'Garden Cottage' and I have no idea where it goes. Everything is just so charming or elegant or cool."

"I assume the door goes to the Garden Cottage."

"Don't burst my balloon. It's adorable up here!"

"Don't blow all your precious funds at Panzers."

"Humph. Where are you off to?"

"Oslo."

"Interesting."

"Hardly," he huffed.

"I was thinking of coming over this weekend, maybe spending a little time with your munchkins. When are you back?"

"Actually Alice is meeting me in Stockholm for the weekend. Her mum is taking the babes."

"Oh," Margherita said, a pang of disappointment. She had barely seen Benjamin and his two little ones since she arrived, and she couldn't help but feel it was always her trying to chase them down.

"By the way, I spoke with your dad. I'm going to try to go to the opening in the spring. Ah shit, my flight is about to board."

"The opening on Mustique?"

"Yes. Gotta run. Be good."

"Ciao," she said, dejectedly, as she hung up and carefully crossed Wellington Road. She still hadn't gotten the hang of the whole 'look left look right' bit. Or was it look right look left?

Later, sitting in the library room at the hotel in Mayfair, she sent Wesley a message, like a three o' clock snack, to liven up the afternoon.

She'd always preferred a thrill over a candy bar.

Margherita: May I inquire
Margherita: Have you opened my presentation for the Liguria property
Wesley: You are demanding.
Wesley: I like it.

That's definitely flirting, she thought.

He sent her a photo of her laminated presentation, held open with his thumb, which in that moment of chastity, was the sexiest thumb in all of England.

Wesley: Does this count?
Margherita: Sometimes demanding, yes.
Margherita: No this does not count and you know it.
Margherita: If you're not going to look through it, will you put it on Robert's desk
Wesley: Why Robert?

Margherita: Because I sent it to him at his house in France this summer, and he hasn't looked at it yet. So maybe he will think the world is bringing it round once again for a reason.

Margherita: That sounds creepy doesn't it

Margherita: I found his Luberon address and wanted to be memorable

Margherita: I couldn't find your address in Greece.

Margherita: How much do you regret responding to my email at this point

Wesley: One person's creepy is another person's intrepid. I guess…

Wesley: And one person's regret is another person's adventure?

Margherita: So which camp are you in— regret or adventure?

Margherita: (they're both adventures, I think)

Wesley: Adventure. Of course.

Margherita: That's the spirit.

Wesley: I look forward to it.

She sat back into the leather banquet seat as the suited piano man took his seat next to her.

"Hello again," he greeted her with his usual good cheer.

"Hello again!" she replied buoyantly.

Margherita left the hotel around five, when the staff dimmed the lights in the library and set out candles and cocktail napkins. Maybe the drizzle would stop, and she'd be able to walk all the way home to St. John's Wood through Regent's. The autumn hues had begun to make appearances, bathed in glorious tangerine light, especially in the early morning when everything felt pure and majestic.

She called Noah as she made her way up Marylebone High Street.

"Just making sure you're still coming. Don't you dare cancel on me."

"I'm not coming to London *just* for you, you know."

"I didn't say that, but I'm counting down the minutes. You know how I treasure our time together."

"Ha. Yeah. More than my own niece and nephew do."

"Ah, so you're going to the *country*. Don't get stuck there. Remember, they can't drink martinis yet. An impulsive, adulterous gypsy awaits your presence in the metropolis."

"Is that supposed to be you," he said drolly.

"Oh Noah! I feel like I've been brought back to life. I *love* games. I love this feeling!" She swung the string of her umbrella and let the deadweight contraption ride through the humid air as she passed after-work pedestrians on the sidewalk.

"You love to be bad."

"I love mischief."

"You love to set yourself up."

"I love to feel my heart race."

"You love to be entertained."

"I love a little drama."

"You're afraid to be close to someone."

"You're a dick, Noah. Hanging up now."

Passing Daunt Books, Margherita could not deny the allure of the dreamy window displays, and she dipped inside.

Margherita: I'm thinking of taking myself for a drink at Fischer's in a bit. If you'd like to discuss Gehry.

Wesley: That sounds delightful but I'm on my way to the airport.
Wesley: Another time!

Margherita: Okay. Though the weather really calls for that kind of evening
Margherita: And there is also the risk that my future is becoming closer and closer to this:

She sent him a photo of the blurb on the back of *Miss Pettigrew Lives for a Day*.

> **Margherita:** I'll have you to thank.
> **Wesley:** I do feel like middle-aged governess is some distance away for you yet.
> **Margherita:** You'll tell me if my messages meander to too demanding, or too meandering, I hope.
> **Wesley:** I trust you know your limits.

She ha-ed at the irony as she placed 'Miss Pettigrew' back on the shelf. It wasn't about knowing limits, it was about her habit of crossing them.

How many limits had she bounded past? So many she could hardly remember them all. One of her 'crossed limits' was a few neighborhoods away that very minute, managing a team of architects on his latest project.

Jack, who Margherita had boldly introduced herself to when he was transferred to Merrill Bates Lee's New York office eight years prior, was one of the first men for whom she had fallen hard, with whom Margherita felt mystifyingly close. He was also married, with children, a fact that both stained and peculiarly ignited her. Shamed her and intrigued her; an impossible situation with highs and lows, yet a simple solution to her apprehension towards growing entwined with someone: it simply was not logistically possible.

Margherita scrolled through her WhatsApp chats until 'N' appeared. Another 'limit' she clearly did not know. She clicked the chat open. He had not responded to her most recent message, about putting cold butter in the pie, and for once she did not want to go chasing him for answers.

They had spent over a year in New York sending mixed messages that neither revealed nor completely masked their intentions, an endless, indecipherable dialogue. So many memories still painfully scratched at her—the quantity of messages that went completely ignored, the time she finally let herself sleep over and pass an entire weekend with him before he suddenly sent her home at the announcement of his girlfriend coming over, his refusal to respond to a heartfelt letter she had written, in which, for the first time ever, she had deigned to be truthful about her feelings.

But no matter how many purposefully or not purposefully hurtful things Nick did or said, or didn't say, Margherita went back for more. Maybe she always had been, as Noah said, trying to change reality. Trying to win someone over who felt stubbornly out of her grasp.

NEW YORK

March 15, 1987

"Mommy!" Benjamin's voice pierced through the Upper East Side apartment as his little legs brought him from the nursery room to the living room, where Francine sat on the sofa folding a little jumper into a square no bigger than her face. She nuzzled her nose into it before opening her arms to her three-year-old boy as he catapulted his body into her.

She inhaled his soft hair, the dark, gentle waves—the same color as Christos'—and wrapped her long slender arms around his little body, bringing him onto her lap.

"Look what I found!" he exclaimed, in a mixture of American and English accents.

Francine leaned back into the pillows and allowed a little space to come between their bodies. Benjamin held up the G.I. Joe action figure she had bought him a month prior, which they thought had been lost on a trip to the playground in Central Park.

"Oh! You found G.I. Joe! Where was he?"

"He was, um, he was in the treasure chest, at the bottom, where I hid the Karate Kid, because, um, I thought they might fight."

Francine laughed. "How thoughtful you are, Benji. And were they fighting?"

"No, I don't think so." Benjamin slid down from his mother's lap and walked toward his father, who stood leaning against the kitchen island.

Christos' dark, wavy hair had taken on a few wisps of grey, and he shook it gently out of his eyes as he reached his hand down to touch his son's head.

"Make sure you pack him safely, love, if you want to take him to London."

Francine pursed her lips and felt a hiccup in her throat. She had not been able to stop the incessant tears in the recent weeks leading up to that moment.

"Yeah. Yeah, you're right daddy. Mummy, where should I pack Joe?" Benjamin held the figurine up in the air.

Francine wiped a tear running down her cheek. "Here. Give him to me, love, I'll put him in your knapsack."

Benjamin walked back to his mother. He watched her, attentively, as she found a place for his figurine in his knapsack.

Francine held her long hands over her son's buttery cheeks. "Now remember what we said about the phone?"

He nodded vigorously.

"Any time you want to speak to mummy, you call me on the numbers in the little notepad. Daddy or Aunt Bea or Grampa or Uncle Keith or Uncle Rodney will help you with the phone. Wherever you are, you can always call me. Right?" She held his cheeks as he nodded.

Christos folded his arms in her peripheral vision.

"And you remember about bedtime? If you get scared, you count the sheep like we always do at home, right? And pretend like I'm next to you. But you're getting to be a better counter than me, anyway." She felt two more enormous tears roll down her cheeks.

"Mummy…" Benjamin pointed his little finger toward her face and touched one of her tears. "Mummy, why are you sad?"

"Because, because I love you so much, that's all. And sometimes, when you love someone a lot, more than anything in the world, that love is so strong, it can hurt."

Christos cleared his throat. "I think we're ready to roll, right Benji? You'll see Mummy soon."

Francine cleared her throat and ruffled Benjamin's hair again. "Yes. I'll be in London in one month, okay? Just one month. That's thirty days on your big calendar. Now, you be good on the plane, like we talked about. Always hold Daddy's hand. Don't walk away from him in the airport."

"Francie, I'm going to take care of him," Christos said under his breath. "I'm not going to let him wander off at JFK."

She stood from the sofa and pushed the rumples of her acid-washed jeans down her legs.

"Is Tommaso coming over? Don't want to leave you in such a state," Christos said, uncharacteristically pleasant.

"I'm not in 'a state', you asshole, I am saying goodbye to my baby so he can go live on another continent, thanks to you," she hissed.

"Right. Francine—" Christos ran his strong hands through his wavy hair and inhaled deeply as he watched Benjamin reach up to hold his hand. Christos lowered one hand to hold the boy's miniature palm in his own. "I know this is the most difficult thing you can do. But it's for the best. We'll revisit it in a few years. Like we decided."

"Like *you* decided."

"Like *the judge* decided."

"Fuck you," she mouthed in silence.

Christos rolled his eyes and glanced at Benjamin, who looked up at each of them, one and then the other.

"Daddy?"

Francine crouched down to wrap him once more in her arms, tears flowing freely down her stained cheeks.

"I love you, my little lamb," she said, trying to smile for him.

"I love you too, Mummy. Don't be sad. Mummys shouldn't be sad."

She inhaled his scent once again.

"Francie. We've got to go." Christos held onto Benjamin's small hand as his mother embraced him. Finally, he bent down as well, and he wrapped them both in his arms.

When the two adults stood, she looked Christos in the eyes, those eyes that had entranced her nine years earlier on a humid December evening on the Royal Hospital Road, that had held her captivated for too long. Those eyes that had seen her at some of her most manic moments, as she rode his hips, as she listened to him play his guitar, as he stood in the middle of his apartment like a statue while she threw his belongings at him, furious for his disappearing acts or wandering eye.

He held his large hand out, placed it behind her head, touched her long chestnut hair and brought her in to kiss her forehead. Just as he used to do.

"Francie, don't hate me. We're in it for life."

LONDON

October 11, 2021

MARGHERITA STOOD IN the small queue hugging the exterior of the Ginger Pig in Marylebone. It was after one, and weekday lunch-goers enthusiastically awaited the warmth of the carnage within. It was one of those equalized meeting grounds where all sorts and types could be found at the same place: sneakers of varying degrees of exorbitance, flannel button-downs, tall French men in blue suits, older ladies with market push-carts… the magic of the Pig brought everyone together.

She had been hoping to have lunch with Thayer while he was in town, but he was stuck in back to back board meetings from morning 'til evening in Sloane Square.

> **Margherita:** You're sure I can't tempt you with a sausage roll?
> **Margherita:** You're not that far from Marylebone really. Walk through the park, make a right on Upper Berkeley and keep going until you hear French.

> **Thayer:** Pssh I know where Marylebone is, this is My city. And we have catering, what kind of plebeian board do you think I'm on
> **Thayer:** Petrus by Gordon Ramsay
> **Thayer:** Jesus woman, sausage roll…… !

> **Margherita:** ah us plebs stand in queue's for our scraps

Margherita: they toss it at us like Yorkshire pigs

Thayer: pigs eating pig. Interesting. Always gotta watch your back in this world.

An Italian man approached the head of the queue, wearing a wool, plaid suit of myriad shades of blue from ankle to shoulder.

"I want-ah the raw meat-ah," he said quizzically to the young lady ahead of Margherita. "This? For the raw-ah meat-ah?" he asked in very concerned, broken English.

"Oh, no, this queue is for hot lunch," the young woman said.

The plaid Italian stepped inside the small establishment to head straight to the butcher counter.

"Did he just step in front of the queue? Why did he go inside?" a woman, about sixty, piped up from behind Margherita. "We've been waiting! I am waiting!"

"He just wanted to buy raw meat," the young woman turned her head toward the wronged lady.

"I want raw meat!" the lady behind Margherita exclaimed, and purposefully stepped in front of everyone to enter the shop, with great annoyance at everyone in the small queue.

"I guess you don't get in the way of someone who wants their meat," Margherita said to the young woman in front of her, and a 'yikes' expression slinkied through the queue.

How wonderfully civilized, she relished, as she stood patiently in the October sun, knowing that was the most outrageous drama these people would see all day. No wonder her mother had left London for New York. Francine was desperate for the freedom to be pushy, defiant, and outspoken. Margherita, on the other hand, savored the cultivation, the civility, and the superior vocabularies. If only the sad little park around the corner from the Ginger Pig lent itself more to this crowd, rather than sketchy wanderers smoking cigarettes and staring at her as she ate her chicken, carrots, and potatoes.

After the congenial Polish woman served her her regular lunch, she succumbed to the sad park, which was perpetually in the shade, to eat her warm sustenance.

Thayer: By the by
Thayer: I have someone for you to meet
Thayer: You speak to women, right?

Margherita: Hilarious
Margherita: What if I said no?

Thayer: I'd write a screenplay about you

Margherita: I haven't given up on men just yet

Thayer: I don't think my ex-wife wants to date you, but she does want to meet you.

Margherita: Your ex-wife?

Thayer: Yes. Told her about you. You are two peas in a pod, I think. Meet her. Don't take each other's heads off.

Margherita: I don't understand. For so many reasons. Are you two on friendly terms?

Thayer: Yes, we talk every day.

Margherita: Modern divorce. Or is this just par for the course in England? Another example of your superior civilized behavior

Thayer: How's that pig

Margherita: I'm having chicken.

Thayer: Sending her your contact. Play nice.

Margherita: What gave you the idea I'm some kind of woman hater?

Thayer: None. I think you are scared of women. That's why I think you'd get along.

Margherita: whoa! What an accusation. Why am I scared, Dr. Thayer?

Thayer: Because you don't trust female's intentions, and you fear getting close to someone who might turn on you. Psychological trauma hits differently than with a man, who you can somewhat control with sex.

Margherita: You are bold. That's quite a reach.

Thayer: You were badly bullied weren't you? Harassed even.

Margherita stared down at her phone in disbelief. She looked up into the park, her head cocked. *Did I tell him that?* She couldn't recall, but she didn't think so.

Thayer: Am I right?

Margherita: You're starting to scare me. How did you know that

Thayer: Tell me if I'm horribly wrong. But your mum was a flip-flop of intimidation and unintentional frigidity…steely, triply confident, who spent the majority of her adult life surrounded by men. And you haven't any sisters. You never learned the girly thing. Not a bad thing. My ex is the same. Raised by an absent mum. Hence. The meet.

Margherita: Are you in the park right now watching me

Thayer: Ha no. Having a cig outside this meeting. Back to it actually. Meet Johanna. She's fantastic. You'll enjoy her.

LONDON

MARGHERITA ROSE EARLY and wandered east on pumpkin-clad Alma Square to Circus Road, where she made a right down the High Street and crossed over Prince Albert Road, toward Macclesfield Bridge to Regent's Park. Crimson berries flowered in the hedgerows, late blooming chrysanthemums sang an orange parade between pathways, and as she reached the open fields and dazzling meadows, where she spotted Damien Lewis training with his dog, she took giant gulps of autumn air and soaked in nature's benefactions in the form of enormous oaks, London planes, and horse chestnuts. The day was too delicious to spend it inside a dark library room scanning job posting sites.

That afternoon, after a few moments spent with Degas at the British Museum and a sunbath beneath Sir Robert Smirke's enormous Greek temple inspired colonnades, she took herself for lunch at a charming, quirky little restaurant in Bloomsbury with a four-seat bar, window seats overlooking Store Street, and a retro, Art Deco floor.

Everything looked and felt like October, just as it should. All was still green and clear, but the wind had changed, sending long hair dancing and open coats and trenches running backwards. She had braised fennel and a whole branzino, and sat watching people come and go in groups of twos and threes during their lunch hour.

Full and blissful, she did a little googling on Thayer's ex-wife, a woman who had never quite warmed to California and had mostly remained in London while Thayer did his Hollywood thing.

A WhatsApp message flashed across the top of her screen.

Noah: Any updates here?

Margherita: Oh hello
Margherita: No
Margherita: nothing to report
Margherita: how are you

Noah: What happened to the sexy architect with the possible wife

Margherita: We have been flirting a little

Noah: Are you sure it's flirting

Margherita: The thing is. I don't want the reputation I used to have. (I'm pretty sure I used to have one, I never did a formal survey but I am assuming). On the other hand, I think my personality lends itself to it and it's unavoidable. But there is a small chance he might have a job for me one day.
Margherita: And I have a wild crush on him
Margherita: And I would like to have sex with someone who isn't a vainglorious, narcissistic, collector of admirers named Nick

Noah: ah finally faulting him for something. Interesting change of heart.
Noah: So what's next for this tragedy?

Margherita: What's the tragedy here

Noah: The inevitable messiness that will come from this

Margherita: oh golly I love a mess

Noah: Who makes the first move? I guess he should. You're blatant!

Margherita: He really should
Margherita: I've probably scared him

Margherita: Do you think I've ruined it

Noah: He's either down for it or he's not

Margherita: This is the only kind of situationship that interests me
Margherita: I do believe at this point in my early thirties I have a Problem

Noah: I don't know if you have a problem… however does it serve your long term happiness and life goals. Nothing wrong with having some fun.

Margherita: I know
Margherita: But if it's not exciting I'm not interested
Margherita: And then poof it's gone and I'm alone and I'm like, huh that's weird how am I alone? Well duh
Margherita: blah
Margherita: But for right now I need to have sex
Margherita: So. Priorities.
Margherita: What are you doing

Noah: Watching Golden Girls.

Margherita: ohhhhhhh my favorite ladies

Noah: You're a Blanche. Obvs.

Margherita: I accept.

Noah: what are your plans this eve

Margherita: I have a date! With a woman!
Margherita: This guy Thayer, who I met on Mustique, has set me up with his ex-wife

Noah: confusion.

Margherita: yes that was my initial reaction.
Margherita: he thinks we are kindred spirits or something

Noah: What's her story?

Margherita: I googled. Best-selling author, I knew that before. Grew up in Oxfordshire, so I am prepared to be intimidated with fine manners and accents. She's 41. No children. She and Thayer married when she was 31. I listened to a few of her interviews. Really intelligent. Very pretty. No make-up, shiny blonde hair sort of thing. Cheekbones to kill. Jil Sander-ish wardrobe.

Noah: You're more nervous than if it was a man

Margherita: I'm never nervous to meet a man

Noah: ha. Have fun. Keep your wits about you. Take notes.

Margherita: oh eff you, I can socialize with another female.

Noah: can you though?

Margherita: don't be a dick Noah.

Noah: Kidding. I know you can.

Later, four cocktails deep at Noble Rot's sliver of a restaurant bar in Lamb's Conduit, Margherita recounted to Johanna an abbreviated version of her backstory and professional history. Johanna, dressed in skin tight black leather pants and a low-cut black, silk blouse that showed off her impossibly taut upper arms, was a match for Margherita's usual Larry King-style question asking. It was to be expected; authors tended to be quite curious about other humans. Margherita found Johanna impossibly easy to chat with; she was charming, she had a wicked sense of humor, and she exuded a devil-may-care attitude. Thayer was right; they got on smashingly.

Their conversation wafted into anthropological terrain, all the better to reveal themselves to one another; the cultural differences between Italians, Americans, and Brits—men *and* women, their candid thoughts on modern marriage—and divorce, and their quickly discovered shared fear of the 'Female Clique.' While Thayer was a bit more cerebral and contemplative, Johanna was gregarious and fluid. Margherita found herself laughing until her stomach hurt, multiple times.

"Okay Architect. Tell me: which city has the more architecturally interesting department stores?" Johanna asked, tapping her empty glass with one eye on the bartender and a wink in his direction.

"London. By far. I was in Harrods yesterday, actually. Quick stockings trip."

"I was in Harrods yesterday! Food hall. Stop stalking me."

"Stockings are exorbitantly priced here, FYI, if ever you are buying them."

"I shall bear that in mind. Though I am more of a slacks girl come cold weather."

"You know what I love about London, Johanna?" Margherita took a sip from her down-to-the-cube Old Fashioned and regarded her drinking companion as straight-eyed as she could. "How when you leave Harrods there is a tail-coated doorman who opens the taxi door for you. It's just so much more civilized than New York. We should send American men to England for general training."

"Yes, we are a right bunch of princes."

"Speaking of, I've been doing a lot of reading on your people. I have so much to learn about your country. Lady this and earl that." She swung her hands from left to right.

"Oh yes. What resources are you turning to?"

"Oh just the high prose of Tatler."

"Ah, the Bible."

"I've been catching up on the Bathursts."

"A familiar story of woe. An attractive American leads to the downfall of the entire family."

"Shame on the Americans."

"They remain above water. I wouldn't weep for them. Okay so we are classy—" she raised her eyebrows and cocked her head as if this were a dubious claim "—though you should ride the tube after a Chelsea game and come back to me about that then. And we wear tailcoats. But what is your biggest *disappointment* about London?"

"Oh gosh. I really don't have one. Oh! I do! The lack of bars in restaurants! In New York, the best seat is at the bar. It's fun, it's a better vibe—more energy, more interaction. If your date is dull as nails, you have someone else to focus on."

"How *is* dating here? Dare I ask? I dread dating again. I told Thayer I'll never date. I'll wait for clones, and I'll re-make him with an emotional setting more appropriate for my genetic make-up."

"Ha. What did he say to that?"

"He said he would do the same. Which wildly offended me, of course, because what in God's name is wrong with me?" Johanna smiled teasingly.

"I wish I had someone I'd love to clone, with minor alterations," Margherita said as she acquiesced to another drink.

"There's never been a great love? No undeniably sexy, tan Italian?" Johanna held her glass in her slender fingers close to her chest.

"Oh no, there was definitely that," Margherita admitted. "But big shoulders and phenomenal throw-down don't always come in tandem with snuggling and best-friend Saturdays."

"Best friend Saturdays. Those sound lovely, don't they? We had a few of those," Johanna said wistfully.

"A few? Weren't you married for ten years?" Margherita covered her mouth with the ends of her fingers. "Whoops. I googled. I'm guilty."

"Ha. Don't worry. If you don't google before meeting a stranger, you are possibly more psychotic than not. Well, my darling. Here's the thing." Johanna put her glass down on the stainless steel bar. "Thayer and I... well, I suppose I was the grandest of disappointments to him. Worse than his last film disaster. Not nearly as costly—financially, but very expensive emotionally."

"I'm going to need you to elaborate," Margherita said studiously.

"Did he tell you I cheated on him?"

"No," Margherita said, sending her shoulders backward slightly. Thayer had been silent and reclusive when he first moved in to the villa next door on Mustique. There was no way of knowing how much of his inner tumult was due to his recent career flop or his recent divorce, and the norm was: the man cheats. The cheating man is the road to divorce. The cheating wife was not so widely discussed.

"Yes. I did. I did," Johanna pushed her lips forward and nodded her head slowly. "Penny for your thoughts?"

"No thoughts."

"Oh fuck off."

"Okay. Thoughts. Unexpected? And then, but why? I mean, we fully expect to hear about cheating husbands, why shouldn't we hear about wives doing the same? I have to say," Margherita slouched slightly. "I'm growing to dislike the word 'cheating.' It's so irrepressibly dirty and judgmental; leaves no room for complications or grey areas, which is precisely what every relationship is: complicated and grey."

"Yes. Yes. Yes." Johanna nodded her head again slowly, looking through her glass at the bartender with a tattoo on his neck. "Thayer's schedule has always been hectic. More than half the year he's on location, or in an edit room for twenty hours a day, or location scouting. I expected him to be having affairs left and right. In my head, this was my reality. I convinced myself: that's marriage! That's marriage to a famous movie director! Get on board, Jo!"

Margherita rested her chin in her palm, her elbow on the bar, and watched Johanna thoughtfully.

"But, then, alas. I started going on tours a few years into the marriage. My books were doing well. My name was growing. And I was so desperate to do my own thing, to have my own thing, to not be Thayer Howard's wife. Even the word 'wife'—" Johanna visibly cringed. "I hate it!"

Margherita smiled. "I get that."

"Well, long story short—and I tell you this, free flowing, because Thayer speaks so highly of you, and I am a good reader of people, and I hereby agree you are a person of my court—anyway, Thayer is an enormously understanding and empathetic individual. It's what makes him such a brilliant director; he has a magical way of befriending actors and actresses on a set. They call him 'Dad.' He can relate to just about anyone and still command respect. And he was, most likely, more devoted to me than I ever knew. But I didn't know who I was when I married him, and being in that marriage was like having constant interference whilst I was trying to grow."

Johanna placed her napkin on her lap as a plate of raw scallops was placed in front of the two women.

She continued: "I thought when we first married that I would never find anyone more wonderful—brilliant, funny, kind, in love with me. I thought, this must be my person! And listen, Margherita," Johanna pushed her fingers together in a praying formation, "I'd like to say everyone is going to find their person, but I don't know. I think sometimes it takes longer than usual to find *me* or *you*—*my* person. *Me* as a person. Does that make sense? And that's more important or necessary for some than for others. I didn't realize it was necessary for me until mid-way through our marriage, sitting at dinner one weekend away in Santa Ynez. Horses grazing in the distance. A bottle of white wine on the table. Thayer reading an email on his phone. And suddenly there I was with debilitating thoughts like, 'How did I get here?' And: 'I don't feel like myself with this man.' *That* was terrifying. Then the cheating began. Somewhere to run. Somewhere to hide. And it was all down hill from there."

Johanna picked up a fork. "So that's my version of events!" She smiled, as if to wash away any awkwardness.

"I understand. I've never been married. But I really get it," Margherita said. She pushed her lips to the side in a sympathetic expression. "It's Grey. It's Grey All Over."

"I like to remind myself how truly, and I mean *truly*, wonderful Thayer is. I was really lucky. We could have had a nasty, bloody, public Hollywood divorce. Thankfully, his mother raised him well and he's too classy for all that."

"I think you're really strong to do what you did. To come to terms with that truth and make moves."

"Well, I did cheat on the poor man."

"Yeah, but in a weird way, that was your method of wiggling, sending signals. To yourself, or to him."

"Anyway, tell me about you. Dates. Men." Johanna exhaled and placed her palm on Margherita's wrist. "I know you're not my therapist, just FYI."

"Ha. Don't worry. I am fascinated by other people's relationships. You can talk about it all day. Far more interesting than anything in my life. Actually this weekend I am meeting someone new. We made lunch plans. And he said—I kid you not—he said, 'It's a satur-date!'" Margherita smiled at the waiter as he placed before them a Roast Cornish Hake. The scent of salty capers wafted into her face.

"That's fantastic."

"I laughed out loud when he said it. I don't think I'll ever forget it. A Satur-Date! I mean, I can't marry him. My man doesn't say 'Satur-Date.' Just can't be so."

"Maybe, just maybe, your man *does* say Satur-Date, and maybe *that* is the defining characteristic."

"Anyway. My focus is really two-fold in London: The Villa project. And a new job."

"Right. So this is what Thayer had started to tell me about. This Villa. The illustrious Paraggi Villa. You know I grew up going to Sori every summer. That coastline is very special to me."

"Really?" Margherita exclaimed. "Wow! What a small world!" Sori was a tiny town just a few villages south of Paraggi.

Johanna nodded, smiling. "Darling, we have so much to catch up on."

On the way home, more smashed than she had been in ages, she sent Johanna a photo of a drunk man half passed out on a subway bench in Piccadilly where she changed tube lines, his mouth open, one leg outstretched on the platform, his head leant on the subway tiles behind him.

Margherita: I don't know why everyone hates on Piccadilly, excellent place to pick up guys

Johanna: The old sit/lay/stand

Margherita: slay

Johanna: It was lovely to meet you kiddo
Johanna: Hope Saturdate goes well

Margherita: Nice to meet you!

Johanna: Maybe I should ask my ex-husband to set me up on real dates. What a fine matchmaker he is.

Margherita: It actually makes a lot of sense.

Johanna: Though I suspect my therapist would think it a rotten idea.

Margherita: Therapists don't need to know everything.

Johanna: I feel like mine is watching me sometimes. I'm not religious, but it's like when I go in there, I have to make confession. She just knows I'm holding something back.

Margherita: Try going to a man. Maybe they're less prying.

Johanna: ha we are bad women.

Margherita: Don't you wonder how many male therapists have sex with their patients who become wildly dependent and attached to them

Johanna: All the time, I wonder this.

Isabetta Andolini

Margherita: Someone should write a book. Do you know any authors?

Johanna: I only write murder mysteries. So actually this would be quite the plot. Will get on it. Have a good night love! And send me that presentation on The Villa! Will take a good look through this week. Am v curious

A few days later, while Margherita walked to the takeaway sushi across from Panzers, she felt her phone vibrate in her pocket.

Johanna: So the lunch date was not a repeater I assume

Margherita: sigh no
Margherita: is there an inbetween 'Nice, Nerdy, Non-Chemistry, Successful' and 'Fun, Funny, Sexy, Charismatic, KindaBadNews' because I'd like to find this unicorn

Johanna: oh good luck with that
Johanna: have you ever watched the Crazy Hot Matrix? We need the female equivalent of that to be made.
Johanna: It's a staunchly accurate piece of academic research

Margherita smiled to herself. Though they had only just met, it felt so good to have a female in her matrix who clearly understood where she was coming from. Thayer had done her a real kindness. Maybe he really did have a talent for making people feel less alone.

NEW YORK

November 28, 1988

THE COPY MACHINE jammed as the last of the salespeople hustled to the corner of the floor for the morning meeting.

"Fuck, fuckity fuck!" Francine banged the side of the enormous machine and bent down to peer at its opening. She attempted to pry open one of its doors, then another, but nothing led to any clues.

"Trade figures, Francine. Get your ass over there." Jeff eyed the machine with satirical pity, then hovered his eyes over Francine's short black skirt and textured stockings before he flipped his straight hair from one side to another en route to the meeting.

Francine watched his flat bum in disgust as it receded toward the windowed end of the open plan; the 28th-floor trading room was crawling with versions of white-collar, Harvard-educated, Connecticut-raised Jeff's, whose condescension and annoyance toward Francine and her short skirts and her quick-hire sans business degree made some days at the firm an eye-roll marathon. It took all of Francine's might not to bite their heads off.

Thank goodness for the manageable ones—Carl, Frank, Sam, Eddie, and Nan. She had made her crew, the other traders and salespeople with whom she could have a laugh, swear all she wanted, grab an expensive lunch at Michael's or a hot dog from the bodega, share a cab from Upper East Side apartments, or sit next to on the express bus. She had found her own mini world, and it felt damn good.

Isabetta Andolini

It was the Monday after the American trade numbers for that November had been announced, and its 25% drop in one month was enough to send ripples of simultaneous edginess and elation through every floor of every building on Manhattan's southernmost tip. Friday had ended with an enormous steak dinner at Gage & Tollner, Francine's first venture across the bridge, where fax machine menus were all the rage and a seventy-two-year-old southerner named Edna was the new head chop in the kitchen.

Francine huffed at the uncooperative machine, leaving her report on the previous Friday's biggest currency deals from the London office stuck somewhere in the innards of the electric world as she joined the edges of the meeting. In truth, she didn't yet fully understand the banks' play moves with the price swings and she had a hard time keeping up with some of the more advanced algorithms and strategies.

"No set of trade numbers has been so pivotal in the financial markets..." Francine could see half of Bob's face and a corner of his pin-striped suit as he stroked his forehead and addressed the group. "$13.2. That's one of the biggest deficits I can remember in all my years working in this racket. London, Frankfurt, and Tokyo traded the shit out of the dollar from 8:30 a.m. Friday. I went down to the FX floor. Never seen anything like it. And a lot of money was made. And that's great. But let me tell you, since October's crash, the currency world has turned into one big crapshoot. You hear that Eddie? You wanna share your bagel with the rest of us or can it wait? Ya got cream cheese on your face." Bob motioned his fat finger at poor Eddie, who sat leaning into a desk taking big bites of a well-smothered sesame bagel. "We need more skin in the game. And we need to hedge more. The volume of trade in the currency markets is exploding, and it's just going to continue. These poor shmucks couldn't keep up with orders on Friday. A fuckin' frenzy. Royal bank breaking records." Bob narrowed his eyes as he turned around to face the enormous view of Brooklyn outside the floor-to-ceiling glass windows, the light of the day bright and blinding.

Francine inched forward among the layers of co-workers and found herself next to Jeff, who peered down her silk blouse. She eyed him viciously and followed his gaze, but he was unperturbed.

"Best day for the dollar in a long ass time. And that's great. But everyone needs to be aware of how finicky it is. There's a herd instinct out there. Don't be a lamb. Keep sharp. The dollar has fallen below what the value suggests it should be. You know what this means. High interest rates. Inflation. These are things to watch out for."

Her mind began to wander. She wondered if Tommaso would be at home when she returned that evening. He had moved in that summer, after they had spent every weekend together at a rented house in Litchfield County, Connecticut, where Francine had taken to a vegetable garden while Tommaso cooked up flavorful, simple Italian dishes. They'd spend the day reading under an enormous oak tree, making love with the bedroom doors open to the fields, and falling asleep under pitch black skies. Patient, handsome, fun-loving, quirky Tommaso had been her rock throughout her pregnancy, her first years as a mother, the trial and the difficult days and nights after Benjamin's departure. He had sat with her in almost all of the meetings with her lawyer and at every court appearance. He'd even accompanied her to some of her check-ins at Bellevue.

To Tommaso, her illness was part of her package, something which he sympathetically viewed as completely out of her control, just as his hair was black and his skin was fair. It was the way they'd come into the world; not much could be done about it. He had fallen deeply in love with her in a way that reminded her of her father with her mother. He was attentive without being irritating, and she felt both indebted and intrinsically attached. She did not think she deserved him, especially when she thought about how much he did not know—how many stories and tales from her past she kept hidden under her belt—but she had grown so entwined with him, she could no longer imagine her world without him.

More than anything, if she was to have any chance of winning her son back, she needed Tommaso at her side—a showcase of a healthy home, an employed and non-psychotic father figure. Wild and dramatic and corrupt was no longer her life. Sure, they had parties and went to all of the fabulous restaurants—Tommaso was effortlessly charming and Francine remained the spotlight of the evening—but the nights of hard drugs and waking up in other countries was officially behind her. Whether that was due to her regularized pill regimen, the physical distance from her London life, Tommaso's support, or motherhood, she would never really know.

Until her most recent London trip, all had been, for the most part, smooth sailing. If there had been any hiccups between them, the culprit was undoubtedly Francine. And sure enough, their fight the previous evening had been entirely Francine's fault.

———

Before her flight back to New York, upon arriving at Keith's in Kensington to retrieve Benjamin, she had felt something like sticky feet seeing her best friend and her little boy sitting side by side on the front step. Benjamin pushed a stick at a fat worm while Keith looked on.

"What do we have here?" Francine asked as she approached them, trying to minimize the urge to nestle into the space between Keith's knees, to feel his familiar warmth wrapped around her. She hugged her arms into herself, pulling at the ends of her blazer's velour sleeves.

Keith looked up into her eyes and opened them exaggeratedly, as if to imply the excitement of the worm.

I miss you. Nothing feels the same without you, she wanted to say.

When he gradually stood and reached out his arms in a thick cable-knit sweater, she nuzzled into his chest like a mini dachshund.

"Hmmm. There's my Ruby Tuesday," he said, kissing the top of her head.

"Mummy look! I'm helping it to the grass."

"I see that, love! Good job. Does it have friends in the grass?" She looked down at her son with her arm wrapped around Keith's back.

"This worm has never had a better friend than Benjamin. He's kept it company for the better part of an hour."

"Well, to each their own," Francine said, looking up at Keith.

"When is your flight?"

"Tonight. I have to get Benji back to my dad's. He's staying for a week while Christos is in Greece." Francine raised her eyebrows at 'Greece.'

"Ah. Right. I could've dropped him?"

"But I wanted to see you," she said. "Where's whatshername?"

"You know her name." Keith rolled his eyes.

"Sure. Where is she?"

"Sweden for a few days."

"Oh." Francine was secretly glad.

"That's a shame you're leaving tonight. We could have caught up. I'm making a roast. Benji could have found more worms."

Francine tilted her head back and Keith looked into her eyes. He brushed a few errant hairs from her face and smoothed her long hair behind her back.

"Maybe I can change my flight. I don't have to be at work until Monday…"

"Well, don't change it on my behalf. Up to you." His voice was soft and he continued to look at her with his Keith eyes. Kind and comforting and home-like.

"No. It's no big deal. I haven't spent real time with you in ages. Let me make a call."

He smiled. "Okay. So we'll keep the kid for another day?" Keith said loudly enough for Benjamin to hear.

"I can stay here?" Benjamin shot up on his feet and shouted.

"Just until Sunday eve, love, then you go to Grampa's," Francine said as she rumpled his hair and went into the house to change her flight.

She would call Tommaso the next day to let him know. She had no idea he'd planned to surprise her at the airport. She hadn't thought it would be a big deal.

"You could have had the decency of telling me, Francie. I was worried sick," Tommaso said when she returned Sunday evening.

"Don't scold me like an insubordinate child," she said as she stalked past him down the hall.

"More like an inconsiderate adult. I'm in this relationship too, you know. A little thoughtfulness and communication goes a long way." He followed her into the bathroom where she opened the medicine cabinet. Dozens of orange pill bottles glistened in the light. She reached for one and eyed him in the reflection when she closed the cabinet door.

"Okay. I heard you. I'm sorry. I wanted to spend an extra day with my son. And my best friend. You know, I left a whole life in London."

"You're there all the time, Francie. And that was your choice, need I remind you. You say it as if it's my fault."

"My choice. My choice. Yes. Damned if it's not my choice. Damned if it is."

"What does that mean?"

"Your life is nowhere near as complicated as mine, Tommaso. You wake up, you feel fine, you go to work. No children. No other world pulling at you from another continent. You have no stress. You have no fears. No medicine cabinet filled with uppers and downers and hundreds of pills that numb your insides or make you see double or have you pretending all day like you're *not* nauseous."

He huffed and leaned against the bathroom wall with his arms crossed.

"Right. You're the only one entitled to complaints, fears, doubts, bad days… It's all about you. The rest of us glide right along, everything comes easy to us, none of us have any problems that amount to anything compared to yours."

Francine rolled her eyes and walked into the bedroom, where she vigorously pulled back the comforter.

He stood in the doorway, watching her.

"What?" she scoffed, standing next to the bed.

"What do you want, Francie? Do you want to go back? Do you want to find a job in London and go live with Benjamin over there? Tell me. I need to know."

"You know I'll never have the same career over there. I've worked my ass off, I'm doing brilliantly. I'm not going to throw that away. I'm not giving up just because things are imperfect. I've known imperfect for a long time. It follows me wherever I go. Benjamin will move back to New York in a year or two. When the court revisits it."

"And what if he doesn't?" Tommaso asked, more gently.

She glared at him. "Of course he fucking will."

"Don't swear, please," he grimaced.

"Of course he *fucking* will."

"Is it me? Have I done something, Francine, that I'm not aware of? Or do you take this self-absorbed attitude with everyone?"

She got into bed and ignored him, her head facing the window overlooking the rear garden.

"Right. Ignore me."

"I'm knackered, Tommaso, give me a break," she said into the pillow.

"Fine. I'll give you a break."

When she heard the sound of the front door open and close, she sat up in bed. She hadn't expected him to walk out.

On the trading floor that Monday, standing in the assemblage of her co-workers, Francine found herself wondering how self-absorbed Tommaso honestly found her to be. He had never alluded to anything like that before, and he had admittedly been the 'giver' in the relationship. Why had there never been some sort of warning? She needed to be better, or when it was time to re-visit her guardianship status, the court would view her as a single, working mother with a mental disorder—potentially catastrophic.

If she were being truthful to herself, she needed Tommaso by her side for her own sake, too, to be strong and steady. In all of her life, she had never been alone, never without a safety net, even if it was not always to her liking. Whether it was her father, or Keith, or any of her friends, she had always known that there was a stopgap nearby. Without one, she might spiral like her mother.

Every decision she had made as an adult was somehow connected to *not* ending up like her mother. Deeply ill, alone, horridly depressed and disintegrating—emotionally, mentally, and physically—by the moment. Until it was too late. Until the end looked more appealing than the present.

That was what it had come to for her mother. The ending shone brighter than the present. A full pill bottle was all it took.

Maybe if we hadn't left her, had been Francine's first thought when she'd received the news of her mother's suicide. Surely it had been her father's as well.

LONDON

October 18, 2021

MARGHERITA EXITED THE taupe-colored brick building in Curlew Street just before six and looked up at the unusual black metal windows as she wound her way toward Maltby Street. It was a cool neighborhood—industrial—if not a little cold, and it reminded her of where Alexandre had worked in Milan. She had not, truth be told, harbored any feelings for him after she had ended their short-lived affair, and she certainly had not so much as grazed his hand on the business trip to Paris that had been the beginning of the end of her most recent life in New York. The last she had heard, he had exited the jewelry company and was writing his 'memoirs' in Normandy. Pretentious as ever.

At the narrow wine bar in Maltby Street, she found Noah immediately, recognizable in his ubiquitous black trousers, navy AMI tee-shirt, and navy blazer. Los Angeles nonchalant met Bermondsey trendy, the same outfit he had been wearing since they'd met nearly ten years earlier. She hugged him flamboy-antly and he let a smile slip in tandem with an exaggerated eye roll. Margherita greeted the bartender and got comfortable in her high-top seat.

"What can I bring you?" the bartender asked, nodding toward the hand-written chalk menu on the wall behind him.

Margherita eyed Noah's glass.

"Merlot," he said.

"Uhhh… I'll try the I Vicini Grignolino, please."

"Fantastic choice. Lucid, spicy… distinctive, a very unusual grape." He returned with a glass.

"You just described her precisely, minus the lucid," Noah said to the bartender, taking a sip of his merlot.

"Ha. Funny." Margherita slid the glass closer to her. "That's lovely. Thank you."

Noah sneezed into his arm and Margherita gave him a look of horror as they both waited for the second sneeze to come around. She sprayed his hands with her disinfectant.

"What is *that*?" Her face belied exaggerated repugnance.

"Just allergies. Either that or one of the plebs on the plane gave me their cold. Don't worry, I took like three tests."

"I love how it is now totally acceptable to be completely, openly *revolted* by anyone who coughs or sneezes. I used to be like that before the virus and everyone thought I was a bitch. But now it's just commonplace," she said with a shrug.

"You're still a bitch." Noah sniffed his palms and made a face. "Is that lavender? Uck."

"This is my first time in Bermondsey. I like it. Wait. Second time. I came here once for a meeting. I think. When I was maybe twenty-three." She readjusted herself on the stool.

"This isn't technically Bermondsey. It's St. Saviors Estate."

"Oh bah humbug let me be 'hip' tonight. It's a *natural* wine bar, after all."

"So? How was your interview with the Grosvenor Hotel Group?" Noah asked, emphasizing the name of the company for a false sense of star-struck.

Margherita shook her head as she took a sip. "The woman who interviewed me was terrifying. She'd ask me a question and then interrupt me after I was speaking for just ten seconds, with a facial expression as if I had interrupted *her*." Margherita shivered and rolled her eyes to the ceiling as if to shake off the memory. "She hated me."

"I'm sure she didn't hate you. She knows nothing about you."

"She asked me why I started a project with so much vigor and then walked away from it. And I really dislike that question, because it's an unfair presumption. I didn't just 'walk away.' And to tell a potential employer that one must pay their rent and buy food to live is not particularly becoming."

"Why not say you're trying to sell the plans to another architect, that you aren't walking away but that you've laid the groundwork for someone to carry on with it?" Noah asked. "You're only thirty-one, it's not exactly shocking that you're struggling to get such an ambitious project off the ground completely on your own."

Margherita leered at him with furrowed brows and pursed lips. "Don't ageist me," she glowered. "There are plenty of girls my age or younger that have done far more." She shrugged her shoulders. "But I clearly set myself up for this. Whatever the reason, I 'walked away.'"

"It's not over yet. Maybe this woman was in a crummy mood. Maybe a brief she was working on for a year just got passed on. Maybe she'll call you tomorrow for another meeting. And dating? Are you dating? What's the latest?"

"Nothing. The only guy I've met in ages who makes my heart race is probably— though not for certain—married."

"You just want what you can't have."

"That's not always true. I don't want you?" She smirked.

"Maybe date a single guy and pretend like he's not interested in you. And he'll become more attractive."

"Blah. Doubtful approach, but I'll try it. You can't *decide* who you are wildly attracted to. I am fairly certain that was a two-way feeling. There was some kind of really intense chemistry in that room. I definitely felt it. And I know he felt it too."

"How do you know, Miss Humility?"

"Because we've been texting."

"Oh my God, you're nuts. You are walking danger."

"Nothing inappropriate!"

"You met him on a job interview. It is inappropriate already."

"But he didn't offer me a job…" She tipped her head with a raised eyebrow.

"So now what?"

"I don't know." Margherita placed her finger nail between her teeth. "I haven't had sex in a *very* long time."

"That is the umpteenth time you've said that in weeks. Can you go screw something already so we can all move on with our lives?"

She continued to hold her thumb nail between her teeth as she stared into Noah's face, lost in her own thoughts.

"How do you know he isn't just entertaining himself… Maybe he has no plans to cheat on his wife. Maybe you're getting excited over nothing."

"Firstly, we don't know for certain he *is* married. Secondly, the periodic table is a snooze without putting two of those buggers together. Chemistry only exists when it's two sided. And it's pretty hard to ignore…"

Noah bludgeoned a large green olive and brought it to his mouth.

"So you're going to track him down for some sort of sordid, explosive combustion and then what?"

"How's that Grignolino?" The bartender nodded toward Margherita's glass.

She pursed her lips and raised the corners of her mouth in an innocent smile, nodding with her eyebrows raised.

Margherita turned toward her friend with a studied expression. "Do you remember *any* of the elements on the periodic table?"

They sat in silence for a moment.

"Zinc?" Noah guessed.

"The only thing I remember from chem class was skipping it."

"For what?"

"To get drunk and have sex. Duh."

"Well, good thing you got over that phase."

_____

The next day, at her favored hotel in Mayfair, Margherita sat in the library room and sent The Villa presentation to Johanna, who pinged her within thirty minutes.

> **Johanna:** This is absolutely incredible
> **Johanna:** You need to do this. Let me give this a think. I know a few people. But I think you really need to enchant a big name architect. Have them fall in love with the idea so that they can go to work for you. They have relationships—previous clients who might be interested. They know the right people with investment prowess.
> **Johanna:** Have you presented to many firms in London?
>
> **Margherita:** No not really
> **Margherita:** Most of them are completely tied up in their own projects... legitimate briefs/existing contracts come first
>
> **Johanna:** The cost of the villa is not absurd. It's the cost of the renovation and the hotel management that requires a bigger wig. But you could have a private buyer who isn't involved in the hospitality part of it right? Someone who just wants to own it but doesn't know a thing about hotels?
>
> **Margherita:** Yes, as long as they don't become one too many chefs in the kitchen...
>
> **Johanna:** So even better if they don't cook at all.
> **Johanna:** I'm going to have a perusal through my Fancy Contacts.
>
> **Margherita:** Thank you for that. I imagine you have many Fancy Contacts.

Johanna: Yes loads. But sadly to them I am now a member of their 'Divorced Contacts' and that really gets in the way of my former 'Power Player' status.

Margherita: oh fooey fuck them. Everyone's divorced. If you're not divorced are you even living

Johanna: Now you're talkin.

She thought about Robert and Wesley's firm. Maybe she should try her hand again at Robert; he was the one she had originally attempted to contact, and he seemed to be the relationship man of the two, while Wesley was more 'hot, brooding quiet guy' behind the scenes.

Her emails to Robert had gone unanswered, but she had found him on Instagram. It was a very modern and gutsy approach, but this was 2021, not 1953; the world was a casual place. He was not even ten years older than her. He could be her brother.

Margherita messaged him on Instagram.

Margherita: Ciao, I realize this isn't the most professional or kosher approach but you have not responded to my email, and I would be so very appreciative to have your feedback on the presentation I sent you, which I hope was also left on your desk a few weeks ago. You once said in a lecture at Harvard (this coming from a Yale girl, mind you) that sometimes you had to be the loudest person in the room and there was no shame in that if you believed you could make the room a better place. Here, here ☺

She sat back in the leather banquet seat and held her thumb nail between her top and bottom front teeth.

A few minutes later her phone pinged and she jolted toward it with excitement.

Robert: You have gumption, I'll give you that.

Robert: So sorry the lecture was not at Yale

"Ha," she said to her corner of the room. *So he's got a personality.*

Margherita: As am I!

Robert: I'll look at your presentation. Things often get lost on my desk, and I'm not in the office this week. Send it to me again.

Margherita: Gladly. And thank you, honestly. I don't normally stalk across all mediums at once.

Robert: I hope not; this is not America, Margherita. We have class.

Margherita: ha. That made me laugh. It's true. What can I say, we're a bunch of vulgar, lowborn unsophisticates. But we have gumption!

Robert: Send me a message on my mobile so I have your contact. It's in my signature. Responding to your email now.

Margherita: that was too easy Robert.

Robert: Be weary, I might still report you to the queen.

She waited for his email to come through and entered his number into her contacts, then proceeded to send him a WhatsApp.

Margherita: So I've done it. Please don't report me.

Robert: The police are on their way
Robert: How long are you in London

Margherita: Good time to dye my hair then
Margherita: Indefinitely

Robert: What color are you going for

Margherita: Red, obviously.

Margherita: in all seriousness I'd love to hear your thoughts on this proposal. You are the Jack Nicholson of this world; your black book knows no bounds, and this project has massive potential.

Robert: Wesley mentioned he was very impressed. Let's chat soon. Would like to hear more about it before I consider sharing with anyone.

Margherita: Sounds fair. When shall we chat?

Robert: I leave for Hamburg tomorrow. Back next week. Will be in touch.

Margherita twisted her mouth.

Yeah, right, she thought.

Margherita: Shall I hold you to it, or is that too much?

Robert: I suspect 'too much' weighs heavily in your repertoire

Margherita: Just dotting my I's

Robert: I won't forget you. If I do, ping me. In the meanwhile, well done on the stalking. A good hoot is always welcome here.

Margherita: This is not the nickname I was going for.

Robert: ha. Speak soon.

NEW YORK

November 7, 1989

"FRANCIE, WANNA MAKE twenty-five cents on HP? I'm betting they miss earnings."

Francine looked up from her white sheet, one hand on the phone, one hand scribbling away. On the line in Dallas, her biggest client had just made a fortune on Energy Ventures and was determined to buy six hundred more shares at an enormously inflated price.

Carl, the trader sitting directly across from her, widened his eyes in impatience. "Whaddya say?"

Francine held up her finger and stood from her seat as she jammed the phone back on the receiver, tearing her white sheet from its pad. "Sure," she nodded toward Carl as she approached the new head trader at the end of the long desk. Dozens of conversations between starchy white shirts rattled off as she passed.

"The Dow is going to close at least 25% ahead…"

"How much did you make on that trade?"

"Harry, I've got a really good deal for you but it's not gonna last…"

"Who wants in on a hedge against L.A. Gear?"

Francine stood before Pat, the new head trader swept from Lehman after a garden leave, her fingers grazing the desk and her smirk as proud as ever.

"Whaddya got Francie?" he asked, his hand on his beard as he watched over the desk from a standing position.

"Energy Ventures."

"Houston? Small oil and gas outfit?"

"Yes. A total gusher. Returns up to 550%. The teachers fund just bought six hundred more shares."

Pat's jaw twisted into a satisfied grin as he nodded deliberately without looking her in the eye. That was the best she was going to get from Pat, and she took it.

She spun on her heel to return to her seat, stopping at Jeff's desk to let him know the good news.

"You're the best, Francie!"

"I thought I was the best?" the salesperson next to her whined.

"You're only as good as your last trade." Jeff gave Francine a wink. "You coming to Fraunces Tavern tonight?"

"Can't tonight."

"Hot date?"

"Yes, actually." She raised her shoulders playfully as she sat down. Hot date with a new Bottega bag at Bergdorf's. Who knew when her next good trade would be?

That evening, after she hung up the phone with her father in London, who had just spent the afternoon with his rambunctious four-year-old grandson, Francine grabbed a yogurt from the fridge and nestled into her sofa with one of Benjamin's miniature jumpers. She stretched down the length of it, listening to the frenetic city sounds outside the windows. Tommaso was visiting his sister in Carmel, and though he had invited her, she didn't want to take time off work.

In the corner of the living room, a mini play-pen sat forlornly empty, and she brought her son's jumper to her nose to inhale the sweet scent. Apple sauce and gentle shampoo and his own honeyed aroma. Though it did not provide any physical sustenance, she needed it more than the yogurt.

Sighing heavily, she reached behind her head to the phone and its cradle on the side table. Keith didn't pick up after two tries, so she dialed Rodney.

"Do you know what time it is?"

"Is that your standard greeting now?" Francine asked.

"Oh. Francie! I thought it was George." Rodney expelled a great sound of vexation.

"And who is George, pray tell?"

"My latest. Not my greatest."

"Hmm…"

"He was supposed to be here an hour ago. I made arctic rolls."

"Is that code for something I don't need to know?"

"No, you dirty bird, it's a dessert."

"Still potentially sexual."

"Well, true."

"Anyway, what else is new? Besides George's disinterest in your arctic rolls."

"Maybe I'll call Bea. I'll have too many leftovers otherwise."

"I don't think she'd be interested either, darling."

"Francine—they are *dessert*. I assure you. I'll post you the recipe."

"Don't bother. My fridge looks sadder than mummy's did." Francine's eyes lingered over her empty, quiet kitchen. Not even a single banana on the counter. Scenes of her mother's basket of decayed pears crossed her mind, and she suddenly missed her so much she felt a lurch in her chest.

"You don't need to cook. You're in Manhattan. With an expense account."

"True."

"What's new with that pratt father of your child?"

"Nothing at all. I'll be in London next month. Tommaso is coming with me actually. That shall be interesting." Francine smoothed her palm over her stomach. Each day she ran her hand over it, terrified of its growth and already planning how she would hide it at work.

"Oh wonderful! I adore your Italian. That hair. What a dish. You really lucked out."

"Yes. Yes I did."

"I've never seen a more natural father."

"Yes, yes I know."

"Speaking of. Have you spoken to Keith lately?"

"Not for a few weeks, why?"

There was silence on the line and Francine waited with eyebrows suspended.

"Hello…" she said.

"Well, maybe he should give you the news."

"Spit it out." Francine sat up, forever nervous at the mention of any sort of 'news' in connection with Keith after the accident.

"Well. Don't tell him I told you. He might want to tell you himself. But it's too late now that I've opened my giant gob. He told you about Ulla, right?"

Francine rolled her eyes. "The gorgeous Swedish girl ten years younger than him, yes I heard about her."

"She's due in May."

"Due for what? Her GCSE exams?" Francine retorted.

"Come, Francie. Let's not be childish. You should be happy for him."

Francine clenched her jaw and bore her eyes into the corner play pen. "They've only been dating a few weeks. How can she be pregnant? Is she going to keep it?"

"They've been dating a lot longer than that and you know it. He's happy. She seems sweet. They will make a gorgeous baby, that's for sure. And who will be a better father than Keith? Look what a dear he is with Benji."

Francine's heart throbbed so forcibly, it was practically in competition with the incessant sirens on Lexington Avenue.

"I have to go. Enjoy your dessert. Love to Bea."

She smacked the phone onto the receiver and tried deep breathing for twenty seconds with her fists clenched.

Deep breaths. In. Out.

Oh this is bollocks.

KISS MY JAGGED FACE   337

In the bathroom she swung open the medicine cabinet with a clang and reached for a valium, which she swallowed with two gulps of Nolet Reserve Dry before taking off all of her clothes and climbing into bed.

Three minutes later she shot her eyes open and cringed. How much longer could she self medicate like that with a fetus growing in her womb?

They were due only months apart.

Ulla. *Ulla.* She hated her. Keith would make a life with someone else. The idea made her see red.

LONDON

October 20, 2021

MARGHERITA WANDERED DOWN Well Walk toward the Heath, "Big Cat" by Wild Beasts calling the pace through her AirPods. She held her gaze straight ahead as a beagle and its owner passed on the narrow sidewalk. The wooden gate on the periphery of her right eye was half open; it always was.

It doesn't matter. It won't do anything for you.

As soon as the beagle passed, she turned around.

Oh what difference does it make, she thought, as she crossed the street to walk through the gate and descend into Gainsborough Gardens. She slowly walked in and out of the historic community garden, admiring each of the stately homes on the oval crescent. A vibrant Japanese maple was planted in the driveway of her mother's childhood home, the precise address of which she had discovered while organizing knick-knacks in Francine's dressing room a few months after the funeral, an antsy day that had sent her mindlessly rummaging through her mother's belongings.

Margherita stopped in front of the brick home and shamelessly stared through the windows. Not a lick of movement. John Le Carré had been across the crescent, though Margherita was not sure of his exact address, and according to Francine, he used to have her over for tea. She would choose a book from his bookcase and pretend to read while she watched him write. He let her be in the calm and quiet sanctuary of his private library, a very different environment from the indecorous scenes her mother was making across the garden.

She walked slowly around the oval and then back again before exiting through the shortcut to the Heath, just across a main road. On the other side, a young woman with chestnut hair had just stepped into the tall grasses of the path leading to the park.

Margherita's heart leaped nearly across the road itself.

Mom.

She waited impatiently for two cars to pass before she dashed across and onto the path, running over thick roots and beaten-down weeds before coming out onto the open fields. Margherita swept her head right and left, but the chestnut hair was gone.

Hand on her chest, as if she could control the vigorous swells, she heard a cat-like whimper exit from her own mouth. She bent down over herself, hands on her knees, hair touching the grass, and kneaded her fingertips into her forehead.

Stop it.

Behind her, the sound of cars on the two-way road. How many times might Francine have crossed that road? The thought made Margherita's stomach flip, and she welcomed the distraction of a man in a Barbour coat and knee-high wellies, his two standard poodles sniffing the tall grasses gallantly.

Standing upright again, she tipped her head backward to face the gloomy sky, its outward expression an overlapping of whipped mashed potatoes. It was one of those typical London days of drizzle that came and went from morning to night. She had never seen her weather app rattle off so many notifications. 'Rain will start in your location at 15:32.' 'Rain will stop in twelve minutes.' 'Rain will start in your location at 16:01.' She debated turning the notifications off but was mildly charmed by the sheer, ridiculous quantity of them, so she let it be.

I'm lonely, Mommy.

She trudged through the wet grass. Thoughts of Francine drenched her all the way through.

She wanted to have someone to write to in that moment, to ask if he fancied an evening of take-away and an old Robert Redford film, or maybe something silly like *Shampoo* with Goldie Hawn and Warren Beatty. Maybe they would debate the choices, exchange a few witty but familiar messages, and she would know that, wet as her boots were and white as the sky was, there would be a warm body who loved her waiting at home.

Maybe she *was* being inappropriate, like Noah said. Maybe, like her mother had once clipped, a mischievous flirt might be cute at twenty-six, but not so much in her thirties.

She decided to try a different approach with Wesley. The verdict was still out on his marital status, and she wanted to know once and for all if she was, as always, the toy, or if he was simply more aloof than he realized.

Margherita: Three songs for you.

Margherita sent an assemblage of tracks. Nina Simone included.

> **Wesley:** 'Baltimore' is great. Can't believe I've never heard it. How are you?
> **Margherita:** It's a goodie.

Enervated, she slogged through the slippery grass toward the Downshire hill exit, her boots covered with wet strands like a linoleum floor after a haircut.

> **Margherita:** May I ask you something
> **Margherita:** to temper anything that might potentially need tempering. And this might be a wildly inappropriate question, excuse that, but... am I sending (mostly blameless) meandering messages to a married man

Wesley: definitely blameless
Wesley: and please don't worry
Wesley: as you can imagine—it's complicated

Margherita: So… that's a yes

Wesley: I sense you know the answer. 'Yes.'

Margherita sent Noah a screenshot of the chat.

Noah: he hasn't heard Baltimore by Nina Simone?

Margherita: god I love you
Margherita: thatsssss the most important bit
Margherita: I should be so turned off by that alone

Noah: yeah seriously. Shameful.

NEW YORK

June 1990

ONE NEW YORK Plaza was particularly windy that early June morning. It was nothing compared to the winter months, when the plaza would set up ropes for workers to hold onto as they made their way to the front door, lest they be knocked over by the gusts coming off the river, but it was enough to blow Francine's new short hair-do into disarray.

She ran her hand over the front of her long, wide shouldered, Chanel suit jacket. The spring-weight tweed had come in handy on the unusually chilly day, her first in the office after a three month maternity leave. She hadn't slept the previous night; the electric currents in her chest and anxiety over what her new stature might be as a 'mother of two' had given her night sweats. She couldn't stop thinking about how differently she would be treated. How differently she might feel.

"Francie. Look who it is! How you doing?" Carl jumped into the elevator with her, his ubiquitous paunch below his suit jacket.

"All good, yeah. You all right?"

"Yeah. Not a great week, as you saw. Everyone's got recession on their minds. The jitters. I keep telling 'em, it's gonna be nothing. No big deal. Little dip. Bound to happen. Hey—speaking of. Was thinking of buying some gold today. You want in?"

Francine watched the needle climb above the elevator door. "How much?"

"Twenty-five cents."

"In it on a skinny, hell of a way to start."

"Hey, gotta jump back in somewhere."

Francine huffed as the doors opened and the cacophony of the trading floor hit her like a gust of sea air tracking the stern of a motor boat in the Caribbean Sea.

She smiled widely. Back to her niche.

"Fine, Carl, but you're buying the drinks at Des Artiste Thursday."

"Deal!" he yelled as he strode across the enormous floor, beneath the overhead international clocks, through the hundred or so traders and salespeople—sitting with three small monitors apiece—and cutting through the never-ending phone calls, the yelling, the shouting, the laughter, the grievances, and the lightning-speed scribbling.

"Francine, welcome back." Jeff took a sip from his Dunkin Donuts coffee and eyed her as she sat down at her desk and logged into her computer. The shimmer of the jagged diamond band she had bought herself after her civil wedding to Tommaso caught her eye. It was the first time she had witnessed her hands at work with a ring on her finger.

There was more to prove now. A wife. A mother.

She regarded Jeff and his minging styrofoam stained cup with a curt nod.

"How's the new kid? What's his name?" Jeff badgered on.

"*Her* name. She's gorgeous. Now bugger off, the market's about to open."

———————————

Later that evening, as Tommaso put Margherita down for the night, Francine took the phone onto her bedroom balcony overlooking her neighbors' rear gardens. She scratched her neck restlessly and proceeded to dial long distance. Her phone bill was enormous but she could afford it.

"Hello?" a woman's gravelly voice answered, miffed from the start.

"Oh. Hi. I… it's Francine. Ulla?"

"Yes?"

Francine chafed at her irritability. "Right. May I speak with Keith please?"

"It's very late, Francine. I do not know if you are aware, but we have a newborn."

"I am aware, congratulations. I'm sure you're zonked, not used to motherhood. Don't fret. You'll get the hang of it. Just want to speak with my best friend of twenty-three years? Thanks."

She could practically feel Ulla's convulsions across the Atlantic.

"Francine…"

"Ah! There he is! Gosh it's become rather gruesome getting through to you. Aren't you allowed to answer the phone yourself anymore?" She gripped the metal banister and watched an older woman in the garden kitty-corner to her sit down on a bench with a cigarette, staring at her peonies.

"Francine, it's after midnight. You could have woken Lisabet. You can't call this late, come on. You know that."

"I know. Don't be upset. I can't call you during the day; I'm at work. And I have a baby too, you know." She spun around toward the doorway leading to her bedroom that she shared with Tommaso, where beyond it, in the small nursery, a three-month old Margherita was hopefully asleep. Her mind went to Benjamin in London.

Two babies, she thought.

Keith yawned into the phone and Francine turned back toward the rear gardens, grasping the cradle until her knuckles turned pale buttercream, stifling the desire to blurt out how much she missed him. How much it bothered her to hear Ulla answer *his* phone.

"How is Margherita?"

"She is delicious. Tommaso is in heaven. If he could breast-feed, I'd be redundant."

"I'm too tired for your self-indulgent pity, Francie."

Harrumph. "That wasn't very nice," she said, ever so slightly bruised. On her left hand on the banister, the western sun bounced off the jagged ring. She stared at it. "How are you doing? Besides tired."

"I am… in love. Completely blown over. Ridiculously unprepared. I'm a father. This tiny little pink creature with enormous blue eyes watches me like I am an alien, and I look at her like she is an alien, and every minute that I leave the house I feel like I am missing out on the most momentous twinkles of my life."

"Twinkles."

"Francie, it's… it's the single most strange, most unnerving, most frightening and humble thing on the planet."

"You're going to be a brilliant dad."

She stood in silence, looking down at her ring, thinking about Benjamin. Of all of the minutes that she did not spend with him. Of all of the momentous twinkles she was missing. The date for her full custody appeal was approaching, and in combination with a new infant, she felt more edgy and uneven than she had in a long while. There were moments, such as when Margherita would wail her little head off in the middle of the night, when Francine desperately wanted to pick her up in her crib and scream in her cherry-red face. And there were moments when she desperately wanted to crawl into bed with her mother in Hampstead, or with Keith in Kensington… anywhere where she could be coddled. Where she could hide and no one would expect anything of her.

Her chest contracted and she covered her heart's surface with her outstretched hand.

"How's Tommaso?" Keith asked, always polite.

"He's well. Yeah. How's… Ulla?"

"She's well. Tired, of course. Understandably. Lisabet hasn't been sleeping since we got home from hospital. I try to take most of the night shifts. The weather has been fantastic, so I sit with her on the porch, and the night air seems to calm her down a bit."

Francine could hear her friend smiling through his words. She pursed her lips and scratched her forehead.

"Keith?"

"Yes."

Do you ever wonder? she wanted to say.

"I'm really really glad for you."

"Thank you, love. Listen. I've got to go. I promised Ulla I'd run her a bath."

"She can't run her own bath?"

"She can. Be nice. We haven't had any one-on-one time in two weeks, and—"

"Right. Okay. I'll let you go."

"Francie."

"Yeah."

"I miss you, Ruby Tuesday."

"Yeah."

"Give my love to Margherita and Tommaso."

"Yeah."

"Come. Don't give me that. Say goodbye."

"Goodbye, Keithie."

His beautiful voice sang a Stones line softly in her ear.

Her throat hollowed, like an empty pipe had suctioned it.

She sang back, quietly, watching the old woman eye her peonies forlornly.

When she hung up, she remained on the terrace, studying her hands. The jagged ring on her left. Her mother's serpent ring on her right. She pushed her cuticles down and entwined her fingers, lapping one thumb nail over another. Over and over. Then the sound of a screaming baby.

Hers.

Life is unkind indeed, she thought, as she turned toward the door into her bedroom, the sounds of Margherita's wails growing louder as she approached the nursery.

But Tommaso was already there, reaching into the bassinet

and lifting her ever so gently, like the porcelain doll that she was.

Francine silently stroked her own neck as she watched her husband soothe their daughter. She turned toward the living room and sat on the sofa with her legs curled beneath her, staring out the window idly, thinking about the chasm between her old life and her new life—how many tetherings she had permanently linked herself to on both sides, how impossible it had become to enjoin them—and wondering where in the world she belonged.

LONDON

AFTER AN UNEVENTFUL day sending out personalized letters, applying to jobs she was not interested in, and ignoring a stern email from the lawyer in Italy looking for outstanding payments, Margherita opted for the tube over walking home in the drizzle. She felt tired; the peak of the Wesley excitement having been reached, the inevitable disappointment of a crush-gone-nowhere having been felt, her credit card approaching its maximum, and no breakthroughs or sheer luck as of yet, all contributed to a fog layer of exhaustion.

After a scalding hot shower (Beauty Reel Queens ignored: Bad for the hair! Bad for the skin!), she lay on top of the bed's plushy comforter in the St. John's Wood flat and would have liked to read a book, if only there had been a bedside table with a lamp on it. The ceiling light was too bright and invasive, even with a dimmer. It was the only grievance she had with the flat. That and the upstairs neighbors who had late night sex.

She was in the mood to chat mindlessly about both the tedious and the profound with someone who would make her laugh and make her think.

Nicky.

Since her arrival in London, plentiful distractions and energetic, positive moods had rendered him temporarily less important. For a few weeks, if she came across something intriguing or funny or completely random, she desired to share it with Wesley—a change, a welcome respite from wanting to share the bits and pieces with Nick. She wondered why she felt compelled to share at all. No one in her family had the same reoccurring compulsion. Francine was too hard and fast to share much of anything except razor-sharp opinions and peppery cocktail-hour banter. Tommaso was more an elicitor of news than a giver of personal thoughts, and Benjamin was a freezer door that required a hard pull to release its suction closing.

Beyond the spontaneous sharing of unrelated moments, there was the undeniable addiction to the *other* category of thoughts that immediately prompted tingling sensations. Even from afar, even across an ocean, the pulsating warmth was only a mind's image away.

Just thinking about him sliding her toes into his mouth one by one drove a purposeful breeze through her tummy down to her groin.

It hadn't escaped her, however, that she had not heard from him. Even after his unexpected, out of nowhere messages.

She gave in.

Blame it on pulsating warmth, she thought as she began a new chat.

Margherita: You haven't said a word.

Nick: Hello.
Nick: About what

Margherita: Are you serious
Margherita: About your most recent messages

Nick: Oh.
Nick: You haven't said a word either.

How much could he possibly mean what he said, then? If this is the level of interest in this topic? It was déjà vu from their first exchanges. The dance. The 'I said something but I'm not going to elaborate until you say something.'

Margherita: Do you know the song "Baltimore" by Nina Simone
Nick: Of course.

Humph.

She waited for him to approach the bench. Explain himself. Tell her *why* he had been silent. But of course he didn't say anything.

Margherita: Have you ever lived a London autumn?

She sent him a few photos from Regent's Park that morning, where burnt orange leaves covered the promenade like a sheet, and the parallel ombre trees grew lighter and brighter at their ends, like dozens of stars oozing glow. Charcoal-colored benches lined the Broad Walk, more elegant than Paris, and stretching out from the North-South promenade, narrow gravel paths led to noble weeping willows that appeared painted into the setting. Margherita couldn't resist a wander over to the central pond, where long-necked swans skimmed the water closest to the tall grasses, a smattering of maple leaves in their path. She sent him a photo of the glimmering water as a swan cleared a passageway through.

Margherita: The colors this morning were so romantic.
Margherita: So literary-like.
Margherita: Everyone was just walking on their way to work or jogging along like nothing special or extraordinary was happening around them, and so really, this must be the place.
Margherita: I'm in love.

He sent a few unsatisfying heart emojis.

> **Margherita:** What's new with you, Chatty Cathy?
>
> **Nick:** ha sorry
> **Nick:** I am slightly overwhelmed at the moment.

She was already frustrated with herself for instigating the exchange. Their chats were so one-sided, as they had always been, unless the subject was their own dysfunctional 'situation-ship.' Never did he ever volunteer anything about his life or what he was up to, how he was doing, or anything at all to build off of for even a bare-minimum catch-up. Never did he ever reach out to ask her any of the above. And yet, she was somehow convinced that there was potential comfort in talking to Nick, that eventually he would crack and they would have the friendship she had indoctrinated in her head.

She turned her Spotify to shuffle, beginning with "Bird's Lament" by Moondog, and lay her phone down next to her. On her side, hands layered beneath her cheek, she stared blankly out the window at the newly trimmed trees on Alma Square. Ready for winter.

> **Nick:** I didn't want to take up real estate in your head
> when you've just landed in London. I wasn't sure if
> you even wanted to talk about it.

At least he acknowledged it, she thought.

She inhaled deeply and bit the inside of her cheek, her jaw tense. What she wanted was for him to care enough to *not care* where she had just landed.

> **Margherita:** how would you know if you didn't ask?

Maybe if we ever, EVER, spoke about anything in-person...

In all fairness, she had never actually, substantially responded to him. But it felt, after years of being sidelined, like nothing more than bullshit. Maybe he was lonely or bored. It was the same knee jerk reaction she had when he first admitted to not being able to get her out of his head. *Well where have you been then?* As much as she wanted him to say the things she wanted to hear, she knew that she could never believe him. The hurt could not be erased; the drawn-out confusion and its layered damage had been done.

If he can't support what he said, it was a shallow confession.

Nick: You are in London. I am in New York.
Nick: We each have our own worlds going on.

A maddeningly weak and pathetic excuse. She decided to flip the switch. If she wasn't worth so much as a phone call, what should he care?

Margherita: Right.
Margherita: Well, in my world, I've been trying to be "well-behaved."

Nick: meaning?

Margherita: Can I be honest? No judgment.

Nick: of course.

Margherita: okay here goes
Margherita: I met a man, who is married, and nothing has happened. And it won't. Because he is married, which I just learned, but I am pretty sure I also knew it all along. And I was feeling quite guilty about it, which is new, because I don't think I ever felt guilty before. I think I always approached this kind of situation with an 'oh well, that's life/relationships are complicated' sort of attitude. But something feels like it's shifted, and it's unsettling, because one minute I am excited

KISS MY JAGGED FACE   353

and love the high and the next I feel a little noxious. Like I'm making a fool of myself and more aware of it than ever.

Margherita: And what's strange is I can't tell if all of this is a positive thing, like am I "growing up" or is this a strange negative, because it means I'm sort of losing a confidence I once had, and that is a little disheartening.

Margherita: I feel like, and this sounds maybe really pathetic, but that flirtatious devil-may-care girl was so much of my spirit, and without it, I'm almost.... A little lost? Like I don't recognize myself. Does that make any sense? Blah. Don't answer that.

Margherita: I would go back to therapy but I find them all terribly judgmental.

Margherita: And in addition to all of this, I'm feeling very sexually frustrated. I can't concentrate on anything. All I think about are very seductive little scenarios all day long, and it's becoming quite challenging Nicky.

Nick: You've no reason to feel pathetic.

Nick: I don't think you are losing your confidence, I think you are gaining different perspectives, which is something most people don't have the bandwidth to do. And it doesn't mean any one of them is particularly 'right' or particularly 'wrong.'

Nick: Relationships are complicated. People are complicated. Don't view it in so black and white a lens—it's not a positive nor a negative, just a period of reflection.

Nick: You can still be flirtatious and spirited but with different goals, whatever goals you feel comfortable with at the moment.

Nick: Maybe ask yourself why the shift? Or why now.

Nick: And I'm sorry to hear about the frustration.

Nick: I wish I could be of help..

Margherita: Yeah. Thank you ☺ Appreciate you listening to me whine.

Margherita: Do you think you could be a friend for a few minutes?

Margherita: And walk through a little fantasy with me?

Margherita: I'll start…

Nick: You're not whining.

Nick: And go ahead. I'll pick up where you have blanks.

Margherita: Okay. Thank you.

Margherita: This is what I'm imagining…

Twenty minutes later, she felt a not-inconsequential release of pent-up energy and lay on her side with her phone next to her.

Nick: I'm pleased you feel safe with me

Nick: To be authentic

Margherita: Ha are you

Nick: Yes

Nick: It's an honor

Margherita: Shut up

Margherita: I really wonder what you think of me

Nick: I think really good things of you

Nick: A brain

Nick: A beautiful girl

Nick: With good taste

Nick: And big dreams

Nick: And the confidence to actually get out there

Nick: And a delicious sexual appetite

Margherita: I don't do this with anyone else, you know that

Nick: I know. That's why it's an honor.

Margherita: I feel bad you've gotten the brunt of my 'need a moment to vent' messages lately

Nick: Don't feel bad at all
Nick: I like the directness
Nick: And realness

Margherita: Okay good ☺
Margherita: Will you promise me something
Margherita: Will you tell me if you're seeing someone seriously enough for my directness, on this last subject in particular, to no longer be appropriate

Nick: I 100% will.

His response was too quick. It scratched her like a nick from a passing branch. His random confession not even two months prior felt all the more shallow.

She rolled over onto her stomach, propped up on her elbows with her thumb-nail between her teeth.

Margherita: It's probably not a good idea that I send any of these messages at all is it

Nick: ?? But they're great

Margherita: I think in a weird way you're like my crutch.
Margherita: And it's not so smart for me.

Nick: I suspect
Nick: That I'm an outlet
Nick: For thoughts
Nick: At times when they're bubbling up
Nick: And you want to share them
Nick: And explore them
Nick: And it's quite sexy
Nick: I doubt it's holding you back from anything else
Nick: Or blocking anything
Nick: Is it?

Margherita: No

Yes, she thought.

Isabetta Andolini

Margherita: But it feels one sided

Nick: Oh

Margherita: Maybe that's why after a few years I still want to talk to you… I barely know you. So it hasn't gotten old yet.

Margherita: But still I don't like the feeling of, I want to share something with you randomly and it's a one sided feeling

Margherita: That's not a friendship—that's not an anything really

Margherita: I don't want to want to share things with you. I want to want to share things with someone who wants to share them back. And yeah maybe it does unknowingly block me in some strange way. Because I know you're there somewhere in the universe to receive my bubbling up. So maybe no more, I think. Which is something I've tried to do before I know but maybe I try again

Nick: well

Nick: I suppose I am just quite consumed with my day to day life

Nick: and what I need to figure out that's right in front of me

Nick: and I AM here, as it so happens

Nick: somewhere in the universe

Nick: and I will always receive your bubbling up, if you want to bubble this direction

Enough. She knew it needed to stop. In the same way she knew it needed to stop all those dozens of times before. The temptation to be buoyed and dipped—whiplashed, even—had been a hypnotic force in the face of her grief. Distraction it had been, that first year back, but savior it was not.

You are bold, you are courageous. You don't need a crutch. You don't need to bubble up to anyone. Bubble to yourself.

"You are bold," she said out loud as she lifted herself from the bed and stood before the mirror.

The magnificent sun the next morning was like a lifeboat over the evening's thoughts; it gave her an uncanny sense of independence from the situation as she ventured out toward Regent's Park.

You don't need a crutch. You don't need a crutch.

But at about 6 a.m. his time, back in New York, he wrote again.

Nick: I don't feel it's so one sided.
Nick: I just don't know what to say sometimes.
Nick: I never know where we stand
Nick: it seems to always shift

Well that's not good enough, she thought, as she smiled widely at the dogs off-lead, running into the blinding morning sun.

Hours later he wrote again.

Nick: Do what you feel is best for you
Nick: But I dislike the thought that you want to cut yourself off from me
Nick: I don't strive for that

What do *you strive for?* she wondered.

Isabetta Andolini

NEW YORK

December 27, 1991

"TOMMASO! CAN YOU answer that!" Francine shouted over her shoulder and bore her fingers into her temples in an attempt to concentrate on her enormous monitor. Working from home was a ridiculous notion which she did not support, but Tommaso had guilted her into a full week off, especially with both kids there for the holidays.

"It's for you." Tommaso appeared in her office doorway, Margherita on his hip.

"Bloody hell." Francine pushed her chair toward the telephone at the far reaches of her expansive desk and extended a cashmere arm.

"Yes?"

"It's your father," she heard Tommaso say as he returned to wherever he had come from in the new townhouse. Hopefully unpacking the boxes that had been sitting in the upstairs den for a month, filled with his architecture books he'd promised he would organize.

"Oh. Daddy. Sorry. Was just trying to squeeze in a few hours. I hate losing so many days in a row." She leaned back in her chair and held her fingers over the cord. "What are you up to?"

"Francie, darling, you have to give yourself a break sometimes. Benjamin starts a new school next week. Why not spend some time with him? He could be nervous. He's not used to New York kids."

"I know. I know. Giving it a rest soon. What did you do today?"

"Keith just left. He brought over a crumble he made with Lisabet. Adorable little creature. Blonde as a blinding sun. Keith is glowing just as bright."

"Oh? I didn't know he was going over to see you. That's nice." She wrinkled her nose. "Was Ulla there?"

"No. No Ulla."

"Good."

"Oh, Francine. Don't be childish. There's no reason to dislike the woman."

Francine muttered to herself and scornfully cast her eyes over the framed photo on her desk: her and Keith on the floor of his Kensington living room, high on something, laughing, limbs entwined.

"Anyway, I wanted to say hello and tell Benjamin that I am sorry his gift is late. I put it in the post two weeks ago. I hope it arrives today. Poor lad."

"Oh, don't worry. He'll survive. I think he's watching a film; shall I fetch him?"

"Yes, yes, put him on."

"Daddy. I wish you had come. You could have flown over together. And then you wouldn't have to be alone this week."

"I am fine! Greta left just yesterday; I wouldn't want *her* to be alone, would I? And this time of year is lovely for long walks in the park. All is cheery and calm."

Francine nodded slowly and quietly, studying her nails which needed a manicure. "What film will you watch New Year's Eve?"

"Oh, I haven't decided yet."

"Nothing sad."

"No, no of course not."

"No more Auntie Mame."

Her father sighed. "Gosh, how many times we have watched that. Still not as many times as Mummy."

Francine puffed her lips. "Yeah. I miss Mummy. All that baking she would do. Like a sugar storm."

"Yes. She was frightfully productive this time of year. I miss her too. Now go on, get my grandson on the line."

"Okay. I love you."

"Love you too, my big city girl."

Francine placed the phone down on the desk and rose from her chair.

"Benjamin!" she shouted as she walked down the long hallway, still unpainted. They had moved in before the final bits were done; eager to get out of Francine's too-small apartment on seventy-first street.

In the downstairs den next to the open kitchen, a nearly seven-year-old boy with his father's dark locks and his mother's emerald eyes rimmed in gold, sat on the rug with one leg beneath him and one leg bent, one small hand resting limply on a toy truck and an open-mouth expression toward the large television screen.

"Darling, Grampa's on the phone and would like to speak to you."

Benjamin didn't look up.

"Benjamin. Can you come say hello to your grampa? He's calling all the way from London just to speak to you. A very important phone call. Man to man."

Benjamin moaned, eyes glued to *Duck Tales.*

"Come, three minutes. In my office. Won't be long." Francine held out her long fingers and waited for her son to rise from the floor. He ran ahead of her toward the hallway and down its length. His tiny legs like a paddling duck.

How big he was getting.

Family Court had been a seemingly endless process, but the judge had finally ruled in her favor, thanks to her stable relationship with Tommaso, their marriage, the birth of Margherita, and the townhouse large enough for two kids. Francine had established that she could create and maintain a healthy home environment for her children, with a committed partner and a good report card from her doctor at Bellevue. Benjamin would remain with Francine and Tommaso in New York, though Christos had threatened to weasel him away somehow, determined to send his son to an English boarding school. Ironic, because he had never even attended university.

In the meanwhile, Francine had one more extended limb on her side of the pond, and she felt both satisfied and fearful; there was a small part of her, if she were honest, that had been comforted by Benjamin's immersion in her London life. Her father, her friends, her culture. She had often wondered: Was that a better world for him? What did she know? She was just his mother. Just the body that built him. Did that mean she knew what was best for him? She couldn't help but doubt it, in the crevices of her fickle mind.

LONDON

October 24, 2021

As MARGHERITA SAT at the glass table in the Alma Square flat, scrolling through job postings in one tab and copying, pasting and personalizing outreach emails to potential investors in another, her phone pinged an Instagram message in response to that morning's Primrose Hill sunrise.

Jack: You're in London?!

Margherita: Facticity!
Margherita: You have a fine city
Margherita: Octobering has never been so glorious

Jack: Not bad is it
Jack: How long are you here for?

Margherita: I'm not sure
Margherita: Technically I suppose I am legal

Jack: Ah the chummy realization of being legal somewhere

Margherita: how are you

Jack: fraying at the seams sometimes
Jack: the job is killer
Jack: I need to do something a bit easier

Margherita: nooo that's no fun
Margherita: a little fraying does you good
Margherita: what are you working on?

Jack: I am split three ways between a new terminal at Lisbon airport, a bank client's new London tower, and a performing arts center with enormous community grounds in Lausanne. Exhausting.

Jack: what about you?

Jack: I saw you were back in Italy for a few months. Working on a new hotel project?

Margherita: Wow! All sounds incredible. Bravo.

Margherita: ah yes… italy. It's on a bit of a pause.

Margherita: So here I am in London Town. In need of a job.

Margherita: do you require an additional designer?

Jack: yes

Margherita: Don't tease a girl

Jack: we can work very closely together

Margherita: or closely but from a distance

Jack: nooo

Margherita: Yes I presume it would be the most productive combination of physical selves

Jack: shall we go for a spiffing lunch?

Margherita: I like spiff

Margherita: Can we take a cloaked-wander down the Broad Walk afterwards? It is at its peak. Would add great enchantment to our spiff.

Jack: I haven't been up there in ages.

Jack: You're talking to a below-Thames man

Margherita: You are deprived.

Jack: I am. I see your photos every morning. You appreciate London more than we Londoners do.

Margherita: As to be expected.

Jack: TBD on lunch.

She smiled to herself but shook her head. Yet another blast from her past creeping up on this post-COVID year. It was as if in her off-the-grid-ness, her heart had played with the chronology of romantic interests and was throwing them all back at her in quick succession. Try, try again!

She had not seen Jack in nearly eight years, but their familiarity was a rarity so obvious, so constant, she would not deny herself one innocent spiffing lunch.

NEW YORK

April 21, 1992

"Fuck. Fuck!" Francine bent down to scoop up the pills that had spilled all over the marble floor.

"What happened?" Tommaso peered into the bathroom.

"Nothing! I snapped the lid off a new bottle and they exploded everywhere."

"Oh God, Francie, let me help you. Can't have Margherita waddling in here popping—which ones are they?" He looked up as he crouched down to push dozens of cream-colored pills toward one central area.

"Valproics."

"Hmm."

"I'm late."

"I'll do it. You go."

Francine stood. The door to her medicine cabinet was wide open, and bottle after bottle after bottle stared back at her. She shut the door and caught herself in the mirror. Long hair in need of her colorist. Creases beneath her eyes. Thinning lips. A single crease in her forehead.

"I'm getting old, Tommaso." She pushed up the skin above the forehead crease.

He rocked back on his feet and looked up at his wife.

"You're forty-two."

"Exactly. Fuck forty-two." She clinked past him in her stilettos and Tommaso looked up her short pencil skirt.

"Saw that," she yelled behind her as she walked through the bedroom.

On the west side of Second Avenue, just above 88th Street, Francine gave Elaine two kisses on the cheek and rushed over to Keith, waiting at her usual table nearby Elaine. He rose from the table and she walked into his outstretched arms.

"Look at you. My gorgeous best friend." She pushed him away, her hand on his chest. He wore a wide-shouldered, boxy, brown sports jacket over a black tee shirt, and cream-colored trousers.

"Woody Allen is here," Keith said as he sat back down.

"Is he? He's here all the time." Francine waved her hand in the air. "I don't care. *Keith* is here." She smiled widely at him. "Tell me everything. Except anything about Ulla. I'm too jealous." She puffed up her hair nonchalantly.

Keith threw his head a few inches backward, shaking it as he laid his napkin on his lap.

"Come, I see you one night in a blue, blue, blue moon. I want you all to myself. Is that so unreasonable?"

"Francie, darling. She's my wife. I don't forbid you to speak of Tommaso, do I?"

Francine ran her fingers through her hair again, crimping it upwards. Keith reached out for her hand.

"Christ, you're shaking. What's the story with this?" He held her quivering palm in his warm fingers.

"Oh. It's fine. I made a mistake with my pills this morning. Tried to fix it. I probably made it worse. I'm fine." She pulled her hand into her lap and slid it between her thighs.

"Francine, what are we drinking?" Elaine stood behind her chair. "Linguine tonight?"

"As always!" Francine said, tapping Elaine's plump hands. "You know we don't come here for the food, Elaine darling."

Keith shook his head. "Rude as ever, my darling best friend, isn't she?" He smiled warmly at the proprietor of the infamous restaurant.

Elaine laughed. "Honey, I fill these people up for weeks with my crowd alone. I don't give a damn where those clams come from."

Her eyes were already roaming around the room, eyeing Michael Caine at his usual table. When Elaine moved on to greet her other patrons, Francine took a few gulps of water and blinked excessively, trying to block out the nausea and the beginnings of a migraine.

"You don't look so well," Keith said, leaning his elbows into the table.

"I'm fine. Just the usual."

Keith shifted his lips to the side and opened the menu. "You know," he began. "Benji told me you've had three different housekeepers in the past few months. He rattled off their names and expiration dates like they were hamsters."

"Oh. Yes, well. It's hard to find good help in the city."

"He said you screamed at one of them and threw a carton of eggs at her face?"

Francine rolled her eyes. "Benji doesn't know what he's talking about. He's just a boy."

"He's not *just a boy*. He can see things, Francie. He can pick up on things. You ought to be a little more careful. Kids have memories like dolphins. You *do* remember the odd scene or two in Gainsborough, do you not?"

"Are dolphins more intelligent than humans now? This is news to me." A dirty martini in a rocks glass was placed before her. "And I was a teenager when my mum started acting up. A lot older than Benji. And fuck off about my mum. I work twelve hours a day, the kids hardly see me anyway."

"Should you be drinking?" Keith asked.

She waved him away. "Okay, love, enough out of you. Quit the babysitting. I'm a shit mother. We've established this. Can we talk of other things?" She smiled flirtatiously and took a sip from her drink, her hand shaking so much the gin spilled onto the table.

LONDON

November 1, 2021

BLACK CAB. DRIZZLE. Boxes of varying sizes, some opened and some not, suitcases of varying dimension, innumerable canvas bags and Panzers carry-alls. Laundry she had nearly forgotten to take out of the machine stuffed into a Daunt Books tote. The usual suspects.

"Don't worry, little miss. We're gonna make it fit."

Margherita smiled and nearly hugged the sixty-something taxi driver who patiently and graciously carried each weighty item from the doorstop of the Alma Square flat to his cab. By the time she'd finished carting everything downstairs, there was just enough space for her. On the ride from St. John's Wood to Hampstead, just up the hill but seemingly in another universe, they exchanged stories. She told him of the year's endeavors, of all of her 'try, try, again-ing,' and her many moves.

"Well, hey. You're young. And you seem very content. So don't give up. Keep funneling that energy into something. Don't get complacent. And it will all work out."

"Yeah. I like that attitude." She smiled out the window as drops hit the glass, running backwards down the hill. "I feel terrible, I have all of this stuff to get inside in the rain."

"Don't you worry, little miss Margherita. We're gonna make it work. Everything will be just fine."

On Fitzjohn's Avenue, just south of Perrin's Lane, the taxi driver pulled into a driveway opposite her new address and instructed Margherita to watch over the cab while he carried each item one by one in the now pouring rain. Fifteen minutes later, when he had taken the last item and returned soaked through, he held his hand out as she stepped onto the pavement.

"Alright, little miss. Keep it up. You've got pizzazz. You're going to be great. I can just tell."

She smiled big. "Are you my guardian angel?"

The flat was on the top floor of an old mansion. It was a little worn, but it had a glorious view of treetops and neighboring gardens. She'd make it work. Like a treehouse above London. Besides, she'd be out and about all the time. Meetings and dates and hopefully a new job.

LONDON

October 30, 1993

SATURDAY ON LIME Avenue was a confluence of interactions: immediate and extended families on a long walk after a picnic, running groups beginning or ending, dogs out for the week's longest adventure, and friends who had not seen each other in too long wandering as slowly as possible, savoring the kaleidoscopic sun rays through the still-leafy tree tops overhead.

"You should have brought her. I'd have loved to spend the day with her, you know," Francine said, her hands in her jacket's deep pockets, looking down as she carefully stepped over the raised roots in the wide path.

Keith stepped carefully as well. "Next time. I wanted you all to myself today. And besides. Ulla is a little protective of her lately."

"What does that mean?" Francine spat out, looking sideways at him.

Keith ran his hand through his layered, dirty blonde locks, a few grey wisps above his ears. Watching his strong hand float through the air, one hand in the pocket of his Ryan O'Neal coat, Francine longed to stop beneath the lime trees and wrap her delicate fingers around his neck, to feel the warmth and comfort of his skin.

In her pockets, she clenched her fists.

"Oh. I don't know. She's gone a bit barmy lately. Doesn't want Lisabet out of her sight. And you're not exactly… her favorite person."

"Ha." Francine scoffed and smiled sarcastically. "That's ridiculous. That's ridiculous, Keith. Say it out loud. She's scared to let me spend time with her child? That's ridiculous."

"Stop. She's not scared. She's just… going through a phase. Attachment anxiety. Or whatever. And she's jealous of you, so what? You intimidate her. You don't need to be contemptuous about it; it just *is*."

"She sounds like a real pain in the ass, Keith."

"Let's change the subject."

"No, this is your wife. Obviously things aren't going so swimmingly. We *should* talk about it."

A whippet darted in front of them and they stopped short to let it pass before they carried on.

"Relationships are tough. This too shall pass," Keith said as the autumn wind rippled through his hair. Francine pulled hers into a momentary ponytail in one fist and stopped to look at him as she let it fall.

"Keith. How bad?"

He stopped and met her gaze. Shrugged dismissively. Looked eastward down Lime Avenue. "I think it will pass." And he kept walking.

"How old is she now? Thirty-three? Gosh, she's just a baby. Does she want more kids?"

"It seems she does not."

"What do you mean?"

He shrugged again. "I asked her about it. A few times. She insists she's happy with one."

"Really? What about you?"

Keith squinted down the wide path. "I would like more. But… what can I do?"

"That doesn't seem fair. Did you ever talk about this before?"

Keith shook his head. "I guess, I don't know. I guess I just assumed."

"I'm really sorry, Keithie," Francine said with a scrunched face.

"Let's talk about something else. Mariah Carey. CDs—those ghastly things. Fuck—I feel old lately."

"No, let's talk about why you bought my son that idiotic Game Boy thing that I can't pry from his hands. I brought him here to spend time with his Grampa and all he wants to do is stare at a two inch screen."

"Ha. Sorry. You know I love to spoil the little lad."

Francine swatted his flannelled arm with the back of her hand and Keith brought her in close, his arm around her shoulder until they exited the park.

The warmest feeling. Her most favored form of ecstasy.

LONDON

November 5, 2021

Every rapid test and PCR that Margherita took that week came back negative, but she was convinced she had the virus all the same. Three nights of high fever and chills, followed by days of whiplash exhaustion, a wicked headache, and blue lips led her to her own conclusions. If only London had the same amount of delivery options as Manhattan, she would consider herself a full-on Greta Garbo recluse.

> **Margherita:** I have been bed-ridden for four days and I've made a discovery.
> **Margherita:** Don't make fun
> **Margherita:** But I now firmly believe that Gilmore Girls is more enjoyable as an adult than as a fifth grader
> **Margherita:** For the next time you get covid
> **Margherita:** There are like 371733 episodes a season, don't know what kind of crack WB was on in year 2002.
>
> **Nick:** Oh, wow.
> **Nick:** That's great.
> **Nick:** I've never had covid.
>
> **Margherita:** Well, groove is in the heart.
>
> **Nick:** Where are you
>
> **Margherita:** My bed.

Nick: I'm in London

Nick: What zip code is your bed in

Margherita: Nice try.

If you wanted to see me, why are you just telling me now? Why didn't you reach out to me first? she thought as she looked out the window, aggravated at how easily he made her feel unimportant.

Nick: Seriously.

Margherita: I have covid, I don't think I'm ideal company.

Nick: I'm here for a week. You could feel better soon…

She buried her phone under her pillow and nestled her cheek into its plushness. The treetops sang an autumn lullaby as a memory of Francine swayed in. Francine listless in bed, facing away from the doorway, where Margherita had stood so many times, studying the form of her back and holding her breath until she saw her mother's shape rise and fall.

Signs of life.

CONNECTICUT

FRANCINE PUSHED THE handle down on the French door leading into the kitchen with a dozen tomatoes in her basket.

"They're doing brilliantly," she said as she passed Tommaso and Margherita at the banquette.

"Yeah? How much basil is out there? Maybe I'll make a pasta tonight."

"Daddy! That's *my* half!" Margherita placed her chubby, soft little arm down the center of the oversized coloring book.

"I'm only trying to help you, Marghe!" Tommaso said playfully. "Fine. Your half," he said to her inflated pout.

"Tons." Francine dropped the tomatoes into a colander.

"Tons what?"

"Basil!"

The phone rang as Francine was rinsing the tomatoes, and she turned the faucet off.

"Hello?"

Tommaso looked up at her as she stood leaning into the desk in the corner of the room, looking out at the neighbor's horses.

"Oh. Darling. How *are* you?" Francine smiled widely.

"Smashing, Queen Francie. I'm in Surrey. Nathaniel is making chicken pailliard like we had in Provence last summer. My dahlias are as boisterous and abundant as gays on Old Compton Street. I am tan. Making pottery in my dairy shed. But I missed you. How are you? When are you in London?"

"You're tan in Surrey?"

"Don't be daft; we're just back from Sardinia."

"Ah. You have a dairy shed?"

"Soon I'll be hedge-laying and making cider. So? I have twenty before supper is ready and thought I'd check in."

"Oh. You were bored."

"Of course not. I'm in love. I'm never bored. How are you, sweets?"

"Well! All is well. I'll be in London in a few weeks, to collect my son from his weasel father before school starts."

"Who is it?" Tommaso mouthed.

"Rod-ney," Francine mouthed back, her palm over the receiver.

"Oh that's right. Bea told me she flew him over. Like an escort."

"You are so strange, Rodney. She was here to visit and I booked him on her flight. She's not an escort. Least of all my nine-year-old's."

"So. Have you heard from Keith lately?" Rodney's tone changed.

"No. Not in a month or so. I hate when you do that. Drop these ominous foreshadowings. What now?"

"Well. You didn't hear it from me."

"Of course I did."

"Okay. Well. *Apparently*, big problems in Ulla-land. She's been having an affair."

"What!" Francine shrieked and turned around, facing the long, graceful bodies of the horses in the distance.

"What!" Tommaso squeaked from behind her.

"Poor Lisabet. Good thing she's only four. They're fighting over her like a vintage Van record. Ulla wants full custody. She's gone total nutter, Francie. To-tal. Wretched little trollop. She's met a filthy rich American banker and is moving in with him in Holland Park. Keith is beside himself. They were having problems, but I don't think he saw this coming."

Francine held her palm over her mouth. "I can't believe it. Poor Keith."

"Yes and now his wagon is hitched to this American tosser and crazy Ulla for the rest of his life. They'll be fighting over Lisabet for a century."

"Why hasn't he told me?"

"I only found out because Bea saw them out to dinner in the City one night and immediately called Keith, not knowing if he knew or not."

"And did he?"

"Yes."

"Oh, Keithie. My heart is broken for him. Why hasn't he told me?"

"Anyway. Let me go. Nathaniel will be looking for me. I'm meant to be cutting wildflowers for our table."

"Yeah. Sure. Thanks for calling, love."

Francine hung the phone back on the receiver and stood frozen.

When she turned around to face the room, she took in the scene. Margherita's head leant into Tommaso's chest, father and daughter side by side on the banquette, Tommaso's hand stroking her soft brown ringlets. She should have felt relief in that moment, at how lucky she was, but she only felt guilt.

How unfair, after everything, that she should be washing tomatoes for dinner with her doting husband and wonderful father to their sweet girl, kind and endlessly giving to her son from another man—all in all a perfectly wondrous culmination—while Keith, so much more deserving of a fairytale ending, seemed to have the most rotten luck of them all.

LONDON

November 10, 2021

A FOUR-PERSON LINE at Artichoke was enough to make the charming shop feel crowded and jovial. Hampsteaders and their small dogs overlapped like lanyard as one arm reached for England-grown lettuce and another went diagonally for organic, green grapes that came, ironically, from Italy. Margherita waited patiently to purchase her few items: a bag of pre-washed spinach, a cucumber, celery, fresh ginger, and a lemon. She had felt energetic enough to go for a slow wander into the Heath and was ready to feel her way through a day where she—hopefully—didn't crash back into bed.

Outside the shop, above the hilltop village, the sky quivered like a frightened puppy just fallen into a pool. It was not sure if it should whimper and retreat into itself, or shake off and excitedly run a lap around the yard. She crossed her fingers the rain would at least hold off until she reached Mayfair, where she intended to sit and work for the afternoon.

Her phone vibrated on the side of her leg, affixed in its yoga legging pocket. Margherita didn't have enough hands to check it until she returned to her flat, where she let the produce tumble onto the countertop, eager to be rinsed, crushed, and imbibed.

Tommaso: how do you feel?

Margherita: Each day slightly less catatonic

Tommaso: this is good.

After she blended everything, she stood in front of her window overlooking the ever-changing treetops of the neighbor's yards below. The light in the sky changed by the second, as if a carnival was suspended somewhere in the air, and a Ferris wheel of lights turned round and round, changing the hues of everything in its vicinity with every full circle.

Energized by the greens and emboldened by the 'turning of the corner' of whatever COVID or non-COVID virus had taken a raucous ride through her system, she typed out a message.

Margherita: tonight?

He wrote back within a few minutes, and Margherita could feel the space between her legs take on its own Ferris wheel.

Nick: yes.
Nick: what time?

Margherita: 7?

Nick: perfect.
Nick: I'm at my sister's in Chiswick
Nick: cool spot down the road… I'll send you the address?
Nick: I think it will be up to your standards

Margherita: you would know…

Nick: I wouldn't, would I

Margherita: not really.

Nick: ok. I HOPE it will be up to your standards. How about that

Margherita: ha I trust you. I'm easy

Nick: ha sure.

Margherita: be nice or I won't make the trip all the way to Chiswick

Nick: if you told me where you lived I could make it easier for you?

Margherita: no no it's fine. See you later ☺

She took the day one hour at a time and decided that if she relapsed into imminent dormancy, she would simply cancel. She didn't *need* to see him. She didn't *need* to force herself.

She just *wanted* to see him.

Later that evening, after reapplying a bit of make-up and nervously checking her reflection in the Mayfair hotel's ladies' room (as if she would look precisely the same after the tube ride through the rainy evening), she took the Jubilee line from Bond Street to Westminster, where she changed to the District Line. At Chiswick Park, she exited, inflated her umbrella above her head, and followed her Google Map southward to the pub. It was dark and young parents herded their excitable children away from sports activities toward the dry warmth of their homes, toward dinner time and homework and a hot bath. Pajamas that matched on top and bottom and flannel sheets with stories and characters sewn into them. Rain that pitter-pattered outside their windows like lullabies.

And there was Margherita, walking toward what she imagined would be an evening of too much gin, ravenous sexual tension, and—quite inevitably—the hollowing after-effects of time spent with a boy who had never loved her back.

The rain strengthened as she turned a corner, the wind not doing her any favors, and she felt fat drops hit her right side. Her dainty umbrella inverted and she turned around to let the wind push it back to its rightful position, cursing it as two children skirted by. Cheeks wet and hands dripping, she swung open the door to the pub and pushed back the velvet curtain that further protected against the evening's cool temps.

Nick stood from a stool he had been leaning against and approached her with arms outstretched. Margherita collapsed her umbrella and shook herself off as a warm smile grew in strength across his face.

"I'm all wet. I don't think you want to hug me," she said into his shoulder as he brought her in for an embrace.

"I'm quite used to you all wet," he said into her ear.

"Funny." She looked into his azure eyes. Ever so slightly drooping at their outer edges, but energetic all the same. His lips upturned. His expression always an invitation to play. Play what? She hadn't ever gotten it right. But it was always some sort of game. Some sort of dance.

"I've been trying to find two places to sit, but it's fairly crowded at the moment." He turned to survey the room. The stool he had been hovering over had been quickly stolen, and all of the oversized leather chairs were occupied.

"It's a good night for a long pub hang," she said, shaking her hair out.

"Hi there, we're two." Nick held up two of his fingers to the hostess. "Are you feeling optimistic?"

The young hostess, a bun on top of her head, looked around the room, craning her neck so as not to miss any of the pub's crevices. She winced.

"I'm afraid not. I'd guess about an hour's wait? But I can't be sure."

"I should have reserved, shouldn't I?"

"Yeah. I'm sorry!" The hostess winced on.

Nick turned to Margherita. "So odd to me, reserving seats at a pub. My sister's is down the road… they're away. We can go there? She doesn't have a *full* bar, but I think we could make it work."

Margherita bit the inside of her cheek.

"What?" He cocked his head, that big smile. Those white teeth.

She eyed him suspiciously.

"We don't have to do anything you don't feel like doing. If that's what you're thinking." He raised his eyebrows at her.

"Fine...." Margherita groaned, and she turned to exit, umbrella in hand, ready to get wet again.

Once inside the brick, semi-detached house in Grove Park Terrace, they hung their dripping coats and left their shoes in the narrow entrance hall.

"Where are they?" Margherita grazed her eyes down the hall, which led to an oversized den and open kitchen.

"Visiting my parents. They took the kids. So I have it to myself."

"Why didn't you go?"

"I did. Just got back today."

"Oh."

He led the way toward the kitchen at the back of the house. Glass doors reflected their bodies and Margherita went to cup her hands around her eyes and peer out.

"Looks like a nice little patio."

"Yeah. Perfect for weather like this. What would you like to drink?"

She spun around and leaned her elbows into the kitchen island while Nick retrieved two tumblers from a glass cabinet.

"What are you having?"

"Gin? Soda water?"

"That's fine for me."

"So how do you feel?" he asked as he opened the fridge in search of soda water.

"So much better. Not one hundred percent. But I stayed out all day today, so that's huge."

"Huge!" He smiled widely at her as he snapped off the metal top. She returned the smile and rolled her eyes.

Isabetta Andolini

"So strange to see you here," he said as he walked over to the bar cart and bent his knees, leaning backwards, to read the different bottles.

"Is it?"

At the counter again, he mixed their drinks and handed her a glass.

"Cheers. To a very wet night at home."

She smirked behind her glass and eyed him. They each took a sip in silence.

Margherita turned around to survey the den. She approached an enlarged modern artwork on an empty wall beside the sofa.

He stood next to her. The only sound was the rain outside and his breathing.

"Interesting. What do you think it is?"

"I think it's a fish pushing through the ocean floor. My nephew thinks it's his little sister trying to share bathtime with him."

"Aw. That's cute. Clearly wants his alone time."

"Oh yes. He's very independent. He's four."

They exchanged another glance.

More upturned corners of mouths.

Margherita bit the inside of her cheek.

She placed her glass down on the side table below her right hip.

Nick watched her. He placed his glass down as well and faced her.

She faced him in silence.

Neither touched the other. Neither said a word. Just intoxicating eyes. Just testosterone and estrogen. And an empty house. And rain.

With the back of his fingers, Nick grazed the edge of her jaw and up to her ear.

She stared into his eyes.

He placed the imprint of his thumb on her temporal lobe, where she often massaged herself after a bad night of TMJ. His other fingers gently touched her hair.

She watched him.

"I said we don't have to do anything you don't feel like, but I don't know what you feel like." His voice was quiet.

She continued to stare into his eyes.

"What do you feel like?"

She looked askance.

Margherita slowly took his hand in hers, her thumb pushed into the center of his palm, and held his fingers straight upward, pointing toward the ceiling.

She pushed together the pointer and middle finger, separating the pair from the ring and pinky fingers, and slowly brought the former to her mouth, guiding the two joined fingers along her tongue, toward her throat.

Nick watched her in silence, his mouth slightly agape.

She guided his moistened fingers towards the hem of her dress, up and underneath it, toward the top of her tights.

She brought them beneath the elastic and up inside of her. She eyed him as she did so, her mouth slowly opening until a small moan released.

His eyes remained locked on hers as his fingers slid deeper inside of her.

She brought them out slowly. They were slick.

"You tell me, what do I feel like?"

He put his hand on the back of her head, pulling her hair gently backwards so her chin tipped upward, and he kissed her jawline. Then her lips.

"Wet," he whispered.

She kissed him energetically, her leg riding up to wrap around his waist until he picked her up and kiss-walked her toward a downstairs guest bedroom.

Sex with Nick felt simultaneously slow and deliciously drawn out. There was an awareness to each moment, in the moment, but as all things did, it ended. Margherita always desired more, while Nick enjoyed the adrenaline-washed aftermath and seemed to relish a blissful transition from climax to the chilled-out sensation of encircling oxytocin and dopamine.

He reached for his phone in the pocket of his jeans, which had been kicked to the floor beside him. On his back with the screen in the air above him, he scrolled through his Spotify.

"Otis" by The Durutti Column rippled through the silent room.

"Love this one," Margherita said lazily.

He looked over at her, on her stomach, her arms overlapped beneath the pillow, one cheek down.

"Me too."

"Let me see." She held out her naked arm.

He brought the phone close to his chest, as if it held a secret.

"Oh come on, I'm only in it for the music."

"Fine." He handed her the phone.

"Lots of Philip Glass."

"Yeah. Good for working."

"Love him." Margherita scrolled through his library. "Gosh, I hate choosing tracks. It's like my Sophie's Choice."

Finally she chose "A Rose for Emily" by The Zombies.

"Sad song. Are you Emily?"

Margherita scrunched her face. "Mean."

He turned onto his side, so that they faced each other, and he stroked her soft forehead with his thumb, grazing it outward toward her hairline.

Suddenly she felt tired. Lethargic. It had been a long day, her most active since she had been ill. And his touch on her skin. It was too much.

"Don't do that," she said, her eyes closed.

"Why?" He pulled back, an incredulous smile on his face. His nostrils flared.

"Because."

"Because why?" He reached his hand out again, moving a

strand of hair behind her ear.

She shook her head and turned to face the ceiling. "Because I don't want you in my head."

"Oh?"

She turned to face him. "If I'm not in your head, I don't want you in mine."

"Who said you're not in my head?"

"Not just when I text you my random fantasies."

"Not just when you text me your fantasies."

They lay there looking at each other in a stand-off.

She sat up.

He remained lying down and rolled his eyes at the ceiling.

She leaned her hand into the mattress like a kick stand and turned to watch him stare back at her.

He shrugged. "Lie down for a second."

"Why?"

"Why not?"

She lay down, despite the voice in her head telling her to call an Uber and go home, and he rubbed his hand up and down her arm.

"What is your biggest pet peeve?" he asked.

She thought for a moment. "I have many. I'll name one. People who blow their nose at the dinner table."

"Disgusting."

"People who talk on the phone on public transport."

"Horrendous behavior."

"People who don't ask questions."

"What do you mean?" He smiled facetiously.

"Ha. Very clever."

"I ask questions, I think."

"Not with me. Maybe with other people. I hope with other people."

"I ask you questions. Come on. That's not fair."

"You do not. Let's be honest. I'm used to it, don't worry."

He didn't say anything.

"One of my sisters got dumped yesterday," he said.

"Oh no! That's awful. I'm so sorry for her." Margherita winced.

"Yeah. She's shattered. Heartbroken. Completely gutted. Been crying all day."

Margherita pouted. "That's rough. How long were they together?"

"Five years. He just sort of stopped loving her, I guess. I never liked him, so I think she dodged a bullet. But I'm not going to say that of course. Not helpful in the moment."

"She will meet someone else one day."

"Yeah. That's what I said."

"I can't imagine having a sister." Margherita watched the ends of his fingers run back and forth on her arm. "So strange to think about it. What would a sister of mine be like?" she enlarged her eyes, still looking down.

"Do you wish you did, have a sister?"

She shrugged. "Yeah. I guess. It could be nice. Do you ever wish you had a brother?"

"Sometimes. I did growing up. I think it made my dad and I really close, but three sisters is a lot of sisters. They all fight with each other but I think I've always been a little jealous of how close they are." He fingered the serpent ring on her finger.

"You can hang out with my brother. You just have to schedule it like, four months in advance."

He pulled his head backwards. "You have a brother?"

She raised her eyebrows and nodded slowly.

"How come I didn't know that?"

She shrugged. "Anyway, I'm really sorry about your sister. I'm sure she'll realize it was for the best once she meets someone new. Best way to get over someone is to fall for someone else."

He eyed her apprehensively. "Yeah. When was the last time that happened for you?"

Margherita's eyes enlarged in thought. "Gosh. I don't know."

"Well, when was the last time you fell hard?"

"When I was in kindergarten, I was so in love with this boy named Joseph who wore corduroy pants. I remember them so well." She smiled teasingly.

"No, come on. Be real."

"I don't know!" she laughed.

He gripped her hand. "Tell me. Be honest."

"It's been a really long time. The End."

"You are so difficult."

She shrugged.

"I'm going to start touching your forehead if you don't tell me."

"What difference does it make?" she asked, still smiling.

"When was the last time you fell for someone so badly you lost your appetite? I'm genuinely curious."

"You know the answer to this. You just love to have your ego stroked don't you?"

His eyes went large in mock offense. "I do not."

"Don't be an ass."

He tipped his head. "Marghe."

"The last time I fell for someone and lost my appetite, everything went pear-shaped. And you were there, so, recap not necessary."

His face belied nothing. He squeezed her arm and leaned over to kiss her.

She pushed him off gently. "You just wanted to hear that out loud, didn't you?"

He climbed on top of her and made an exaggerated scene of rubbing her forehead with both of his thumbs.

"God, you're annoying," she laughed. "Stop it!"

He lowered his face to hers and kissed her hairline, then her lips, and they had sex once more, before she called an Uber and went to sleep in her own bed, not having discussed any of the texts throughout the previous months, nothing about The Villa, or what she was doing in London, nothing about what he was up to in New York; nothing at all of any consequence between them.

A few days later, with the return of full energy after COVID, she awoke with zeal and practically chased herself out the door for the first gentle jog in weeks. Nick was back in New York, not a peep had been heard from him since she had left his sister's house— and she was, with her post-COVID energy, determined to replace thoughts of him with cheerful things like energy balls from Artichoke and glorious North London sunrises.

It tore Margherita to shreds to have to make a decision between parks in the morning. Daybreak on Primrose Hill, approached from the north, was a painting come to life: the stark outlines of the trees against the luminous sky caused her to express elation out loud, to absolutely no one. When, from the top of the hill—sixty-three meters above sea level according to her encyclopedic brother—a wash of yellow dashed across the London Eye, The Shard, and the BT tower, she felt a surge of life itself.

This is it, she could hear her mother's voice in her head.

The grass was the brightest of greens beneath a blue sky. Oh how London loved its rain; how verdant and luminous it could be. How the dogs relished it even more; they'd leap jiggedy jaggedy down the hill, sprinting with all their might toward scents and squirrels and dancing leaves; it was such a simple scene, but at the same time, extraordinary, and it cast the widest of smiles across Margherita's face.

Then there were the beams dancing between the consecutive, elegant trees along Broad Walk, at the north side of Regent's Park, just over Regent's Canal. An older gentleman and his collie throwing a stick in the meadow to the left. Dogs galloping in and out of the spaces between the ancient oaks. A carpet of yellow and orange leaves on the grass, a smattering across the paved center passageways. The bright yellow light that clung to the ground, reflecting off the foliage, hues as vivid as an Edward Henry Potthast oil painting. Everything had a glow, every human form was a shadow against it, or bathed in it, or walking into it, crossing through it, moving within it. The way the sun backlit people dressed for work, making their way southward toward duties and phonecalls and meetings with other humans. Decisions to make. Schemes to illuminate. Pupils to enlighten.

But oh, then—of all of the cinematic scenery in London, what could be more transcendental than the mist rising off Parliament Hill? Margherita raced across Downshire Hill to enter the Heath, past the swimming pond, past the spectacular golden tree on the right, up through the darkened path, and out into a mystical abyss, where spirits flowed from east, west, north and south. Dogs skipped, chased, and leaped across the intersection, catching up to each other with grins on their faces, front legs in the air, practically dancing at the day.

And there! There was the glittery, moistened grass on the hill, and there crossed a human at its crest, as if on the edge of the world.

On days when the fog held its stubborn head down along the wet terrain, it was a different kind of literary spectacle, equally magnetic and romantic. Curved paths through the meadows led to layered trees and forests that looked, from afar, as if they had been doused in mist, like visible cologne. Some trees lost leaves while others sat tenaciously green with a streak of orange, like the dyed head of an alternative teenager. White labs, spotless upon entering, ran wild through mud and slippery leaves and left blissfully amuck. In lesser frequented fields, where tall grasses grew and wellies sunk into the earth, men in hunting caps strode slowly with their hands chastely clasped behind their backs, their head down, or their heads up, either way, it was straight out of Emily Brontë's Yorkshire Moors, or Jane Campion's *Bright Star*. It made Margherita leap; the purity and the beauty. No wonder all of her favorite authors were British. Everything made so much more sense.

Except of course her life at that moment. Not much about it was making a whole lot of sense.

LONDON

August 5, 1995

FRANCINE STOOD IN line at the newsagent on King's Road as
Benjamin tapped a ball on his knee a few feet away, and Bea
counted each bounce excitedly.

She rubbed her temples. A new anti-depressant was giving
her the worst migraines of her life and she was desperate to see
her doctor at Bellevue to change her prescription back to the
former pill, which had started giving her double vision. She
figured the former was more manageable, as long as she wasn't
driving.

Francine thought of her mother, of that first year when her
medications had begun wreaking havoc on her body, and she
shivered at the thought that this might be the beginning of a
similar, dark period.

The newsstand was flooded with supermodels: Claudia
Schiffer's face was on every cover imaginable, and if it wasn't
Claudia, Linda, or Naomi, it was O.J. Simpson. When it was her
turn, she scooped up an *FT Weekend* and a *Times*, paid, and
folded them into her bag.

"Right. That's done. Off to the park," she said to Benjamin,
who, at ten-years-old, was nearly as tall as her. She ruffled his
soft, dark hair. He dodged her hand.

"Oh, no. Not the hair," Bea laughed. "Benji, did you show your
mom the medal you won last week at the tourney?"

"What medal?" Francine asked.

"It's nothing. Everyone at camp got one." He kicked the ball up into his hands and the threesome made their way toward Burton Court.

"A medal is not nothing! Why didn't you tell me?" Francine asked.

"You weren't there. I forgot to tell you," he said moodily as he ran down the sidewalk.

Francine's eyebrows furrowed in hurt. "Careful!" she yelled after him.

"He's a little upset, I think. Keith promised he'd play with him today but he's not coming anymore." Bea pushed her hair into a ponytail, a giant scrunchy held wide around her fingers.

"Oh? This is the first I'm hearing of it. Where is he?"

"He's got Lisabet for the weekend, last minute. Ulla the ice queen went to Paris. A surprise anniversary gift from her tosser husband, who I swear is cheating on her. And she dropped her off at Keith's this morning, unannounced. So typical."

"How do you know he's cheating on her?"

"Oh come on!" Bea groaned. "He's in New York every other week. You think he doesn't keep a stash of gormless girls over there?"

Francine narrowed her eyes down the sidewalk, increasing the step in her stride to catch up with Benjamin.

"I assume Keith took Lisabet to Cornwall for the weekend." Francine asked.

"Yep."

She felt her face go long.

Up ahead, her son turned into the park. He kicked the ball far out into the field.

"Personally, I'm relieved to be Aunt Bea to everyone. You parenting folk sure have a lot to gripe about."

"Yeah. I suppose we do." Francine pushed her fingertips into her temples.

"You've been doing that all day." Bea waved her finger at her friend's forehead.

"Yeah. I suppose I have."

"By the way," Bea said slowly. "Benjamin mentioned something about Brighton College."

Francine's eyes scrunched together and she looked at Bea.

"I guess he has mates who go, or are starting next term. Not certain of the details. But he's brought it up a few times this summer."

"In bloody Brighton?" Francine exclaimed.

Bea nodded slowly. "Christos took him a few weeks ago. For a tour."

"What the fuck? Why didn't you tell me?" Francine's eyes shot toward her son as her heartbeat quickened.

"It's not my place, Francie. I was hoping one of them would have said something. But I guess they haven't."

"Fucking mother fucker. I can't believe him."

Bea inhaled and exhaled and sucked her bottom teeth. "Francie. It's not the worst thing in the world, you know." She watched her friend timidly.

"He hasn't even hit puberty and you want me to send him to boarding school in bloody fucking Brighton?" She rubbed her temples again.

"My brothers went away to school from age ten. Keith did too. Tons of boys do. It's not unusual. And he's so happy here." Bea watched Benjamin kick the ball into the net. "He says… well, he says he doesn't like Browning. The Upper East Side boys—"

"The Upper East Side boys are no different from the Brighton boys. Trust me."

"It's a different culture."

"It's a different country!" Francine raised her voice. Benjamin's face turned toward the two women. Bea waved at him.

"Talk to Benji. And Christos. It's so near to London, Francie. He'd be close to your dad, and to all of us, and maybe it would be better for him. I know you're… stressed, with work and—"

"Oh, fuck off Bea. You don't know anything. You don't know what it's like to be a mum. Or to have a job as demanding as mine."

Bea nodded her head up and down as if the damp air was molasses. "Francie, I'm not trying to upset you or tell you how to be a mum. I know, I don't know anything on the subject. But the more stress you're under, the worse for wear you are, and I just don't want to see Benjamin resent you for growing up so far away from where he clearly feels more at home, and meanwhile you're never around. He has more friends here. He fits in better here. *We* are his family, too. Just think about it."

Francine rubbed her temples vigorously, as if trying to remove a stain. "I hate being a mum, Bea. I hate it sometimes. It's fucking hard. The hell if I know what to do. I don't fucking know. So Benjamin goes to the boys' school in Brighton. Then what do I do with Margherita? Let her fall victim to my shit attempt at motherhood? Shall I pitch her off to boarding school too? Tommaso will *love* that."

Bea wrapped her arm around her friend and rubbed her shoulder. "Francie, love, you don't hate being a mum. I see you. You are a wonder. You make them laugh, and they're always thinking of you, what can they bring you, what can I make for mummy, how can I make her smile? Margherita doesn't know any differently from New York, and Tommaso is an incredible father. She has a nest there already. She doesn't have to worry about not feeling at home."

LONDON

November 15, 2021

MARGHERITA LAY ON her stretch mat in her attic flat. She pulled at her right leg and watched a crack on the ceiling as if it were about to expand, like something out of a cartoon she used to watch.

"What the fuck am I doing here?" she said out loud. "You think I'm an idiot, don't you? You want to say, 'I told you so' so fucking badly."

Her phone lay dormant next to her. What other contacts did she have in London who could possibly help connect a few dots? What had happened to Jack? She typed out a message in her phone.

Margherita: spiffing lunch

Jack: let's do it
Jack: are you free next week?

Margherita: I am unemployed, the world is my oyster

Jack: I'll find a place

Johanna's name floated to the top of her chat list.

Johanna: Hi darling how are things?
Johanna: I'm in NY this week, let's chat when I'm back
Johanna: Am having dinner with a friend at Hart Browne tmr eve

Margherita scrunched her eyebrows together. Hart Browne was one of the biggest architecture firms in the world, let alone New York.

> **Margherita:** Ciao! Wow that's impressive! An old friend or a new friend? Are you buying a penthouse I should know about?
>
> **Johanna:** New friend. He's my editor's brother. Very artsy family aren't they!
>
> **Johanna:** I've gone through your presentation a few times and watched the virtual walk through, I think I've gotten wrapped up in the romance of it. I plan to scrounge his brain. Maybe I can be of use. Or maybe he can. Either way, I promise not to return without an email address for you, my fabulously resourceful and enterprising friend!

Margherita smiled big at her phone.

> **Margherita:** I expect nothing, but thank you nevertheless! That is so kind of you to think of me. I hope it's at the very least a fantastic evening with an interesting man ☺
>
> **Johanna:** Kisses. Be good, or if not, have fun ☺

LONDON

November 19, 2021

"So you're not going home for Thanksgiving?" Thayer spread his napkin on his lap and grazed his eyes across the triangular common. It was a clear autumn day, and London was looking particularly brilliant.

Margherita followed his gaze across Chelsea Common, landing on the fishmonger, where a young man carried crates from a white van into the slippery shop.

"Home?" she asked, confused.

"Your dad is staying on Mustique? You're not going to meet anywhere?"

Margherita sighed and shook her head. "He's busy. And it's never been that big of a holiday for us. You know, my mom thought it was silly. She opted for her British patriotism every time Thanksgiving rolled around."

"Your mom sounds brilliant."

"She was that."

A young couple, holding hands, walked past their sidewalk table and approached the windows of the tavern, though they were covered with thick velvet curtains and it was impossible to see inside. Elystan Street hung tight to its snobbery. The couple quietly debated entering, and Thayer gave them a polite closed-lip smile as they ultimately decided against it and crossed the street to the less expensive-looking pizza place.

"Hand-holders," Thayer pronounced slowly. "Are you a hand

Isabetta Andolini

holder?"

"Hmm… maybe. Probably not. But possibly." Margherita looked up at the waiter who appeared then, and her eyes followed the plate of salmon and grilled vegetables set before her.

Thayer breathed in the steam from his Chateaubriand, served in a piping hot cast-iron oval dish. "Mmm. Heaven. I am a hand-holder. Johanna was not."

"Gimme a piece," Margherita immediately stabbed a slice of the tender meat with her fork. "Mmmm," she moaned happily as she chewed on the classic cut.

"You could have had it," he said, holding his knife and fork over the oval dish. "Miss Virtuous over there."

They took a moment to enjoy the first bites, always the best, and Margherita relished the cool breeze skipping up the Chelsea streets from the River Thames. What she had missed the most on Mustique were the seasons. An autumn breeze. Possibly more delicious than the first bite of a tender steak.

"So, what do you mean, probably not, possibly? Don't you *know* if you're a hand-holder?"

She shrugged. "Not really."

"When was your last relationship?" Thayer had yet to ask her this question, and she simultaneously wondered why it had taken so long and dreaded its imminence.

"Well, the pandemic wasn't ideal for single people," she deflected.

"No no, before the pandemic." He drew rewind circles with his knife.

She hesitated. She had become reluctant to open this can of worms; the few times she had been truthful in the past, it had not done her any favors. She had unknowingly cornered herself into a certain reputation, and people were so unforgiving, so determined to keep someone glued to a characteristic that one chapter in their life had portrayed. Why was it not acceptable to change, or grow, or develop new habits?

"I've had a few romances but nothing near marriage," she offered, vaguely.

"And did you hold hands in these romances?" Thayer asked.

"Once in a while." That was the truth. Once in a while, a man had taken her hand, though it was usually in secret in the dead of night.

"So, I hope you don't mind my asking," Thayer prefaced, mid-chew, "but do you *want* to marry?"

She felt her salmon lurch in her stomach. "I have this weird aversion to that word. I find it so—" She clenched her hands in the air and winced. "Airless." She pushed her hands and arms outward beyond her body, to emphasize or clarify her personal space. Thayer looked at her as if entertained. "And beyond the claustrophobia, it's like trying to nail down a moving target. Remember that tracing paper stuff with the designs on them that changed?"

"Um. No."

Margherita shuddered and picked at the zucchini.

"I think the whole point is, it *is* a risk. People are liable to change. You are liable to change. We're all throwing pennies in the fountain."

"Yeah, kind of anxiety-provoking," she grimaced.

"Do you want to meet someone?" Thayer put it to her.

"I don't know?"

"Of course you do." He put down his fork and knife and leant forward slightly.

Margherita placed her elbows delicately on the edge of the table and clasped her hands. "Do you know how rare it is to meet someone with whom you fall in love, who makes sense, who falls in love with you back, and with whom you want to build a life—together? Do you know how rare that is? And now think about what a firecracker love is, true love, real love, big love. How simultaneously hypnotic and painful. Surreal and too good to be true and terrifying and stomach flipping and potentially irrevocably heartbreaking in so many ways. Now take that person away. That rarity of a creature, that unicorn. That life you built together. That haystack of emotions. Burn it down. Imagine that for a second. I don't want that."

"You can't lose someone you never had. You are going worst case scenario before you've gotten to the ticket booth."

"Self preservation."

"No way to live."

Margherita leant forward and lowered her voice. "Your wife left you two years ago. You spent a year in exile on a tiny island where you rarely changed your clothes or spoke more than five words a day, and now you are here giving me advice on love and marriage?"

"Yeah. I am. You can have a rhino hide and still be vulnerable. You can be vulnerable and go on to have a rhino hide."

"How do you figure?"

"Fleetwood Mac made their best album when they were all fighting and getting divorced and ripping each other's hearts out."

"So why haven't you made a movie in the past three years? You could have been flourishing in the face of heartbreak."

"Nothing inspires me lately."

"What happened to the project you were location scouting for in Italy?"

"Nope. Can't have the lead I want, or the art director I want. And so, no go."

"Of all the actors in the world, and art directors, you can't be satisfied with Plan B? They could surprise you."

"It's like your theory on falling in love with someone who loves you back. It's got to be fucking magic in this business, or I'll be out on my ass times two." He picked up his wine glass and leaned back in his chair, glancing around the square again.

"I think you are blocking yourself on purpose," Margherita said resolutely.

"Right back at you!"

"I think we both need Johanna to kick us in the ass," she smiled.

"Do you know Zuckerberg tried to sue her for defamation in her latest book?"

Margherita ha-ed out loud. "Are you kidding? Someone needs to cancel that twerp. I assume she won."

"Yup. And who would run our world if not for the little twerp?"

"Elon."

"Well, the devil you know."

The waiter came to refill their wine glasses. Thayer watched the Haut-Médoc splash into his glass. He twirled it as he regarded Margherita curiously.

"Favorite Cat Stevens song," he queried.

"Oh." She darted her eyes past his face, thinking quickly. "'Oh Very Young.'"

"'Moon Shadow.'"

"'Peace Train.'"

"'Sitting.'"

Margherita sang a lyric or two. Thayer laughed and clinked her glass.

"You are a treasure, my darling."

She smiled. "Now if only I can find someone to treasure me."

"Marriage!" he spat out enthusiastically.

"No!" she exclaimed. "Just treasure-ment."

LONDON

November 22, 2021

ON THE TUBE to Holborn, she thought about that phone call eight years ago, when Francine had told her about the handsome architect she had just watched being interviewed on the news. She replayed her mother's words as she walked the twenty minute stretch from the tube stop to the gastro-pub in Clerkenwell, gritting her teeth against the wind biting at her hair, and the rather insistent rain dampening her from every direction, no matter where she placed her umbrella.

"Go introduce yourself," Francine had said. She had suggested it so... suggestively. So encouragingly. Like the more adventurous, more naturally gregarious friend encourages the wallflower to say hi to a boy. She had felt that her mother was disappointed in Margherita for being less 'in your face' than Francine, less socially impressive and bold.

And then, in Italy, when Margherita had gained a confidence she had not felt before, Francine had seemed bitter, as if she were angry that Margherita no longer *needed* her mother, no longer went searching for her, or as if Margherita's confidence wasn't being used in the environment Francine had had in mind. She couldn't win.

She had woken with a last-minute cancellation in mind; everything in her felt lackluster, the weather was off-putting, and she could not help but second-guess Jack's intentions after nearly eight years. In her mind, men wanted one thing from her:

excitement in the form of flirtation and sex. And in the month or so since she had communicated with Jack, her demeanor had shrunk from the Margherita these men counted on for that satisfaction, to a stripped-down version she was embarrassed to bring out onto center stage. No one liked a dejected girl, an unsuccessful, unemployed, insolvent, mildly depressed girl. *That* was not exciting. Nor was it sexy or appealing. That was not what said men signed up for.

She arrived just before twelve-thirty, and after shaking herself off like a wet dog in the vestibule and leaving her duck-head umbrella by its drenched lonesome, she glanced through the pub, past its wooden bar, to where sweater-wearing patrons sat in groups at large tables, already halfway into their pints. They eyed her merrily though curiously. London never missed a millisecond; by eleven a.m. Monday morning, the pub was their oyster.

No Jack. Ample opportunity for a moment's refreshment in the loo.

Undereye concealer reapplied, hair brushed and flipped, and a good hand wash later, she looked at herself in the mirror and forced herself to smile.

Put it on, she thought. *Just put it on for a few hours.* She unbuttoned her trench coat and unwrapped her scarf. That way she would not have to spend too long awkwardly de-robing. She stepped back out into the main room.

And there he was.

Standing tall at the bar in a long dark coat, with a cleanly shaven face, milky white skin, cheekbones high, and a head of dark hair, was Jack.

Jack who had sent her heartbeat roiling day after day for nearly two years. Jack who had flooded her consciousness the moment she stepped into the office building in West Soho and every time she left her desk to make a copy of a plan, visit the materials room, go to the bathroom, or leave for lunch. Jack, whose round eyes would bury into her as they sat at coffee shops safe distances from their co-workers.

Jack, who had been her comfort, her peer, and her confidante in the years before she knew how to be her own comfort, her own peer, her own confidante.

She wheeled her hand to her hip, stomped her toe outward, and tipped her body to the side, her head cocked with her eyes on him and a closed-lipped, mischievous smile on her face. He imitated her playfully and they approached each other, his arms outstretched. Immersed in a satisfying hug, Margherita immediately felt her whole being absorbed into his warmth. How she missed that man. How she missed that feeling.

They were led to an upstairs table at one end of the room with a row of empty chairs behind them, convenient for draping long coats and scarves and extraneous layers. They sat against the window overlooking the lane below, no other patrons around them.

"You look exactly the same," she said, smiling at him. He might, he just might, look even better, but she was not about to say that.

"*You* look exactly the same!" he exclaimed. "You are resplendent."

She smiled. His subdued, evenly pitched voice sent a zephyr through her insides, clearing any of the doubt or apprehension she had felt when she woke that morning. Sitting across from Jack, hearing his voice; she felt inflated again. At ease.

A waitress approached with menus and wine glasses. Margherita had assumed the lunch would be slightly awkward, more to the point of the agenda (job contacts and perfunctory catch-ups), more formal, more innocent. But Jack's eyes scanned the wine menu with equanimity.

"I can't believe you're here," he said, leaned forward slightly, his forearms entwined, his elbows on the table. "What made you decide on London? Italy looked so deliciously glorious…"

"Yes; Italy is beautiful. But—I don't know. I missed a bit more speed. I missed being surrounded by an abundance of opportunity. And for my project, for finding capital or partners, London makes more sense. And, truth be told, I'd like to find a job. I'd like to stay. Certainly there are a great deal more jobs in architecture in London than in all of Italy."

"Hmm." He pulled at his lower lip with his thumb and fore-finger. "Have you been applying to anything?"

"Yes. Oh yes. But it feels a little slow right now…"

"Yes, sadly." He looked out the window at the rain, still fall-ing heavily. "After the pandemic, and now with another rise in cases… It's putting a freeze on everything."

"Hi there!" A curly-haired, petite waitress approached their table, and Margherita and Jack looked up to greet her. "Have you had a chance to look at the menu yet? Any questions?"

"We have not," Jack said slowly. "But I think we'll start with wine?" He glanced at Margherita.

With two glasses of Rioja before them, they carried on.

"So, you are cataloguing the most beautiful areas of the city quite thoroughly. A love letter to London."

"I can't keep up with all there is to admire. Autumnal goodness of the 'this is so charming, I could just *squeeze* you!' variety."

"This autumn has been a marvel, I agree."

"And then of course I am enamored of every free-range dog in the parks. And sunrises on hillcrests and the *architecture*; oh!" she threw her eyes back in ecstasy.

"Free range dogs. Like eggs."

"Oh! And the Harry Potter-esque pathways! The high stone walls and the autumn leaves growing on their sides. Mazes! From another century! Gosh it's too good," she raised her shoulders in supreme satisfaction.

The waitress appeared again to take their order. They still had not studied the menu.

"We promise to concentrate," Margherita said, as she and Jack dived their noses into the descriptions.

"What is mooli?"

"I was wondering the same," he said in his quiet, warm voice. "Ohh, Devon crab. Singlet Dell ham hock terrine," he purred. "But what is piccalilli?"

"This is a very English menu indeed," she said, reading each line carefully. There was salt marsh lamb with celeriac purée, white bean cassoulet, and thyme jus, pan fried Devon hake, Hereford onglet steak with triple cooked chips, Gressingham duck supreme with Armagnac and morel sauce, or Galloway beef with Guinness pie… Dorothy was not in Italy anymore.

"I can't have any dairy or gluten, so I'm going to have to be rather dull I am afraid," she said.

"So no wild mushroom millefeuille, truffle scented leeks, and Parmigiano milk for you, I presume?" He pronounced Parmigiano in the British way: 'Parme*san*.'

"Parm-i-giano," she said with a thick rolling r.

"What are you thinking?"

"I'm leaning seared tuna, I just need to decode this mooli. And then maybe the Devon caught scallops."

After they ordered, Jack stroked the neck of his wine glass as his eyes grazed Margherita's eyelids.

"From horseback riding on the beach to the shepherd's paths of Hampstead. You have lived quite a life this past pandemic."

"Ha. This past pandemic. Like an annual vacation. Well, you make me sound like a real high-flying brat. In truth, Mustique is very low-key. Colonial-style. No pretense. And Hampstead is just darling, like a storybook."

"Yes. Two very unpretentious, fanciful places to hang your hat."

"It's good to get out in the world."

"It is! I envy you. Your freedom. I wish I could just…" He looked out the window, frustration on his face, and shot his arm out into the air across the table. "Go! Just… venture!" He glanced at her. "Like you. With you, maybe."

She felt his stickiness in that moment. That sticky stuckness that comes with family and commitment. That three-legged, or five-legged race.

"You can venture once in a while. A week here, a week there. Everyone needs a little…" she spread her arm through the air in the same way he had.

"Hmm." He looked down at his wine glass.

"Hmm," she agreed.

"Well. No grass grows under your feet. You should write a book. A memoir. On this past pandemic alone. A year or two in your history."

"If I wrote a book about this year it would be a specimen of fragmented confusion shrouded in beauty. It would be a poem." A ray of light from the slightly brighter sky cast a glow across Margherita's face and her eyes grew big. "For Mustique, a dream scape of infrared energy, water vapor, and humidity. Bananas and frangipani and starfish—characters of the Grenadines. Liguria would be a sonnet of oily focaccia, the scent of baking rosemary, the sound of slapping water at the port. For London: tailcoats, crisp autumn days—wet ones too—moist, hydrated, very happy skin, the jolliest dogs, the most glorious light, and fiery hues, golden hues, the brightest of hues. Charm and elegance and old worldliness. A resurgence. Hope. A search. That would be London." She raised her wine glass and took a sip. "Though now with December coming… a slightly different vibe."

"You are a wonder."

"But you are happy here, aren't you? You've been non-stop. Projects around the globe. I've been following along," she said.

He sighed heavily. "Yes. Work is going really well. Really well. I've led some phenomenal projects. We've won a few awards over the past few years. The firm is gaining oodles of recognition. Everyone is doing brilliantly. My wife is in a really great place at work. Her career has never been stronger, and she's happy. The kids are good. Boisterous. Getting big."

"I saw! Wild! I can't believe how time zips around." In her head, each pronouncement was a too-hard ping on a funny bone. Success at work. Happy, successful wife. Happy thriving children. A contented family.

She braced herself for additional moments of knee-jerk reality and mirror-holding.

"My son's voice cracked the other day." His eyes went large as he shook his head in disbelief. "They're teenagers now."

"Get ready…" she teased.

"I know. I can't be silly anymore. I *embarrass* them. Last weekend I was making breakfast, and I made some silly joke about pancakes. I can't even remember what it was. My daughter looked at me like I was a leper. And she didn't laugh. She used to laugh!"

"Aw. She will laugh at your silly jokes again one day. Maybe not for a few years. But she will come to appreciate them again, I promise."

"I hope so." His bottom lip protruded slightly, and Margherita reached across to squeeze his arm. She could feel its strength, and she had a sudden impulse to climb into his lap and fall asleep.

Later, on their second glass of wine and main plates, the conversation drifted to their beginning.

"Have you stayed in touch with anyone?"

"Noah. My Forever Noah. But other than that, no not really. My boss disliked me immensely. What was her name—I can't even remember. Bev? Bev. She hissed every time I dared use the ladies room. If I wasn't glued to that drafting table…" Margherita leaned into the back of her chair as the waitress arrived with the first plates.

"Yes. I remember her. A bit intense."

"Yes."

"I remember you striding across that floor. So much allure. And zest. You lit up the room. You still do."

"I don't remember it quite like that," she laughed as she took a bite of the seared tuna.

"It was exactly like that!" he insisted.

"Well…"

He took a sip of his wine.

"I remember feeling a little stagnated. I desperately wanted… I don't know actually. Wiggle room. Unencumberment."

"You wanted to leave New York. I remember that. You were set on it."

"Yes. Somewhere new. Some place fresh." She folded her lips one over the other and shrugged.

"That's your thing, isn't it? To search. I worry about you."

"You do?"

"Yes! Of course I do. Constantly moving. Constantly leaving. What do you think you're looking for?"

She took a sip of wine and set her glass down slowly. "Who knows? I suppose I'll figure it out once I find it."

"Well, when you went to Italy for example, what did you have in mind?"

"Hmm… something big."

He smiled. "Something big."

"Yes. I suppose… I suppose I fear an average life. Predictable. Unexciting. Being in the same place for too long. The same work for too long."

"Your mother worked in the same industry for decades. Lived in the same city for decades. Same husband. Right? And she was big."

"But *she* was exciting. *She* was unpredictable. So far from average," Margherita said, her eyes widening at every 'she.'

"And she was struggling," Jack said.

Margherita shrugged and glanced out the window.

"Were you happy in Italy?" he asked, concern in his eyes.

"Umm. I was when I lived there before. In my twenties. This past stint was a little different, a little more stressful. It didn't feel the same, you know, with the pandemic. Italy survives and thrives on tourism, and without tourists, it's just sad."

He frowned sympathetically.

"And carrying your own venture, investing your own money, doing everything yourself, is a bit less carefree than going to work for someone else. At least in my case it was."

"But you were smashing it. And you will continue to be smashing. It's who you are."

"Well, thank you." She tipped her head. "But anyway, I'm happy to be in London. It feels right."

"I think London is perfect for you. And your brother is here?"

She nodded with hesitation. "Yes. But, he's busy. He works a lot. Has a family."

"And your dad?"

"He's good! Completely immersed in the Mustique hotel. He's happy," she smiled.

Jack watched her carefully. "I read, by the way, that article in the *Journal* about your mum and the new library at Yale. I'm sorry I didn't say anything sooner; I didn't know she made such an incredible donation."

Margherita clasped her hands together and licked her lips. "That article was really unnecessary. It should have been about the new library, not her. How much female empowerment can one tout and encourage from six feet below? They should have left her out of it," she said dismissively.

"I think it was lovely. She was clearly an extraordinary person, and extraordinary people are always worth celebrating, wherever in the earth they may be resting."

Margherita shrugged her lips. "By the way, I saw you went to a concert at like, nine in the morning last week. You are officially cooler than me."

He nodded slowly, perhaps realizing her eagerness to change the subject. A smile crept across his face and he held his hands in the air to demonstrate the enormity of his enthusiasm. He looked adorable, handsome, sweet. "It was incredible. I went twice last week! I don't think I've been to two gigs so close together before. Must be the latest incarnation of midlife crisis. I went to sixteen concerts last year. Not bad for the second year of COVID. *Three* Stones concerts."

"Wow! So sad about Charlie Watts, though. That hurt."

"I know. Awful. Do you know how many Stones concerts I've been to in my long, old life? My favorite band of all time."

"You know how we constantly refer to the glamour and rock and roll of the generations before us? Well, a little bit of your generation too, I suppose."

He dropped his chin and eyed her. She smiled in silent banter.

"Who will my kids talk about? The Stones will be so far back. The Who. The Monkees. Fleetwood Mac. Morrissey. The Smiths even, will feel like a dreaded visit to the ancient ruins to them. Who will they bring back from the grave? The Kardashians?" Her eyes grew larger as she spoke, and he nodded along, shook his head in turn.

"I know. It's horrid. A disgrace. Have you ever listened to the lyrics of today's music? They sing about DM's. Those aren't lyrics. That's not Cat Stevens. Leonard Cohen. Springsteen. John Lennon."

"Lou Reed! Paul Simon!" she exclaimed. "*Those* were lyricists."

"Joni Mitchell. Bob Dylan."

"And what do we have… "

"Oof. Was there a more heartbreaking lyricist than Joni?"

"She takes the cake. When I hear Joni Mitchell, I think… love lost. Poor gal."

His eyes followed her glance down to her plate. "What about you? You must have had tons of boyfriends."

Margherita could tell he had been waiting for the right moment for that one. She shook her head a centimeter left and right and smiled at the waitress who came to clear their plates away.

Isabetta Andolini

"Oh come now, you must have broken a few hearts."

"No… I don't think so. Disappointed maybe, but I never dated anyone long enough for heartbreak to be a possibility."

"No? Why not?"

"I don't know." She leaned back into her seat and looked out the window. "The whole concept terrified me. A relationship!" she said with widened eyes.

"So there hasn't been anyone of any consequence? I don't believe you."

She looked down at the bottom of her glass and shrugged her shoulders.

"Were you in love?" he asked, gently grazing his lips with his thumb and forefinger.

She shrugged again.

"Were you?" he asked again in that quiet, warm voice.

"I suppose," she admitted.

"Have you gotten over him?"

She tipped her head and glanced out the window again. A young man walked down the alley toward the pub, smoking a cigarette.

"I hope so."

Jack cocked his head. "Doesn't sound like it. So what happened?"

"I learned to live with it, I suppose."

A memory sprang to mind from an evening in Nick's bed. They were naked, facing each other, lying on their sides. Her left leg draped over him and his hand gently tickled the skin of her outer thigh.

"Does anyone in your world know that I exist?" she had asked in a soft voice, enveloped in the sounds of Lemon Jelly's "Soft."

"No," he had said, equally soft.

She had looked down at his hand. He stopped tickling her skin and brought it back to the mattress, where he slid it under his pillow, palm down.

How unsavory she had felt then. How alone.

In the gastro-pub in Clerkenwell, she held her palm over the base of her glass.

"You're not as happy as you let on," Jack said. He covered her hand with his large palm.

She bolted her spine upright in attention. "I've heard that exact sentence before!" she exclaimed, as if just realizing a clue to a puzzle. Her mind shot to Thayer.

"Have you?" he asked in his usual calm, Hugh Grant-like voice.

"Nobody is," she quipped, as she watched him turn her hand over. He massaged his thumb into the underside of her knuckles. "As happy as they seem."

Jack tipped his head. "But you have a talent for fooling most everyone."

"*Most.* Everyone," she smiled facetiously and he smiled back. "Do you have to go back to the office? What time is it?" She unzipped her purse and checked her phone. Nearly three p.m. She had not realized so much time had passed. "Oh my goodness, have I held you hostage?"

"Not at all. Though I'd gladly let you hold me hostage, anytime. And there's hardly anyone in the office today anyway."

They glanced out the window as the sky shifted from layered grey to snippets of hope and back to darkness again.

"You know when your phone feels dark and you realize the screen light is way down? That's what winter in London is, except you can't slide the screen light up when you want to," she said.

He placed his hand over hers once more and regarded her with unnerving intimacy, as if he was listening to her thoughts out loud. She excused herself to the ladies' room when the bill came, carefully taking the stairs one at a time, realizing only then how tipsy she was.

Upstairs again, he watched her approach the table and held his hand out, grazing the back of her leg.

"Shall we?" she asked.

"We shall," he stood.

How handsome he was in his v-neck sweater, how lovely and familiar his long fingers were as he reached for a final sip from his wine glass. How *good* it felt to stand next to him.

They both inched toward the chair in the corner behind their table, where they had draped their coats and scarves, an elegant pile of their outer layers. She readied to inch out of the way so that he could trade places and retrieve his, when she saw an animal expression coming toward her.

"Why am I suddenly aware I'm in a corner?" she laughed, a mischievous smile on her face as he wrapped his hands around her cheeks with a serious, concentrated expression.

He slowly pulled her in for a passionate kiss. He tasted of Rioja and desire, and in the corner of the restaurant, they embraced fervently, for what felt like forever, her leg inching upward, aching to be lifted, his large hand on the back of her thigh.

They let a sheet of air come between them.

"I've been wanting to do that for seven years," he said, going in for more.

At the sound of the waitress on the wooden steps, Margherita pulled away, a provocative smile on her face. Jack's lips remained parted as he watched her slither toward the stairs.

"Where are you off to?" he asked once they were outside.

She wrapped her scarf around her head. The rain had finally stopped and the afternoon was reversing its mood; a rivet of blue sky revealed itself and she felt unnerved by the day's many shifts.

"I have a tea at The Stafford in St. James Street."

"Right. Well." He stood above her, looking out over her head and debating modes of transport. "How about you come back toward St. Paul's with me and you can get the tube from there."

He led the way up to Farringdon Road, holding her hand tightly. She felt his long fingers wrapped around her small hand;

it was always an odd sensation to her, so unaccustomed to the practice. She thought of her conversation with Thayer. Hand-holding.

His strides were long and she had to walk quickly to keep up with him. Suddenly he stopped, in the middle of the empty sidewalk, and grasped her cheeks to bring her in for a kiss once again.

And then they were off. "We'll get a taxi. Easier." At Farringdon Road, she told him about her difficulty in remembering which way to look first before crossing the street, and how many times she had nearly been run over.

"We can't have that," he said, looking both ways as they crossed together, her hand in his.

In those few moments, she felt joyously looked after. Taken care of. Calm.

The short taxi ride was as steamy as the last few moments in the gastro-pub, instigated by her own greed.

She took his large hand and placed it on her upper thigh, where he began to knead and squeeze and rub, and between Farringdon and St. Paul's, she managed to half straddle him across the leather seats.

Outside again, they wandered in the direction of the church, where Jack stopped to spin her around, his hands on her shoulders, pointing out historical facts of its creation. Information she had learned at Yale, but she relished his pride in re-telling the history of his city all the same.

"I don't want to go back in there. I want to go somewhere with you," he said, having spun her round again.

"But you must. You have universities to build. Libraries. Hospitals. Ski resorts. And I have jobs to get. You *promise* you will call a few friends? Poke around a little for me?" She poked his abdomen beneath his coat.

"I promise. I'm on the case. We'll sort you out."

"Will you? Sort me out?" She smiled coyly.

"Fuck." He threw his head back.

She laughed.

"You have the naughtiest laugh," he said, as he glanced up toward his office building, a gust of wind against his cheeks.

They walked a few meters apart. She turned sideways to smile at him tauntingly, her hands buried in her trench coat pockets.

They stopped and faced each other, maintaining a distance between themselves. She nodded toward the glass office building in the corner of their vision.

"If ever I have something real to talk to you about, and I don't want you to be distracted, I'll bring you here," she said, smirking widely, nodding toward his office building.

"Yeah. An invisible fence."

"You can't do anything here," she said, shaking her head, still grinning.

He bent down to hold her neck with one hand, his long fingers wrapped behind her ear. How warm his hand was. How fine she felt beneath it. How anchored and full, in that moment.

He brought her in for a kiss goodbye on each of her cheeks. His hands were shelter.

"Goodbye you," he said, walking backwards.

"Ciao," she said.

She felt his body drift farther and farther away, back to his office. Back to his life. Later, his family.

And she, alone again.

As she turned in the direction of the tube, not especially eager to reunite with her own reality—the job applications, the unanswered query letters for The Villa, the increasingly hostile emails from the Italian lawyers, and her overextended credit card—she felt herself shaking.

Her boot slipped on the first wet steps of the tube entrance, and her right leg bent beneath her, with her knee the first thing heading down the steps. She yelped as she threw her arm out to the metal railing.

Karma, she thought, as she shakily righted herself. *Karma.* She was fine, thank goodness, but she was certain it was the world's reminder of her unscrupulous tendencies. How devious and counter-productive she could be. How very little it did for her in the end.

Resplendent. Bold. Courageous.

She felt none of those things.

And she had forgotten her duck head umbrella.

LONDON

December 10, 1996

IN THE CAR park, with Bea waiting outside, Francine rummaged in her purse for a valium. Her heart had not stopped racing since she had received the awful phone call five days before, and she was not sure how she would possibly face him.

She swallowed it dry and brought her shaking hand to her hair, to smooth it behind her shoulders.

Car door open, she stepped out into the blustery afternoon, the wind coming off the canal below Kensal Green sending bursts of chilled air up her long black skirt. She shivered.

Bea held out her arm. She looked more fragile than ever, her bald head wrapped in a silk scarf below a faux fur hat to ward off the chill. Though she had only just started chemo, the fear of what might come had taken a toll on her friend's color and spirit, and Francine found it especially difficult to look at Bea with her own chin up, to see beyond the newly shaved head and thinning eyebrows. And yet there she was, holding her arm out, the same friend Francine had known since childhood, since balloon birthday parties on the Heath. Francine hooked Bea's arm with her own and held onto her friend's bony hand.

"I hate this. I hate this. I hate this," Francine said.

Bea was stoic. Francine eyed her. She stopped suddenly.

"The flowers. Fuck. We forgot the flowers. I can't believe it."

"Bea. It's okay. It's really okay. We'll come back tomorrow with flowers."

Bea began to cry, and Francine wrapped her arm around her friend's spindly back and kissed her cheek.

"Come, now. We're late."

Inside the gates of the cemetery, Francine saw Ulla first, her blonde hair fading into the whiteness of the day, and her body as slight as ever, like a thin black Sharpie standing on its end in a grassy field. She was surrounded by other black-clad bodies: her disgusting, pot-bellied American husband, her catty friends, and an older woman Francine assumed to be her mother. Only when Francine and Bea drew closer to the crowd of mourners did she see the bouncy ball shape of Ulla's protruding belly.

She felt her throat drop into her esophagus.

"Yeah. I forgot to tell you that," Bea said, catching Francine's horrified expression.

"I thought…I thought she didn't want any more."

"Apparently, she does. Or, it's a safety net for her next divorce."

And there *he* was. Listening to someone speak, someone who was crying, who Francine did not recognize. His skin looked too pale, and his eyes were swollen, his shoulders stooped. He stood with his weight on his good leg and raised his hand to this person's shoulder, squeezed it, rubbed their back.

So like Keith. To tend to someone else, to care for someone else, when it was he who needed the support.

Francine stood frozen in place on the cold earth. She could feel it creeping upward into her black boots. The deadened ground seeping through her bones, suctioning her into its lifelessness.

He looked up then. Sensed her, perhaps.

She stared back at him, her lips parted, her eyebrows ever so slightly furrowed. As if she were about to cry. But her heartbeat was too vigorous to let her nervous system act.

It was he who approached her. It was his arms that rose before hers, to embrace her before she embraced him.

"You were right, Francie," he said into her ear, his weak voice muffled by her coat.

"About what?" Her voice was barely above a whisper.

"Life isn't all it's cracked up to be."

She wrapped her long fingers around the back of his head and held him there, the way she held Margherita when she was tired or upset. But with Margherita, she seemed to know what to say to make it better, and with Keith, her best friend, the love of her life, she had no idea.

Of all of the pain she had felt in her life, she knew not the pain of losing a child.

LONDON

November 23, 2021

THE DAY AFTER her unexpectedly eventful lunch, in her flat high above Hampstead surrounded by the darkness of a London sky, Margherita felt edgy and ever so slightly hungover. Jack lingered in her mind, and with thoughts of him came contrasting feelings of melancholy. The afternoon had been so far from what she had imagined it would be.

It had been wonderful.

But something about its wonderfulness stroked her the wrong way.

Margherita: Do you remember Jack Nathans

Noah: Not as well as you do.

Margherita: How!!!
Margherita: Did I tell you about that once??
Margherita: Jeesh I miss you
Margherita: I had lunch with him yesterday

Noah: Yes you told me. I was wondering when that would eventually happen

Margherita: Oh gosh
Margherita: Well I assumed it would be a very innocent above the line 12:30 Monday lunch
Margherita: But then he ordered wine. You really are a nation of boozers.
Margherita: And it turns out, he's just as charming

Isabetta Andolini

Noah: Even you were drinking?

Noah: And it's not my nation anymore. I have a green card remember

Margherita: I haven't stopped drinking since I set foot on this isle.

Margherita: I have gained 300 pounds

Noah: Welcome to my world

Margherita: It's awful, I want to stop and everyone's like, let's go get drinks and let's eat late dinners and I just want to say, NO, let's drink tea and go to bed at 8.

Noah: And what happened at lunch? Or after?

Margherita: We were left alone in the upstairs dining room and he cornered me

Margherita: I must be going to hell I swear

Margherita: where is MY man

Noah: You made out in the restaurant

Noah: Is he single

Margherita: No

Margherita: still married

Margherita: do you still want to be my friend

Margherita: do not repeat that obviously. Trying to get a job in this town. And not ruin people's lives.

Margherita: a very serious chemical attraction that doesn't die after 7 or 8 years, that doesn't happen often. Just commenting, not justifying

Margherita: And he's such a great person and great dad and so smart and wonderful and is genuinely concerned I am floating and unhappy and it just makes me sad because A) why does he have to be married and B) where is my Jack and C) why is this wonderful human cheating on his family

Margherita: or D) does everyone cheat and I'm just an idiot trying to figure out a moot point

Margherita: If it was so natural to be one hundred

percent fully satisfied by one other human being, then why have we been talking about affairs for centuries?
Margherita: I've never been married. They say it's hard. Who am I to judge?

Noah: Your problem, my dear, is that once in a blue moon you want something more, or different, than what these historic cheaters want.
Noah: find your own Jack.
Noah: read up on self defeatism

LONDON

November 30, 2021

Margherita: It is the coldest damn day here and I'm standing in line outside OUTSIDE for almost an hour in some awful neighborhood I've never been in waiting for a goddamn booster
Margherita: freezing my ass off

Noah: Oh wow yeah it's cold in LA too. Like 65.

Margherita: oh fuck off

Noah: Why is the line so long

Margherita: freaken socialism

Noah: which one are you getting

Margherita: I don't know, maybe Pfizer. Is there a Xanax add-on available yet?
Margherita: I just want to go home right now
Margherita: to a house a grew up in
Margherita: I have 20 dollars in my bank account and it's not even mine

Noah: Ah, any job prospects?
Noah: You'll even this all out
Noah: You're young. Anxiety is part of life. You'll be fine
Noah: And if not, I'll remember you fondly

Margherita: My nerves are so rattled lately I think I am going to rocket off into space.

Margherita: is it normal to have such swings in mood or do I just live in denial until reality sucks me dry again

Margherita: Tomorrow I am seeing a Colombian guy I went out with once in 2018 and he is here for one night on a layover from Africa where he is working

Margherita: And omicron or not I'm having sex

Margherita: Enough of this abstinence shit, it's not good for the nervous system

Margherita: Did I tell you I saw Nick? Pretending that didn't happen.

Noah: pretending you didn't just say that.

Noah: Where do you find these international men

Noah: Is he married

Margherita: I thought he got married, but I see no evidence of it, and he hasn't said anything about it

Noah: how old is he

Margherita: early forties

Noah: I wonder at what age you will invert and start dating young guys

Margherita: I too am starting to wonder this. Am starting to see why women do this. Those bodies.

Noah: When I was 19 I dated a 38 year old

Margherita: was that your Ayurvedic doctor you once told me about?

Noah: Different crazy.

Margherita: Oh. At least the crazy ones are memorable.

LONDON

December 8, 2021

MORNING RUNS BECAME darker and darker. The time of year when night goggles were necessary before eight arrived like a shock, but having the street down to Primrose Hill to herself and being one of the first to witness the fuchsia skies in Regent's Park was among the most glorious segues into a dismal December day.

She hurried back to the attic apartment to await a package which did not make an appearance.

Hours later, after a phone call with a recruiter that went nowhere as soon as she admitted to never having worked on residential projects, she lay on her stretch mat, staring at the ceiling and not doing the one-hour at-home pilates session she had promised herself she would do. Mindlessly scrolling through her phone was less of a commitment.

> **Margherita:** Ugh I've been at home ALL day waiting for fedex.
> **Margherita:** *Send out for whiskey, send out for gin*
>
> **Noah:** what's in the package
>
> **Margherita:** necessary ingredients for a child-less existence
>
> **Noah:** ah. So it *is* important
> **Noah:** what's the latest with your men
>
> **Margherita:** blah

Margherita: do you think Wesley knows Jack?
Suddenly wondering if this will ever get back to him.

Noah: I think he knows you do

Margherita: what??! How would he know about that?

Noah: everyone at that firm did and they've all dispersed in the past eight years, so make yourself a hierarchical graph and do the math.

Margherita: oh for gods sake

Noah: don't fuck where you work

Margherita: boring

Noah: seriously. Be careful.

Margherita: I am
Margherita: I am confined to the very ironic joke of fedex's estimated delivery hours. No havoc wreaking.

Noah: you're going to get fired or you're going to get hurt

Margherita: one needs to be employed to be fired
Margherita: do you think I am bound for a Sylvia Plath-ish life

Noah: You can't afford Chalcot Square. Nor Fitzroy Road.

Margherita: preposterous because it is shockingly close to the train tracks

---

That evening, between job applications, google searches of peripheral details of her mother's London life, and one bold, cold call to a firm in Canary Wharf, she entered a 'whatever' state of mind. Or, according to Noah, an arena of self-defeatism.

Margherita: Hypothetically... if one was wanting a friendly cocktail with a friend, what might a friend like you say, hypothetically

Jack: I'd say what a great idea

Margherita: have you heard of Archibald Chisholm by the way? Or seen a copy of his gossip column Men and Matters

Margherita: what a title. Wonder how juicy that got.

Jack: extremely juicy. A financial gossip column. Everything historic leads to twitter.

Margherita: he lived in Gainsborough gardens. And so did john le carré. Did you know john died from a fall?! After such a life. A Fall.

Jack: yes. What a legend.
Jack: where did this train of research come from

Margherita: Just reading about the previous notable residents of Gainsborough

Jack: so this will be a boozy and friendly lunch
Jack: it was quite friendly last time
Jack: If I recall

She bit the inside of her cheek. *Flirtation and sex*, she thought and sighed heavily, staring out the window toward the barren treetops.

Margherita: it stupidly hadn't crossed my mind that we might have v different interpretations of the word Friendly

Jack: don't worry, I knew what you meant

Margherita: words are silly meaningless things aren't they

She returned to her stretch mat, stomach down, did five counts of upper back stretches, and harrumphed into the comfort of her folded forearms. Staring at nothing, eyes unfocused, felt like the right thing to do for a while.

NEW YORK

FRANCINE COULD HEAR voices.

She slowly opened her eyes, unsure where she was, or where the voices were coming from. Inside her head?

Everything was white. White door. White walls. She looked down at her body. White sheets. Starch.

Hospital.

She tried to swallow, but her throat was too dry. She tipped her head toward the IV drip next to her. Then she heard her name. A man's voice. Speaking softly. Another man's voice.

She shifted her body up the narrow bed. Her muscles felt weak and her stomach felt empty.

She heard her children's names.

She closed her eyes. But even then, everything was white.

Fuck me, she thought.

Still here.

LONDON

Margherita stood on the sidewalk down the block from the Ginger Pig, across from the block-long construction site for a new luxury condo, adjusting her AirPods and unknowingly scrunching her face into a slinky as Johanna spoke.

"I'm speaking to my bank about the details of the loan, so that's TBD. But Hart Browne… Margherita they'd be fantastic. Take another look at the hotel they did in Madrid. I know it's urban, but it feels like a similar aesthetic. I think they really get it. They would be my first choice, maybe my only choice, since my little in-road contact gets me a big fat discount."

"Yeah, they're incredible. I don't disagree." Margherita looked down at her phone screen, watching the seconds add up, feeling her project in which she had invested so much slipping away with every increase. Two minutes, eleven seconds. Two minutes, twelve seconds. Two minutes, thirteen seconds.

"Would you consider working for them? If I made that a clause of the contract? They'd have to agree of course and essentially hire you, but that could be brilliant for you. You're looking for a job. They're such an impressive firm."

"Yeah. No. Definitely, they're incredible. But they're in New York…"

"Yes. I mean, that's home for you. So that would work, right?" Johanna's voice was chipper, so positive-sounding, as if she had solved the puzzle for Margherita.

Margherita opened her mouth to speak as a crane lifted half a dozen cement slabs in the middle of the construction site. Those slabs had a lovely view of Marylebone; they could see more clearly than anyone on the ground.

"I… yeah. I mean, yeah. I just don't want to get ahead of myself. Let's see what your bank says first, right?" Two minutes, forty seconds.

"Yes. Yes. Crucial step. Oh, shit, my publicist is calling. Right, listen, I'll call you after my meeting at the bank next week. But think about all of this, okay? I think we're onto something here!" Johanna exclaimed, and she ended the call.

Margherita inhaled as the crane lowered the slabs again, out of sight behind the temporary divider wall. She brushed through her WhatsApp chats, wishing someone would suddenly write her and tell her what to do.

She wandered listlessly toward La Fromagerie, with its charming Christmas lights and friends sitting outside catching up over turnip soup and tea. She went inside for no reason at all. Frenchies dashed around her, wearing wool scarves and color-ful socks, speaking significantly more French than Margherita could muster on a good day and buying heaps of fromage. The shop had always been one of her favorites, for its charm and its coziness, and she wanted to be a part of its neighborhood conviv-iality, but no matter how many times she went in, she remained just as lactose intolerant as she had been on the previous visit and always ended up scut-scuttling next door to the Ginger Pig. At the butcher, happy, well-dressed, civilized Londoners exited with bags of expensive cuts, prepared for dinner parties and real meals. Lots of protein.

As she walked toward the High Street, with a gander around Daunt in mind, she texted her brother, feigning a sense of excite-ment for a prospect that was quickly creating a circular pit in her stomach like a dust storm.

Isabetta Andolini

Margherita: guess what

Margherita: I might have a little traction with the villa

Margherita: Thayer's ex-wife is speaking to Hart Browne in NY about pursuing the project. She wants to buy the villa. She went to see it last week and now seems quite hooked on the idea of this project

Benjamin: Oh that's brilliant. Keep me posted

Margherita: that's it?

Benjamin: what else?

Margherita: I've only been working on this for a year…. But ok cool. I'll keep you posted.

Benjamin: why do you need a cheerleader?

Margherita: never mind

Benjamin: Can't you learn to be proud of yourself? And that's enough sometimes?

She stared at his message.

Fuck you, she thought. *Can't you show a little interest sometimes?*

Inside Daunt, Margherita placed her palm over her heart. Palpitations were the norm, as if her hand had buried itself beneath the organ and sat between it and her skeleton, disabling it from ever settling fully.

Back to New York, she thought. *Could I stomach it?*

She stared at the novels on the shelves, organized alphabetically, hoping the sight of bound spines and fictional friends would calm her. Around the shop, locals politely glided around each other's shoulders, reading blurbs, pointing titles out to friends and loved ones, keeping small children quiet. Scenes of everyday people—who were not in that moment hiding anything, such as extreme debt, or extramarital affairs—innocently perusing new and older titles, sent a wave of anxiety from her stomach to her head.

She needed to quieten her nerves. Their hyperactivity fought her productivity.

On her phone, the clandestine chat with Jack that usually stirred both adrenaline and comfort suddenly made her depressed.

> **Margherita:** you know when the vices that once helped you relax start to have the opposite affect
>
> **Nick:** 100%
>
> **Margherita:** I need stronger drugs
>
> **Nick:** exercise more
> **Nick:** refocus
> **Nick:** unplug
>
> **Margherita:** you're my personal podcast Nicky
>
> **Nick:** lol

She waited for him to say something else, to ask how she was doing, how was it going… anything at all. But he said nothing.

> **Margherita:** how are you doing
>
> **Nick:** good
> **Nick:** tired

Cool, she thought, visualizing a thumbs up.

> **Margherita:** your country is depressing me. When does it ever get light again?

She didn't *need* a cheerleader, but it would be nice once in a while. Francine had never given her that satisfaction; she had suggested any yearning for it was some sort of weakness.

"Don't get comfy leaning on anyone, Marghe. Learn to stand straight," she'd say. "And if you start to tilt in the wind, use your own brawn to right yourself."

NEW YORK

January 2, 1997

FRANCINE GLARED AT the nurse icily. The nurse glared back.

"Dr. Bronsson always lets me use the telephone," she said, gritting her teeth.

"Well, he's not here, and it's against the rules," the nurse said as she hung the chart at the end of the bed.

Francine sucked in her cheeks. "What if I paid you? I will pay you five thousand dollars to bring a telephone in here."

The nurse harrumphed. "I'll be back with your dinner."

"Don't bother," Francine spat out.

The nurse glided past Tommaso as he entered Francine's room, raising her eyebrows at him in warning.

Tommaso approached Francine's bed warily. She lay half upright, propped against five deflated hospital pillows, wearing her glasses and holding a pad of paper.

"They'll allow me paper but not a pen. Apparently one cannot take their own life with a sheath of paper, but it is indeed plausible to kill myself with a fucking ballpoint pen," she said crisply to her husband. "Is that not the most fucking absurd thing? Can you get me a fucking pen? And a fucking telephone?"

Tommaso exhaled and sat in the arm chair against the wall, near her IV drip, facing the bed. He clasped his hands in his lap.

"Francie, why don't you just rest?"

"Because I am not an invalid."

He looked down at his lap and made a teepee with his thumbs.

"I need to make a call," she said coldly.

"No, you don't," he said, weak and tired.

Francine inhaled and exhaled and stared at the wall in front of her. She closed her eyes, her head against the sad pillows.

"Can you please leave me be for a few hours?" she said quietly.

Tommaso slowly stood and exited the room, closing the door peacefully.

SOUTH DOWNS

December 18, 2021

MARGHERITA FELT HER phone vibrate in her back pocket. She took it out; a message from her father.

"This isn't really what I should be doing today," she said, as she slid her phone into her jacket pocket and watched her wellies sink into the damp grass.

"What *should* you be doing?" Thayer asked, raising his chin ever so slightly and squinting as he looked down across the fields.

"I don't know. Job search."

"It's one week to Christmas. England is officially on holiday."

"In New York we'd all be at work until the twenty-third."

"We pride ourselves on putting Spain and Italy down but really we Brits are just as lazy as the rest of Europe. Don't let the stiff trench coats and three-piece suits fool you. See that stone wall up ahead? That's a fine spot for a picnic, you reckon?"

Margherita raised her head to look out before her. The sky was already turning shades of yellow as the sun began its three o'clock melt into December dusk.

"Sure."

When they reached the stone wall, Margherita noted its beautiful, classic construction—the kind of stone wall people tried to recreate all over Connecticut and beyond. She hoisted herself up onto the cold stones and crossed her legs. Thayer sat facing her, one leg to each side, like a ten-year-old boy. He retrieved two apples from his backpack and then placed the sack behind him.

Margherita held the pink apple in her hand.

"What will you do for Christmas?" she asked.

He took a bite from his apple. It was a good crisp one, Margherita could tell. "Mother's," he said as he chewed a big chunk.

"Looking forward?" she asked, watching his cheek engorge with pieces of apple.

"Mm." He shrugged. "She's looking forward," he said, as the pieces in his mouth got smaller.

"Mm."

"You want a family? I don't think I've ever asked you that."

Margherita sat the apple in her lap. She wasn't in the mood to crunch.

"I don't know. Maybe."

"Your brother's wife is poppin' them out like Pez."

"Ha. Oh my God. Pez. I never liked Pez."

"Me neither. Shit candy."

"I don't know. My brother has always done what he's supposed to do. What everyone else does. What he expects himself to do."

"All very predictable."

"All very judgmental."

"Tends to go hand in hand," Thayer nodded as he took another bite and looked out at the sky getting lighter right before it got darker.

"Yeah," Margherita sighed.

"I think that's changing a lot, though. This notion of 'what you're supposed to do.' I think expectations are changing every day. Especially after COVID. It's thrown a detonator into rites of passage and everyone's timelines."

"What would Edith Wharton say?" She rested her hands behind her and leaned her weight into them.

"To give her the damn tightrope."

Margherita laughed. It was a famous Edith Wharton quote: 'Life is always either a tightrope or a feather bed. Give me the tightrope.'

"She deflected expectations quite profoundly," Thayer said.

"I hate this whole subject. What I'm supposed to do. What I thought I'd do. What I'll probably never do. I'm sick of it. I'm sick of thinking about it, of contemplating it, of trying to figure it out, of feeling like I'm farther and farther and farther away from ever getting there."

"Getting where?" Thayer asked casually, taking another bite of apple.

"There!" Margherita thrust her arm out into the cold air, ineloquently gesturing toward the open fields, the world. Thayer followed her gesture.

"You'll never get 'there.'" He mimicked her motion. "The sooner you come to terms with that the better."

She looked at him sideways and twisted her lips around to the side.

"Margherita, I'm forty-five years old, divorced, watching my bank account—which I worked so damn hard to build—deflate with every lawsuit pay-out from my latest career disaster, with no idea really what I'll do next, if I'll ever make a movie again, and I have three houses in three different countries I never use, and no children to teach anything to or learn from, and I am living in the same fucked up universe you are and don't have any answers. But I am sitting on this stone wall in the middle of the stunning South Downs, having a fucking fantastic Pink Lady apple with a human I really appreciate, and so… that's it. That's literally it. It's complicated and shit gets weird and you just have to wade through and sometimes you feel the impulse to make moves and be brilliant and sometimes you just want to sit on this fucking wall and watch the sunset and be really cold but enjoy it anyway."

Thayer looked momentarily exasperated. Then he took another bite of his apple, and the only sound between them was his crunching.

"I've never heard you say so many words at once."

"Yeah. Don't get used to it."

"Ugh. Ugh!" Margherita screamed, aggravated, at the sky.

Thayer repeated her tormented cry. "Argh!" he yelled, shaking his fists.

Margherita looked at him. Her incredulous smile quickly turned into furrowed brows. She wasn't certain whether he was mocking her or offering companionship in aggravation. "Arghhhh!" she screamed louder.

He screamed louder.

She glanced sideways at his face staring out at the downs. His eyes glistened.

Margherita took the first bite of her apple as Thayer put his core down next to him.

"Where are you from, Thayer? I've never asked."

"Wiltshire. Raised knee-deep in cow parsley. High chalk downs. White horses. Lush valleys. Castles and chapels and dovecotes. Oh my."

"Sounds dreamy. Do you think you'll go back?"

"Hmm." He stared out at the sea of pasture before him, the earth at a complete opposite of Wiltshire's fields of bluebells. "It's hard to go back, isn't it? You want to. But it's almost impossible. Comes with so much... over-thinking."

"Yeah."

"Do you think you'll go back to New York?"

She took a big bite out of the apple and passed a long beat chewing, thinking of Hart Browne and Johanna's tentative proposal.

"I don't know," she finally said.

"But it's New York!"

She shrugged.

"Well, what don't you know?" he asked.

"I don't know what I don't know. I feel like I should. My insides are equally averse to both possibilities. I suppose—this sounds a little obtuse, but—maybe I'm scared to let go of an idea, or daydream, or past chapter. I think that's what makes me feel sick sometimes. Like physically ill. The room is shaking. If I move away and stay away and we're never in that same place again…" She shuddered. "It's just over. It's done." She glanced at him.

He listened patiently, relaxed.

"Well. If I never go back. It's in the past," she continued. "My life with her in it. Everything I knew." Margherita looked down at her masticated apple, the insides quickly turning yellow. "I don't know where to be to be close to her, but not be, you know? To not cut myself off, but cut myself off."

"I sense a Jackson Browne song here," Thayer said.

"These Days," Margherita replied.

"I suppose you'll feel her more there."

"Yeah. I don't know. That's the worst part, right? I feel her everywhere. Everywhere I am, she is. And so ironic, right?" Margherita shook her head at the fading daylight. "She was never there before. And now, she's everywhere."

―――――――――

The next day was a variation on a theme: dark morning followed by one hour of bright light, followed by cascading bleakness. Margherita decided, with the holidays on everyone's heels, to do a little exploring.

> **Margherita:** holy shit I am walking from mortlake to Barnes and omg the planes!!!
> **Margherita:** They are deafening!
> **Margherita:** How do people live like this
> **Margherita:** What are you doing for Christmas
>
> **Noah:** Staying in LA. In-laws are here for five days.
> **Noah:** what are you doing
>
> **Margherita:** staying in London watching my ass grow
> **Margherita:** winter here is depressing

Margherita: my eyes now hurt, like actual pain, when it is NOT dark out

Noah: what are you eating for Xmas?
Noah: did you buy cheese?

Margherita: a sweet potato
Margherita: I don't eat dairy
Margherita: what are you eating

Noah: Halibut
Noah: ugh, dull

Margherita: I'm alone, I don't need to cook

Noah: Spoil yourself

Margherita: What for

Isabetta Andolini

NEW YORK

January 3, 1997

IT HAD BEEN three days since she had been admitted, and the doctor on her case had finally taken her off the IV drip, enabling her to move without a wheely plastic bag. Francine scratched at the spot on her arm where a swath of blue tape had been stuck, ripped off, and replaced over and over again.

When the inpatient floor at Bellevue went dim and tranquil for the evening, Francine rose from her squeeky, starchy bed and lackadaisically walked down the hall toward the nurse's station, where she knew the night shift nurse would be getting her first cup of tea. Francine reached over the counter, unplugged the jack from the desk wall, bunched up the cable cord in her hand and swiftly carried away the phone in its cradle.

In her room, she plugged it into the jack and prayed it would work for a long distance call.

Sitting on the cold linoleum floor with her back against the wall, the heater next to her, she listened to the comforting sound of the foreign ring.

"Hello?"

"I know it's nearly five a.m. but please don't hang up," she said hurriedly.

He said nothing. But she could hear him breathing.

"Please say something," she said. "I need to hear your voice."

He said nothing.

"I'm still in hospital. Did anyone tell you? I asked the nurse to tell Dr. Bronsson to call you. They won't tell me where he is. It's driving me mad. I've been his patient for over a decade, and he hasn't shown his face. Can you believe it?"

"Francie, it's not all about you."

She looked down at the floor between her two flat feet and ran her finger over the plastic of the telephone cradle.

"I know," she said.

"Do you?"

"I just want to see you. And hear your voice. And lie next to you. And—"

He cleared his throat. "Please don't call in the middle of the night. I'm sorry to hear you're in hospital. I didn't know. But you sound alright, so I'm going back to sleep."

"No! Don't. I, um…" She swallowed. "I overdosed. New Year's Eve. Quite a party," she said ironically.

"Francie. I'm sorry." His voice was stern. Chilly. "I really am. But—"

"Do you know why?" she interrupted. "Why I wanted to see white so fucking badly? Why I wanted to give up on this shit show? Because. Because I fucked everything up." She started to cry and her throat grew thick. "I always do. I always have. I always will. It wasn't even a case of being off my meds. I did it as sober as Elton John."

"Francie—"

"No. Fuck! Let me finish! Lisabet would be alive, if it weren't for me. You would've been able to save her. The Keith I knew at university. The Keith I knew when we were young. So strong and so dashing and so vital. So full of everything that I ever wanted. You would have jumped into the water with both of your fucking legs and you would have swum like crazy until you found her and dragged her through the current back to shore. It's my fault. I ruined you. Like I always told you I would. And Keith, you're the most important person to me. You're my person. And the fact that I've ruined your life so fucking irreversibly. Well I… I don't know how to live with myself. And since I'm still here, on this side of the dead grass, all I want is to see you."

He didn't say anything.

"Please say something."

"Francine. I think you and I shouldn't speak for a while."

"What?" she whimpered.

"It's better that way. I need time. The truth is, yes. Maybe if I hadn't been in pain from the accident, I'd have been in the water with her. And it wouldn't have happened. But I wasn't in the water. And it did happen. And neither of us can play the 'what if' game. It's exhausting and no one wins at it. But I need time now, to make sense of everything. If that's even possible. And to not be worrying about you. My life can no longer be about supporting you or helping you or saving you or forgiving you. Save yourself, alright? Goodnight, Francie."

Click.

It sounded in her ears for decades.

LONDON

December 25, 2021

Noah: Happy Christmas

Margherita: Happy fucking Christmas

Noah: You've turned into a Brit with that greeting
Noah: You'll be calling me a c-word next
Noah: What's your plan?

Margherita: No plan
Margherita: Gypsy woman

Noah: Where's your brother?

Margherita: At his in-laws

Noah: And he left you alone?

Margherita: I told him I was having lunch with Thayer

Noah: Where's your dad?

Margherita: At my aunt's house in Carmel

Noah: Whoa, you turned down a trip to Carmel?

Margherita: It would take me over twenty-four hours to get there door to door.

Noah: So you'd rather be alone eating a sweet potato.

Margherita: I'm not feeling very people-y at the moment

Noah: Do you have a good book at least?

Margherita: I have lots. I'll go for a walk in the park. All will be fine. I can survive a holiday by myself. Surely there are worse things in life.

And there were worse things in life than an early run in the chilled morning stillness. She ran all the way down to Marylebone, and, not feeling tired, continued on to Hyde Park, which felt sadly barren and flat compared to the Heath. Holiday walkers trickled in, and as Margherita's pinky toes began to bleed from wear and tear inside her muddy sneakers, the sky turned a shade of unfamiliar blue.

She looked up and smiled, despite herself. Everything looked slightly brighter beneath it: the pond swans more elegant, the birds more charming, other joggers more companionable. Looking around, she noticed a man and his little boy sitting on a bench before the pond in full cycle gear, a bike on either side of them. The father pointed off into the distance, perhaps up into a tree to point out a bird, and the little boy followed the direction of his finger. It was such a simple moment, but at the same time, it had the potential to be one of those moments, or mornings, or Christmases that each of them would remember forever.

There was extraordinary in the ordinary, which was not very ordinary at all, but monumental in all its micro moments, in all its splendor. It didn't always have to be big to be brilliant.

She headed north through Hyde Park, the sun streaking across the wide grassy expanses and sending delirious, if fleeting, ecstasy down her sweaty spine. The whiplash power of rays and simplicity.

Margherita ended her run just south of Regent's Park and decided to walk the rest of the way. By the time she reached the cross light on Marylebone Road, the sky had returned to grey mashed potato. She stood next to a middle-aged man speaking Italian into his cell phone, waiting for the walk signal.

"Sempre grigio. Tutto giorno. Grigio," he said forlornly, annoyed. *Always gray. Every day. Gray.*

Margherita smiled to herself. How confoundingly depressing London must be to an Italian.

She decided to call her brother as she passed the boating lake, looking glimmer-less in the bleak light.

"No Christmas burgers," she said in a small voice.

"No," Benjamin breathed sympathetically into the phone. "No Christmas burgers."

"It still feels so weird. Like it's not a real Christmas. Even if she went back to work the next morning."

"Yeah."

"Couldn't *wait* to get out of the house."

"Obsessing over her career gave her a focus. It gave her a bar by which to judge her success in fighting her illness," Benjamin said.

"I suppose the bar of motherhood was less appealing." Margherita looked around at the families who had come out for an afternoon meander. Small children in big coats and parents holding take-away tea cups.

"There is no possible barometer for motherhood. Not even a sane mother knows where that is. It's a shit show no matter what, and one day you will realize that."

"Hmmph."

"Anyway, got to run. Speaking of sanity." In the background, a tiny person wailed and a dog barked. "Fuck me."

Margherita smiled. "My how your life has changed, my high-flying, bespoke-shirted brother."

"Yeah. Where did *that* guy go?"

"Merry Christmas, Benji."

"Happy fucking Christmas, Marghe."

Walking north through Belsize Park, Margherita gave herself a pep talk. The remainder of the day would be spent pleasantly with a book and a movie. It would be lovely. There would be

Isabetta Andolini

no crying. There was nothing wrong with spending Christmas by oneself, with a book and a movie. Companionship came in all forms.

Margherita: happy Xmas to you, hope you got a good dictionary or something equally enlightening

He didn't respond.

NEW YORK

January 4, 1997

"MARGHERITA, WHAT ARE you doing?" Francine could hear Tommaso's voice outside the bedroom.

"Waiting for Mommy. I thought we could color together. When she wakes up from her nap. And play Parcheesi."

Francine rolled over to face away from the door, where her seven-year-old daughter evidently waited on the other side. To color and play Parcheesi.

She eyed the phone on the bedside table.

She never wanted to color again. How would she tell a seven-year-old that?

"Mommy might not be ready to play for a little while. Why don't we go downstairs? Maybe Benjamin will color with us." Tommaso's voice. His sweet, kind voice.

"But I only want Mommy!" Francine heard the beginnings of Margherita's needy wails. She pulled the comforter over her head and held her hands over her ears.

But no amount of layers would drown out that click. That horrible click.

LONDON

December 27, 2021

SITTING IN AN old metal chair on her roof, Margherita stared at the full moon swathed in clouds, as if it wore a shawl it kept readjusting. She tugged a thick cashmere sweater around her and propped her feet up on the wooden bench that lined the outer wall of the balcony. It was a strange sensation to sit outside at December's end. In New York she wouldn't have dared; it would have been freezing. London's winter, with the exception of the day she'd stood in line for her booster, had been so mild. It was just the lack of light she found so challenging.

A winter night in London was another time of day altogether. It was not dusk, with its dull bus beams extending funnels of light through the mist, nor was it that nearly living organism before-sunrise, with its darkened branches slowly revealing themselves beneath a thickening mauve hue; it was brighter than both. The winter night sky felt thick with an energy not even the dismal day possessed; something phosphorescent stirred, pushing the clouds around like pieces on a Scrabble board, making her thoughts and reflections weightier and more pithy than usual.

Margherita: I'm having a day
Margherita: turned night
Margherita: do you ever have a Day

Nick: tell me
Nick: I'm in London by the way

Margherita: do your friends tell you when they're feeling off
Margherita: like do they talk about it and elaborate
Margherita: I feel like people don't have the same quantity of 'feeling off' days that I do lately
Margherita: which makes me wonder why
Margherita: I think everyone has things just much more figured out than I do and I don't know why or how that happened
Margherita: you appear to have everything well figured out

Nick: Sort of
Nick: I want to take my career to the next level
Nick: and find a real babe
Nick: and have the kind of family that makes everyone say ARGH

She rolled her eyes.

Margherita: I'm sure you will.
Nick: I'm sure you will too

The murky sky shifted above her head. Clouds over clouds.

Margherita: I don't see it
Nick: you can't see it until it happens
Margherita: I don't see any of it

Her face turned into a simper. The damn tears that kept on coming.

Margherita: did you know Sylvia Plath killed herself by sticking her head in the oven
Margherita: in an adorable house in Primrose Hill

Margherita: what determination

Nick: It will come together

Margherita: I'm going to be lost girl forever

Nick: what makes you say that

Margherita: I've always been lost girl

Nick: one day you will meet someone who feels familiar
Nick: and you'll look back on the times you felt lost and it will feel very far away

Margherita: yeah

She wasn't convinced. And besides which, the thought of relying on another human being, who could potentially hurt her to make her feel 'found' was just as terrifying as the thought of feeling permanently lost. Sniffling, she made herself stop crying.

Stop it, she said to herself. *Stop the pity.*

Margherita: I just want to make a home and feel connected and not feel like I'm floating anymore, and I want to fall in Big Love, and these are my goals.

Nick: well start somewhere. Stop moving. Make an effort to do things that connect you.
Nick: put a quarter in. See what comes out.

Margherita: yeah.
Margherita: I know I sound like woe is me, and I hate myself for it, but this all sounds easier said than done.

Nick: maybe you've never tried hard enough
Nick: maybe you quit too soon.
Nick: maybe you run away at the first sign of friction and pain and if you waded through it, you'd come out on the other side and you'd be relishing and thriving anew

Ouch, but fair, she thought, as she carefully stepped back inside and laid down in her bed.

Margherita: this is all v possible

Nick: is it accurate

Margherita: maybe.

Nick: no matter where you fly to, Marghe, whatever is going on inside of you is going to be right there with you.

Nick: In your carry-on.
Nick: In your pocket.
Nick: It's not going anywhere until you make peace with it. Or learn to live alongside it.

A tear threatened its reappearance in the corner of her right eye.

Margherita: I know

Neither said anything for a moment.

Nick: I wonder sometimes why my responses have so much consequence

Margherita: You don't get scared away
Margherita: And I feel like you understand me without judging me, or at least you do a fine job of covering it up if you are.

Nick: I'm not judging

Margherita: Can I ask you something
Margherita: Why don't you want to see me
Margherita: Why bother telling me you're here at all, I don't get it
Margherita: at least pretend like 'would love to see you lets try to figure it out!' Lie at least
Margherita: I sometimes feel like, you only respond to me when I appear to be most needy, or when I am putting potential sex on the table, and there doesn't appear to be anything else between or beyond these two very different topics.

Isabetta Andolini

Nick: well. I have all my family and school friends here
Nick: And covid has made everything harder
Nick: And I don't really agree with this last thing
Nick: Stop trying to dissect us

Margherita: okay

Right. Maybe I am dissecting. She put her phone down next to her as she stared at the line where the wall met the ceiling.

Nick: I like talking about this stuff

Margherita: You like listening to me be a crybaby?

Nick: It's real. Instead of lip service

Margherita: I save my lip service for most everyone else.

Nick: I want to hear your plan for how you're going to get where you want to be

Margherita: well I'm probably not going to stick my head in the oven
Margherita: process of elimination
Margherita: I mean, can you imagine

LONDON

December 22, 1998

THE WIND WAS skin-splitting and fierce as Francine climbed the terrain toward the crest of Parliament Hill. She shifted the wool hat on her head and held her mittened hands over her ears.

"Fuck, it's windy today!" she exclaimed as she reached Bea waiting on the bench overlooking the City.

Bea turned; her skin whiter than milk and her eyes sunken. The hat on her head looked three sizes too big.

Francine sat down next to her and enveloped her frail body in a hug.

"Look at you!" Francine said enthusiastically.

Bea rolled her eyes. "Or don't."

"How are you feeling?"

Bea shrugged and tried to smile. "I'm well now that you're here!"

Francine exhaled into the bench and wrapped her arm around Bea's shoulders, rubbing her arm up and down for body heat.

"My dad is making scones with Margherita and Tommaso. I'm all yours today."

"Rodney said he'd come to lunch."

"Oh fabulous!" Francine exclaimed, turning to Bea with a smile. "I haven't seen Rodney in two years at least! Gosh I can't believe it. And... um..."

Isabetta Andolini

"No." Bea shook her head. "He won't. He won't even see me. So. It's not just you. I've called dozens of times. Have gone over. I don't even think he's here for the holidays. I think, actually, I don't know for sure—but I swear he went to Mustique."

"Really? With who? How do you know?"

Francine eyed a chocolate cocker spaniel as it daintily strode by one meter from their feet, sniffing the damp, barren ground.

"What a beauty," Bea said, watching it go. "Look at all that hair! Gosh, I'm jealous!"

Francine tapped her friend's head. "It will grow back, love."

"Yeah. Anyway, Rodney said he heard from someone in his gossipy grapevine that he's gone for a month. Rented a cottage for himself. I don't know, Francie. I'm worried about him. He's so different. So…" She shivered. "Stony. Silent. Mean, even. He's gotten mean!" She grimaced.

Francine bit the inside of her cheek and eyed the cityscape she knew so well in the distance. Everything she knew so well seemed to gravitate farther and farther away.

"Has he come to see you during this last round of chemo?"

"Nope. I'm telling you. He's gone to wood. Harder than it, actually. Woody. That shall be his new name."

Francine scrunched her nose up and Bea held it between her fingers.

"Wonk!" she said.

Francine smiled.

"I miss you, Bea."

"Let's be off, shall we? I can't *wait* to hear about Rodney's new boyfriend," Bea said, as she stood and held her hand out to Francine.

"Yeah. Let's be off."

LONDON

December 30, 2021

Margherita: When do you go back?

She hated herself for sending it, but why the hell not. She lay in bed and watched him come online, read the message, then go back offline.

She moaned to herself, wishing she hadn't said anything.

LONDON

December 31, 2021

NEW YEAR'S EVE. Margherita stood in the supermarket in the hour before its early closure, staring at a basket of plantains. They reminded her of Mustique.

She thought of Francine, of her mother's many New Year's Eves on the island before she'd moved to New York. How much Margherita would have loved to witness one of those evenings.

Holding her phone, she opened her contacts and began to type 'Mamma,' but the search came up empty.

She had done it hundreds if not thousands of times in the few years since that phone call in Milan.

"Marghe…" her father had cried into the phone. Margherita had never heard her father crying before—full-on crying—and before he said another word, she knew.

"She's gone, isn't she?"

In front of the plantains, Margherita's eyes welled.

———

Back in the attic apartment in Hampstead, Margherita went out to sit on the wooden step on her little terrace. She wrapped her thickest sweater around her and let the wind whip her hair around. In her lap, she opened WhatsApp on her phone and clicked on the archived messages, where she opened a very old chat with a phone number no longer in service.

The last few messages were from Margherita: a few photos of a beautiful Sunday on Lake Como.

Francine had never opened them.

She clicked open a different chat.

Margherita: you love to ignore me don't you
Margherita: like you're putting me in my place. I swear that's what it is.
Margherita: don't let Margherita think you're going to give her too much attention

Nick: what the hell

Margherita: I dislike how you ignore me whenever you feel like it. There I said it.

Nick: I'm not ignoring you

Margherita: oh?
Margherita: you come to London, don't say a word to me, don't have any interest in seeing me, I say all these personal things to you, and I'll probably not hear from you until the next time it's convenient for you to pretend to care.
Margherita: I realize I don't have to write you and I certainly don't have to confide in you, but I do, and I did, and I hate how you make me feel like you could go either way. Talk to me or not talk to me. See me or not see me. I'd never hear from you if I stopped writing you. Like persona non grata. Except for the sex bit, because I swear you keep this door open so that there remains an easy fuck once in a while.

Nick: where is this all coming from

Margherita: from the realization, for the millionth time, that you are just as self-absorbed and self-serving as you were when we met

Nick: okay that's enough Marghe.

Nick: I'm not going to sit here and let you throw darts at me because you're bored and upset with your own life

Nick: I'm not going to always respond to you right away. It doesn't give you the right to go off on me

Margherita: yeah treat me however you like. Promise to not be affected by it.

Nick: And it takes two to sleep together. I've never forced you into coming over, have I?

Nick: Don't you think it's time you own your actions a little

Margherita: you really are an ass.

Nick: okay you know what

Nick: don't freak out at my saying this

Nick: but I imagine myself not being very important to you, and if you occasionally didn't answer me for for a few days, I wouldn't be upset

Margherita: what is that, some backhanded way of saying I'm not important to you?

Margherita: you really are the most enormous jerk

Margherita: how do you get away with this? Do you treat everyone like the insensitive jerk that you have proven yourself to be, time and time again? Or save it just for me?

Nick: fuck off. I just landed in Brazil. And I am high on a beach right now. And you're throwing darts at me.

Nick: Sometimes I think you will do anything in your power for a consequence.

Nick: Poke someone and criticize them until they grow ugly with you.

Nick: Fuck someone's husband.

Nick: You want trouble.

Nick: Or punishment.

Nick: And pity. Endless fucking pity.

The wind kicked up then, and the blustery breeze on her fore-head felt like a wet smack. She put her palm to her skin as if to protect herself.

Consequences. Her father used to refer to 'consequences' during Francine's manic episodes. When she'd booked herself a last minute vacation to Mexico for a long weekend and left the next morning, when she'd driven up to Rockport on a Saturday in November and purchased a three million dollar house on the sea. When Tommaso had found the receipt from an embar-rassingly large shopping spree at Bendels that cost more than Margherita's freshman year at Spence.

"There are consequences to your euphoria, Francine. Why aren't you taking the lithium?" or "Why aren't you taking the valproic acid?"

Francine had acted out of mania and a lack of control, while Margherita acted out of—what? Misdirected anger? Loneliness? Lack of a mother?

Margherita: Fuck You
Nick: Fuck you!

She climbed inside and lay down on the bed, where she shoved her phone underneath the pillow and curled into herself.

What she wouldn't give to sit on the top step of her parent's brownstone and hear Francine's St. Andrews accent wax on about the view from the breakfast nook in Rockport. The house Tommaso had put on the market the very next day.

Hours later, she woke to a low ba-boom. She had forgotten to silence her phone.

She pulled it out from underneath the pillow. It was just after midnight.

Nick: Happy new year Marghe
Nick: I'm sorry.
Nick: You are important.

LONDON

January 4, 2022

SITTING ON HER roof deck, her feet resting on the outer wall, she opened her chat with Johanna. She hadn't heard from her in weeks and wondered if her excitement about the Villa had been shallow and falsified. Or maybe she was giving Margherita space to come around, like a game of hard to get.

A new message floated to the top.

Noah: Are you doing good?

Margherita: I don't know if I'm DOING good, but for sure I'm BEING good. alas it's only Jan 4 so we'll see

Noah: I mean, don't be too good, or too sane. You'll lose your essence

Margherita: I'll never be sane, who am I kidding

Noah: Glad to hear ☺
Noah: What's the latest?

Margherita: I think I'm going to have to make a hard decision soon. And possibly a commitment.

Noah: Not your forte.
Noah: turn up the Nina

LONDON

January 6, 2022

MARGHERITA AND THAYER found an empty table at Ginger & White in Perrin's Court, the Hampstead café where moms crammed in for eleven o'clock cappuccinos and strollers lined the brick lane.

On that Thursday morning, the oddly matched friends were surely the only childless patrons. Margherita ordered a smoothie bowl while Thayer opted for a tea.

"Do you eat? I feel like you don't eat," Margherita said, as she swirled her spoon across the full bowl of thick green liquid.

He watched her utensil as he wrapped his large hands around his tea. His expensive sneaker sat outstretched below the table and Margherita eyed it on the brick next to her own converse-clad foot. He belonged in Hampstead more than she did.

"I do eat. You're the one inhaling pulp and powder. Next they'll be serving liquid greens intravenously."

"Pretty sure they already do that in California," Margherita said as she swallowed a spoonful. She looked at him quizzically. "Did you cut your hair?" She motioned to the sides of her head. "Just the sides. Even your ears look like Morrissey! Are you his younger brother by any chance? Same mother, different fathers sort of thing?"

"Hairdresser on fire." *

"That was a *dumb* song."

"'Heaven Knows I'm Miserable Now' was by far the best lyrics. Obviously in the age of The Smiths."

"Are you kidding? 'This Charming Man!'" she exclaimed, head pushed forward over the table.

"That was all Marr."

"Very possibly."

"Anyway. I have to go to California next week, speaking of intravenous kale. Quite looking forward to it actually. Dreary London is never less charming than in these short days, which, all things considered, could be considered a godsend." His eyes scanned the blonde, spandex-wearing moms with their thick ponytails and scarily thin calves as they exchanged overloaded smiles and air kisses. "Darkness!" he hissed.

"Yes, I'm jealous. I need some sun."

"Yes, you do, my little depressed friend," he said with a smile, watching her take another spoonful. "Are you sure you don't want a piece of toast or something?" He mimicked biting down on something, his bottom teeth meeting his top teeth.

"Do you need company?" she asked. "On your trip?"

"No, sadly. Will be in a three-day board meeting the whole time for this podcast company that's more successful than my last two movies combined. Maybe one day for horse-back riding in Malibu. Have you ever done that? Fantastic. Might do a little plasma sculpting, maybe a little stem cell lift, while I'm in town. Thread lift... you know... when in Rome."

Margherita scrunched her lips and bit the inside of her cheek. Thayer's dry sense of humor wasn't strong enough that day.

Thayer ran his fingers through the tall hair on his head. "When's the Mustique hotel opening? March? You do need a break, I think, out of this extremely boring torpor," he said wryly.

She blew air out of her nose.

"Can't be your fellow wallower forever," he said.

"Yeah. Get off my cloud already."

She looked around at the moms. She couldn't help but feel jealous of everyone around her. Thayer, for having the means to be so free, to escape and rejoin as he pleased, and for all of his connections in far flung places; the moms for being so damn happy, for having such organized and comfortable lives.

She was jealous of anyone who seemed to have it more figured out than her. She was jealous of anyone with a home, of anyone with more than one hundred dollars in their bank account, of anyone with a partner or a spouse, of anyone with a big group of friends, of anyone who knew what it felt like to no longer be searching. Scavenging.

Of anyone with 'Mamma' in their contacts.

She felt tears well in the corners of her eyes.

Thayer bent toward her over the table. "What's happening?" he whispered, staring into her glassy eyes.

She drilled her fingertips into her hairline and inhaled deeply. "Oh my God make it stop. I don't know. Have you ever woken up and thought to yourself, *I am so fucking irrecoverably unhappy.* And just hated it? Like you want to shake yourself and run away from your own mind, your own body? I just want to escape *myself.* Can a person do that?"

Thayer shrugged.

"Anyway." she sniffled. "Plus I am some sort of emotional masochist, three years with the same idiot boy in my head, and that's not helping." She shook her head as if to rid herself of the moment of weakness.

"Horrendous combination overall."

She tried to smile and pulled at her upper lip as Thayer enlarged his eyes, a half smirk on his face, clearly trying to reverse her slippage into self-pity.

"So who is the heartbreaker? You've alluded to him before but have not dished."

Margherita looked at Thayer as if she didn't know what he was talking about.

"Give it up." He wrangled a blueberry from her bowl and pinged it at her face.

"Ey!" she yelled, as the blueberry rolled under the table, where someone would surely step on it and imprint violet everywhere for a day or two.

"He's... a long, old story." She dragged her smoothie bowl closer for protection.

"Do you still talk?"

"Yeah," she said, regretfuly.

"Does he know how fake happy you are?"

She laughed in a small way. "Yes. I believe he does."

"So you can talk to him about it?"

"Yeah. Sort of."

"That's nice! Sort of," Thayer said, as he watched each spoonful of lumpy green smoothie go from bowl to Margherita's mouth.

She nodded slowly as she swallowed.

"But..." Thayer prompted.

"But... he disappears. He doesn't really care or—"

"Or he'd check in."

"Yeah." She stirred the soupy green liquid slowly.

"So he doesn't seek you out."

"No," Margherita dragged it out, as if curiously.

"Yeah," Thayer said casually, looking beyond her down the lane, the athletic moms again. He took a sip from his tea. "That's shit."

"Yeah."

He lit a cigarette.

"That's shit," Margherita said, tipping her chin toward his cigarette.

Thayer inhaled and exhaled slowly.

"Yeah," he said. "Well... it's all a bit shit isn't it."

"We're in Hampstead."

He exhaled a thin line of smoke and regarded her with

Isabetta Andolini

dismissive, furrowed brows. A judgmental, peeved Morrissey in five-hundred-pound sneakers.

"We don't smoke in Hampstead," she said, holding the spoon upward in the air.

"These women are probably high off their asses as soon as their kids go to bed."

"Yeah, but they're not smoking cigarettes."

"Oh come off it, Girl, Interrupted. One and done."

"Gosh that movie was so depressing."

"Precisely, *Winona*," he enunciated, his eyes burning into her sad face. "Have you heard from Johanna, by the way?"

NEW YORK

December 30, 1998

FRANCINE STOOD IN the doorway of Margherita's bedroom, taking in the sight of her daughter beneath flannel sheets with snowmen on them in different-colored scarves, her mouth half open, her breath even as she slept. Francine hadn't spent any time with her little girl in days. Work proved to be the most sturdy distraction at the holidays, when too many memories and thoughts of the people she had loved and lost crept into her mind too often, and too overwhelmingly.

She returned to her office downstairs and sat in the chair staring at the framed photo of herself and Keith. Aged twenty-something. Lying on the floor of his flat in Kensington. Their limbs entwined. Such smiles. Such laughter. Such happiness and youth and what may or may not have been a carefree moment in time.

It felt so long ago; her twenty-something years. Even her thirty-something years. Those distant moments in Kensington, in Chelsea, in St. John's Wood, in Hampstead. With Rodney and Bea and Keith and Christos. Her limbs so free of sun spots. Her hair so full and healthy. Her eyes so bright and eager. It all felt so very far behind her.

She picked up the frame and held it in her hand as she dialed the long distance number she had scribbled down on a post-it note.

"Oh, hi! Is this Basel's Bar? It is. Oh wonderful. I used to spend many a holiday at your bar. The reason I'm calling is, I'm looking for someone, and I wonder if you can help. Is Keith there? A man named Keith? It's his best friend. Or, well…yeah. My name is Francine. I know you're going to go all high-Mustique privacy and discretion on me, so if he's there, can you just tell him I'm on the line, and ask if he'll say hello?"

Francine waited for the hostess to return to the phone. She sat up straighter when a voice sounded in her ear.

"Oh. Sure. No, of course. I understand. Right. Thank you, anyway."

She brushed her thumb over his body behind the glass of the frame.

"Never in a million years, Keithie. 'Please send her my best,'" she mimicked what the hostess had said. "You really have become like wood. When will you ever forgive me?"

LONDON

January 14, 2022

THE HEATH LOOKED particularly stick-like and threadbare that morning as Margherita made her way across the hilly, wet expanse past the Tumulus, toward the ladies bathing pond, "The Killing Moon" blaring in her AirPods. A whippet ran in circles around a bare magnolia tree, trying to catch something that moved along the damp ground, the grass peeled out and ripped up in patches like a bad rash on a hairy back. Margherita stopped to watch the dog, so much energy and determination did it have. She closed one eye and tried to imagine the scene at the height of spring, when the magnolia tree would be a burst of pink flowers edging towards cream.

Felicity and innocence and new beginnings and all that.

She typed out a message to Jack, who she hadn't heard from since before the holidays. He'd gone north with his family, and she had fully expected radio silence for a few weeks. It did however bother her that he essentially only messaged her within Instagram rather than WhatsApp. She knew why, of course, and like a twist of the knife, it made her feel rotten every time. Once in a while, he'd call her late at night from his attic, voice low, barely above a whisper, and she struggled with the yearning to crawl into his arms, to feel his gentle voice and his lovely words envelop her, and at the same time, the bottomless emptiness the whole scenario swallowed her into; his family downstairs, his teenage daughter

Isabetta Andolini

who might one day be forced to reverse the image of her father she had had in her heart since birth. The imperfectness of him, the humanness of him. Did he make her feel more or less lonely? She didn't know.

But as she made her way up a damp and dreary Lime Avenue, a shell of its autumnal splendor, she changed her mind and started a new chat.

Margherita: I feel like a horrible person.

Nick: Uh oh. What did you do

Margherita: okay. Incoming.
Margherita: I went to lunch over a month ago with a man I used to know when I was in my early twenties. I was a little bit in love with him then, and we had a very innocent non physical office affair, and then we lost touch for years and years, and I never got him out of my head. And then last month… it was like no time had passed at all, and also that all this time had passed, and that we somehow had the same, undeniably strong feelings, sitting there at the table with us, making us drink a bottle of wine faster, sending hands across plates, chemicals mixed in with winter root vegetables
Margherita: And he's married of course, with three kids of course, and it makes me sad because he is really a wonderful human, and so kind and sweet and such a fantastic dad, and so smart. And he knew me before, and he makes me feel at home just being next to him.
Margherita: Here is someone I could really love, and I can't have him. And I want to know, where is *my* Jack, you know? And why do I keep ending up in these married situations

Nick: I think
Nick: You may not like what I say

KISS MY JAGGED FACE 475

Nick: But I think you're forgetting that you can say no to these married situations?

Nick: You don't have to participate

Nick: I think you like the allure of a challenge. Someone who can't give themselves to you, for whatever reason. And in turn, you get a barrier of protection for or from whatever it is you seem to be afraid of. It's less constricting if you can't have them, or if they don't want all of you. Less claustrophobic maybe. And then you get frustrated by the results as if it's a sudden surprise that that person is exactly who they were when you met them.

Nick: I don't know Marghe

Nick: Maybe an older, married man gives you a false sense of family

Nick: It's interesting how you enjoy the drama but it makes you feel dissipated, like a lesser version of yourself

Margherita: I wouldn't say a lesser version. Just makes me sad.

Nick: Hate to say it, but you're doing this to yourself

Margherita: I get it. It's up to me to re-direct the sail. And to face the realities. Which is so boring and unromantic by the way.

Nick: You don't have to bind yourself to situations that don't fulfill you just because for a second or the duration of a cocktail or the stretch of a lunch you feel magic. Just keep going.

Nick: Don't read into chemicals too much

Nick: Chemical connections are physical. Sexual. But a human connection is like trust. It's something you build. I know I'm one to talk, but I too, am trying to form better habits

"Daisies are truer than wildflowers," her mom used to say.

Margherita: good sex can happen with the wrong people.

Nick: Can you be serious. For once.

Margherita: I know. I get it.
Margherita: but seriously, you can really fall for someone, sex aside, and sometimes it's the wrong person.

Nick: Then that's an error of casting and that's mainly on you.
Nick: You waste time and energy when you let your emotions misguide you, and you also insult someone who's being true to himself

Margherita: who are we talking about here

Nick: Don't read into it
Nick: If you want to be in love, and you don't want to be alone, don't let excitement and forbidden fruit warp your vision

Forbidden fruit. She imagined a prickly pear.

Margherita: who decides what's forbidden

Nick: You do. Based on how it makes you feel. Are you ill afterwards or are you nourished

As Margherita approached the village with its hamlet-esque houses and miniature bakeries squeezed between overpriced eyewear and soap shops, she grazed her eyes over the half-formed adults and buttoned-up toddlers. The strollers and the rucksacks. Somewhere along the way, she had caught up to the age group of that 'young parent' category, only now, instead of celebrating her self-inflicted exclusion, she watched them from the periphery like a non-accepted member of the club. For so long she had snubbed her nose at anything resembling societal norms: relationships, marriage, children, motherhood. If she wasn't going to be one of them for a while, she needed to tether herself to something else that was meaningful. Or she'd be endlessly meandering in someone else's field of fruit trees, vainly searching for sustenance.

The Villa. That was her best hope of tethering at the moment.

She looked down at Nick's last message. *Nourishment.* That was what she needed.

LONDON

January 18, 2022

FROM INSIDE THE Walbrook building, Margherita could see both the spires of St. Stephens Walbrook and the Bloomberg building directly across from her. The windows of the latter were impenetrable, but she knew from memory what lay on the other side of the glass. She thought of the day, only a few months prior, when she had sat on Wesley's office sofa, going on and on about it, his large hand on the cushion between them, like a doorstop she wished she could kick out of place.

A hard copy of her original Villa plans sat on the black marble table before her, over which a man from Hart Browne extended his crisp white-shirted arm. He traced his finger over the kitchen layout as he spoke to Johanna and a person from Johanna's bank about potentially leasing out the culinary aspect to a third party. They spoke of timelines, of licenses, of hiring an existing hotel management company or creating a brand new entity with an undecided CEO. A second and third gentleman from Hart Browne, with their American accents, contributed to the discussion with thoughts on splitting the building team between the New York office and the team of a firm based in Italy. They considered internal demolition costs versus rehabilitation costs. Johanna listened intently, asked smart questions, and fixed her eyes in an expression of determination.

Margherita sat at the table, her ankles crossed below the black swivel chair, her hands folded over one another in her lap, imagining herself on the porch in Mustique, where she had grown and nurtured the Villa idea. She imagined herself swimming in the turquoise waters of the baia, seeing it in the distance beneath her water-splotched sunglasses. She imagined herself in her twenties, on the deep curves of the road, walking from the beach club back to the train station in Santa Margherita Ligure, eyeing the driveway, wishing to know what stories lurked from decades earlier.

Every time one of the gentlemen at the table mentioned licenses or permits, her stomach twitched at the thought of how much money she had wasted on the pursuit of them the previous summer. Every time someone mentioned other members of the senior team in the New York office, what they would bring to the project or for what would they be responsible, Margherita felt herself pushed farther and farther away.

And across from her, through and beyond the floor-to-ceiling windows, were other windows so close she could touch them with a curtain rod, through which she could not see in.

"Thank you again, so much, for making the trip," Johanna said, as everyone stood, neatly tucked their crisp shirts carefully downward again, pushed the swivel chairs into their original spots and smiled awkwardly and politely first at Johanna and then Margherita.

"So, Margherita, I'll have Myra in HR send you an email in the next few days. We'll hash out a few details first, and then we'll get right back to you," one of the men said. "I'm sure you're eager to get back to New York and get started."

Margherita didn't know how to respond to that sentence. Fifty percent of it was so absolutely wrong. But the other fifty percent of it was what she knew she needed to do. Get started.

Outside, standing near the car park area in St. Stephen's Row, watching employees leave buildings in the lanes to retrieve lunch, some in pairs or groups of three or four, some laughing, some concentrated, Margherita was quiet as Johanna inhaled from a cigarette.

"I think that went brilliantly. What say you?" Johanna asked.

Margherita bit the inside of her cheek. "Yes, it went really well. You made it happen! I can't believe it. I guess I'm a little in shock."

"Well, my fine credit made it happen. And my wonderful, generous bank. Who, I'm sure, won't be wonderful and generous for long. But really, none of it would be happening without you!" Johanna put her hand on Margherita's shoulder and squeezed.

"Well…" Margherita shrugged.

"What is it? Don't tell me you don't want to do it. You've changed your mind or something."

"No—it's not that." She exhaled, her mouth a round tennis ball. A quick burst of air exited. "I just. Gosh this is going to sound horrible, and I don't want you to feel like I'm ungrateful. This is a huge, massive thing you're doing and I want you to know that I am behind it. But. New York… I really didn't have that in mind. And now, it's like… that's what's happening, and it feels. I don't know. A little overwhelming?"

Johanna stamped out her cigarette and regarded Margherita with curiosity, her lips sucked inward. "What's overwhelming? It's not like you've never lived there before."

"No. No, it's not that. It's not the city itself. It's more like, well I didn't have that in mind, for myself, for a while at least. I suddenly feel a little like… I'm in the backseat, at a time in my life when every year counts so much. Like each year is so precious all of a sudden, and there's so much pressure on what I'm doing, or who I'm with, or what I'm accomplishing, or where I'm going. Because soon it's not so easy and not so free. These are the years. When it all sort of gets decided by a few decisions. Your twenties are tosses in the bucket. Drops of water in a big open field where the grass never stops growing. But I feel now this scary pressure or foreshadowing or whatever it is, like… soon it will all be sort of irreversible."

Johanna nodded patiently.

"Or… nothing at all will happen. And I'll be someone whose life never… bloomed. And then it will be *real* sad." She smiled ironically.

"Whatever made you think this way?"

"I don't know. Life. Watching people I know. In their forties or fifties. Wistful-seeming, like they're trying to grasp things they no longer can, because of decisions they've already made. My mother even, who was so successful, but I can never figure out if she always wished she could've gone back to London, if it wasn't for me. If she hadn't had me, she might have been more free, she could've lived with my brother and her friends and family. Life happens and then you're sort of a slave to it."

"Has my life stopped?" Johanna's nose scrunched up more than Margherita had ever seen it. She had the distinct feeling she had insulted her in some way.

"No! That's not what I meant."

"Am I no longer able to take chances or go on adventures or change course, now that I've reached the arid fields of my forties?"

"Not at all, Johanna! That's not what I meant. I'm an idiot. I'm sorry. That's not where I was going."

Johanna nodded her head vigorously. "Alright. Forties talk aside, though I *am* slightly offended, I do understand where you are coming from in this moment, and I've got to say, I think you're doing a real psychological number on yourself. You take jaded to another level. But cut it out or life *won't* happen. Most people are scared to jump. You have the opposite problem. You're scared you're not jumping *enough*. If you never stick to your guns or commit to an idea or a dream, if you never put your feet down on steady ground for more than a *minute*, you will be alone. You can still dream and go places and change your mind, to certain extents. Drops of water in a big field and all that. But you have to have the guts to lay the groundwork and stick around to watch it grow. Committing is just as frightful sometimes as bolting, I get it. But how about this, you commit to something, you deal with its challenges, and when you get satisfaction out of the results, *then* you experiment again, when you know what you're capable of."

"So you think I should take the job."

"What would your mum say, if she were here?"

Margherita looked up at the Bloomberg building. The windows no one could see through. "I think," she said, as she exhaled, "she'd say take the job."

"No." Johanna shook her head with a pursed-lip smile. "I think she'd say: 'Margherita darling, I'm so proud of you.'"

An hour later, after Johanna had gone home and Margherita had wandered the little lanes between Bank and Cannon tube stops, she sat with Jack on a bench outside a café on Queen Victoria Street, their heads leant into the glass, faces to the sun. She had sent him a last minute message knowing his office was nearby. He'd come down to meet her for an espresso and a winter sun bath.

"This feels amazing," she said with her eyes closed.

"Mmm," he moaned. "So needed."

"I wish I could go back to your office with you. Put me to work for the day." She opened her eyes and turned her head toward him.

He opened his eyes and put his large hand on the top of her crossed legs. Margherita looked down at his wedding ring.

"Me too. Though I'd have an impossible time concentrating with you in the building."

She smiled and closed her eyes again. "You'd just have to get used to it, then."

"How was the meeting, by the way? You haven't said."

"Oh. It was… good. Went well."

His hand gave her thigh a gentle squeeze. "Anything else to add?"

"The firm is based in New York." She shrugged with her eyes closed. "Can't seem to crack the surface here."

"You will. Give it time."

Give time time, she thought.

"How much time should one give time?" she asked with her eyes closed.

"Margherita?" Benjamin's voice.

Margherita opened her eyes and saw her brother in a fine navy suit, holding a leather bound folder, standing before her on the sidewalk. Another suited gentleman stood awkwardly next to him, a half-smile on his face.

Jack slipped his hand back into his own lap and wrapped it around his tiny paper cup.

"What are you doing here?" Margherita asked. She had no choice. "Jack, this is my brother Benjamin, Benjamin this is my friend Jack."

Benjamin didn't introduce the man at his side, who continued to look on dumbly. Her brother nodded coldly at Jack and regarded Margherita with furrowed brows.

"What are you up to?" he asked, condescendingly.

"Just taking in a little sun," she said, squinting up at him.

"I better run, actually." Jack turned his head toward Margherita. "Good to see you."

"Yes, thanks for the coffee." She hadn't wanted to be interrupted so soon. She had wanted to ask his opinion on Hart Browne, and the imminent job offer, and New York.

"Nice to meet you, Benjamin." Jack rose from the bench and walked toward the crosswalk, where he carefully looked both ways before striding across toward Cannon Street. His long legs. His perfectly proportioned back. Margherita felt like someone had stolen her cupcake.

"I'll catch up to you, Jimmy," Benjamin said to Jimmy, who Margherita assumed was a co-worker.

He continued to glower at her.

"What?" Margherita shielded her eyes from the sun by making a visor with her palm.

"What the fuck? He had a ring on."

"Oh, Benjamin." She rolled her eyes and stood up from the bench.

"Who is he?" Benjamin demanded.

"He's an old friend."

"Yes I can see that. A married friend with his hand on your thigh. What is that about, Margherita?"

"Stop it," she hissed.

"What the hell are you doing in the middle of the day having some sort of rendezvous with a married guy approaching fifty?"

"I had an espresso. Hardly a rendezvous."

"Answer the fucking question, Margherita."

"Don't talk to me like that. I am an adult. I can do what I please. I don't need your permission. Just ironic that one of the three times I've seen you in the last six or seven months is when I happen to be with Jack."

"What kind of relationship do you have with this Jack?"

"We do Mad Libs and exchange sticker books and braid each other's hair," she said as she walked to the rubbish bin to toss her paper cup.

"Don't be facetious."

"Mind your own business, Ben."

"You think you're going to have some sort of relationship with him? Mum told me about the guy in Italy. What is it with you? Can't you find someone who *doesn't* have a family? Do you *aim* to be a self-indulgent home-wrecker?"

Margherita shot her face up toward her brother and eyed him with venom. He stood over six feet in his polished, burgundy Oxfords, and even in her heeled boots, he hovered at least eight or nine inches over her.

"You have no right to insert yourself in my relationships, no matter what kind of relationships they are. You don't have the right to have an opinion. You barely know me. You have never given me the time of day. Jimmy, whoever he was, probably has a better relationship with you than I do. I'm just your pathetic little sister, *desperate* for your life guidance and a fifty pound note. Well, fuck you, Ben."

She brushed his arm as she stalked past him, toward the same crosswalk by which Jack had escaped. Benjamin quickly caught up to her.

"Don't get so hacked off by the truth. You think a man fifteen or twenty years older than you is going to take better care of you just because he could in a technical sense be your parent? Are you trying to replace the parent who wasn't 'parenty' enough for you?"

"That's ridiculous."

"Is it?"

"You're the king of simplistic. Black and white. Wrapped in smugness. That's how you control everything. He knows me. He cares. Do you know he is the only person who has ever asked me, straight out, after everything: 'Hey Margherita, are you okay?' And looked me in the eyes and really meant it. Everyone keeps saying, 'Oh you're so brave, you're so courageous, you're so strong and yada yada yada…' but no one asks me what's underneath that. No one cares."

"No one has the guts to ask the hard questions. Lower your expectations and you'd be less disappointed in people."

"Well, whatever, Jack does. And he knew me before."

"Before what? You think knowing someone before life experiences and events makes for a stronger, more magically meaningful relationship?"

She shook her head dismissively.

"You don't understand. You'll never understand." She mentally willed the crosswalk to turn in her favor so she could storm off.

"Oh? Why's that?"

"You've always known who you are, Benjamin. You've *always* known. And you probably always will. And you've always had a girlfriend. And now you're married, and your wife got to meet Mom a few times. You have a family. You're insulated. You have built-in love and company and comfort. All figured out. Sure-handed from day one."

"Margherita, have I missed something? Are you an only child? Are you an orphan? Do you not have a single friend on the planet? Don't you think you're taking the pity party a little too far?"

"You've not a clue. Just drop it."

"There are ups and downs. For everyone. Moving countries or moving cities or sleeping with an unavailable man is a band-aid. You've got to make a life for yourself, of your own doing. You've got to stop waiting for a ghost to accept you and your choices or make up for lost time. She's not coming back to fix everything that went wrong. She's not going to reappear for a do over. A rewrite. One without a mental disorder. Not happening. It is what it is. That was the mom you had. You've got to face that or you'll never move on."

Margherita didn't say anything. The crosswalk light turned green and she hurried forward, leaving her brother and his thirteen hundred dollar shoes filled with judgment on Queen Victoria Street.

That night she called Jack from her sofa.

"I'm sorry about today. My brother can be a real prick," she said softly.

"I'm just sorry we had to cut our coffee short. I like seeing you. Spending time with you. I wish we could do it more."

"Me too."

Neither said anything for a moment.

"You seemed a little sad today," he said gently.

Margherita sucked her teeth and swallowed.

"Oh. I don't know. Sometimes I feel like I've lost the track. Have you ever felt that way?"

"Yes. Many times. What makes you feel that way now? You've done so many amazing things this year; you've set out goals and you've worked toward them. You've been fearless. Self-possessed. And dazzling."

"Well, thank you. But I'm not so sure. I wish sometimes that I was more… I don't know—normal. Like I had a job, whatever it was, and I stayed there for years, and I celebrated co-workers birthdays and Fridays we had bagels and weekends were mostly the same and maybe I had a nice enough boyfriend and we had a dumb wedding, and we live in a house in Somewheresville and it's all fine, and none of it bothers me or bores me or freaks me out." She raised her arms above her head and clenched her empty fists. "I wish I didn't have this annoying *yearning* all the time. More than ever I feel this frustration… I haven't gotten where I want to be yet, with the person I want to be with. Wherever and whoever that is."

"You are a seeker. I don't think you have much choice in this. You know Joseph Campbell? He said, follow your bliss. It's an essential piece of advice, and it's like oxygen, for some. But he didn't say there aren't costs. Courage is the other essential. And clearly you have it! Chin up, Margherita. You're doing brilliantly."

Isabetta Andolini

LONDON

January 30, 2022

"YOU'VE BEEN VISITING quite often. Is that normal for you?" Margherita wrapped her hands around the oversized tea cup he passed to her. She shifted the pillows behind her to sit more upright and tried to take a sip. "Oh. Hot. Hot-ta." She placed the cup on the bedside table.

Nick climbed into bed next to her. "Yeah give it a minute. Um, yes and no. It's been a mix of work and family."

"And me of course," she said teasingly, with her hands cupped over her cheeks in exaggerated sweetness.

He ha-huffed and placed his hands over her hands.

"What's the latest with the Villa?"

"Oh. It seems I've stumbled upon a buyer. She got a sizable bank loan, a business loan, and hired a firm in New York to take it on. They're reviewing the plans. Making changes, I'm sure."

"That's amazing!" He tapped her leg eagerly.

She rolled her eyes. "Yes… though it wouldn't be totally my project anymore. This firm will get all the credit."

"But it might actually happen this way, as opposed to not happening."

"Yeah. I know. It's just not the Big and Brilliant solution I had in mind."

"Do you want my advice?" he asked.

"Yes. *Sing into my mouth.*"

"Don't look at it that way. Look at it like the first big step toward something else even bigger and more brilliant. Think of it like, once it gets under way, you'll be onto the next idea anyway. This could give you more flexibility."

"Yeah. That's true."

He leaned in toward her and kissed her forehead.

"I think it's amazing," he said.

She shrugged, a small, humble, pursed-lip smile on her face.

"I think your mum would think it's amazing."

Margherita squinted one eye closed and made a face, a half up-turned smile.

"Anyway, what's new with you?" she asked.

"Well wait, before you change the subject, does that mean you'd go back to New York? Or go to Italy?"

"I don't know." She shrugged again, taking a sip of tea. "How's New York lately?"

"Do you *want* to go back to New York?" he pushed on.

"I don't know," she said.

He watched her, waiting.

"You're doing that thing. Where you zip up." He mimicked the zipping up of a jacket.

"That thing?" she repeated, tipping her head to the side and smiling.

"Yeah. That cagey Marghe thing. Don't do that."

"I'm not doing anything!" she laughed.

"You were cagey Marghe when we met. And this past year you've been so... different from that girl. It's weird. I feel like, by seeing you so infrequently over the past few years, but by being in touch, it's like watching someone grow. It's been really wonderful actually."

She stayed silent.

"I can almost see inside your head right now. You're trying to decide whether to talk or close up again. A little ongoing war in there," he said as he placed his pointer finger to her forehead.

She scratched at a piece of lint on the blanket, trying to free it from the material.

He pulled her hand away and held it tightly. "You can trust me, Margherita. I'm not going anywhere."

Margherita looped her thumb around his and squeezed hard.

"As long as you don't tell me I'm the most self-involved asshole you've ever met," he added with a smile.

"I did not say that."

"Yes you did. I'll show you."

"I never said that in those words. I might have said it in other, classier words."

He began to scroll through their WhatsApp conversation in his phone. It seemed to have no ending and no beginning.

"Oh my God, how long is our chat?"

He glanced at her and raised his eyebrows, a half smile on his face. "Three years long."

"You've *never* deleted it?"

"No? Why would I?"

"Are you kidding?"

He shrugged and his nostrils flared.

She glanced at the screen but then covered her eyes. "I can't even look. So many things I wish I could un-say."

"Why?"

"Weren't you ever worried your girlfriend would see? That is a long backlog of some really inappropriate content. Images included."

"I think I deleted a few of those." He smiled, embarrassed. "Here. Look."

She shifted onto her elbows, just as he was.

"Why am I saved in your phone as 'Margaret?'"

"Ah. I did that in the beginning. Just to be safe." He peered at her without turning his neck entirely.

She raised her eyebrows and swallowed, slowly nodding her head. Having lost interest in being proven wrong, she rolled over onto her back and sat up.

"And you never changed it?"

He leaned his weight on one arm. "No. I suppose I didn't."

Margherita pursed her lips and stood from the bed.

He didn't say anything as her eyes scanned the floor. One pair of underwear. That was a start. She walked around to the end of the bed, where she found her crumpled jeans and sweater in a heap. She continued around to where he lay sideways, now facing away from her. There was her bra.

She put everything on, one by one.

"Margherita. Come on. I didn't keep it like that purposefully."

"No? You know my name's not Margaret, though…"

"It's insignificant."

"Am I?" she asked plainly as she pulled her jumper over her head, flattening her hair. She ran through it with her fingers and zipped her jeans as she walked out of the bedroom, down the hall toward where her coat hung on a rung.

He followed and stood in the hall in his briefs as she slid her arms into her wool coat.

"I said 'it' not 'you'. And yes. *It* is not significant enough for you to storm out."

"Be honest. You still think of me that way. Don't you." She flipped the back of her hair above the neck of the coat and let her hands hang at her sides.

He didn't say anything.

"I'm still the secret." She raised her shoulders and shook her head minutely. "I'm still the random girl you think is easy enough to have sex with once in a while. Check in, check out, ciao. Easy peasy, *Margaret*."

"Not at all."

"Why can't you even acknowledge me truthfully in your own phone then?"

He narrowed his eyes. "I really think you're over-reacting."

"Do you know how badly I needed you as my friend this past year?" She shook her head toward the ceiling. "Not even

Isabetta Andolini

just this year. Since we met. That's really all I ever wanted, was a *real* fucking friendship. And you push me aside to this secret corner, far from the world you'll never let me into, where all the rest of your friends live, where all the stuff you do with them and the places you go live, and I'm 'Margaret!' I'm that girl you met when no one else you knew was around, who gives you a headache once in a while but is still pathetic or idiotic or naïve enough to give in." She shifted her top jaw out of line with her bottom one as she imagined her mother scolding her for her affairs. "I hate thinking that anyone, *anyone*, thinks of me that way. The insignificant fuck." She picked up the handles of her tote and wrapped the long leather strap across her body as she went toward the door.

"I don't think of you that way. At all. Never have. Maybe you think of *me* that way!"

"Maybe I do," she said, as she left and shut the door behind her.

In the tube on the way back to Hampstead, crossing from south to north on the transport's deepest, most cavernous Northern line, she stood at one of the car's end doors and leaned against the felt siding, her face a diagonal reflection in the dirty glass. Other people in the car laughed and chatted or read books, equally submerged in the solar plexus of the city; unable to do or change anything in the world until multitudes of escalators sixty meters below propelled them to actionable life once again. Her indifference to either universe had never been more discernible.

She was literally in a rut. Emotional paralysis. Stickier than glue.

In her AirPods, raised too high for comfort to drown out the human interactions around her, Lower Dens sang "To Die in LA." She looked down at the album cover on her phone. A myriad of colorful pills.

She exited the train at Belsize Park to let the night air and that eerie, low-hanging, cloudy night sky diffuse her mood. There was something lonely about wanting someone who didn't reciprocate; lonelier than never wanting that person in the first place.

In her apartment, she watched herself in the full length mirror as her hands tugged at the ends of her jeans, extricating one leg from the material and then the other. Muscles she could not recall controlling reached for the hem of her thick cashmere sweater and pulled it over her head. With a handful of material in her hands, she let everything fall out of her palms onto the top of the dresser. Facing the mirror again, she took off her bra and her panties and pulled an oversize tee-shirt over her head. It fluffed out her hair and she wiped it from her face with the back of her forearm, like a toddler.

To the bathroom. One leg in front of the other. She washed her face, half aware of the feeling of wetness. She brushed her teeth, her eyes barely open. In her room again, she pulled back the blankets and slid into what was beginning to feel like her crypt.

Her phone pinged as she closed her eyes.

She could not recall where she had set it down. It pinged again. She opened her eyes and concentrated on the sound. When it pinged once more, she peered up toward the dresser.

A fourth ping.

Fine, she thought. *But this will be some sort of dagger. I know it.*

Nick: I think you're overreacting
Nick: Sometimes I feel like you act like we are dating and I don't think it's very fair
Nick: You have these unrealistic expectations
Nick: Why can't that have been remembered as a lovely afternoon

Nick: Why must you turn every interaction between us into some bitter fall-out
Nick: You're so determined to pick it apart and find something to feel hurt about
Nick: You have become the most irrational, predictable pattern.
Nick: You're only perpetually hurting yourself by doing this. I'm not trying to hurt you. You're the one trying to hurt you.

She tossed the phone onto its belly on the heap of her clothes and got back into bed. Tears sprung to her eyes as she thought of her mother.

There had been times, when she was younger or in her early twenties, when Margherita had envisaged a serious boyfriend meeting Francine. Her future husband perhaps. In the imagined scene, he would be enamored of her charming, witty, beautiful mom. He would be swept away. She would laugh and flirt with him, challenge and tease him, and he would blush and hold his own. And Margherita would sit on the edge of the chair, or listen in from the kitchen, and she would feel pride. For having such a vibrant, singular mom. For finding someone Francine so clearly enjoyed.

There would be no such scene. Ever. And how impossible it was to describe a personality like her mom's, a force like Francine, to someone who had never known her.

Morning appeared, or at least she assumed it did. The thick, velvet curtains let in a trickle of light that bounced off the full length mirror, and Margherita lay motionless with her eyes open, staring at it. After an hour of this, she rolled over on her side, her face smooshed in her pillow, and lay that way for another hour.

Finally, she swung her feet around. She had to pee.

When she returned to her bedroom, she looked for her phone on the dresser. Eight notifications from Nick had arrived while she had been in her awake, comatose state.

Nick: Hey
Nick: Let me rephrase
Nick: I hate that you feel that way. That I think of you as a random, flimsy 'Margaret'
Nick: You're gorgeous and funny and interesting and an amazing person with feelings and value that I recognize
Nick: You're not a random at all. Just like you weren't a random 3 years ago
Nick: Our association grew in the weirdest conditions. In my own dark secret cave. And I'm ashamed about that. And maybe I associate you with that guilt or murkiness. Which is my fault and my prerogative.
Nick: I never intend or expect for us to sleep together. The fact that we do implies nothing about your value or my respect for you. Just a mutual impulse that's quite wonderful

The messages felt condescending and she hated him for it.

He continued to type, and she watched message after message appear.

Nick: The truth is
Nick: I've just started dating someone
Nick: It's new, but I shouldn't have allowed myself to sleep with you yesterday. I don't want to be 'that guy' just as much as you don't want to be 'that girl.' I want to do things right this time, and respectfully, without hurting anyone in the process.
Nick: You and I started in such a weird way, and continued in such a weird way, and I don't think either

one of us will ever be able to fully untangle ourselves from our history.

Nick: I'd like to not feel like I have to misspell your name in my phone. And if we stay in each other's lives, in this non-way that we tend to do, I fear you will always be saved as Margaret, and our chat will continue to grow, and the thorniness of our strange relationship will always be there, the sporadic ugliness and chafing, and even if somehow the next day it washes away, we will always be in this odd, viscous puddle, and neither of us will have a healthy relationship.

Nick: I suspect you think I'm a massive jerk, and we might never come back from this.

Nick: And maybe I subconsciously did that on purpose.

Nick: But I think, or I hope, it's for the best.

LONDON

March 1, 2022

MARGHERITA STOOD AT the window watching a bright blue bird flutter in the tree, its high-pitched chirp causing her to smile. Her phone began to ring and she looked around the apartment for it.

"Happy thirty-second birthday to the marvelous Margherita. How do you feel?"

"Strong and able, sane and stable," she said.

"Jolly good. I'm coming to get you. Wear your wellies."

She zipped herself into a Patagonia and put on her highest Hunter boots.

On the front stoop, waiting for Thayer, she tilted her head back to take in the morning sun. It was still cold, but the sky was clear. March had turned a corner. Spring was coming.

With warm cheeks, she looked down at her phone again and typed out a message.

Margherita: I was in love with you.

Nick: hi.
Nick: Why didn't you ever say so

Margherita: I did. Maybe not in those precise words. But in other combinations of words. And I think it was pretty obvious.

Isabetta Andolini

He typed and stopped for a minute.

Finally, he sent something.

Nick: Nothing about you is obvious.

"You know what is one of the great perks of getting older?" Margherita said, head tipped back again.

"Fuck me, no. Can't name one." Thayer removed his sunglasses and used his shirt to rub them clean, squinting into the sun.

"You get to know yourself. What works and what doesn't. When you need a fix of something and how many frozen toes you're willing to risk for the reward."

"What counteracts a rapid heartbeat."

"Restless sleep."

"An overflowing head."

"And you know what the answer is?"

"Richmond Park."

"Yes. Tall grasses. Reindeer. Magical light."

"That's why I brought you here."

"I know."

"All you needed was a little walk in the light."

She patted him on the back playfully. "You've been a lot of light for me, Thayer, you know that."

"Just waiting for you to be the American in the *Tatler* story of my eventual demise."

"Who will play us in the biopic?"

"Me: an aging Bradley Cooper. You: a mischievous unknowable Zooey Deschanel."

"Hmm."

"TBD."

In the car, driving east toward central London, the evening

dark around them, the night lights of the city reflecting off the Thames as they crossed Putney Bridge, Margherita stared out the passenger side window.

She tried to remember the last birthday she had spent with her mom. It had been five, maybe six years. Had her mother been tracking the years as well? Wishing her daughter had been blowing out candles at home on the Upper East Side instead of in a chic restaurant in Milano? Margherita had always tried to punish Francine for making her feel a runner-up to her life, her work and independence and her closeness with Benjamin. After her death, she had felt an angry bitterness for being abandoned, sharpened by guilt for all of the attitude she had given Francine, all of the vociferous resentment.

Margherita clearly remembered, however, the last time she had spent Francine's birthday at home with her parents. She had woken early to go for a run in Central Park, having spent the night in her old bedroom instead of her apartment downtown, and Francine had been upstairs still when she returned. She assumed her mother was sleeping off the previous evening's festivities—a small party with fifty of her mother's friends and co-workers in their back garden. A fifty-first chair was annually left open for one of Francine's old London friends who, year after year, never showed.

By ten a.m., when her mother still had not shown her face at the espresso machine, Margherita gently opened the door to her parents bedroom. Tommaso had gone out to food shop for the day, and Margherita held a birthday card behind her back as she scanned their empty bed.

"Mom?" She remembered the strange sensation she'd had as she padded across the plush dressing room carpet into her mother's bathroom.

"I found my mom once. Unconscious," Margherita said, looking out the window at the Thames. "I've never told anyone that."

Thayer didn't say anything for a moment. He glanced in his rear view mirror as he changed lanes, but remained unaffected.

Then he said: "You know that Rodriguez song. 'Cause.'"

She turned to face him. "Yes."

"Endlessly, Margherita. You can plant flowers forever," he said quietly, glancing at her once.

Back in Hampstead, having declined his invitation for sushi, Thayer pulled up at her flat on Fitzjohn's Avenue.

"So, back to the nest this week. Mustique," she said as she opened the passenger door.

"Yeah. Easier to visit after you've regrown your wings. Listen, happy birthday. Cheers to another year of good mistakes and adventures."

She smiled and shook her head. "Ha. Yeah. Ciao." She shut the door and reached for her key fob.

"Hey!" he shouted from the driver seat, the passenger window rolled down.

She spun on her heels.

"Dust yourself off. You ain't done yet."

She huffed a smile and turned back around.

LONDON

March 4, 2022

"Why do you keep checking your phone?" Thayer asked as he gripped the instrument and yanked it from her grasp. "We don't have time for that."

Margherita looked up at him with annoyance. "I liked you better when your Morrissey hair did most of the talking."

"I am a clam. I've opened." He held her phone in the air. "What is your obsession?"

"I am waiting for a response that will never come like the daft bird that I am."

"What did you say? If it was political, you'll definitely get one."

"No. It wasn't political. You know I don't go there. It was… emotional."

"Oh, even worse."

"I just want, so badly, to not be in love with him anymore. What if I'm in love with him forever?" She rolled her eyes and moaned. "Fuck me, I feel like such an idiot."

"Love and idiocy are one and the same, my dear."

"This is what withdrawal feels like, isn't it?" she asked.

"That's precisely it," Thayer said, zipping her suitcase. He leaned into the gleaming aluminum with his elbows and looked up at her. "How long has it been since your last message?"

"Thirty-six hours," she said.

Thayer raised his eyebrows and jolted his head back, making a mocking expression at the severity of it.

"Do you not understand my natural level of discipline in life? It is approximately zero."

"Good job. When you get to thirty days, I do believe your name goes on the wall at the community center," he said as he leaned into his feet and stood up. "By the way, are you one of those people who are abnormally impatient to exit the plane? I don't fuck with people who exit the plane before the people in front of them."

"I can feel my liver."

Thayer scrunched up his face in an 'I get it' expression. "That's your nervous system. The Liver-Brain Connection, too. Real phenomenons, mind you."

A moment passed, Margherita staring at her dark green Rimowa suitcase, Thayer with his hands on his hips looking at it as well.

"Johanna got the loan," Margherita said lackadaisically. "For the Villa."

"I know."

"You know?" She looked up at him.

"Of course."

She nodded. "Of course you do."

"How do you feel?" he asked.

"I can feel my liver…"

"Excited?" he asked, eyeing her.

"Not especially. I'm tired of suitcases and boxes," she said, looking around at the random boxes stacked against the walls, the suitcases she'd barely managed to hide behind or under furniture that wasn't hers.

"Think of it like a vacation from your boxes."

"The only vacation I want to go on right now is to a house—or a home—*my* home, with all my belongings in it."

"Come on. It's almost four and I've got a meeting before my flight."

"Ah…is your name on the wall?" she asked, a snide smile on her face.

"You bet your fuckin' peripatetic ass it is."

IN THE AIR

March 4, 2022

WHEN MARGHERITA WAS a child, she and her father had played cards on plane rides. Her mother would either be sleeping (due to self medication) or working (also, truth be told, due to medication) and it had been left to Tommaso to entertain her. Which he did with great joy. She could clearly remember learning to shuffle, asking her father to do it over and over and over again. He'd oblige, but as quietly as possible, aware as always of the people around him, not wanting to disturb anyone.

How different they were. Tommaso: a humble homebody who was content to go along in the world surrounded by his work and his family, doing for others more than he did for himself. Francine: vibrant, charming, direct, seemingly self-involved, always wanting something out of her reach, always ready to rock a boat to get it.

Francine would not have cared if she disturbed anyone, shuffling the cards.

Margherita walked around her brother's legs to go to the bathroom. He was immersed in a long document, a pen behind his ear like a poser. Margherita had wanted to smack him with it for the past four hours. Instead she every so often regarded it with disdain. Who put a pen behind their ear?

When she returned from the bathroom, he looked up at her and watched her sit down.

Isabetta Andolini

"What?" She wondered how they had managed to book the one old-fashioned plane where the first class seats were still right next to one another.

"We have six more hours. You're not planning to speak to me at all on this flight?"

"What would you like to talk about, Benjamin?" She folded her hands on her lap and smiled in false pleasantry.

"Right. How is the job search?"

"I stopped looking. Chew on that for six hours." She returned her attention to the white sky out the window.

"What do you mean?"

"I mean, I haven't been looking lately."

"You just said that."

"Very good, Benjamin!" She clapped her hands together.

"Oh fuck off. Okay. Next. Any interesting dates lately? With single men, I mean."

"No."

"No?"

"What do you want?" she clipped at him.

"Margherita. Can you please give this teenage anguish a rest. It's exhausting. I have two children at home. I'd like to speak to you like the adult that you are."

She raised her eyes to the ceiling of the plane and shook her head to herself.

"I don't want to date. I want to be in love. Big fucking enormous love," she said dryly.

Benjamin harrumphed.

"What?"

"Well—don't jump down my throat— but if you want to fall in love, what are you doing toying around with all these silly ticking bombs? It's beneath you."

"I wouldn't say it's beneath me. Or anyone. Everyone is entitled to flirtation and a little fun. I lead with my nerve and my freedoms. So what? I refuse to be shamed for that. It's more that what used to satiate me isn't doing the trick anymore, for some reason, and this sounds kind of cheese-ball, but I'm not as terrified anymore to share myself with someone. But not just anyone. It's got to be magic. Magic or else."

"Magic is for the movies."

"Magic is for believers."

Benjamin pushed his head back into the leather pillow affixed to his seat and huffed a closed-lip smile at her.

"Touché. So how's this guy Thayer you've grown so close to?"

"I wouldn't say we've grown so close. He's just been a bit of a buddy. Solid sense of humor. We get on."

"A good buddy, I hope. What about that other guy you used to work with, who moved to LA? Do you still talk to him?"

"Noah. Yeah."

"Isn't it interesting you seem to collect variations on a theme. Dry-humored men who don't quite fit in."

"How would you know? You don't know them. And what difference does it make? I 'collect' people who accept me, who I get along with."

"Sure."

"'Sure,'" Margherita imitated, her mouth twisted. "What is your attitude all about Benjamin? I'm so extremely sorry that I'm not up to snuff. But if you didn't stick up your nose at absolutely everything I say, it would make the next few days a lot more bearable."

"Well, add to that, don't assume I'm thinking the worst of you every time I respond."

"K. Whatever."

"Mature."

"Right back at you."

"When are you going to stop resenting me for being me, Margherita? For knowing her longer? For working in a similar world to hers? For being successful? I'd love to know."

"When you stop making me feel like I don't have a prayer of

amounting to even ten percent of what you two deem respectable."

"Margherita, Mum and I are not the same person. I don't know when or how you came to that twisted conclusion, but we are not one mind. I don't see everything the same way she did. And vice versa. You put words in my mouth. And hers. No one thinks as lowly of you as you do of yourself."

She swallowed hard and her head trembled from left to right as she whipped around to focus on the passing clouds.

Benjamin opened his laptop and proceeded to type away. The fact that he'd let the argument drop right there irked her. He didn't care. He never would. A tear escaped down her cheek and she swatted at it.

"Margherita." She could feel him peering around at her. "Stop that. Don't bloody cry."

"Oh, okay. I won't," she snipped. "Thanks for the advice."

He sighed grievously. "You're not alone in your feelings of neglect, you know. You got to grow up with her. She was there. All the time. When you didn't feel well. When you woke up Saturday morning. She saw your dirty dishes in the sink. Maybe she helped you make your bed once in a while."

"Betsy made my bed. Betsy was there when I didn't feel well."

"She was there, Margherita. Even if she wasn't *there*, she was somewhere nearby. She was more aware of everything. Don't forget, we didn't have FaceTime or iPads or cell phones even. I waited by the phone Tuesdays, Thursdays, and Saturdays like an idiot."

"But she never missed a call, did she?"

"No. But sometimes they were five minutes long."

"Always trying to make it up to you."

"Margherita, you can't compare her dedication to each of us like an XY chart. Our situations were inherently different. You will somehow feel like you had the short end of the stick, and I feel the same."

Margherita continued to stare out the window with arms

folded, jaw clenched.

"How about this? Neither one of us got to say goodbye. So at least we are even there."

She turned to look at her brother. Her brother whose life was so incredibly different from hers. So organized and responsible and respectable. A wife, two offspring, a house fully paid for. A big job, a big salary. No credit card debt. A known purpose. A fully rounded sense of belonging.

And just as motherless as she was.

"That's a terrible way to call a truce," she said quietly.

He patted her on the head and ruffled her hair. "I'm the only brother you've got. Get used to me already," he said affectionately.

She pouted her lips and picked up the colorful packet in her lap. Airport kiosks were the only place she bought cheap candy.

"Starburst?"

He reached for a pink one, and she buried her finger in for the red one beneath it.

"Fucking disgusting," he said as he noshed his teeth into the gummy block.

"I know," she giggled, red rubber wrapping around her back teeth.

After the propeller plane had transported them from St. Vincent to Mustique and they'd settled into the same cottage where Margherita had passed the majority of the pandemic, she left her brother with Tommaso. They had always had an easy relationship, Tommaso more fatherly than Christos had ever been—softer, more open to vulnerability, more loving—Benjamin tended to loosen his buttons around him.

Margherita decided to stretch her legs and breathe in the island air. She walked down to the beach that fronted Plantation House, the path lined with wild orchids, bromeliads, incredible fern trees, enormous elephant ear plants, low hanging figs, and ombre hibiscus. It felt glorious to be back.

Thayer: landed!

She smiled down at her phone. How strange life was. When she'd first arrived, she'd thought Thayer was cold, sad, and unfriendly. And he was—all of those things. But perhaps because of it, they had forged such a lovely friendship. Misfits or not. Once a kindred spirit was found, the term misfit no longer applied.

Margherita: Whoooopeee!! The gang's all here!
Margherita: We flew in with Meredith. That woman never misses an event, does she?

Thayer: how's her new neck lift?

Margherita: let's inspect it later together. She'll love that.

Thayer: yeah. Gather a panel.

Margherita: score cards

"Hey!" She turned around at the sound of her brother's voice approaching her on the beach.

"What are you doing? I thought you were going for a walk with Dad?"

"Yeah, I will. In a bit. But there's someone I'd rather like to introduce you to first." He waved her over toward the golf cart on the path.

"Me? Who do you know here? This is *my* island!"

"I have people, too."

They rode through the palm-infringed roads, the balsam trees draping overhead, toward the northernmost point of the tiny island.

"Who is it?" Margherita asked, as the wind swept her hair into her face.

Benjamin pursed his lips. "An old friend. Of Mum's. And mine too." He glanced sideways at her.

KISS MY JAGGED FACE   509

She knitted her brows in confusion.

"I don't get it."

"Your dad told me, a few weeks ago, that an old friend of Mum's has spent a great deal of time here, and has been here permanently for the past few years. He hadn't known when he arrived, but, apparently, the two gentlemen had dinner one evening at Basil's and history revealed itself."

"So who is it? Then I would know them too?"

"Yes and no. It's a man who knew Mummy very, very well," Benjamin said slowly, as if explaining a simple concept to a child. "But they fell out of touch, you see, and this man had a bit of a rough go of it."

"Of what?"

"Of... life. Dealt a tough hand. And he never had the chance to get to know your dad. But, when Tommaso told me he was here, he knew that I actually knew him, when I was just a lad. And, well, he was really important to Mummy. I just wanted you to know him. That's all."

Margherita's eyebrows remained furrowed as they pulled up to a small cottage.

On the deck sat Woody.

———————

Margherita approached slowly. She eyed her brother's incredulous expression. The smile that spread from ear to ear.

Woody rose from his deck chair and smiled. The biggest, most genuine smile she had ever seen on his drooping face.

"Benjamin." He stood tall on the wooden porch, hands in fists on his hips. His head shook slowly in disbelief.

As Margherita drew closer, she could see the tears engulfing Woody's eyes.

He held out his arms as Benjamin stepped up the two risers to the porch, and the two men embraced tightly, for a long, layered moment. Benjamin buried his head in Woody's bony shoulder, his arms wrapped around his back.

Margherita felt goosebumps run up her arms and legs.

What the fuck is going on? she wondered.

When they took a step apart, Woody held his hands on Benjamin's shoulders and looked him up and down. "My word. What a man you've become. I can't believe it."

Benjamin wiped at his eyes with the back of his hand.

Is he crying? Margherita tried to catch her brother's glance but he would not look at her.

"Margherita. It's been a while. Welcome back." Woody turned his attention to her, to where she stood beneath them on the grassy patch before the cottage. "Francie's babies. So grown up. Come. Come sit." He waved them over to the chairs.

Margherita picked up the book that had been left on one of the seats. "*Bonfire of the Vanities*. That's one of my favorites," she said, holding it.

"Yes. Mine too. I read it once a year. Makes me laugh. But also quite sad. The horrific fall from the top."

Margherita nodded. "Indeed."

"This is a great spot, Keith," Benjamin said as he looked out over the front yard toward the sea beyond.

"It's rather lovely here, breeze comes all the way up from the water."

Margherita glanced from one man to the other. "Keith?"

"Ah. Yes. That's my real name. Woody was something your mum's friend Bea started calling me after… well, let's just say, she thought my heart had turned to wood. She used to say it teasingly, but it stuck. And it was quite accurate, actually."

"Oh. So, you're the Keith who Mom used to talk to in her dressing room. I remember, when I was really, really little, going in there and she'd shoo me out." Margherita seemed to be putting two and two together. But then she shook her head again. "I'm just so confused. Is it just a coincidence that my dad got this project here? And you're here?" She looked to her brother.

"Coincidence entirely!" Keith, or Woody, said. "We used to come to Mustique all the time. Your mum, and Bea, and Rodney, and I. And whoever any of us was dating. Every year, for New Year's. We'd be on the first plane out of London after Christmas lunch. Couldn't get away fast enough. I wasn't sure if your father knew, actually, and when he didn't say anything for so long, it felt strange to suddenly ask him about it. And then finally, one night at Basil's, we were the only ones, and I just felt like… gosh, if Francie were here, she'd slap me for being such a wuss. So I sat down next to him. Sure enough, he knew it was me the whole time. Didn't want to make me uncomfortable. And didn't want to rock your boat either. Your dad is the classiest. Most thoughtful. I told him a bit about her before-New York life."

"I- I don't understand," Margherita said again, a hollow in her throat building like a slow but powerful wave. "Why didn't Dad want me to know?" She wanted desperately for Woody to take it all back, to stop talking about her mother in a way that made her feel like he knew her so much better than her. And yet, she also wanted him to tell her everything. To never stop talking about her.

"You look so much like her. When you and your dad arrived, and I saw you at Basil's that first night, holy hell, I thought someone had slipped me half a dozen quaaludes. Like it was 1975 all over again, like it was another January eve with Francie and the crew after a boozy day at Macaroni. With your green eyes and the dark wavy hair parted in the middle, and those dimples and the facial expressions. You scared the living daylights out of me."

Margherita felt a tear in her left eye that she pushed away with the heel of her hand.

"I look that much like her?" she asked. "When she was my age?"

"Yes, yes you do. The same eyebrow manipulations, the same lip movements. Imagine. I never thought I'd see those again," Woody said, gently shaking his head in disbelief.

"How…when…how did you know her? When did you meet?"

"I met Francine in 1966 on her first day at St. Andrews. She was the most effortlessly charming, gregarious, and mysterious woman I had ever encountered. The queen of debauchery, the center of every dial, the fearless girl who didn't care who rode in her wake. And then... ah, then she was quiet and inward and sensitive. Sad. Evanescent. Everything about her was evanescent." Keith turned the book around in his lap, picking it up and putting it down, a tool with which to see scenes fifty years old.

He continued. "Your mother was a magnet with both a positive and a negative side. Depending on her mood. I used to call her Ruby Tuesday—not for all her men, but for all her moods. It was our little joke. She was either Rosalind Russell, life's a party, or Bette Davis, it's going to be a bumpy night. And then... well then of course, the suicide Tuesdays that lasted ten days, only in poor Francie's case it couldn't all be attributed to X. One morning we all woke up and she was nowhere to be found. We didn't pay much attention to it, assumed she was sleeping it off. Mick found her on Petit Mustique. That's a mile from the lagoon. To this day I don't know how she got there," he laughed.

Benjamin swatted at his eye again, and Margherita glanced at him in total disbelief. She couldn't remember the last time she had seen her brother cry.

Margherita sat in silence, her heart racing a thousand beats a minute. She had never heard anyone speak about her mother in the way Woody was. She felt an immense wave of guilt for her father as she wondered if he had ever known that side of Francine. He must have known her as Woody described her. He must have fallen in love with her in that way, not knowing of the burden to come.

"Your mum was one in a million. I've never met anyone like her. She really struggled with that. Being her. Being Francie. She was at constant war with herself. It didn't matter how much we all loved her." Keith looked down at the book.

"Why didn't you ever know my dad? If you two were so close?"

"Well, she left London. She had to. It wasn't doing her any favors. She went to New York. Head held high as a skyscraper. Got herself a job that kept her mind occupied. She met your father. Benji came in to the world. Her job was intense. Eventually she stopped coming to Mustique for New Year's. She couldn't be loosey Francie anymore. Wild and free. Flighty and frightful. And she didn't want to be. She wanted to be big, and she couldn't be big if people saw her being vulnerable, being messy. I saw her a few times in London, a few times in New York. Always impeccably dressed, effortlessly so. That was Francie. She'd glide into La Grenouille, forty-five minutes late. I'd be huffing and puffing, fuming in the ears, and she'd sashay in and hold me by the shoulders and kiss each cheek and smile and say 'Sorry doll, it's been a Day. What are you drinking? You look gorgeous.' And she'd have this crinkle in her eye, and you suddenly remembered how easy it was to love her and to pity her at the same time." He paused, as if reflecting on one of those moments, thirty years prior.

"At least she showed up for lunch. Most of ours she clear-all missed. Couldn't make it. Something's come up. Start without me. Benjamin is just like her. I bring a book to any supposed lunch with him." Margherita cocked her head toward her brother.

He smiled and laughed under his breath. Then he noticed Margherita's facial expression and slowly crept back the smile. "That's a shame! He was the sweetest little boy..."

"Oh," Margherita said, as if caught in a trance, still confused by it all. "Did you know Christos?"

"I met him a few times, yes. He and Francie were two peas in a pod, especially when she was manic. He was wild and endlessly energetic. Scared the crap out of me. Preposterously intimidating Greek god. I hated his guts, to be honest. Sorry, Benji. Francie was so in love with him. So taken by his music. And his energy. But his was mostly due to youth and sex appeal and the confidence of being dealt that deck. While Francie's was a bubble ready to burst at any second. And when it did, he wasn't too interested in her."

Benjamin shifted uncomfortably.

Margherita's eyebrows were fixed in a furrowed knot, and she felt she hadn't breathed in a number of minutes. She ran her hands up the length of her neck and dug her fingertips into the back of her skull in an effort to calm her nerves.

"Margherita, I don't know you. And I wasn't very close to Francie in the end. My own fault, really. My wooden heart. I went on more pills than your mother for a while. Over-corrected myself. Not even Francie wanted to talk to me. She told me I had a heart of metal, and I blamed it all on her, somehow, and—" Keith looked up into the sky and shook his head. He exhaled deeply before continuing. "I'll never forgive myself for cutting off your mum. Anyway, that's not the important bit. The important bit, for you to know, is she did her best. With you, with Benjamin, with your dad, with herself. She did the best she could. Not everyone is born equipped with an equal set of tools. Some people are, and life takes them away one by one. We're all fucked, basically. That doesn't mean her love wasn't as strong as any other mum's, I'm sure of it."

Margherita's heart somersaulted and her eyes became puddles. She cleared her patchy, water-logged throat. "I always felt like she didn't really like me. She loved me in a perfunctory way, like, that's my child and I have to, but I felt like she didn't like *me*."

Benjamin tusked his lips and shook his head.

"That couldn't be farther from the truth. If anything, it was the other way around. I knew your mum better than anyone, and I know how hard it was for her to let someone see every side of her. She wasn't sure even herself which side was her and which was the meds. Francie was afraid of love not because she didn't want to get to know someone or be vulnerable with them, but because she was weary of feeling itself. Of euphoria. She couldn't trust it. She was hyper aware of feeling *too much*. There was no way for her to differentiate, you see, between the euphoria of love and the euphoria of her illness. It made her fiercely self-protective and fearful. Lonely. Swimming in a body she could not always recognize or navigate. There were a few of us who knew her since she was just coming up. Bea, Rodney—did you ever meet them? And others who came and went. She had loads of friends, always highly social, but trusted only a handful of us. Everyone else received a careful *version*. The version she thought they wanted to see. So paranoid to show someone any sort of mood other than the one that would get her ahead with that individual. It's one of the reasons she was such a spitfire at work. It was like her own little stage. She controlled it to a tee."

He seemed to recall a vivid memory at that moment and huffed out a beat of reflective air.

"Anyway, I'd have regretted it forever if I hadn't said anything to you. I hope you don't mind. An old man has ghosts too, you know?"

"My mom." Margherita cleared her throat again. "Our mom. Was she happy? When you knew her? I mean, I know—not all the time. But, did you see her—happy? Because with us, it was all work, and when it wasn't work, it was only because… she *couldn't*, you know."

Keith reached out across the table and lay his long slender, sun-spotted hand over Margherita's.

"Your mum was happy a great deal. Very happy. She was a wonder. And a wonderful human. Your mum was such a wonderful wonder."

Margherita let the tears slide. "It's not fair," she said, wiping her face. "I wish I knew—I wish I saw that." She sniffed and sucked up the tears, looking out at the water's edge. "I wish I had your memories," she said.

"I'll share them with you," Keith said. "They're yours to keep, darling."

In the golf cart, riding south toward Basil's, where the group planned to convene for an evening of casual fun before the following day's hotel unveiling, Margherita's head was a tumble of unanswered questions.

"You know when Keith said that he cut Mom off, what did he mean? Did they stop talking?"

"It's a very complicated story. My dad told me once, what happened, but you know my dad… can't always trust his memory. Everything is soaked in gin. Keith had a little girl, born the same year you were. He took her to the beach one weekend down by Land's End. Apparently his hip was acting up… You know he had his leg amputated after a bad accident. He had problems with his hips ever since then, and he took a bunch of pain killers. It knocked him out for a few hours. When he woke up… he couldn't find Lisabet."

"What happened? Where was she?"

"She waded into the water at high tide…"

Margherita gasped. "And what happened?"

"She drowned, Marghe."

"Oh my God, that's horrible."

"Yeah. Keith blamed himself. And then he started to blame mum. If it weren't for the accident, he wouldn't have taken the pain killers. If it weren't for mum's manic episode the night of the accident, there wouldn't have been an accident."

Margherita's eyes filled. "Was she there?"

Benjamin hesitated. He took advantage of a moment at a turn, looking carefully to the left around a sharp curve before moving the golf cart into the road. "No," he finally said, looking in his rear view mirror. "She asked him to come get her one evening. Late. She was mad at my father. Keith was—" Benjamin shook his head and shrugged. "Her savior. Always. Always coming to her rescue."

"So what, he cut her off?"

"Eventually, yeah. By the time I went to university. He cut all of us off. Me. Mum. Bea was gone by then. He became this—other person. So un-Keith. Someone totally different. He was… broken. Mum was the culprit. I was a healthy, vital young man, still on this side of the dirt. That was a painful, bitter pill to swallow. It was all too much for him."

"What did Mom do? She must have been beside herself."

"I assume so. She lived with all of that guilt for a really long time. I think it's part of the reason she sent me back to England… to be like a surrogate child to Keith. They were best friends. In the biggest, most unique way. In fact I'm quite sure she—" He stopped himself and cleared his throat. "But you know, between her meds and her brick walls, she put up a tough front."

"She what? What were you going to say?"

He shook his head. "Nothing. It was a really messy, difficult situation."

"I can't imagine cutting someone off like that, who's been such a big part of your life."

"It's a little evil, but when you're heartbroken—completely destroyed—you do what you think is the quickest route out of it. Not necessarily the best in the long run. But in that moment, it's just about survival."

LONDON

March 19, 2022

It was an unusually sunny morning when their plane landed at Heathrow, and though she managed to evade the chipper taxi driver's chit-chat—her brother having gone straight to the office—she felt a new sense of calm as the black cab made its way through west London and northward, toward her temporary flat with its stack of worn and weathered boxes.

When she arrived, she sat down at the kitchen table and made a list of everything she needed to do.

You are bold. You are courageous, she repeated to herself. *You can do this.*

After the FedEx pick-up took away most everything, she looked around the lifeless flat with her hands on her hips and was making her way toward the swing window in the bedroom, to sit on her little roof terrace one last time and let the chilly air and bright sun play hopscotch on her cheeks when her phone pinged.

Jack: Fancy lunch this week?

"Ha," she said out loud.

Margherita: I fly back to New York tomorrow.
Jack: oh? For good?
Margherita: For now. For good isn't familiar territory yet.

Her phone began to ring.

"Good morning," she said, as she sat down on her bed and watched herself speak in the reflection of the mirror.

"Good morning. What do you mean, for now? What's happened? Soured on London already?"

"Ha. No. Not at all. Quite the contrary. I adore your city. But I've had someone take a rather keen interest in the Villa. A writer actually, who has decided to buy the property and fulfill the plans I've made. She's propositioned it to a firm in New York, with myself on board, and they have taken the bait. Contracts signed."

"I can't believe it. That's incredible news. Really. You must be chuffed."

"I'll be back soon, I'm sure."

He sighed into the phone. "I suppose it makes sense. Though I can't believe a London firm didn't snatch you up. Our job market isn't the most robust at the moment, I'm afraid."

"Alas. Can't cry over socialism."

"Ha. No."

"How are you?" she asked.

"I'm fine. I'm good. Bloody cold out there today. I woke up to go for a run and felt how cold it was and went back to bed."

"It's freezing out. But gorgeous. The sun shines on, after all."

"I saw two robins this morning. I went out in my bathrobe to give them a bit of bread and they flew away. One robin is beautiful but two is incredible."

"Magic." She rubbed her leg up and down, blinded by the reflection of the sun in the mirror.

"I tried to show my kids, and they were like 'Yeah who cares.'"

"You did a good thing."

"I'm sad you're going."

"Are you?"

"The UK will miss you. You're like someone in a movie, one day you're here, the next, poof you're gone, up and away."

"Like fairy dust."

Isabetta Andolini

"I feel like, with you, you're either in my life with this electric presence, or you're very far."

"It's flames or nothing. I've always been that way. Bit of a curse."

"Hmm. I've been thinking about our lunch. It was so natural and magical and bound to happen. I would have liked to see you again before you left."

"It's better this way," she said, carefully.

"Why?"

"For a multitude of reasons, for you and for me… real life calls," she sighed.

"Yeah. What about unreal life?"

"It's a tough thing, that unreal life."

"I always thought it would be quite great there, given that anything could happen. I've thought about it a lot. About spiffy lunches. And what we would have done for dessert."

"Oh gosh, dessert." She pushed her lips to the side and eyed herself in the mirror. That wasn't really what she wanted to hear.

"Yes. Delicious delicious dessert."

"Is that all I am to you, my charming handsome friend? Dessert?"

"Oh no, you are much much more than that. But you are still delicious. You are funny and sweet and delightful and clever and very, very beautiful."

She smiled at her reflection, embarrassed.

"Let me know if you're ever in my country," she said.

"But will you want to see me?"

"Of course. But not if it's only for dessert."

"No. Of course not. Good luck, let me know what happens."

"The future is bright," she said, more to herself than to him, as she winced into the blinding rays bouncing off the mirror.

"Yours is."

"Yours is too."

LONDON

March 20, 2022

On her last day, she wandered down from Hampstead to Primrose Hill and back, taking her time and appreciating the first signs of Spring. It wouldn't yet be so temperate and colorful in New York, so she took extra care to appreciate the narcissus and buttery yellow daffodils.

On Belsize Park Gardens, a forty-ish-year-old dad stopped with his tricycle-riding toddler to say hello to a snail on a white ledge.

"See the snail? He's in no rush there. Just moving along real slow," the father said.

"Yeah," the little boy said, placing his pointer finger close to the snail.

"Well, let's go. We'll probably see him on our way back. He'll probably still be there. Say goodbye to the snail," the dad said sweetly.

"Bye snail," the little boy said.

Margherita smiled.

"Bye, snail," she said to the little creature. She looked behind her at the little boy and his father walking toward Primrose Hill. "Goodbye, Ruby Tuesday.

Still, I'm gonna miss you," she said. To herself. To her mom.